Desert Star

LINDA CHAIKIN

HARVEST HOUSE PUBLISHERS

EUGENE, OREGON

All Scripture quotations are taken from or adapted from the King James Version of the Bible.

Cover by Koechel Peterson & Associates, Inc., Minneapolis, Minnesota

DESERT STAR
Copyright © 2004 by Linda Chaikin
Published by Harvest House Publishers
Eugene, Oregon 97402
www.harvesthousepublishers.com

Library of Congress Cataloging-in-Publication Data

Chaikin, L. L., 1943-
    Desert star / Linda Chaikin.
      p. m.
    ISBN 0-7369-1235-5 (pbk.)
    1. Women pioneers—Fiction. 2. Virginia City (Nev.)—Fiction.
    3. Actresses—Fiction. 4. Nevada—Fiction. I. Title.
    PS3553.H2427D48 2004
    813'.54—dc22

                                                                        2003020994

Printed in the United States of America

04 05 06 07 08 09 10 11 / BC-MS / 10 9 8 7 6 5 4 3 2 1

For Steve, my beloved husband.
Philippians 1:3

Linda Chaikin
is an award-winning writer
of more than 20 books, including
Desert Rose and the popular A Day
to Remember series.

Prologue

*R*ick Delance sat at the desk in his upstairs room in the spacious hacienda-style ranch house. Although his father, Lucien Delance, was a wealthy cattleman, that in no way altered his expectations to see his youngest son enter Harvard Law School two years down the road.

Rick drew his dark brows together trying to concentrate on his reading while enduring an aching arm and, at the same time, attempting to ignore his disappointment. Here he was buried in law books when all the action—and trouble, was just beginning. He ought to be out helping his brother, Alex, and the cowhands rounding up the cattle for the big drive east to Abilene.

What a time to get laid up with a busted arm! Alex was shorthanded some of his best wranglers because some of the hands in the bunkhouse had gotten sick mighty fast. It made no sense. The odd sickness left even a strong man doubled over with pain in his belly, too weak to ride. More of the Triple D hands than he'd care to admit had allowed the fear of cholera to spook them, and some had even slipped away in the night leaving the ranch shorthanded. Lucien couldn't understand the cause of the sickness, nor could anyone else. Curly was sent out yesterday to Fort Craig near Santa Fe to get Doc Kinny, but that would take several days.

The sickness sure is peculiar, Rick mused, tapping his pencil on his desk. Ol' Elmo, the chuck-wagon cookie, hollered he had nothing to do with makin' the boys sick. "I done tasted ever'thing

I cook," he insisted, hands on hips, "an' if'n it were in the goods, I'd be down in the bunkhouse with the rest of them rascals."

Lucien said he'd never come up against anything like this illness. Rick supposed he could take solace in the fact that there was no mystery about his broken arm—except it'd become the subject of a good laugh among the ranch hands. If he hadn't been so quick to tackle that ornery line-back dun, and get himself thrown, he'd be out on the range now, just when Pa and Alex needed him most.

But it did a body no good to sit around mooning about it. He'd wanted that stallion from the very first time he'd laid eyes on him, and he still wanted him. He'd try talking nice to him while his arm was healing. Next time when Rick was ready to saddle him, that horse wouldn't be bucking him! "You and me are going to be friends," he'd told the horse, "one way or another. Our traveling days, boy, are just beginning."

Through the open window he heard the thud of horses' hooves entering the wide front yard with its two giant pepper trees. Rick got up from his desk and put his law books away. That would be Alex returning from the emergency meeting over at Dan Ferguson's ranch. Rick wondered how things had went. Had they gotten the cowpunchers they needed for the drive?

Out front, below the veranda steps, he heard his father call up to the open window: "Son, come down to the kitchen! Alex is back. Dutch is with him, too."

Dutch was the manager over at the Ferguson ranch. That he'd ridden back with Alex to talk to their father was a hopeful sign for getting extra cowboys to replace some of the Triple D's who were recovering in the bunkhouse.

Rick appreciated the fact that though plans existed to send him East to become a lawyer, his father wanted him to know he would remain an important member of the Triple D by including him in the meetings on ranch business. His father set great store by city-bred education, though Rick didn't think much of it himself. Not that he and Alex were unlearned by any means. Their father had left France as an educated young man to emigrate to America and settle in Louisiana. Dreams of gold and tales of the Western Territories however, had lured him to the California gold rush, then on toward Texas. Along the way he'd settled in New Mexico, where he'd staked claim to what was now one of the largest cattle ranches west of the Rio Grande.

While Rick had grown up in an all-male culture on the ranch, Lucien had made sure his two sons were well schooled and taught gentlemanly manners. He'd also instructed them himself on everything from the Bible to European literature. Although Rick had learned the ways of a gentleman from his father, he'd learned survival and the raw ways of the West from the plain but dauntless men he'd become friendly with in the territory, rugged men who had filled his ears with the ways of the Apache, Comanche, and the Kiowa. As boys, he and Alex had learned to read "sign," to be able to track man or animal when most folks wouldn't notice that anything had passed as silently as phantoms in the night. Rick had learned how to find water holes for the cattle drives, what cacti were useful for survival, and which plants were used by the various Indian tribes for medicine. Rick had also picked up many of their views on valor and justice...and how to handle a gun.

Rick came down the stairs into the large, square room furnished with leather and dark Spanish furniture. He wore a neatly pressed blue-shield style shirt with a row of buttons down each side, a black bandanna kerchief around his neck, black, Spanish style trousers with silver buttons, and polished hand-tooled boots. At sixteen he was already a strong young man who would soon catch up in height with his brother, who was five years his senior.

Rick, with his right arm in a sling, entered the big bright kitchen.

His father, Lucien, was there looking more like an old-world aristocrat than the rugged cattleman he'd become. He was tall and somber, with white in his sideburns and a neatly trimmed Prince Albert beard. He'd become a widower at thirty and never remarried, taking instead to turning the Triple D into what it was today and finding his loneliness assuaged in raising his two sons.

The Bible, he had told them, was one of the few possessions he'd carried in his carpetbag when he'd first come to America. Rick recalled how, when a small boy, he'd watched his father skillfully remove the small Bible's worn cover and make a handmade replacement with a cross tooled into the leather. His father made much of the fact that the leather had come from the first steer on the Triple D.

Rick's mother, Rosette, had found life hard in the territories. Already of fragile health, she died at twenty-eight, leaving Lucien with two small boys. They had laid her to rest beneath the shade of a willow that grew by a year-round creek.

"Well, boys, what do you think we should name this creek where your fair mother rests till our Savior returns for us?"

"Angel's Creek," Rick had said almost at once.

And so it was called.

Rick's memory of his mother was not as clear as Alex's, but he held images of her as smiling, gentle, and affectionate. He remembered sitting on her lap and being hugged. Of course, that wasn't a memory he shared with the all-male household, though Alex and his father must have had their tender memories, too. They silently determined to tough it out, three men alone, though always together. There was very little rivalry between Rick and Alex. Being five years apart, it had seldom seemed necessary.

His father was talking to Alex now, as Rick entered the kitchen for the meeting. Salvador, the house cook, or "Sal" as they called him, brought in a big urn of coffee. Rick walked to the long table and poured himself a cup, all the while glancing at the stranger who had returned with Alex and Dutch from the meeting at Ferguson's ranch. Rick would recognize most of the cowhands working there, and he also knew by sight the men working at Tom Hardy's ranch. He'd heard talk around the bunkhouse that Hardy had hired some new men out of west Texas—several of them with reputations not too comforting. It was a thing with Tom Hardy to butt heads with the Triple D, though he was friendly with the three Delance men. Sometimes Tom was hard to read. He owned the second largest ranch in the Cimarron area, but Rick believed he wanted to be the largest. He wanted rights to Red Creek, which formed one border of Triple D and was considered part of its property.

Rick took slow measure of the tall stranger who had an inch in height over his father and Alex, both six-footers themselves. The man had wide shoulders and coal-black hair turned under in a smooth pageboy that reached to his wide muscled neck. He apparently set a great store by his drooping mustache, for it was well-oiled and perfectly trimmed. It wasn't his appearance that Rick noticed so much as the quick, alert eyes, and his fancy, tied-down, pearl-handled pistols. His father introduced him as Zel Willard from Texas.

Rick, who was laid-back and quiet, was looking at those six-shooters over his coffee cup. He didn't know what Alex or his pa thought, but he'd already decided this stranger was no ordinary cowpuncher. When he glanced at the man's face again, Rick found that he was under the same scrutiny by Zel Willard. Rick let his gaze slide. Willard looked as if he knew Rick could be a man to reckon with in a few more years. Rick was confident he could handle himself, even now, in most situations.

Alex, always the fast talker and center of attention in contrast to Rick, was telling their father that while he was at Ferguson's ranch, both Tom Hardy and Zel Willard had come riding up offering a crew of seasoned cowhands from Abilene who were anxious to work. Rick could see from the look on his pa's face that he was by no means convinced he should hire them.

There were two other men there besides Zel Willard. The six-foot-four fellow with yellow hair and gaps between his big front teeth was called "Dutch." Rick had never much liked him, but evidently Tom Hardy did. Dutch was the manager over at Hardy's ranch.

The other cowboy was Hank, his father's own trusty top hand, a lanky redhaired fellow, easy-going—a true gentleman from the Panhandle region of Texas. He had been with Lucien from the early beginnings of the Triple D. He was as casually welcome in the kitchen as Sal and his fifteen-year-old daughter, Marita. Rick noticed that Willard's quick eyes had already found the girl, and he kept glancing in her direction.

Rick turned his attention back to his brother. Alex was no fool when it came to sizing up a man's character, yet he looked enthusiastic about the prospects of bringing the herd to the railhead with the help of Dan Ferguson and Tom Hardy. Ferguson had offered five of his own cowhands, and Hardy had sent Zel Willard with an offer of even more seasoned men to ride herd. All in all, they would fill in for the Triple D's shortfall due to illness.

"Rick, what's your say on this? Pa always sets a big prize by your take on things. You heard what I just told him."

"That's right, son, let's hear what you think now."

Aware that the eyes of Zel Willard and the other men had circled and stopped on him, Rick straightened from where he'd been leaning.

"Seems mighty neighborly of Tom Hardy to be worrying about Triple D cattle getting to the railhead on time for a sale."

Zel Willard's eyes flickered with amusement.

"I'm representing Tom Hardy," Zel drawled. "Being neighborly is just a right nice thing to do. Especially since we'll be seeing a lot of each other from now on. You see, I'm going to marry Tom's eldest daughter, Miss Tina."

Rick just looked at him. His father's head turned, and Alex, too, was surprised. This was the first Rick had heard about it. Tina's younger sister, Sue Hardy, was Alex's girl.

Rick couldn't resist. He'd seen the way Zel Willard had looked at little Marita. "Comes as a shock. I wouldn't have taken you for an engaged man."

Zel's eyes shot a cold look even while he smiled. "Most folks don't know how to take me, but they learn." He turned to Rick's father. "Now, Mr. Delance, both me and my future father-in-law want to start out on the right foot. With Alex here likely to marry Tina's younger sister, we're going to be brothers-in-law. It's fitting we lend a hand when you're in a tight spot. No reason neighborly competition has to be unfriendly."

"He has a point, Pa," Alex said. "Especially with the grazing land getting crowded."

"We've got to get our cattle to market," Lucien Delance agreed. "I have a buyer waiting in Chicago now."

"Buck Bodene has a tough crew," Zel Willard said. "They know their business."

Rick had never heard of Bodene. He looked at his father to see his response. He seemed thoughtful.

"Does Bodene and his crew come with Tom's recommendation?"

"They've not worked for Mr. Hardy before. But I'll tell you one thing, sir. If we needed them on the Hardy Ranch we'd sure hire them. Bodene says times are rough in the Panhandle, or he'd not have ridden this way looking for work. Ranchers there been taking a toll from the drought and Indian raids. Bodene carries a recommendation from a rancher you know in west Texas."

Rick saw his pa's curiosity.

"Oh? What rancher is this?"

"Mr. Clyde. Billy Clyde."

Rick tried to place the name. He knew his pa had friends in west Texas.

Alex turned to his father. "You remember Billy Clyde, Pa. He was in Santa Fe last year, too. When Tom Hardy mentioned Billy Clyde at Ferguson's ranch tonight I knew you'd recall him."

"Yes, a fair gentleman." His father stood. "Well, if Bodene and his bunch come with Billy Clyde's and Tom's recommendations, then that's good enough for me. We're in a difficult pinch right now with illness putting down some of my best men. I'm sure Alex has already spoken about that, Zel."

"Yes, unfortunate. I hear some of your hands have been spooked by the thought of cholera."

Rick kept silent. He didn't know why, but there was something he didn't like about this. Still, Billy Clyde was a decent man and a friend of his father. And Alex was pleased about getting the extra hands so the drive could start at the end of the week. With his father and Alex agreeing they'd hire Bodene and his crew, Rick knew Alex would think he was being presumptuous to question the decision so he went along. The Triple D was playing against time.

In the next few days, with the new cowhands working for the Triple D, the roundup was going as expected. Pa had elected to stay at the ranch instead of going on the drive as he usually did, and Rick knew why.

"Don't stay on my account, Pa. I've plenty to do, and that stallion's starting to turn his head in my direction now when I go down to the corral to talk to him. I aim to ride him soon."

"Don't try it till that arm heals good and strong. As for staying, it's time Alex handled a drive on his own. Besides, some of our boys still need care." Lucien rubbed his chin. "Strange thing, there. Doc Kinny is baffled. There's no accounting for what ails them. I've asked Elmo, and he still claims they're all eating the same grub."

Two of the hands had died, and Rick knew of eight others who were recovering but were still too weak for work. Two of their best leads remained in their bunks, even after a month.

"Doc will have something to put in his research notes," Rick said easily, and he stood from the front porch where he'd been sitting on the steps. "I still say I ought to be going on the drive. A busted arm isn't going to keep me from riding. The least thing I can do is help Elmo in the chuck wagon."

"No, son. Not this time. We're both staying on the ranch. You tackle those books." He dug an envelope from a shirt pocket beneath his leather vest. "I haven't told you yet, but maybe I should. I've a letter from Mr. Charles Bingham."

It was clear the letter from school pleased his pa, but Rick felt the old disappointment.

"Because of your high grades you'll be permitted to enter prep school a year earlier than we expected. Come September, on your birthday, you'll be heading for school in the East. Mr. Bingham's arranging for you to have a room in his home."

Rick looked at him, feeling as though a hanging rope had just been tossed over the highest branch above his head.

"Pa, it's just not in me to be a lawyer. I belong here with you and Alex, with the cattle and horses, the mountains—"

"Son, the Triple D will always be here for you. I'm leaving it to you and Alex. But one of my sons ought to have a formal college education. You took to reading at an early age, so with Alex sure to marry Sue Hardy, and you still single and better at books than him, it's fitting that you attend college. You'll be an asset to Alex later on. This land will continue to grow. One day New Mexico Territory will be part of the United States. Some extra knowledge will come in handy around here for all of us." He stood, smiling, putting his arm around Rick's shoulder. "Let's go inside, son. Sal has made one of your favorite desserts, and Marita has the coffee on. We'll discuss your going off to college another day."

Rick hoped that day would be a long time coming. *Prep school!* Why that hardly gave him time enough to break his stallion in.

Three weeks after Alex and Bodene's crew had started the cattle drive to Abilene, Sal came bursting into the hacienda calling: "Senor Lucien! It's 'Cookie.' Elmo's come riding in alone. There is bad trouble, senor, I think so!"

Rick raced out onto the front porch, and his father quickly joined him from the library.

"We been 'dry-gulched,' Mr. Delance. It were that Bodene and his crew. Them cattle was stampeded and rustled. Across the border into Mexico is my guess. Ever' last one of the Triple D men was shot up or trampled. Some shot right where they slept; others caught in the stampede." The old-timer was weeping now. "Alex was shot in cold blood, Mr. Delance, by that fella who called himself Bodene and another named Abner. They didn't give Alex a chance. Rattlers in the camp, they was. Just shot him down. If I hadn't crawled behind that rock I'd be dead, too. Bodene and Abner….Never seen a man draw as fast as Abner."

Rick, dismayed, turned to his pa. Lucien had turned white, and his shaky hand reached for the porch pillar. He retained his somber dignity.

"When?"

"Nigh two weeks ago, Mr. Delance. Took me ridin' day and night 'cross Injun country to get here. 'Most killed by Comanche, and I 'most killed my horse with ridin'. In the end I had to shoot 'im. This mule were one of the pack mules for the chuck wagon. She got me the rest of the way, she did. It were an evil time, Mr. Delance."

Rick's heart beat steadily, a slow, boiling anger rearing up in his soul.

He went to his father, taking his arm gently. "Sit down, Pa," he said quietly, but his father refused the porch chair. He was trembling as he looked off across the miles of ranch land toward the distant red-brown hills of Cimarron, as though he could relive the scene somewhere near the Texas border in his mind.

"I blame myself for this."

"Don't. There was no way to know," Rick said, attempting to comfort his father.

"No, I shouldn't have trusted Buck Bodene. I left everything to your brother. I was too anxious to give him his lead, to let him test his abilities in running the Triple D. I should have insisted on seeing that letter of recommendation Bodene claimed he had from Billy Clyde. There's a chance Bodene never knew Clyde and that he lied to Tom Hardy."

"I never liked that Zel Willard. Wouldn't surprise me if he wasn't in on it from the beginning."

"No, son. Tom Hardy and I are competitors, but he'd never go along with murder and rustling."

"Maybe Zel didn't tell him."

His father shook his head. "I can't see it. Tom would be very careful about the man marrying his eldest daughter."

True enough, but Rick wasn't convinced about Zel. He'd seen the way the man wore his guns tied down.

"Bodene," Rick's voice was hard as steel, "and Abner. I'll get them, Pa. I'll kill 'em both for this. They'll pay for sure."

His father's gaze turned and locked horns with his son's.

"You'll do no such thing, Rick. You're going East like we planned. You'll go sooner now. I want you away from here."

Rick stared at him, frustrated. "They killed Alex! You heard! They shot him down in cold blood!" He turned. "Isn't that right, Elmo? You saw it? For sure?"

The old-timer was grim as death. "I seen it. He crawled out from under the wagon where he was sleepin' soon as he heard shots and the cattle stampedin'. Then he was a bucklin' on his gunbelt as fast he was shoutin' for Hank. First we thought it were Comanches. But Bodene and that Abner were awaitin'. Them reprobates shot him more'n once."

His father sank into a chair, head in hands. The wind stirred a dust devil in the yard, and the silence captured them in a moment of deep grief.

"No man gets by with evil, son," Lucien said a minute later. "No matter how he tries to cover his tracks. There's no hiding from the Lord. He knows all; He sees all."

Rick knew that. *Still...*

"*But Pa!*"

"Though justice may not reach unrepentant, wicked men in this life, the day will come when they must stand before their Maker and give account of every thought and deed. Vengeance belongs to the Lord." Lucien Delance's voice was even.

Rick's hand tightened on the porch post where he stood. "Their sinful souls belong to God to judge. But I'm bringing earthly justice to their bodies now. They're going to pay, Pa, and no one is going to stop me."

Lucien looked up with a pained expression. "Don't talk that way, son. We've lost Alex. Do you want me to lose you as well?"

"You won't lose me. I'm not going East, Pa. I'm staying. I'm going to hunt them down. You wanted me to study law. Well, the highest law comes from God. I've read that God ordains rulers who bring terror to the evil, who bear not the sword in vain. But there is no law here yet, Pa. And until there is *we* are responsible to establish the law! How many times while growing up did Alex and I hear you say that?"

"Maybe once too often…and it's true, there's no denying it. But there is Clay Billings in Santa Fe, and I'll be riding there to see him."

Clay Billings was a Santa Fe lawyer and a judge. He was also a friend of his pa.

"And I'll talk to Tom and Ferguson, too." Lucien stood, pulling his shoulders back. "They need to be involved in this."

Rick struggled against frustration. "But Pa, it was Zel Willard who recommended Bodene and his crew. And Zel's going to marry Tom's daughter. We need to do some talking with Zel."

"I'll do the talking with Zel Willard."

Rick dropped his clenched hand from the post and met his pa's steely gaze.

"I'll go with you. There may be trouble." Rick turned to go to the hacienda for his hat and gunbelt. He felt the ironclad grasp of his father's commanding hand.

"You'll stay here, Rick. You're sixteen; remember who's in charge."

Rick clenched his jaw. "Pa! I'm not a kid anymore. I'm fast with my guns, I—"

"I know you're fast," his father's voice came quiet and cool. "I've seen you practicing a few miles from here. I trailed you."

"Trailed me?" Rick searched his face, surprised, then hurt. "Pa! Come on! What was there to hide from you? Alex and I have practiced since we were twelve. You're the one who taught us! I couldn't practice my shoot'n round the hacienda now, could I? Naturally I'd ride out farther from here. There's no shame in using a gun for protection against killers. If it isn't Bodene and his crew of rustling renegades, then there's Comanches."

"Of course. But this is different. This is a matter for the law to handle. I don't want to hear anymore arguing, Rick. You'll do as I say. Do you hear me?"

Rick let out a breath and stepped back. "Yeah, I hear ya, Pa."

"Good." There was a moment of strained silence. Then his father spoke more gently. "You're in charge here until I get back from Santa Fe."

"There's no marshal in Santa Fe," Rick said stubbornly. "While we're wasting time, Bodene and his men are getting away—"

"*Rick!*"

Silence came between them again. Rick met his father's gaze and knew the matter was settled. He nodded.

His father nodded, too. "I'll see what Clay Billings has to say. He may be able to legalize a posse...maybe from Fort Craig. You saddle up my horse for me. Tell Sal and Marita to get some grub together for me. I'll be gone a week or more."

Rick's gaze followed him through the door into the hacienda, then he turned to Elmo.

The old-timer was still resting his arm on the back of the mule. He pushed his beat-up hat back, showing a grizzled gray mane that breezed his skinny collarbone. His hard, lean brown face looked more like worn-out boot leather than skin.

"What do you know about this man named Abner?" Rick's voice was low and hard.

Elmo shook his head. "Talk goes he's a gunfighter. He hitched up with Buck Bodene back in Abilene. He didn't show up on the cattle drive till we was a week into it. Then he comes ridin' in one night to the chuck wagon. He was there drinkin' coffee when Bodene rides in. Like two rattlers, they got on with each other, but kind of touchy too, if you know what I mean. Abner was quiet, hardly ever talked. I 'member your brother talked to him when he first come in and asked him a mess of questions. Things seemed to go okay for a few days, and he punched cows. And then like the blue blazes ever'thing went bad.

"Alex and Hank, they'd done their part and was turnin' in, leavin' the guard to Bodene and his sidewinders. In the middle of the night shots was fired and Bodene's men were yellin' like Comanches. Them cattle just took off like demons was after 'em. Alex was up quick. Bodene and Abner appeared. There was words but I couldn't make 'em out. I grabbed my rifle, and next thing I knew Bodene and Abner was shootin' at Alex and Hank. Hank went down right off. I got off a shot at Abner. After that I had to run for it. Them cattle was coming straight through—" he paused, ran an arm across his eyes, shook his head.

"Then, well, I went back later…found Alex—buried him. Never did find Hank's body." He removed his hat.

Rick stood there. His gaze lifted to the far-off cinnamon-brown hills.

That night in the hacienda Rick couldn't sleep. It was late when his father returned from the meeting with Tom Hardy and Dan Ferguson, and he was somber.

"Tom says Zel took a few good gun hands and they're out looking for Bodene. Zel hasn't returned."

Rick wasn't satisfied. "Took Tom Hardy long enough to tell us that."

"You're jumping to conclusions." Lucien sank wearily into the kitchen chair and motioned for Sal to pour the coffee. "He was just saddling up to ride over when I got there. Tom was upset. I could see it was genuine."

Sal and his young daughter, Marita, were looking on sadly. Marita's eyes were red-rimmed from crying. At fifteen she was a pretty girl, and Rick had suspected her of having unspoken feelings for both him and Alex. She brought Lucien a plate of eggs and peppers. Her hand shook as she put down the plate. Lucien looked up at her kindly, as though he knew and understood.

"Thank you, Marita." He reached over and patted her hand. It was all the understanding she needed, and two tears ran down her cheeks. She turned away and hurried to the big stove. Sal sniffed loudly and wiped his eyes on a handkerchief.

Rick narrowed his gaze. "Pa, what did they say about it? About Alex?"

"Tom didn't see the letter from Billy Clyde, either. It was Zel who handled the matter of Bodene and his crew."

"See? Just as I suspected!"

"Hold on. We all unwisely took Bodene's word, including Zel. Tom says that Zel is taking the news hard."

Rick scowled. He pulled out a chair and plunked himself down, arms resting on its back. "Who is this Zel Willard anyway? How did he get tangled up with Miss Tina?"

"He's a distant cousin of Mrs. Hardy. She and Miss Tina are taking this bitterly. Of course Miss Sue is broken up about Alex…"

The silence lingered.

"What about Mr. Billings and that posse?" Rick asked restlessly.

"Tom's already sent several men with Zel to help out. So did Dan Ferguson. I'm leaving first thing in the morning for Santa Fe."

"By now those cattle are across the border in Mexico."

"We'll find those responsible."

Would they? Rick was already suspicious of their neighbors.

Later that evening his pa left for Santa Fe, and Rick went up to his room. He paced, thinking, then went to his closet and opened the door. He stood looking at his gunbelt. He fought the temptation of taking the pistols out, remembering what he owed his pa. He shut the door again and walked over to his bed thinking of Alex. He unbuttoned his shirt and draped it over the back of a chair. If it had been me instead of Alex, what would Alex do?

He'd listen to Pa. No doubt there. Alex has always been the easy-tempered one.

Rick flopped down on his bed and somehow, finally, drifted to sleep.

It must have been toward three in the morning when he awoke suddenly to the sound of horses galloping and gunshots. A bullet smashed into his bedroom window and shattered the glass. Another bullet broke the lamp and a third thudded into the wall above his head. He dove for his guns and struggled to belt them on with his left hand. Outside, riders were circling the ranch house spraying bullets and smashing windows. Flames shot up from the bunkhouse, and men's voices were yelling and horses neighing, their hooves tearing up the ground. Rick had his boots on and threw open the door when Sal and Elmo came rushing from the back kitchen area, both carrying rifles. Something crashed through the window and a flame spurted up.

Rick rushed down the stairs, a pistol in his left hand. Sal was trying to beat out the flames, and Marita was running about throwing water from jugs she'd hauled from the back porch. Rick heard other windows being smashed and smelled smoke from one of the rooms.

"Delance! Come out with your hands up!" a voice shouted from the yard.

"Don't trust him, Rick," Elmo whispered. The old-timer had his rifle in a window and plugged off a shot.

"Your pappy's dead, boy," someone else shouted, "come out and we'll let you go!"

Dead?

The flames were spreading. They were caught like chicks in a ring of foxes.

"Senor Rick, come! We will all die in the fire!"

"Don't go out there Sal!"

But Sal grabbed Marita's arm and headed for the door. The girl struggled to free herself, yelling at her dad not to go out, but Sal was paying no heed to the warning. No sooner had Sal stepped out calling, "No shoot, senor, no shoot—" then a spray of bullets cut him down. Marita screamed. Rick caught sight of one of the attackers on horseback among the trees and fired a shot. The man lurched back and fell from his horse.

The next moments blurred into confusion as the heat and smoke turned deadly, and as bullets hurled into the room through windows and the open front door.

Was Sal dead? Where was Marita?

"Elmo...the kitchen, quick—"

His father had a cellar built in case of an Indian attack, and Rick caught Elmo's arm and drew open a small door beneath the kitchen table. He held it open while Elmo climbed down into the opening and onto a ladder. Rick followed, pulling the door shut and thrusting the bolt into place.

He felt his way down the ladder into cool blackness until his boots met the stone floor.

Rick lit a candle and handed it to Elmo, freeing Rick's good arm. He went to one end of the cellar where he slid some shelves away from the wall, revealing an opening.

Elmo followed him into the entrance of a small tunnel dug through dirt and rock. "Well if'n that don' take all," he said, awed. "Looks like a mine."

"It leads to the stables. Pa was worried about Comanches. Quick, Elmo, help me pull these shelves back into place."

Hunched over, they moved slowly in the low tunnel, and then they sat down and waited out the danger above them.

Pa dead! Was the renegade lying? Or had they come upon him as he rode to Santa Fe? Rick dropped his head into his hands and prayed silently, fervently, that God would spare his father's life.

"Please, Lord Jesus, don't let them kill him. I know all things are possible with You. The Scripture says 'My times are in thy hand.'"

Perhaps fifteen minutes passed before Rick led Elmo the rest of the way through the tunnel to the outer exit near the stables. All was quiet except for his and Elmo's breathing.

He slowly raised the cover, listening for anyone in the stable. He heard nothing except the horses. A cover of dry hay fell on his face as he opened the hatch. He brushed it away. They were alone. Rick climbed out, and Elmo followed. It felt good to walk upright again. Rick led the way to the open stable door.

The night was hot, and the big yellow moon was beginning to set behind the Sangre de Cristo Mountain range. In the distance they heard voices and horses. The sound of a bullet mingled with the roar of flames. They must think everyone is dead, caught inside the burning hacienda. Fire and smoke filled the air.

"Can you shoot?" Rick whispered to Elmo as they left the stable and crawled behind some low bushes.

The old-timer's eyes snapped in the moonlight. "Best shot in Texas!"

They circled back behind the trees to where the renegades had concealed themselves, but they'd ridden off. The bunkhouse was crackling and burning, and the bodies of the cowhands who had been confined to their bunks with sickness were strewn across the ground, riddled with bullets, still lying where they'd tried to run for it.

"Them yellow-bellied snakes in th' grass," Elmo muttered.

Rick's anger settled into something cold and determined.

They neared the hacienda, and Rick searched for Marita and Sal. Sal was still breathing when Rick managed to drag him farther away from the charred, smoking porch to the pepper tree, but his voice rasped and his eyes glazed over with shock.

His hand reached to grasp the front of Rick's sweat-stained shirt as his last breath came in a hoarsely whispered prayer.

"Marita—find my little Marita…"

He and Elmo searched the grounds. There was no sign of her. Rick, grim and deadened with loss, believed he wouldn't find the young senorita until he located Bodene and his rustlers.

The sun was coming up in the topaz-blue sky with the rustic mountains etched against the horizon in the color of sienna. Rick saw riders approaching. Tom Hardy and a few of his cowhands drew rein near the sycamore trees, but Zel wasn't with them. Tom, a rugged man with pale eyes and gray in his brown hair, surveyed the devastation in grim silence. Rick faced him from some feet away, his rifle resting on his slinged arm. Elmo was out of sight behind the pepper trees.

"Did you see the men who did this?" Tom Hardy asked dourly.

Rick wasn't about to give away what he knew—or didn't know."

"I'll find them."

Tom didn't look pleased, and it was clear he wanted him out of it.

"When Sal opened the door last night to escape with his daughter, they thought it was me and shot him down in cold blood. They carried Marita away with them."

Tom Hardy's square jaw went rigid. "We're getting up a bigger posse. We'll hunt 'em down, boy, and we'll bring 'em in."

Rick didn't know whether to believe him or not. Tom Hardy wore two faces.

"You do that, Mr. Hardy," he said evenly, never taking his finger from inside the rifle trigger guard. Tom Hardy noticed, as did the sober-looking cowhands with him, including the big blond fellow, Dutch. None of them spoke.

"You look for them," Rick repeated. "I'll be looking, too, in my own way. They killed Alex and my father and destroyed the hacienda. Our cattle's been rustled into Mexico most likely, and most of the horses in the barn were run off. The sick men in the bunkhouse were shot down like mad dogs. I'm hunting those hombres down, Mr. Hardy. And when I find them, I'll kill them."

Tom Hardy looked down at him for a long moment, his calloused brown hands resting on the saddle horn. The horses stomped their hooves in the dust, and there was the creak of leather as some of the men shifted uneasily in their saddles. Rick looked at each one of them to see if he recognized any of them from last night.

Tom Hardy gestured his head toward the still-smoldering ranch house. "That won't do you much good now, boy. At sixteen you should be getting schooling in the East. That's what your pa wanted. This property is too much for any young fellow to manage. I'll buy you out at a fair price. You can take the money and build yourself a new life somewhere else. Become an educated man like Lucien wanted."

Rick's anger boiled with the thunderheads gathering above the mountains. He felt the sweat bead on his forehead.

"The Triple D isn't for sale, Mr. Hardy. I'm keeping it intact, and that goes for Red Creek, too."

At the mention of Red Creek, Tom Hardy's face turned ashen. His eyes snapped with temper.

"You can't handle this land alone, boy. You need to listen to me!"

"You'd be next to the last man I'd listen to now, Mr. Hardy. I'm not forgetting it was you and Zel who suggested Pa hire Bodene's murdering rustlers for the cattle drive. Now I don't know yet whether you had anything to do with what happened or not, so for the moment I'll give you the benefit of the doubt. My father taught me that. But one thing's for sure, I'm not selling you the Triple D. And Mr. Hardy…" Rick's voice turned quieter. "…if ever I do find out you or Zel was involved I'll be coming back with a loaded gun."

Tom Hardy leaned forward in his saddle, his knuckles white as he gripped the bridle's reins. "I had nothing to do with what's happened here—not on the cattle drive and not last night. If I find Bodene, I'll hang him from the highest limb I can find."

Rick considered, then gave a curt nod. "All right. But does that go for Zel Willard, too?"

Hardy didn't like the question and he straightened. "Whoever is to blame will bear his judgment. We want this territory to be law-abiding." He turned in his saddle. "Boys, help bury the dead." He turned back, eying Rick.

"You're not going to be able to manage this rangeland," he said again.

"Maybe not, Mr. Hardy. Not now, anyway. Far as I'm concerned, since I've no more cattle, it can just sit a spell till I'm good and ready to rebuild and settle here. A good sabbatical won't hurt the land any. Meanwhile I'll have time to hunt down the killers of Pa and Alex…Sal, too."

Tom Hardy didn't like it, but he said no more. And after measuring Rick with a glance, he jerked the reins, turning his horse, and rode off toward his own ranch.

When the dead were buried, the Hardy cowhands left. Rick, still dazed, returned to the smoldering ruins. He searched within the scorched adobe walls for anything that had survived: Some clothes and boots were charred but still usable, Alex's favorite pistols that had been put in his trunk earlier were in good condition. He went to where his father's room had been…and little remained. Then he saw it—how it survived he could not say—his father's Bible with the handmade leather cover and cross. Except for charred edges and darkened leather, it was intact. He placed it into his saddlebag.

Feeling only emptiness in his heart, Rick mounted his strawberry roan, which Elmo had found not far from the hacienda. He rode to Angel's Creek to his mother's burial site. He dismounted and leaned against the willow tree looking down at the grave. The creek water tumbled over the rocks and the wind walked through the drooping branches. He leaned there, hat in hand, turning it around silently between his fingers.

He stood there for a long time, then rode back to where Elmo waited. Rick saw the line-back dun and paused.

"He just came alon' nice 'n easy like," Elmo said at Rick's questioning glance.

Rick took the rope and tied it to his saddle. He sat there a moment then looked down at Elmo.

"I'm going to Santa Fe. I'll report what's happened to Pa's lawyer, Mr. Billings. Then I'm riding to Fort Craig to talk to the army colonel. I'll see if I can find out how Pa was killed and what can be done about it."

"He was dry-gulched like Alex. That's what the boys said from the Hardy Ranch when they was buryin' the hands. Ferguson's men found him on the trail. They buried him close by at Red Ridge Gulch. There's a marker with rocks, they said."

Rick wanted to bring him back and lay him to rest beside his mother with Scripture words and a prayer, but he didn't know if he had the courage.

He drew in a deep breath and settled his hat lower on his dark head. "I need to alert the fort about Marita, too."

Elmo nodded. "I'm trailin' after ya, Rick. Wherever you're goin' I'm agoin', too."

Rick looked at him steadily. "For a time, maybe, Elmo, but then I've a different road to travel. Where I'm going, I wouldn't want anyone to follow."

Elmo looked at him warily. "That won't be an easy way to ride, Delance."

Rick's gaze hardened. "No, but it's the way I'm choosing."

Rick turned the reins and urged the strawberry roan ahead, leading the line-back dun with a tether. After a mile on his way toward Santa Fe, Rick looked over his shoulder. He saw Elmo on a mule trailing him. Rick paused under the lee of a red canyon ledge and waited for him.

One

Nevada Territory, 1862

*T*he Wells Fargo stage, after making stops at Van Syckles and Genoa, came slowing to halt in Carson City on its way to Virginia City. The dusty driver swung down and jumped lightly to the ground, followed by the man riding shotgun. The driver opened the doors.

"Won't be here long, folks, 'cause we're runnin' late. So's if you want to stretch yer legs and get some coffee, best go to it."

The passengers stepped down from the crowded cab and headed for the stage eatery for food and coffee. The four women and three men were all part of the Perry-Ralston Theater Company out of San Francisco. After they'd gone, Callie Halliday O'Day stepped from the coach, accepting the lifted hand of the renowned theater star, Ashe Perry. She was uncertain how she felt about returning to Virginia City after a seven-month performance in Sacramento and more recently the Golden City by the Bay. She'd been staying with Aunt Weda until her aunt had departed to help Uncle Samuel care for Callie's younger brother, Jimmy. Callie had moved then from Sacramento to the luxurious Palace Hotel in San Francisco where she'd met Ashe Perry. She was thrilled to have joined his theater company at his personal invitation. She'd also been given the opportunity by Ashe to buy into the Perry-Ralston Company, and she now owned a third of the shares.

I can't believe I'm returning to Virginia City as a star in my own right! And imagine being escorted by Ashe Perry! Callie knew a prickle of pride. Why who'd have thought Callie Halliday would be playing opposite one of New York's famed golden boys?

She felt the breeze ruffle her dark hair. She'd taken extra pains this morning to arrange it in a cascade of curls, as was the fashion, beneath her new, blue-satin bonnet. Two heavy trunks hoarding a dozen positively gorgeous gowns, bonnets, matching slippers, and crinolines galore were to be shipped from her hotel room in San Francisco to the newly built Halliday Mansion in Virginia City. All of her new gowns were to the praise of the French designer Sebastian in San Francisco. She hadn't needed so many of course, but she'd bought them for the satisfaction of being able to do so. She spent lavishly as she sought to quench her early years of deprivation, but each new gown, necklace, or set of earbobs she acquired seemed to do less and less to satisfy her thirst—so she bought more. Now she even had her own personal "secretary," Mrs. Elmira Jennings—thanks to Ashe, although Callie wasn't all that sure whether she should thank him.

Ashe's mother knew Elmira and had pleaded with Ashe to find a suitable position for the widowed woman. So when he'd asked Callie in San Francisco if she would mind terribly in hiring his mother's friend, Callie, anxious to make a good impression on Ashe, had agreed—to her own grief of mind.

Elmira was a tall, somber woman who always wore black and seldom spoke. Callie supposed the woman was somewhere in her forties. She spoke of herself as a "Pennsylvania Dutch woman." Callie wasn't sure why that should have anything to do with her ways. Elmira didn't look Dutch, though. She had very black, deep-set eyes, and hair as dark as a raven's wing. She wore no makeup, and Callie had the distinct notion that the woman disapproved of her and her wardrobe. Elmira drank weak tea smelling of anise seed. She drenched a handkerchief with a too-strong eucalyptus oil for her constant sniffles, and then stuffed the hanky inside her black bodice. The constant smell was giving Callie a headache.

Callie thought defensively, *I'm a silver heiress. I can afford to do most anything I want! Why shouldn't I have the kind of secretary I want instead of this cranky old feline?* She was used to getting her way. She'd learned quickly that people treated her differently as soon as they learned she was someone *special*— that is, *rich.* They were anxious to please and coddle her. Of the correctness of it, Callie's mind remained undecided. But then, she didn't need to decide. Not now, anyway. She was having too much fun. She'd made all her plans, so why interrupt them? She plucked at her glove. She hoped Uncle Samuel didn't lecture her. Aunt Weda had been bad enough in Sacramento, constantly warning about smooth-talking gents out to take advantage of her because she was not merely pretty but an heiress. Maybe so, but fiddlesticks! she was smart enough to see through a no-account ladies man.

She looked at Ashe and dimpled. He stood by the stage offering his arm to assist her down.

The powder-blue sky above the brown, barren hills supported a few puffball clouds. There was a promise of a hot summer already whispering on the dry spring wind, like envoys of trouble to come. She pushed such depressing thoughts away and touched her expensive new bonnet to make doubly sure everything was in place.

Ashe Perry smiled at her. His sandy, wavy hair and light-blue eyes obviously contributed to his successful acting career. "You look charming, Callie, my dear. Come along out of the sun. I think the summer will be extremely hot this year." He looked around at the hills and sagebrush as though it gave him cramps, and then walked her toward the eatery.

Callie felt the eyes of folks turning their way. It gave her a feeling of pride to walk beside such a talented man, knowing there wouldn't be anyone in Virginia City who could compare with him. There would be no dusty, smelly, poor-speaking miners for her! Ashe Perry had been educated back East. He spoke well because of his experience on the theater stage, and his warm, resonant voice had taken on a slightly British tone that carried with it a ring of proficiency.

His polished manners had been displayed on their first dinner date in San Francisco when he'd ordered their expensive meal by speaking to the waiter in French. He was older than she by perhaps eight years, and she'd been awed by his sophistication from the start.

As they walked together to the eatery he was mannered and neat in his white hat and dark jacket. She noted his straight shoulders. Even after the long, hard travel through dusty country and dry winds he looked well-dressed and refreshed. If he'd had a silver badge on his shirt, he would have made an ideal, handsome sheriff.

She was still smiling as she turned her head and noticed a rough-looking man standing out in front of Johnson's Dry Goods store. She saw him clearly in the brief moment their eyes met. He had a broad, rock-hard face and big yellowish teeth that showed as his lips spread in a rude smile, his eyes raking her. His look gave her a shudder. She turned her head away pretending not to have noticed, but not before spotting a Z-shaped scar across his leathery neck. From the corner of her eye she saw him mount his horse and ride slowly away still glancing at her and at Ashe as well. Ashe apparently didn't notice.

Callie saw the scarred man riding in a direction leading out of town, possibly toward the Carson River area where she knew of placer miners working along the river panning for gold.

She had an odd sensation that he'd been waiting for the stage just to watch who got off, but why?

"Come on, Ashe, I could use that coffee," she commented, determined to forget the distasteful moment.

Virginia City

The rugged young man wearing a buckskin shirt and breeches rode into the silver boomtown on a Saturday morning, trying not to draw attention to himself. Someone had been on his trail lately, tracking him as an Indian would. Someone who wished to kill from the shadows.

It was hard for Rick Delance to not be noticed. He was a good-looking man, six feet, weighing a solid one hundred eighty pounds, with an air of mystery surrounding him. Was he a gunfighter? An outlaw? He'd been on his own since he was sixteen, and was often misunderstood, though much of the uncertainty was intentional on his part. Delance had ridden the old outlaw trail with men of dangerous reputation in order to share their campfires, always hoping to pick up a name here or there in casual talk that might lead him to the men who'd ridden with Bodene that night five years ago. Except for Abner and Bodene, the others were shadows. Abner, Delance now believed, was a loner like himself and may no longer be riding with Bodene.

Rick rode down C Street to the barbershop. He stopped and dismounted. After tying his horse to a fence rail he went in. Twenty minutes later he came out clean-shaven, got on his horse, and headed for Beebe's Livery. The burly hostler looked up when he rode in. Delance thought he eyed him watchful like.

"How-do, Delance. Pony ain't rode in yet. Hope there's no more Paiute trouble. All we need is another dead Pony man. Everyone's anxious for news. They're bettin' over at the saloons on if'n there'll be war with the Rebs or not."

The Pony Express, delivering mail, was two days late. Delance had come to town every morning this week expecting a letter from Mr. Billings, his father's attorney in Santa Fe. However, he avoided mentioning Santa Fe to most folks. He wanted to keep his New Mexico connections quiet, a wish that might already have gone astray. Helvey, the mail clerk at the Wells Fargo Pony Express Office, knew he was expecting a letter, and where it came from, but there'd been no choice in that matter.

Delance walked over to the stalls where the horses were kept and casually looked them over. Beebe watched him. Delance found the horse he'd expected. It was a big dappled gray, and this one had come far and was in rough shape—in need of rest and good feed. Delance noted the Spanish-style saddle nearby, typical of many he'd seen in New Mexico, and similar to one he'd owned in kinder times. He looked the tired horse over, then glanced at the saddle again. The saddle was the real give away. From the looks of the horse, whoever rode him had likely won him and the saddle in a card game. Or taken them from a victim? Any hombre treating a good horse this way wouldn't bother with an expensive saddle like that except to steal it.

Beebe gestured. "That horse is a good'un. But he's come too far. Ridden thoughtless like. Hate to see a good horse treated like that. In fact, makes me madder'n a wet hen." Beebe shook his head with disgust. He picked up a cloth and began rubbing the horse down. "I do this even though that feller didn't pay me to do it."

Delance saw all he wanted, including the broken shoe on the horse's left front foot. He belonged to the man trailing him all right.

"Did the rider say where he came from?"

Beebe forked some hay for the big gray. "Fella hadn't any mind to waste on being friendly." He paused, leaning on the pitchfork. "You know him?"

Delance read the puzzled curiosity that showed in his eyes. While folks in town sometimes didn't know what to make of him, a few like Beebe and Helvey over at the Express Office were casual and friendly in spite of his reputation as a fast gun. Most tended to shy away, even though it was known that Brett Wilder had deputized him for a time for the gunfight with Hoadly and his men.

"Don't know if I know him or not. He's been trailing me off and on, but he's not too smart."

Beebe scratched his red locks. "How do you reckon that?"

Delance gestured his dark head. "That broken horseshoe left trail sign. If he was worth his salt, he would have known better."

"Trailin' you, huh? He's a mean-looking sidewinder."

Delance left the livery and stepped out on the boardwalk glancing down the street. He removed a cigar. Now, where would he have gone? One of the saloons, most likely. He struck a match and lit his smoke, all the while his eyes were busy looking for an ambush. He walked toward the Wells Fargo Stageline and Express Office. He slowed his pace when nearing the new Stardust Theater. Mighty fancy place. Tom Maguire from the San Francisco theater world was going to build a theater here in town as well, but the Stardust across the street belonged to Callie Halliday. She was to have her opening night there soon. Delance leaned a shoulder against a post, thinking things over.

The brick building with its gilded ornamentation had been under construction since last year and was undergoing its final decorating. He saw men working. Red velvet carpet was being laid.

He straightened from the post, stepped down into the dirt street, and walked over to the theater just as Gordon Barkly came out the front entrance. Gordon started to cut across the street to his small newspaper office near the Pony Express when Rick caught his eye. Gordon paused, reluctantly, Rick thought.

The young newspaperman had come from Sacramento in '59 to start his own paper. Word was that he'd first courted Annalee Halliday—now Mrs. Brett Wilder—before showing interest in Callie.

Gordon's face settled into stony coolness as Rick walked up. Rick was amused but didn't show it. Gordon knew of his partnership with Brett Wilder and Flint Harper in the Threesome Mine out on Gold Canyon, and he believed Gordon was hesitant to offend anyone who might soon become one of the town's silver barons—even though he didn't like him. Gordon was the type of man to pretend a false friendship if he believed he'd need to get on with the individual—in this instance, Delance.

Gordon nodded his head in greeting.

"Hello, Rick. How are things at Threesome?"

"We're shipping ore. It's starting to pay off." He gestured his head toward the Stardust Theater.

"Fancy place."

"Very well done, indeed. They open in two or three weeks I believe. Miss Halliday, or should we be calling her Miss O'Day now? will be performing, along with Ashe Perry. Looks as though she's doing well for herself. She owns a third of the Perry-Ralston Company and half of the Stardust."

"Who owns the other half of the theater, Ashe Perry?"

"No, same man who owns a third of the acting company, a gentleman by the name of Ralston from back East."

Delance looked at him sharply. "Ralston?"

Typical of a newspaperman's thirst for information, Gordon Barkly noticed his response.

"Yes, Hugh Ralston. From New York, I think. Do you know him?"

"Heard of him, if it's the same man. May not be." But Rick was uncomfortable with the notion of Callie forming a partnership with Hugh Ralston. Hoadly had mentioned Ralston once or twice, except Hoadly had said Hugh Ralston—a crooked theater man—was dead. Hoadly must have gotten it wrong.

"Is Ralston also an actor with Miss Callie and the Ashe Perry group?"

"That I haven't heard."

"How did she happen to become partners with Hugh Ralston?"

Gordon raised a brow of disapproval. "She might have met him in San Francisco through Ashe Perry. I can ask, I'll be doing an interview with her before her opening night." He looked down the street toward Wells Fargo. "I've heard a few unpleasant things about Ashe Perry. Maybe I'll telegraph some friends of my father back East and see what they can shake out."

Delance thought it would be well to light a fire under the newspaperman's feet. Gordon could check into matters better than he could.

"What falls out might be a nest of rattlers."

Gordon's gaze swung back and measured him a moment. "Oh? What makes you think so?"

"I don't know much about Ashe Perry. But if Hugh Ralston is the same man I've in mind, he knew Macklin Villiers and his lawyer, Colefax."

Gordon's mouth dipped down. "Callie's cousin...who was shot by her father Jack Halliday. Yes, I know all about Macklin Villiers and Colefax. Two clever minds bent on havoc."

"It might be wise if you did some looking into Ralston as well as Ashe Perry."

Rick saw the greed for information on men he didn't like or approve of kindle in Gordon's eyes.

"You bet I will. I'll look into it all right. Callie's quite independent now that she's come into her own inheritance, but she's young enough so that Samuel should know about this as well."

Delance remembered how Gordon had jealously tried to stir up trouble for Brett Wilder on the ranch land out at Grass Valley. Gordon had long been overturning rocks and poking around for stories. The thought of him nosing around about Hugh Ralston, and even Ashe Perry, didn't give Delance any grief. If anyone could dig up the facts it would be Gordon Barkly.

"The stagecoach will be in soon. I'll see you later, Delance."

Rick watched him hurry across the street to the *Barkly News* office. Delance stood there a minute longer thinking, and he didn't like what was stirring in his mind. Callie was a silver heiress, but also beautiful. Ambitious men with plans would naturally gravitate toward her. Could Ralston have been involved in Macklin Villier's past plans to take control of the Halliday mine?

Rick tried to recall exactly what Hoadly had said about Ralston back when Hoadly had ridden into Tucson looking to hire Rick's gun for a job here in Virginia Town. Delance had not liked Hoadly, a cheap gunslinger with a murderer's heart, but he'd left Tucson believing the silver rush would eventually become a magnet to draw the men he was looking for.

They hadn't come, but things had been stirring recently. He thought of the horse with the broken shoe in the livery. Delance believed things were heating up because of Billings' recent contacts with him over his father's will and his right to the Triple D.

Could it be that he'd been wrong all this time? What if the killers he'd searched for these years had never left New Mexico? If word was out that he was returning, those same killers would want to stop him before he ever left Virginia City.

Delance started toward the Wells Fargo Stageline and Express Office, then changed his mind. The stage wasn't due in from Carson for another hour, and if the Pony had ridden in people would be shouting the news. There was time now to talk with Callie's uncle, Samuel Halliday, the circuit-riding preacher.

Rick turned and walked toward Sun Mountain.

Delance approached the small, newly built Grace Chapel that was erected midway up Sun Mountain. In the early days of the silver strike, Samuel had stayed in a dugout cave in the side of the mountain, but he wasn't living in the old dugout anymore because money from Jack Halliday's half of the Halliday-Harkin mine had permitted a mansion, though Rick had heard the ostentatious house had been all Callie's decision.

The Christian chapel was of simple brick construction with a cross, yet even so, Samuel had insisted on a stained-glass window. When sunlight shone through the glass it glimmered like a mixture of jewels. "Better than the shine of silver," Samuel liked to say, "even though, by the grace of God, silver's what let me build this chapel."

Delance stood looking at the colorful window, noting that the scene of the resurrection of Christ seemed identical to the one in the church his pa had taken him and Alex to during their childhood years. When he saw it, he remembered things from his childhood: prayer time with Alex and his pa, the sound of his father's voice reading from the Bible, the prayers of thanksgiving around the evening supper table in the spacious hacienda....

Rick stirred from the memory as Samuel spoke from behind him.

"Good to see you, Rick. Come in and sit a spell. I'll put us some coffee on. Nothing like that bit of a kitchen I've got built onto the parson's study."

"Hello, Samuel. I hear your niece is coming home."

"Today, in fact." He shook his head. "Don't know how long Callie will stay, though. She's got stars in her eyes. She sees the glamor of Broadway and New York. I don't like it; I don't like it at all. I worry about that little one."

"Will Hugh Ralston be with her?"

"Now, I wonder."

Delance followed him to the chapel and up the wooden steps to a double door with a silver plaque that read, "Sirs, what must I do to be saved?" It was followed by the apostle Paul's answer in Acts 16:31: "Believe on the Lord Jesus Christ, and thou shalt be saved."

Delance didn't come here on Sundays. He knew the folks, especially the ladies, wouldn't look kindly on a man known as a gunfighter sitting in one of their new pews. He had that knowledge from his own growing-up days in Cimarron, when there'd been scowls from some in the little country church he'd attended with his pa and Alex. A man of reputation had come one day, and the folks got all upset 'cause they didn't want his "kind" around their daughters. Not that he blamed them.

When Rick came, it was late on Saturday nights when Samuel's lamp was still glowing in the parson's office as he was preparing for the morning worship service. On some of those Saturday nights, when lonely, Rick had ridden in from Gold Canyon to see if the lamp was burning in the window. After a time he began to think Samuel guessed and deliberately lit it in case Delance rode by. Samuel would always greet Rick in a relaxed and friendly way and make him a cup of coffee. Now and then he'd say a few words about the Lord, but he hadn't pushed him. Rick wondered how much Samuel knew of his past in Cimarron. Certainly he hadn't told him.

Delance felt drawn to Samuel because he was rugged and practical in his faith. He'd never told Samuel about his pa's Bible, and that sometimes he'd take it out of the hidden corner of his saddlebag and read it when alone at his cabin on Threesome.

Samuel never talked down to him about his reputation or pushed him to put away his gunbelt. In fact, he never talked about his past at all. There'd been times when Rick had come close to telling Samuel about those dark events on the Triple D and what he intended to do about them, but he had yet to cross that threshold. He thought he already knew what Samuel would tell him—likely the same thing his pa had said when Alex was shot down in cold blood. Delance wasn't willing to change his plans now. He lived for the day when he'd find Bodene and Abner and face them on the street.

Over coffee, in the small kitchen, Samuel told him that Jimmy and Weda were down at the stage waiting for Callie's arrival.

"Callie's moving ahead too quickly with this Ashe Perry. Hope I can reason with that girl to hold off on an engagement."

Delance affected calm disinterest. *Engagement? Already?* Secretly, he was disappointed, yet angry too. He wanted Callie for himself, and he was going to get her. Perry or no Ashe Perry. Callie would be mighty shocked to know that.

"That's what I wanted to talk to you about, Samuel, Ashe Perry and Hugh Ralston."

Samuel's greenish eyes from beneath black-winged brows touched with silver seemed to sparkle. There was a time or two when Delance had an uncomfortable feeling that Samuel sensed the attraction he'd felt for his niece from the first time he'd laid eyes on her. Samuel had commended him for protecting Callie from her cousin Rody Villiers the night of her father's death, and had nothing good to say about Gordon Barkly who'd failed to protect her.

But Rick was no fool. With his reputation, he knew that neither Samuel nor Callie's aunt would look favorably upon his interest in her. He hadn't made up his mind yet to try changing their minds. It would depend on whether she was in love with Perry.

"Do you mind if I ask what you know about her partner in the Stardust?"

"Hugh Ralston? Not a thing about him, except she wrote Weda she'd met him through Ashe. Ralston's lately come to California from back East." Samuel looked at him long and hard. "Why? You've heard something otherwise?"

It was like Samuel to know where he was headed and then come straight to the point.

"If it's the same man I'm thinking of, he kept company with some bad hombres. Hoadly mentioned a Hugh Ralston to me back in Tucson. Though he may not be the same man."

Samuel leaned across the table. "Hoadly! That murdering coyote!"

"Uh-huh. Said the man was a friend of Macklin Villiers."

Samuel just stared at him. Delance finished his coffee and set his cup down. He stood. "Thing is, Hoadly said Hugh Ralston was dead."

Samuel looked up, furrowing his brows. "You don't say....A friend of Macklin's," he repeated. He rubbed his chin. "Now I wonder why Hoadly would mention Ralston to you?"

Delance picked up his black flat-crowned hat. "At the time I didn't pay close attention. Wish I had. You might want to discuss this with Miss Callie...and Gordon Barkly, too."

Samuel was still seated and looked up at him blankly. "Gordon? Why him?"

Rick smiled. "His father's in politics. He knows some important people in the East. Gordon's planning on looking into Hugh Ralston's background." He moved to the door. The Pony should be in by now. He wanted to get that letter from Billings and then ride to Carson to see Bill Stewart about what he could expect from his father's will. Rick wondered if he still had rights to the Triple D. It had been abandoned these past five years. Stewart, an attorney, could tell him.

"Just thought you should know," Delance told him.

Samuel stood, still looking dazed. "Yes…yes, thanks, Rick. I'll surely look into this myself. If Callie's partnering with a friend of Macklin's, then I'd better know what it's about."

Samuel walked him outdoors. They paused under a newly planted birch tree already making some shade. The sun was hot for April.

Rick walked down the mountain to C Street and toward the Express Office. He hoped Callie had more sense than to fall for Ashe just because he was a theater name. He grinned. If not, well, then he'd just need to convince her otherwise. Could he get her for himself? He was going to try, but he would need to move carefully.

Two

The boy of ten, with olive-green eyes starred with black eye-lashes and wearing a red cotton shirt, sat in an open-top buggy beside a small, frail lady of barely a hundred pounds with white curly hair and clear gray eyes. They were parked near the Wells Fargo station in the bustling silver boomtown of Virginia City, Nevada.

The boy moved restlessly, taking a brown hat from his dark curly head and putting it back on again.

"Pony's bound to come today, Aunt Weda. Sure makes a person mighty curious. Pony Bob was due days ago. Maybe an Injun got him."

"You never-your-mind about the Pony Express, Jimmy boy. It's the stagecoach from Carson bringing your sister concernin' us."

"Sure will be glad to see Callie again after a whole year."

"Been longer than that for you and Samuel."

"She's a mighty big star now, just like Mama was." It was hard to keep the pride he felt from affecting his voice.

Aunt Weda wrinkled her slim nose as though pestered by a fly. "About time she came back home, too."

"She doesn't really consider this home, Aunt Weda. She even mentioned moving back East in a letter to Uncle Samuel. First, though, she wants to go to the New Mexico Territory to see Annalee and Brett."

"Well that girl better mind herself to be sure. As pretty as she is, and rich to boot—well, there's no counting all the scalawags who'd try to take advantage."

Jimmy knew that Uncle Samuel worried about the same thing. Callie wrote a month ago from San Francisco saying she was coming back to Virginia City to play the new theater, but she wouldn't be staying. Interesting thing was, she said she wasn't coming alone, either. There was an actor-friend coming too, maybe a whole host of acting folks she'd met in San Francisco when she'd played the theater there. Jimmy thought the actor's name was strange, something like "Smoke Berry," but Callie was sure taken with him. She'd said he was mighty important in places like New York and London. Callie seemed powerfully impressed that she'd met him and even acted with him in some fancy play or two in San Francisco.

"Hope we can see Callie when she does a play at the new theater," he said. "I looked in the door when it was open and there were men working inside. It's big! With lots of fancy red rugs and drapes and lots of silver and there was a big chandelier, too. One of the workmen said it came all the way from Vienna."

"Chandeliers…chandeliers don't impress me much. Don't know what your mama would say about Callie taking to the stage like this." Aunt Weda heaved a tired sigh. "Lilly never did set much store by the notion. Callie was pestering your mama since she was only fourteen to become an actress like she was, but Lilly had better ideas for your sister. She wanted Callie to teach school in some nice, quiet little town instead of this wild and woolly Virginia City! Why, your mama will be turning over in her grave when she sees what Callie's up to."

Jimmy looked at her. "She can't turn over in her grave, Aunt Weda," he said soberly. "Mama's not there now. Uncle Samuel said she never was. He read to me about how she's been carried into the presence of Jesus from the moment she died, in Second Cor—Cor—"

"Corinthians. I know, I know. Was just a figure of speaking. Now don't go gettin' me off the subject. Your mama wanted Callie to be a plain girl and settle down and marry a good fella, raise a bunch of good kids. Now she's all for glittering gowns, jewels, and applause." She shook her head, cotton bonnet jiggling, and whisked her fan at a fly. "Least Samuel got her to come back."

There was satisfaction in her voice, but Jimmy wasn't even sure about that. Callie wrote she wanted to come back for a short time to perform with that theater star in the Stardust Theater.

"That last trip Samuel made to San Francisco to talk to her seems to have worked. Still, it's worrisome."

Jimmy didn't know about that, and he didn't much care about Callie raising a bunch of kids, or even being a teacher, but he did wonder about the Pony Express.

"Sure seems like Pony Bill ought to have come by now. In the Paiute war in '60, when you were still in Sacramento, one of the Pony riders was shot through with arrows. I saw him come in and there was blood coming even from his mouth—"

"*Jimmy!*"

"Rick Delance must be a mite curious, too. I seen him come riding in from Threesome Mine every day this week to check on the mail."

"You circle clear round that boy when you see him. Mister Delance is a hired gunfighter."

"Not anymore. An' he's mighty big to be called a boy, Aunt Weda. Why, he's as tall as Brett and just as strong, too. I'd say six feet and a hundred-and-eighty pounds—"

"That's neither here nor there. It's what's in the heart and head that matters to God."

"Yup. Know what? Delance is mighty fast with those guns of his, too. You should'a seen him. He sure taught Cousin Rody Villiers a lesson. Not only beat him on the draw, but aimed at his gun hand, then dumped him in the water trough out front of the Virginia House Hotel." He grinned at her. "But that was before you came, Aunt Weda."

"Doesn't sound like I been missing much but a heap of trouble."

"Yeah, but you know what? It was Cousin Rody who started it. Rick was minding his own business, but Cousin Rody was mean to Callie. Then he was going to shoot Delance right then and there—Callie saw it, too. She said Delance drew like lightning."

"That's nothing to brag about."

"It is when the other gunfighter's bad—and he's goin' to kill you, too. Delance was so fast Rody was stunned. He just stared at his broken wrist and began to cry like a baby."

"Well I'd cry too. It must have hurt plenty."

"Oh, Aunt Weda! Rody wasn't crying because of that, but because he wouldn't be able to draw his gun fast anymore."

"Either way, tush. Both them boys are cut from the same piece of cloth as far as I'm concerned."

"That's not fair, Auntie."

"You can certainly find better heroes to think about. Your Uncle Samuel for instance. Up before dawn with the Bible, readin' and prayin'. Walked with the Lord all these years, too."

Jimmy nodded soberly. His Uncle Samuel was a hero, all right, and a brave man, but even he carried guns and was the best Indian tracker around, except maybe for Rick. But Jimmy knew better than to argue, nor did he want to trouble his aunt. She was like a beloved granny and had come to Virginia City a year ago at Uncle Samuel's request just to help look after him. That was shortly after the death of his pa and the going away of his favorite sister, Annalee. Annalee had treated Jimmy something like a mother would, though he'd not come out and say it. She and Brett had left for his ranch in Grass Valley and got married, then they went to New Mexico to the sanitarium ranch Dr. Wilder was going to start up. Annalee had what folks called "consumption," and she was trying to get well.

Then Callie went away too, just a few months after Annalee—except Callie had gone to Sacramento to play the theater. Jimmy had been left alone with Uncle Samuel. Jimmy loved Samuel like a grandpa, but there was no denying he'd gotten mighty sad after all that happened with his pa and with his sisters going away. Then Uncle Samuel had written for Aunt Weda to come.

The gray-haired woman, dedicated to her baking, cooking, and sewing, had seemed to be all that Jimmy needed to snap him out of his doldrums. He'd been comforted by her arrival. Aunt Weda was not new to him. He and his sisters and mama—Lillian O'Day, the theater star—had lived most of their lives with Aunt Weda and her husband Charlie on their humble Sacramento farm. Then Uncle Charlie died on the Fraser River gold hunt, and

Jimmy's mama met the angel of death on the early route from Placerville to Strawberry Flat over the High Sierras. There'd been a stagecoach accident, and she'd been injured. From what he'd been told, his mama died before help could get there....

Things had sure changed since back then, when he, Annalee, and Callie first arrived. All kinds of money came pouring in now from the Halliday-Harkin Mine. Now they had themselves a big two-story house not far from the Mackay Mansion. Uncle Samuel had his chapel built, and Aunt Weda had a shiny buggy that she drove around town calling on the ladies to get a children's Sunday school started. She wanted to pass a law to ban all the saloons, too, but nobody was of a mind to agree.

Yep, things changed all right. Now he had a bunch of new clothes, boots, hats, and what really mattered—his own pinto horse. Uncle Samuel said there was lots of money for his education, too, when he did some growing up. He was to get a third of all the silver money the mine had produced, and it was all being put aside for him in Mr. Williams' bank down the street. Callie already controlled her third, and so did Annalee.

"Elmo says Rick knows all about New Mexico Territory, but he won't talk about it. Reckon he knows all about the area where Annalee and Brett are living."

"Maybe that Mr. Delance has got himself a mighty good reason to keep his stay in New Mexico quiet," Aunt Weda said dryly. "With those guns he carries, it don't surprise me none. He didn't draw first on Rody, that's true, but I hear he killed a man in Tucson, a man named Clegg. And that old codger Elmo is just another scalawag to be avoided. Him and those tales he fills your ears with are just plain nonsense. Says his friend Delance comes from a good family, my foot!"

Jimmy tugged at his hat. "Brett said the same thing once."

"Did he? Well, he was just bein' kind."

"Gordon Barkly says if I come up with a good tale he'll pay me a nickel and put it in his paper, the *Barkly News.* Maybe I'll be a newspaperman when I grow up. Wonder if he'd like one of Elmo's tales about Delance."

"Well you be careful now. You go hanging around these saloons and mines picking up gossip, and you'll get more than a tale or two—you'll likely get a heap of trouble. Now you watch for that stage she'll be on, Jimmy. Seems it ought to be here by now."

"I'll go ask Thompson if there's any news yet."

He jumped down from the buggy and made his way toward the Wells Fargo Station. He hadn't said anything to Aunt Weda but a moment ago he'd seen Rick Delance riding his horse from Beebe's Livery.

The three terraced streets on Sun Mountain: A, B, and C, had few cross streets because property was too valuable to waste. To get from one street to the other, he, like everyone else, had to scramble up and down hilly property.

The town was busy, and Jimmy made his way through the wagon trains and teams of oxen. Back in '59 when they'd arrived to hunt for their pa, there'd been fewer than several hundred people here. Now it numbered well into the thousands, with still more coming.

Jimmy paid little attention to the diverse crowd. He had long ago grown accustomed to the sight of Chinese with pigtails balancing baskets from yokes on their shoulders as they hurried from the Oriental quarter past canvas cabins reeking of tea and the heady odor of red poppies.

He was on tiptoe staring down the dirt street for any sign of the stage. He hurried out of the way of a wagon veering down C Street with barrels piled high. The driver cursed a Mexican vaquero who galloped past with a string of mustangs.

Then Jimmy saw Rick Delance nearing the hitching rail outside the Express Office on his line-back dun. Delance had told him he'd busted his right arm the first time he tried to ride that stallion, which had come from a wild herd roaming New Mexico near the Texas border.

Jimmy liked the stallion, too. He liked its black face, mane, and tail. It had some Indian "appaloosa" in it, so Delance said, and some "Morgan," too. Jimmy didn't know a lot about horses yet, but the way Delance said those two words convinced him it was special. His own horse he'd named "Reb." That might not go over too well with the Yankees in town. He'd heard that Southerners in Virginia City were a bunch of "fire-eaters." He didn't know why they said that, but he'd heard that "fire-eaters" didn't seem to appreciate the new president, Abraham Lincoln, much.

Jimmy hadn't decided if he wanted to be Union or State's rights. He didn't know which he was supposed to be. He wasn't rightly excited about Yankees, but he didn't like the notion of the Southern states quitting the Union, either. Some said the fight was over the wrong of keeping slaves, others said it had to do with a State's right so the federal government couldn't be breathin' down their necks all the time.

Guess I'm still in the middle, he thought, and wondered how many Yankees and Rebs felt the same way who'd still be told to pick up a rifle and start fighting.

David S. Terry, previously a California Supreme Court Justice, was whispered to have plans to seize the Comstock lode of silver for the South. He kept saying, "As the South goes, so goes the lode." If war came and Virginia City did go with the South, Gordon Barkly said Mr. Terry already had authority from back home to be Virginia City's governor. Mr. Terry's "secesh" friends were already calling him "Governor Terry."

"As the South goes, so goes Washoe, so goes Sun Mountain," Jimmy was saying as his boots clambered over the boardwalk toward Rick Delance.

Jimmy saw Rick step down from his horse. He liked to watch him because he always made it look so smooth and easy. Seemed to Jimmy everything about Delance was sort of that way, even the way he wore those guns—Colt 1860 Lawman six-shooters—tied down. Jimmy knew about the guns because he'd asked old Elmo, Delance's friend. Elmo knew a lot about Rick Delance and bragged about him, too. "None better'n with a gun," he'd told Jimmy.

Yup, they was—were—mighty big pistols, Jimmy thought. Elmo said Delance had spent months and months practicing his draw until it was so fast and easy that you could hardly see 'em come out of the holsters. He'd even learned to draw with his left hand, but that, Elmo had told him, "were a secret." *Rick has a rifle, too, in his saddle-scabbard...was it a Henry rifle?* Jimmy wasn't sure about that.

Jimmy admired Delance from afar. "Maybe I'll be like him. I'll grow up and get me a pair of .44 Lawmans."

Delance wore a buckskin shirt and breeches. His hat was black, but Jimmy had also seen him wear what was called Spanish clothes, a wide rimmed hat, a poncho, and boots with big Spanish spurs—Elmo said they wore 'em a lot where Delance came from. Jimmy guessed that meant New Mexico Territory.

Delance was big with lots of muscle. Jimmy liked that, too...being strong. His hair wasn't dark like his own and Callie's, but a lighter brown, and the sun had turned some of it golden-like.

Jimmy walked up, his thumbs under his suspenders eying Delance who hadn't noticed him yet.

"Draw, Mister!" he said in a low, rough voice.

Delance turned, his move so quick and quiet that Jimmy's mouth slipped open and his eyes must have widened as he stared at the barrel. Jimmy stood motionless, gaping, and his gaze lifted to Rick's face.

Delance winced, then released a breath that told Jimmy he was mighty displeased!

Whew, I'd best not do that again. Jimmy offered a shy smile. "Sorry...Delance."

"You do that again, boy, and I won't wait for Samuel to tan your hide, I'll do it."

"Elmo's right. You sure are fast!"

Delance leaned an arm against the saddle and tipped his hat back. "You stay away from Elmo. And you best forget what you saw just now."

"Ah, shucks, Delance! Everybody's always telling me to stay away from everybody else interestin'. Can't see as how I can be a newspaperman if I don't talk to folks. Anyhow, I don't honestly see as how I can forget what I saw, even if I tried hard."

"You'd best try, boy."

Jimmy knew an ornery moment. "Maybe I could sell what I just seen for a nickel to the *Barkly News*. How's this for a head-line? 'Eye witness says Rick Delance draws his pistol in mere sec-onds.'" Jimmy grinned.

Jimmy saw the flicker in Delance's dark-brown eyes and didn't know how to read the glint. Rick might have been amused, then again, he might not.

"You do that, and I'll have a long talk with Samuel. Knowing your uncle like we both do, I'm guessing you won't be too pleased about that talk...or about what'd likely happen afterward. Might not be able to sit comfortable for a few days. And your caption is too long. You'd need to shorten it plenty."

Jimmy swallowed. "No, sir. I mean yes, sir." He changed the subject quickly. "Is it true you know all about New Mexico Territory?"

Jimmy noted another spark in his eyes. "Why do you ask?"

"'Cause that's where my sister Annalee is. Brett, too. Not in Santa Fe but around Pecos I think, or is it Cimarron?"

"I know the area," Delance said mildly. "I've heard from Brett recently. They're doing fine. Mighty pretty there."

"I'd sure like to go there myself and see Annalee and Brett. Callie would like to go there, too."

Rick's quick gaze paid him closer attention. "Callie? How do you know that?"

"She wrote Uncle Samuel about it. If Callie goes, I want to go with her. Maybe Samuel will let us all take the stage. I'd like to travel the Ol' Santa Fe Trail. Hey! That's somethin' I could write about in the newspaper. 'Boy takes historical journey.'"

Rick laughed quietly.

"Callie's coming in today," Jimmy said rubbing his palms together. "Just like old times. Any minute now. She and a whole bunch of theater people from San Francisco."

Then the news that Jimmy had been waiting for broke through the morning air.

"Ho! Here comes the Pony! Make way!"

There was a scramble to clear a path in the street.

"Here he comes!"

Jimmy felt Rick take hold of his arm and pull him back to the boardwalk. Men were jumping out of the street. It wasn't long before the expressman came galloping down C Street from the direction of Six Mile Canyon.

The rider dismounted. Jimmy saw the mustang, foaming at the mouth, being swiftly led away to water and rest.

"Did you see him, Delance? He sure was in a hurry!"

"Yes, he's ridden in from Buckland's Station along the Carson River."

"War!" shouted the Pony rider.

War! Jimmy turned to look at Delance. He looked sober but not surprised.

The crowd closed in, and Jimmy took hold of a wooden post along the boardwalk and stepped up onto a handrail to get a view.

"What's going on?" someone shouted from the back of the crowd.

"War! Those Rebs fired on Fort Sumter!"

Jimmy, standing on the rail, looked down at Delance. "Where's Fort Sumter?"

"South Carolina."

"That's a mighty long ways from here." Jimmy felt a little disappointed. He thought there might be some fighting here in Nevada Territory.

"A civil war will affect every American, North or South," Delance said.

"Then the South is going to fight?"

"Looks like they are," Delance said grimly.

Jimmy gazed down at him. "Which side are you on, Rick?"

For a long moment Jimmy didn't think he would answer. Maybe he didn't want folks to know how he felt?

"I reckon the States joined the Union of their own free will. We're a Republic not a Democracy, though people often think otherwise. If the citizens of a state have a grief with the federal government that can't be reconciled, and the Feds keep intervening, then it's my opinion they have the right to take a course of action decided upon by those who live in that state. That's how I see it."

Jimmy pondered. "You spoke funny—like a lawyer. I like you better the other way."

Rick smiled. "Is that your aunt in the buggy over yonder?"

Jimmy turned and looked toward where his Aunt Weda was gesturing wildly. "Yes, sir, that's her, all right. Now I'm in for trouble. She's come here a few months ago from Sacramento to live with us. We're waiting for the stage from Carson."

"Reckon she's a nice little lady. She's having a fit with you standing here talking to me. So I suggest you do as she wants and go back to the buggy and wait for the stage and Miss Callie. Better tell your aunt the North and South are at war."

"She's going to be mighty upset. We have folks in New Orleans. Lots of 'em. Some in Missouri, too."

"She has a right to be upset. Reckon a whole lot of us will be before it's over."

Jimmy shimmied down his perch too swiftly and landed amid some barrels that toppled onto the street. The storekeeper next to the Express Office ran out hollering, "Jimmy!"

"Sorry, Mister Jakes!" Jimmy was on his feet racing toward the buggy, holding his hat in place.

"War with the Yankees!" he shouted.

Three

≈

Rick Delance left his horse at the rail and began shouldering his way through the throng. Men were scattering with the news of war and someone called out, "Sound the word! There'll be a meeting at Fayer's place tonight. Governor Terry will be there."

"'Governor' Terry? Who elected him?" a man scoffed, and a murmur of discontent arose.

"You'll find out soon enough."

"First it's 'President' Jefferson Davis, now it's 'Governor' Terry. Well, I'll be bound!"

Threats erupted, with some pushing and shoving. Delance avoided trouble by skirting around the hotheads. He came to the Pony Express Office connected to the Wells Fargo Stage Depot.

He stepped inside casually, lingering at the entrance, his glance affecting indifference as he noted those present. There was a line for mail pickup, and Delance walked forward and stood so that he could keep an eye on the door. A woman turned and left with a small parcel, and a man entered. Straw-colored hair hung below his hat. His jaw was jutting forward with stubble, and his narrow chin made his high cheekbones seem more pronounced. His deep-set eyes circled the room, saw Delance, then slid away to an open window. He sauntered there and leaned his shoulder against the wall where he could face the street toward the stage depot.

Delance recognized the man's Texas-style spurs with the big rowels often used in the border areas. The boot heels were unusually high which gave him an odd, forward-tilting stance. Delance had never seen him before but he suspected, having mingled with too many in the past five years, that the man was a bad hombre. This was no miner looking for work nor a hopeful prospector. He looked like a drifter hunting trouble. Or, more likely, a hired gun working for someone in the shadows who wanted to keep his hands clean, just as Macklin Villiers had when he'd hired Hoadly to shoot Jack Halliday.

The man's eyes swerved back, saw Delance watching him evenly, and he straightened from the wall. Turning his shoulder toward him, he bent his head down as he slowly reached into a shirt pocket.

Delance had experience with sleeve guns, often used by gamblers, so he unobtrusively lowered his hands within reach of his gunbelt. No one in the Express Office seemed to notice. He didn't think the man would start shooting in a crowded office, but he'd learned long ago not to bet against some men's folly and blood lust.

The man slowly took out the makings of a smoke weed, taking his time building it—another habit picked up from the border. He struck a match on the heel of his boot. The match flared up and he raised it to the end of the makings drooping from one corner of his mouth. It seemed to Delance that the hard, cold eyes mocked him as his gaze dropped pointedly to Delance's gunbelt before turning again toward the street.

Could this be the hombre who'd been trailing him?

The door swung open—

Delance recognized his friend Flint Harper, owner of one of the larger mule train operations over the Sierras. Walking in, he glanced around, spotted Delance, then gestured with a nod of his head and strode up.

Delance kept an eye on the straw-haired man who was still facing the window with his back toward Delance, smoking his weed, easing the tension.

Flint Harper hadn't cottoned to Delance when they first met in '59. That changed when he saw Delance come alongside Brett Wilder in a showdown with Macklin Villier's hired gunfighters. Now Flint sought his company, and their friendship had strengthened over the past year as they respected one another's strengths. Now they were partners with Brett Wilder in the Threesome Mine down Gold Canyon way. But not even Flint knew of Rick Delance's background on the Triple D Ranch. He'd confided in only a few men, one of them being Brett Wilder, the other, Elmo, the old cookie who'd run the chuck wagon.

"Saw you ride in," Flint said. "Say, is Miller still over at the Threesome?"

"He was when I left earlier."

"Well, I need him to ride shotgun with me on that load of ore we're shipping. Can you spare him?"

"I'll manage. Trouble?"

"Couple of fellers been eying me lately. My cabin's been busted into. Happened last night or thereabouts. Don't know if it was the same men watching me though. I came in late from Silver City, where I'd been staying for two days an' found the door busted in and full of hatchet marks. Looked like a diablo went whirling through my cabin. What they was looking for I've no mind to guess. Maybe they thought I was hiding somebody there they wanted."

Hiding someone? Who would they be looking for? Not me. Everyone knows I'm living out at Threesome.

"Looking for money, maybe?"

Flint shook his head. "Don't think so. I'm known for not keeping money in the cabin. What I have, which ain't much, is in the bank. Anyway, thought I could use Miller on the trip for company, if you can spare him. Some of those trails over the mountain get mighty lonesome. Can become a shooting gallery for the wrong men."

"I'll ride along if you can wait till I get back. I'll be away for a day or two."

"Can't wait, Rick. That ore sitting 'round makes me a mite nervous. Should have hauled it a week ago. Where you going?"

The straw-haired man was still at the window with his back toward them.

"Carson. Look, Flint, I haven't talked about this with anyone, but I'm thinking of making a trip to Santa Fe. It has to do with some land."

Flint looked curious but didn't pry. "Santa Fe? When d'ya think you'll leave?"

"Don't know yet." He glanced toward Helvey behind the mail counter. "Depends on a letter I'm expecting from a lawyer friend of my father. We owned a cattle ranch there."

Flint showed surprise. "Your pa has ranch land in New Mexico Territory?"

"Around Cimarron. He's dead now…both him and Alex, my brother."

Flint looked thoughtful and something like understanding flicked in his amber eyes. "Rough. Didn't know. I won't pry none, but if ever you want to talk about it, both me and Samuel will be ready to listen."

"Thanks." Delance liked him. Flint practiced his Christian beliefs in everyday life so that Delance felt he could trust him the same way he did Samuel. He would have told him more except he didn't want to embroil his few friends in possible bloodshed.

"Samuel says Wilder's thinkin' of selling out at Grass Valley," Flint said. "Didn't take it none too serious though."

"Brett's interested in buying land in New Mexico Territory around Mora."

"Then the talk is genuine. Must say I'm surprised, though. He has a nice place in Grass Valley."

Rick had received several letters from Brett Wilder. On Brett's first trip to Santa Fe with Annalee, he'd met with Mr. Billings, telling him that Delance was in Virginia City. Brett then wrote Rick informing him that he should contact Billings at once about his father's will. The letter from Brett had surprised Delance. He'd been under the impression that everything had gone up in flames on that grievous night, including his father's will, all the family papers, and the deed to the Triple D Ranch. But his father had wisely left these important papers with Billings. Rick had promptly written Billings inquiring about sustained property rights and was now expecting Billings' response.

"With Brett's wife at his father's sanitarium it makes sense for him to be close by," Rick told him. "He tells me that's what Annalee wants, too. She'll be there for some time for sure, and Brett isn't prone to go off and leave his bride. So he said he wants to relocate his ranch. Annalee's doing much better there. Besides," and a note of wistfulness crept into Delance's voice that he tried to mask, "that area by the Cimarron River, the Canadian, and the Rio Grande is some of the best land in the region."

"Never been there myself. That'll be some cattle drive if Wilder goes all that way. Unless he sells and buys new stock out of Texas."

"It can be done either way. I've known of drives like that. My father and brother went to Abilene with two thousand head one year. I was only a kid then, but it's something I'll never forget. We had quite a time with Comanche and Sioux in the Dakotas."

Flint listened, a far-off gleam in his eyes. "If the Threesome struck a bonanza, I'd sure make Wilder an offer for that spread at Grass Valley. Of course, the Lord would need to bring all that together. Don't know much about cattle, but I'd bust a leg tryin' to learn. Then again, dreams are one thing, the will of God is another. He doesn't always give us our dreams."

No, Rick thought tensely, *He doesn't.*

"Ever wonder why?" Rick queried.

"Sure. Some things He just doesn't explain to us yet. And some things just don't have an easy answer, least from our understandin' of it. Sometimes it seems to us God's ways don't make sense, but it's our narrow way of perceivin' that's the problem. If we think the problem is with Him and not with us, well, then we got a heap of pride blockin' our way."

Flint's words, so casually spoken, caught Rick off guard. Who had said this to him before? His pa, of course, though his pa had said it in a more refined way. However it was put, it came out the same. Uncomfortable, Delance changed the subject.

"Lots of money to be made in cattle. Ranching is the thing, and it will only grow with the settlement of the West. It's a hard and rugged way of life though." He didn't know why, but his thoughts trailed to Callie. Callie with her desire for beautiful clothes and the sophisticated ways of the East.

"Nothing like having a ranch of your own and settling down," Flint mused, looking toward the window as if the stage had arrived and Callie had already stepped down, her eyes for him alone.

Delance, reading Flint's emotion guessed what he was thinking. He was a good man, and he was sure to be disappointed.

He doubted that Callie would fall for him. Delance thought of himself and sensed a restless stirring, a stirring that spurred him onward, but produced irritation, too, for he also felt bound to make the past drink its cup of justice. Only then would he feel free to pursue another trail in life—the kind of trail Flint was dreaming about.

"You're mighty young and got a whole future out there just waiting to be plucked like a ripe plum," Flint told him. "Ever think of settling in one spot, getting yourself married? Maybe going back to that land that was your pa's?"

Delance remained silent, though he felt an unwanted yearning, one he couldn't quite deal with or even fully understand. It came sometimes when his fire had turned to coals and the night was silent except for the wind rustling prairie grasses. Or when the great expanse of sky was as black as velvet, with thousands of stars sprinkled in the arms of the Milky Way. His upbringing would tell him it was a longing for a relationship with the Creator whose awesome handiwork displayed His glory. A romantic would say it was a yearning for a precious woman's love and loyalty. Maybe it was both. Maybe he was tired of running from his longings.

Delance felt his jaw stiffening, and he couldn't stop the response. He'd conditioned himself to react this way, to guard his emotions from moments of weakness because weakness would get him killed. It was hard to change. There was a price to be paid, he knew. Did he even want to? It would require a determination to turn around on life's road and go another direction. His father said something similar once, using the word "repentance."

But where would the road he now traveled lead? It seemed these last five years of journeying had already lasted a lifetime. As he attempted to imagine its end, it faded into swirling dust.

If he admitted it now to Flint, settling down with Callie was exactly what was on his mind. It was the very reason he was anxious to reclaim all in his father's will, including the Triple D.

But he changed the subject without answering Flint's question. For one thing he knew Flint had a flutter in his heart for Callie, too.

"I'll tell Miller you want him to ride shotgun when I get back to the mine."

"Hear about the war?" Flint asked.

"Uh-huh. Tough." Delance glanced toward the window again. "Ever see that hombre before?"

Flint casually turned his head. "Don't think so. Looks like he came a far piece. Waiting for the stage?"

Delance wondered. "Someone getting off maybe. Keep an eye on him after I leave, will you? See where he goes, who he meets, if anyone. Someone's been trailing me recently."

Flint looked at him, worried. "Think it has any connection with someone bustin' into my cabin?"

"Maybe. That trouble we had with Rody Villiers and Dylan Harkin could be festering, just ready to flare up again."

"Yeah, I've been thinkin' that recently. Thinkin' about them both. I'm kind of concerned about Callie. Doesn't seem to me Dylan is goin' to stay away from Virginia City forever. Not with him ownin' half the Halliday mine that was Frank's. Wonder if Dylan understands it wasn't Callie's pa who shot his brother, but Hoadly?"

If Dylan showed up what would his attitude toward Callie be? Delance wondered. He felt a prickle of worry.

"Callie's coming on the stage. Suppose Samuel told you?"

"Heard about it," Rick said.

"She probably won't have much use for her old friends now." Flint pulled at his ear. "I'm thinking a silver heiress and theater star will choose herself finer circles now. Me, my grammar ain't too good."

Rick felt a sting of defensiveness. "Out here it takes more than socially polished manners to make a man. I wouldn't sell myself short if I were you, Flint."

Flint looked pleased to hear that. "Wonder if she knows it?" He chuckled.

Delance remained silent. She would need to look long and hard to find a more dependable man, but Delance would like to have suggested that Flint forget her, that she was star-struck, and he'd just end up getting hurt. But Rick's motives could be brought into question if he did. Fussing with another man's romantic notions could get a body into more trouble than a pack of hungry coyotes snarling over a rabbit.

"I was talking to Neil down at the Virginia Opry Theater," Flint was saying. "He heard how Ashe Perry's career on stage bumped into a cactus bush back East."

Rick was interested. "Did he say what it was about?"

Flint shrugged his muscled shoulders. "It was over some trouble of sorts, but what kind he didn't say, and I wouldn't be knowin'. That's why Ashe came West to play the theaters. New York was through with him." He smiled. "Guess he sort of figures we're an easier audience."

"He's right. The people here are hungry for good theater and the finer things that they left so far behind when they came West."

Through the window Gordon Barkly in a business suit could be seen walking across the street toward the stage depot. Delance felt himself in a wry mood. Another man interested in Callie Halliday O'Day.

Flint saw him, too. "His newspaper's doing good I hear. His father's in Sacramento politics."

Delance noticed it was his turn at the mail counter, and he stepped up. "Hello, Helvey. Anything yet?"

"Finally came in." He slid an envelope toward him across the counter. "Gotta sign for it, Delance." He took the pencil from behind his ear and handed it to him. Rick signed neatly.

Delance saw the name plainly on the envelope. "Clay Billings, Attorney at Law, Santa Fe, New Mexico Territory."

Someone hollered: "Here comes the stage."

Helvey used the moment when everyone's attention turned toward the street to lean closer across the counter and speak to Delance in a low voice.

"Fella came in here yesterday asking about you."

"The man standing by the window?"

Helvey glanced toward the window. "No, not him. This fella was part Mex. Dark and handsome gent, with big spurs and a fancy mustache. Had an inch on you and maybe thirty pounds. A real bad hombre, that one. Wearing two six-shooters. I've never seen him around Virginia Town before. Someone called him Cesar."

Cesar…did I know anyone from the Triple D days with that name? Does it have anything to do with Marita?

"Know anything about the one by the window?"

Helvey shook his head. "Never seen him before, either. Cesar was asking about you not more than five minutes after you rode back to the mine yesterday. He asked if you'd gotten a letter from Santa Fe…or was expecting one."

Just as Rick had thought.

"I told this Cesar it wasn't my business to tell him. He didn't appreciate that. He had me worried for a minute. I wasn't sure if he was going to grab me by the shirt collar and haul me over the counter. But then he calmed down and smiled. Had a smile like a tomcat. He just turned and strode out, his spurs jingling."

Delance considered. "Thanks, Helvey."

Rick came to the conclusion that someone back in New Mexico was getting mighty nervous over his recent contacts with Mr. Billings and Brett Wilder. Wilder was no man to mess with either, and there were some ranchers who would look with concern over his arrival and competition. His brother Yancey down Texas way had a name, and two big ranches near each other would make a rumble. The noise would be heard far and wide if he, too, should return to rebuild the Triple D.

Delance turned from the mail counter pondering things. There was only one man in Cimarron who was likely to be worried about the land on the Triple D. That was Tom Hardy. Tom— and his son-in-law, Zel Willard.

Back then, Tom had sworn he'd had nothing to do with the gunning down of Lucien and Alex, but while Rick had no liking for the powerful rancher, and even less for what he remembered of Zel, there was little reason to not believe Tom. Tom Hardy was greedy and proud, wanting to be top rancher in those parts, and justifying his greed by claiming he would bring settlement to the territory. But Delance didn't think Tom was a cold-blooded murderer.

Still, a man had a way of fooling people when they least expected to be fooled. If Zel had hired those killers, Tom might have found out too late and lied to protect his own reputation and that of his daughter Tina. By now Tina was Zel's wife. The

Hardys had themselves a lot of pride. The whole family was that way, even Sue, whom Alex had been seeing. Now, after five years, Sue would likely be married to someone else. But that past pride and conflict between the Hardy Ranch and the Triple D had been noticeable even between Sue Hardy and Alex, though in a playful, teasing way. Sue used to tease Alex by saying she was only marrying him so her pa could gain water and land rights. Even at sixteen, Delance had thought that if any girl said that to him he'd think three times before hitching up with her. Alex had merely laughed. Alex had always been easygoing. He trusted people too much because he judged them by his own heart. Since he wouldn't resort to low means to get what he wanted, Alex hadn't thought other folks would either.

Evil, Delance thought, *should not be underestimated, especially if it could be cloaked in an angelic face.*

There'd been others riding with Bodene's bunch of rustlers who'd been involved in the massacre, but Delance had no names or faces to identify them. He expected to learn who they were from Bodene or Abner when he found them, but he hadn't been able to track them down. What he hadn't considered until now was the possibility that once they were confident he'd lost their trail they might have turned right around and returned to the Cimarron region of New Mexico.

Elmo was a witness to what some of those renegades looked like. But what if Bodene and Abner had lied about their names? What if they were working at the Hardy Ranch right now under different names? Who was to know except Zel and Tom Hardy? And Elmo!

Suddenly Delance was angry with himself. Had he been a fool? If they found out that Elmo alone could identify them, the old cookie's life wouldn't be worth a plug nickel.

He tightened his jaw. It figured. If the killers had returned to the Cimarron area, then whoever had hired them would want Delance dead before allowing him to return to do business with Mr. Billings. This could explain why he was being trailed now. As long as he stayed far from Cimarron, Zel and his bunch would let him waste his years searching for two men who'd vanished, whose names may no longer even be Bodene and Abner. They could all rest easy among themselves at the Hardy Ranch. That could explain why no outlaw had been able to recognize those two names.

"If them two was as fast you say, Delance, their names would be knowed by all of us by now," an outlaw had once told him when Rick had stopped at his campfire.

He hadn't accepted that then, but he was beginning to now. It also explained Cesar's arrival and his asking questions.

Delance looked over at the dusty hombre at the window with the New Mexico spurs. Maybe him, as well. Was he one of those sent to stop him before he left Virginia City? For that matter, could he be Abner or Bodene?

The rumble of horses and the creak of stage wheels drew his attention to the open door.

The Wells Fargo stagecoach came rolling in, covered with dust. The wearied horses looked anxious for the corral.

The straw-haired stranger was still standing near the window, his attention on the stage.

Delance saw Flint Harper out front on the boardwalk. Gordon Barkly was standing off to himself. Both men were evidently waiting for a word of welcome with Callie. He saw Jimmy Halliday running up the boardwalk to greet his sister.

Delance put Billings' Santa Fe letter inside his buckskin's pocket. As he did, the wiry straw-haired man near the window was watching him. Rick felt a quick, frustrated hardening of his emotions. He was weary of sidewinders.

Delance strode quickly toward him taking the man by surprise.

"You been watching me ever since I came in here." Rick's voice came low and icy. "If you have any business with me, you'd better get it over with now. Because if I as much as see you scoutin' my trail again I won't just be asking questions."

The man's pale eyes flared a little like a spooked steer. He took an uncertain step back, but Delance stepped with him, crowding him, making it difficult for the man to reach for his guns at this close range.

"Who sent you here?"

"What are ya? Crazy or somethin'?" the hombre tried to take another step back and came against the wall. "I don't work for nobody."

"Your kind always works for somebody. Men with devious plans who are too smart to get their own hands bloodied, but don't mind if yours are dripping. What's your name?"

"None of your business."

"You'll answer or you'll be picking yourself up from the floor." The man smirked. "Johnny."

"Where you from?"

His eyes chilled. "Supposin' I'm telling ya it's none of yer business."

"I'm making it my business."

"El Paso."

"Know Tom Hardy and his son-in-law, Zel Willard?"

Johnny's eyes were mocking. "Sure, he has himself a spread down Santa Fe way, or thereabouts. Big cattleman. Lots of land. Lots."

He was taunting him, why? Delance studied his face a long moment. "Ever heard of cowardly killers named Bodene and Abner?"

"Bodene? Abner?"

Rick wanted to backhand the smirk from the stranger's face but kept his hand near his holster.

"Naw, never heard of no Bodene or Abner."

"They were yellow-bellied murderers and rustlers. Sure you never heard of them Johnny boy?"

The man's face turned a pasty gray. He trembled slightly with rage. "I said I ain't."

"Got business on that stage? You seem mighty interested in who gets off."

"My business ain't none of yers."

The stage was drawn up to the wooden walk and passengers were getting out.

"But there's an hombre lookin' for you," Johnny said. "A man named Cesar. He's fast." He gave a chortle. "Like a rattler strikin'."

"Where's he from?"

Johnny's stained teeth showed in a slight smile. "Why, Santa Fe."

In the next moments, sounds coming from outside seemed to mingle with the dust and heat.

"I don't know if you're lying or not, but you go tell whatever hypocrite you're drawing pay from that you found Delance. If he wants me, you tell him to come for me himself. Now, if you were wise, you'd ride out of here today."

Beady eyes blistered with rage. "You can't tell me—"

"I'm telling you."

The man's bitter mouth twitched as though it took all his willpower to not go for his gun.

Delance stared coolly, evenly, warning against any move. Then he stepped aside and gestured his head toward the door. "Get moving," he ordered quietly.

"You'll pay heavy for this, Delance, real heavy."

"I'll be around. Your kind never quits till you're buried on Boot Hill."

The man walked to the door, flung it open, looked back with a vulpine glare and went out.

Delance stayed, looking at the door, guarding against any tricks. In Tucson he'd witnessed a killer named Elton walk out the saloon as though leaving, only to turn back unexpectedly with both six-shooters blazing. The other gunfighter didn't have a chance. Tucson and Yuma had been rough places…and still were.

When he was sure the stranger had left the boardwalk, Delance looked out the window. The man crossed the street to a saloon, puffs of dust rising from his high-heeled boots, his long arms swinging wide with an ambling gait. Inside he must be boiling, for the confrontation must have taken him by surprise and ruined whatever plans he'd nurtured, at least for the moment. An evil man with injured pride was worse than a wounded bear.

Delance didn't expect "Johnny" to leave Virginia City, but to at least keep out of sight for a time and then pursue whatever brought him here. He was probably working with Cesar, and both were probably sent by Zel.

Delance opened the envelope from Clay Billings, read, then reread the surprising news of how he'd been trying to locate him for several years, but thought him dead. Why Mr. Billings believed him dead he did not discuss in the letter, but he wrote that he'd learned otherwise from Brett Wilder.

> *...your father was an astute man. He left a folder with me here at my office several months before the trouble out at the Triple D. He owned more financial investments than even I realized. It was always his dream that you would go to the university and upon graduation take control of the other properties while Alex ran the ranch. There is property in Galveston and more of it in Louisiana. There is ownership of shares in a line of riverboats doing business on the Mississippi. Concerning your inquiry, the deed to the land and water rights of the ranch are in my possession. Upon the death of Alex all reverts to you. I would advise you to come to Santa Fe as soon as possible. There are papers for you to sign and a few other business dealings to be taken care of. Once that is done you can take full possession. Or I can send the necessary papers to Bill Stewart in Carson for your signature. Please advise.*
>
> *C. Billings,*
> *Attorney at Law*

Property in Galveston and Louisiana, riverboats, and the deed to the Triple D? Why had pa never mentioned them? Maybe because I'd been sixteen and would have had even less desire to go East to years of university studies. Had Alex known? Maybe. There'd been a time or two that he'd mentioned Galveston, Texas, but I didn't pay much attention.

Rick's thoughts drifted to Callie Halliday....*If she knew my status has changed, would she show more interest? What was Callie Halliday really like?* he wondered. *A man has to be sure of the woman he loves and marries—that it is he himself she loves, and not an image or a bank account. Then again, Callie was a silver heiress, and she too had to be mighty careful. Why wouldn't any promising man want her—and the Halliday mine?*

Through the window, Delance saw a young man step down from the stage. He carried himself well with a certain pride of face. His features were fair, clean-cut, his golden mustache meticulously trimmed. Unquestionably handsome in a delicate, sensitive sort of way, he looked to be a purposeful man, perhaps nearing thirty years. *Rather old for Callie,* Delance thought critically, for he was sure that this was the "great Ashe Perry." Despite the dust of travel on his gray coat, he appeared dashing and sure of himself.

"Your baggage, Mr. Perry," the stage boy called. "Where do you want it sent, sir?"

"International Hotel," came the clear, resonant voice, with a tinge of British accent.

Callie stepped down from the stage. "Ashe! Look at the town. I can't believe how it's changed in a year!" Her voice carried through the window.

"There's much to benefit us here, my dear. I can feel the raw hunger, the eagerness of the young town. This is wonderful."

Rick Delance felt his mouth turn wryly as he scanned Ashe. *"Raw hunger" he wanted, did he? Then he'd like a pack of vultures.*

Ashe took her arm and said something, and they both laughed pleasantly.

Rick Delance's eyes narrowed as he studied the actress. It had been over a year since he'd last seen her. She'd changed all right, but he'd expected that. He supposed any young woman who suddenly become a silver heiress, a successful stage star, and who was also gifted with beautiful looks would be hard-pressed not to let it go to her head. A woman with all that Callie had would need to be mighty mature to handle it all wisely. No wonder Samuel worried. He had a reason to.

Delance, having been raised without a mother in a man's world, didn't think he understood women very well. Callie could be a mite reckless, he knew that. And she didn't have much experience with life, though she probably thought she did now, just for playing the theater in Frisco and dining at flashy restaurants.

Her hair was ebony, and he remembered her eyes being a violet-blue. Just then she seemed to purposely dimple in a too-sweet smile at Ashe Perry. Delance felt an angry dart of jealousy. *The little vixen.* Then he laughed at himself. What right did he have to be jealous—or to even worry about her? She was free to make her own mistakes, wasn't she? He'd little doubt she'd make them. In his judgment the biggest mistake was that slick blond fellow holding onto her arm.

The baggage was being unloaded as Rick put his letter away and stepped out on the boardwalk, drawing his hat lower. He felt a little rebellious. Keeping back from the crowd, he leaned against a wooden column, a seemingly uninterested bystander.

Callie gathered up her billowing skirts, her dress the refreshing color of sapphire blue…and Delance had no notion what it was made of but he hadn't seen one that pretty in a long, long time. Each flounce of her skirt was tirelessly trimmed in what looked like some sort of black ribbon—maybe velvet—and with her gloved hand she took hold of Ashe Perry's arm.

Yet Delance saw more in her face, something he was sure went beyond the outer fluff of a girl her age. There was, he believed, a hint of character not yet honed. Something that lay dormant, ready to come alive under the right circumstances—or was he seeing what he wanted to see? What he hoped was really there?

Others had also emerged from the stage—all theater people, he supposed, for their dress looked city slick, and they congregated around Ashe Perry, who appeared to be in charge.

The sun's rays caught a sparkle of jewels that glinted on Callie's throat, ears, and wrist. Delance again felt an irritation. Quite a show…and quite a temptation to stage robbers. A good thing Ringo had ridden shotgun on this trip. There were some lonely spots on the way from California.

"Howdy, Delance," Ringo called, climbing down from the driver's seat. He dropped to the ground, rifle in hand.

Delance had met Ringo, a fast gun, in Tucson, and Delance had convinced him to take another route with his life. To his advantage and the passenger's safety, outlaws knew Ringo's reputation for handling a rifle.

As Ringo called out his name, Delance saw Callie come visibly alert. She turned her head and glanced quickly through the small crowd until her gaze found his.

Delance smiled knowingly at her, personally satisfied his name had arrested her attention. He winked. She glared and jerked her head away. His smile deepened. She had too much pride, and he enjoyed rattling her. She must think he was a mean hombre who relished adding notches to his gun handle.

Rick saw Flint looking on, sober-faced, when Callie looked right past him as though she hadn't even recognized him. He hesitated over that, seemed pensive, then strolled away, hands in his pockets. He'd just learned the Callie he'd met at Strawberry Flat no longer remembered the mule skinner who'd brought her safely to Carson. Rick felt sorry for him.

Gordon Barkly, on the other hand, had boldly pushed his way through the little throng as though proud to make his presence felt. No humility there. Rick laughed to himself over the scene.

"Miss Callie, how good to have you in Virginia City again."

Callie turned to him, looking doubtful as though she tried to place him, then she smiled, pleased.

"Gordon, oh, hello. How's the newspaper going?"

"Fine. Oh very fine, indeed. Just about ready to run the *Territorial Enterprise* out of business. All ready for New York soon."

"Well, congratulations."

Rick read the doubt and amusement in her voice. At least she saw through Gordon's boast.

Jimmy stooped down and crawled between Gordon's two booted feet, then he stood.

"Callie! It's me, Jimmy!" came the plaintive cry.

She looked down at him, laughed, then stooped, put her arms around him, and hugged him. "You're the best part about coming home, Jimmy."

Rick liked what he heard. She turned Jimmy toward Ashe Perry to introduce him.

Delance touched the letter in his pocket from Mr. Billings, then stepped down from the wooden walk to go to his horse. He'd seen enough. He would ride to Carson to see Bill Stewart and bring him Billings' letter to see what he advised about sending the papers to Carson for his signature.

Callie would need to wait until he had a better day. Would there be one?

Four

⁊ᵒ

"Jimmy, how you've grown in a year. Why you'll soon be as tall as me!" Callie told her younger brother with a smile.

Jimmy grinned, obviously pleased. "I'm going to be like Uncle Samuel—and Delance!"

Delance again. Callie felt a strange prickle. From the corner of her eye she watched him mount his horse.

Why did Rick Delance keep turning up? She didn't like the way he unsettled her. She remembered his reputation as a gunfighter; Rick was a dangerous man. She turned her head and glanced his way again. He wore a buckskin shirt and a dark hat. He was a good-looking, rugged young man with sunlit brown hair and a slow, contagious smile. *Nevertheless,* she told herself, *he represents everything I find objectionable in the West, everything I plan to leave behind when the time comes for me to go East with Ashe.*

How dare he have winked at me like that! And yet, if she admitted it, she…but then, she wouldn't admit she'd been flattered! And he'd winked while she was being escorted by someone as gallant and sophisticated as Ashe Perry. It was almost as if he'd done it deliberately, in order to—what? He was quite bold, wasn't he? Confident. He seemed to know what he wanted. She felt an odd thrill.

Delance was no longer paying attention to her now as he scanned the other passengers who'd gotten off the stage as if expecting someone else. *Who might that be?* Those on the stage were members of the Perry–Ralston Theater Company. Well, perhaps she was mistaken about him showing up to see her after all.

The streets were crowded, buildings were going up, and there was the pounding of the stamp mills and compressors. Virginia

City was booming, but was this what she wanted? Far better to move East.

"You sure look mighty pretty. Your dress shines, an' those jewels—are they real, Callie?"

She smiled. "Of course, Jimmy! Where's Aunt Weda?"

"In the buggy. Hurry, Callie, she's sittin' on pins and needles waiting to see you."

"I don't see Uncle Samuel."

"He couldn't come. But he'll be home for supper tonight. We're having your most favorite. Roast chicken and peas. And Aunt Weda's made a peach cobbler, too. I've been smelling it since I woke up."

Callie laughed, and with her arm around his shoulder, she started through the crowd toward the buggy, Jimmy taking the lead. Over her shoulder she called, "Come along, Ashe. I want you to meet Aunt Weda."

"Better not—not now. I'll go to the hotel, and we'll talk later."

She was disappointed. "Oh, all right, if you must. You'll come to dinner tonight?"

He smiled. "Roast chicken, peas, and peach cobbler? A team of horses couldn't keep me away." He lifted his hat, smiled at her and Jimmy, then made his way through the crowd.

Jimmy looked after him. "Mr. Perry's a big star."

"The biggest Virginia City's likely seen in a long while. Ashe has played New York and even London. He's good, Jimmy, very good—" then she neared the buggy and saw her aunt. Callie smiled and quickened her steps. "Aunt Weda!"

She hurried up to the side of the buggy, and Weda leaned over and they exchanged quick, welcoming hugs.

"Why, just look at you, girl. So fine looking! Why you'd be a star on stage even if you couldn't act. And that dress. Land's sakes! Looks fancier than anything I ever saw Lilly wear."

"It is fancier," Callie said with a laugh, "and a good deal more expensive, too. Mama would be proud of me if she could just see where I am today."

Aunt Weda cocked a silvery brow.

"And you just wait to see the dress I had made for you from San Francisco," Callie told her, ignoring her lifted brow.

"For me?"

"Why, sure, you wear that dress, and I'll need to fight off a pack of silver-haired gentlemen beating a path to your door."

"Shucks, girl, there'll be none of that. I've a broom handy. You didn't go getting me fancy duds, now, did you?"

"I absolutely did," Callie stated, climbing into the buggy. Jimmy clambered into the little seat behind. "And you're going to wear it to my opening night at the Stardust Theater, too."

"What about me, Callie? What'd you bring me from San Francisco?" Jimmy begged.

"Jimmy, that's not mannerly," Weda shushed. "You don't go asking folks what they brought you first thing off. Makes it sound like all you want is gettin' something. Just remember those ten lepers the Lord healed. 'Gimme, gimme,' but only one cared enough about the Lord to return with thanksgiving."

Jimmy frowned and pushed his hat back. "Aw, shucks—"

"Don't say that."

"You say shucks all the time."

"That's different."

"She's just my sister. How long do I have to wait before I ask?"

"Jimmy, I declare."

Callie laughed. "Oh, how I've missed you both. Sounds like home. Don't worry, Jimmy, I wouldn't forget you—or Samuel. I've bought you both the finest silver pocket watches you ever laid eyes on. With your names engraved, too. They come from far away Switzerland."

"Oooh! Can I wear it to the Stardust and sit high up in the balcony?"

"Why sure you can. I own half of that wonderful theater." She clasped her hands together and laughed at Weda. "Oh, Auntie, isn't it *grand* to be rich?"

"Tush. It has its nettles. Too many bees buzzing the honeypot, I say."

Callie was too happy today to let her aunt's usual worrisome ways trouble her. Nothing was going to get her upset.

Aunt Weda snapped the reins and the horse moved out onto the street.

"And I brought you a brooch, Auntie dearest. It's a gold rose with a cluster of pearls. It goes with your new evening dress."

"Girl, if we start sporting around like that, we'll all be robbed for sure."

"In Virginia City?" Callie said lightly. "Why, everyone's rich here."

"I've heard some mine owners will have silver on their horses and carriages, and silver doorknobs, too," Jimmy said. "We all better be careful or President Lincoln will come and take it all for the war. Callie, did you hear?" His voice jumped with excitement. "The Rebs fired on Fort Sumter. Delance says the fort's in South Carolina."

Callie sighed. "Yes, I've heard. Heard once too often to suit my tastes. Goodness, I'm just positively sick of the chatter of war and such, so don't you start, *please*." She turned to Weda. "That silly war talk's kept me and Ashe and the Company from our plans to travel to New Orleans to play the theater. I was even hoping to go pay Aunt Lorena a visit while I was there. Now that door has slammed shut. Who knows when I can go?"

"The Rebs in town say the war won't last any longer than it takes to hit a Yankee with a peashooter," Jimmy said. "They're afraid it will all be over before they can get back home to join the Confederate Army."

"Well, them Yankees have their nerve," Weda said over her shoulder to Jimmy. "Look how they went and declared war on good Southerners. Your Aunt Lorena included."

"Lorena's in New Orleans. She's not likely to see war," Callie stated.

"Delance says it's likely we'll all be involved before it's over," Jimmy said soberly.

Callie looked at him over her shoulder. "You sound mighty friendly with a man who's a gunfighter."

"I've told him and told him to stay away from him," Aunt Weda agreed crossly.

"Aw, shucks, he ain't bad. Why, Delance is friends with Flint Harper and partners in Threesome Mine with Brett, too. Flint and Brett think he's all right."

"And don't say ain't," Weda said. "You need more learnin.'"

"I pick it up from you, Auntie. And just 'cause Delance is mighty fast with a gun don't mean he's a killer. Even Uncle Samuel talks to him often—"

Callie laughed softly looking at Weda, who pretended to frown. "Well you don't want my education, boy, I had me precious little of book learnin'. You want to speak right, like Callie and Annalee."

"Callie says 'shucks' too sometimes."

"Not on stage," Weda said firmly.

"You know what? I saw Delance draw his 1860 Lawmans. He was so fast, I felt cross-eyed."

"See there! What'd I tell ya?" Aunt Weda stated with satisfaction, flipping the reins as the horse trotted faster, keeping up with her emotional energy. "He's been trapped by his own words. You heard it yourself, Callie."

Callie fanned her face with a blue-lace fan that matched her dress. "Oh, never mind Mister Delance. I want to hurry and get home, Aunt Weda. Ashe is coming to supper tonight, and I want everything just so. Oh, this sun feels so hot after San Francisco. All I want is something refreshing to drink and a nice bath. The dust on the ride from Carson was just awful....And you're coming to see me in the new theater. I won't take no for an answer. Besides, Ashe Perry and I are playing together. He's magnificent."

"Who?" Aunt Weda wrinkled her nose. "Berry? Never heard of him."

"Oh, Weda," Callie laughed in toleration. "Ashe Perry. I wrote you about him from San Francisco. Don't you remember?"

"Oh, him, yes. Yes, I very well remember."

Callie glanced at her. She could sense the worry, and sighed to herself, reading signs of trouble to come. There would be difficulty convincing Weda—and maybe Uncle Samuel—that she was going to marry Ashe and move East.

"Ashe will be returning to New York once we've played out here," Callie said, keeping her tone casual. "I may sell out my shares in everything—even the mine. Ashe is interested in opening a theater of our own in the East."

Aunt Weda's head turned quickly and the buggy swayed with the jerk of the reins. Callie quickly reached a hand to steady the reins. "Look out, Aunt Weda! We're going off the road—"

"I know how to handle a horse. Sell your third of the mine?"

She might as well just let the truth come out and have it settle where it may. Better that Uncle Samuel learned now rather than letting things drag out. Besides, the longer she waited, the less nerve she may have left.

"Well, my third anyway. I'll need to find a good buyer first."

"What about the Stardust?" Jimmy asked.

"We'll keep the Stardust for awhile. Hugh will run it."

"Hugh?" Aunt Weda asked with a definite scowl. "First this fella named Ashe, now a Hugh. Land's sakes girl, how many scamps is out there buzzing about? Samuel isn't going to take to this. You know that!"

Callie scowled too, straightening her pretty bonnet. "Yes, I'm fully aware I may get some criticism, Auntie dear. I don't want to hurt those I love, but my mind's made up. I'm going to marry Ashe, and we're selling out and going East."

Aunt Weda heaved a sigh and shook her head sadly, but she offered no words, which was a relief to Callie in and of itself. Would exercising her will be this easy? She felt a trifle guilty knowing she would disappoint her aunt and Samuel, and said quickly: "But it won't be overnight, of course. Ashe and Hugh are going to do what they can to help me find a buyer. That will take a bit of time. Then there's the play…we'll open in a few weeks. I expect it will run a good month. After that, Ashe and I will leave for Santa Fe to see Annalee and Brett. I may marry Ashe in Santa Fe." She glanced at her aunt sideways, waiting for an explosion. None came. Callie arched a brow. *Well, well. Could it be?*

"Then we can come, too, can't we, Callie?" Jimmy asked eagerly. "We want to see Annalee again, too…and Brett…and it wouldn't be any fun if we couldn't go to your wedding, would it, Aunt Weda?"

"'Course not, but Santa Fe's a good long way from here, and I don't think Callie's going to up and marry this Ashe Perry without a good, long, respectable engagement. Isn't that right? A long engagement?"

Callie saw the shrewd glint in Aunt Weda's eyes. Callie settled her skirts on the seat. "Naturally there should be a nice engagement."

"Engagements are for a year. Sometimes two years. Even longer. Nothing less," Weda said waving her hand, "is much respectable or folks will talk."

"Ashe won't want to wait a year, and neither do I. It's way too long. And it won't matter what folks say," Callie said. "We won't know anyone in New York."

"Time flies. Before you know it, a year's past. Anyhow, you need time to get to know the man. And what folks say and think— if they're the right kind of folks—is always important."

Callie was about to protest, then thought better of it. After all, she had gained ground. Aunt Weda hadn't said marriage to Ashe was out of the question. If all the resistance she was going to get from her was about a long engagement, then she'd done better than she'd hoped. Then again, there was still Samuel to deal with.

In order to win Jimmy to her side she said gaily, "Of course you'll come to the wedding, Jimmy. I want everyone there. I don't see why we can't all go visit Annalee in Santa Fe."

"Oh, boy!" Jimmy clapped his hands and began bouncing on the springy seat. "We're going to Santa Fe to see Annalee and Brett!"

"Now you hold on about that big decision," Aunt Weda said over her shoulder. But Jimmy was too excited to calm down easily, and he kept talking about his trip to New Mexico Territory. Callie formed her lips into a small, satisfied smile. The faster she moved things along, and the more expectations she roused, the more difficult it would be for Weda or Samuel to derail them.

The Halliday Mansion, so newly built, was located near the Savage Mansion and the Mackay Mansion, but closer to Flowery Street. There was only one thing Callie was sorry about in having Uncle Samuel arrange for her to buy this land. The mansion was situated close to the site of the Gould & Curry Mine Works, and at all hours of the day and night she could hear the work going on in the mine. Aunt Weda insisted she would soon become so used to the pounding of the stamp mills she wouldn't hear them, but Callie wondered.

Callie planned for the supper that night to be a fine affair, but no sooner had Ashe arrived then matters took a turn and supper was not progressing as she desired. She was pleased, however, to see that Ashe was trying to get on well with Uncle Samuel.

It was after dinner, and they were all in the new parlor with its red drapes and ivory-and-dusty rose rugs. The furniture, which gave the rooms a touch of elegance, had been chosen by Callie in San Francisco and hauled over the Sierras.

"You're a Northern man?" Uncle Samuel asked, sizing Ashe up over coffee and dessert.

"From Illinois, sir. I started my acting career there, then moved on to New York."

"And London," Callie was quick to add, "don't forget how you played the theater for royalty, Ashe. Tell them how important it was to meet royalty."

Ashe looked at her and smiled his appreciation. "A great honor indeed." His light-blue eyes flared slightly. He turned to Samuel. "Your niece is a talented woman, Samuel. She's one of the best actresses I've worked with." He looked at Callie. "One day we'll play New York together, Callie, maybe even London!"

Callie, smiling back at Ashe, became painfully aware of the silence in the parlor. Ashe must have noticed, too, for he said to Samuel, "That is, sir, if you concur."

Samuel lifted his cup and drank his coffee.

Callie stiffened. Samuel was a rugged man, broad-shouldered, wearing a dark frock coat reaching to his knees. His sharp, greenish eyes looked out evenly but kindly, and his thin, hawk nose flared into wide nostrils. His flowing Kit Carson-style mustache was touched with gray. Uncle Samuel had never married, having given his life as a circuit-riding preacher in the hard and difficult gold and silver towns of California, Nevada, and Colorado. Callie loved him dearly, but unlike Annalee who had always been the sweet and submissive sort of girl, Callie found her uncle restrictive. Her decisions tended to clash with Samuel's—and never more than now as she wanted to begin a new life in New York with Ashe, and her uncle showed no enthusiasm.

There'd also been a conflict when she'd first left Virginia City for San Francisco soon after Annalee went away with Brett. Callie had insisted on having her own way and had dug in her heels. She remembered leaving her uncle standing alone at the stage station with the wind flapping his old frock coat. That image of her Uncle Samuel with his rugged countenance subdued in tender sadness over what he'd believed was an error had haunted her for a time.

Now she was back, safe and sound, proving he'd been wrong. She'd met Ashe Perry in San Francisco—the best thing that could have happened to her.

But as Uncle Samuel deliberated over giving his blessing on Ashe's pronouncement of their playing New York together, she bristled. The agonizing silence nettled her. She realized she must assert her independence or risk losing Ashe.

"Of course we'll play New York one day, Ashe. They'll all be sorry they didn't appreciate you when you were the golden lad of Broadway. I should even like to try London." Then she added more kindly for love of her uncle, and because it was true: "But now I'm happy to be here to play the Stardust with you and the others."

Samuel looked up from his coffee. "I understand a gentleman named Hugh Ralston owns the other half of the Stardust."

Now it was coming...the myriad of questions she couldn't answer.

"Yes, I wrote you about him."

"You didn't write to your old uncle, lass, you must have written to Weda."

Callie shrugged easily. "I expected her to tell you. There seemed no reason to write both of you about the same news." She looked over at Aunt Weda for confirmation, but Weda pursed her lips.

"You wrote me about some business shenanigans? Gracious sakes, I must be getting old. Don't remember no words about it."

"Well I *did* write, Auntie. Anyway, Uncle Samuel, Hugh is a friend of Mr. Tom Maguire. You don't come by any better recommendations in the theater world than Maguire."

"Maguire I've heard of," Samuel said, nodding. "'Mr. San Francisco Theater' himself, right? But I've not heard of Hugh Ralston until this morning. What do you know about him, lass?"

Why this morning? She wondered….Again, the questioning of her plans prickled her pride. She didn't want her desires threatened by disapproval or scrutinized for rashness, especially in front of Ashe Perry whom she wished to impress with her independence and maturity.

"Really, Samuel, you must let me grow up sometime. I'm capable of making my own decisions. Hugh is a very smart man. He knows the theater world as few others do, and he's an asset to our partnership."

"Did Tom Maguire personally recommend Hugh Ralston?"

Callie stood and walked slowly about the spacious parlor, her skirts rustling.

Ashe deftly removed a cigar from his pocket, and Weda began eying him with nipping white brows. "If you aim to smoke that cantankerous thingamajig you do it out on the porch, Mr. Perry. That'll stink up the whole house. Charlie used to smoke those things. Enough to make a woman quit her housework."

Embarrassed, Callie felt her cheeks warm. "Aunt Weda—"

"Of course, my sincere apology, Miss Weda, I should have asked your permission. I'm afraid I wasn't thinking." He put the cigar away, a slight smile on his lips.

"Hugh is respected in San Francisco," Callie went on, avoiding Samuel's question. "He moved to San Francisco about—" she glanced over at Ashe for his help "—about six or seven years ago? From St. Louis, wasn't it, Ashe?"

"Er, Chicago." Ashe, too, stood and joined her near the open window where a breeze filtered through the lace curtain—the clear implication being that the two of them were an independent entity standing side by side against the frowning family opposition.

Through the curtain Callie gazed at the yellow moon rising from behind Sun Mountain. Her fingers ran gently along rich, red velvet. She'd chosen these drapes from a large selection in San Francisco and had them sent here to Virginia City, too.

She recalled the cotton curtains in the bedroom she'd shared with Annalee while growing up in Aunt Weda's farmhouse. Shabby is how Callie had viewed them each morning upon wakening to begin each new day. Shabby, old, and ugly. Annalee had rarely complained about such things, but Callie felt depressed whenever she looked at them. Especially after comparing them with the fine curtains in Gordon Barkly's Sacramento mansion or even with some in her friends' homes. Strange how cotton curtains from her past could intrude into her thoughts now when discussing something far more important with her uncle...silly curtains she'd allowed to make her feel insignificant.

Well, I'm not insignificant now. I'm a star and a wealthy woman.

Five

かの

*C*allie stood with Ashe Perry by the terrace in the elaborate parlor of the newly built Halliday home as she faced Uncle Samuel. She managed a theater smile, hoping to win him over.

"Now, Uncle, why worry so? You're like Aunt Weda. You both see me as 'little Callie.' I've got to make my own business decisions eventually, don't you agree?"

"Now, now, little one, your uncle isn't wishing to hog-tie you...though Weda might," he said with a wink at Callie, followed by a glance toward the widow of his older brother Charlie.

Weda had reentered the room bringing dessert; Jimmy followed with plates, napkins, and utensils. She stopped upon hearing her name.

"Horse feathers," Weda snorted. "I always did say you can't hog-tie folks who don't want to stay put. But when the prodigal ends up in the pen with the hogs, well, that's when they learn to appreciate a good home."

Callie cringed. She glanced at Ashe to see how he was accepting Weda, but he seemed to not even be listening. His eyes were fixed on Samuel.

Weda dished her famous peach cobbler, and Jimmy passed it out.

After they'd eaten and coffee was served, Ashe told Weda: "Delicious, Miss Weda. I've never tasted finer cobbler, not even at renowned restaurants in London. Why, with the dinner you've cooked tonight and this dessert, you could open your own fine dining house anywhere."

A faint flush of pleasure touched Weda's wrinkled cheeks. "Why, I'm right thankful of your compliment, Mr. Perry."

Turning to Samuel, Ashe frowned thoughtfully, and with his hands in his city trouser pockets, he paced slowly.

"About Hugh Ralston, sir. I think I'd better declare myself. I can see you're worried about your niece's decisions, and I, for one, appreciate your concern." He looked at Callie and smiled encouragingly, then back at Samuel.

"I've known Hugh from my early days of acting in Chicago. Hugh opened some important doors of opportunity for me when I was just starting out. Callie's investment in the Stardust with Hugh will pay off in rich dividends in the future. You might also consider that Tom Maguire is opening his own theater. He wouldn't be doing so unless he thought it a wise investment—which certainly confirms Hugh's good business sense."

"What about his character?" Samuel asked in a quiet voice. "Can you vouch for that, too?"

Callie fumed. The entire evening had been an embarrassment to her. Samuel was so old-fashioned and homely compared to the interesting, sophisticated people she'd met in the theater through Ashe and Hugh. She felt ashamed of Samuel. Of Weda, too, with her silly expressions of "horse feathers" and such. After the sophistication of San Francisco, with its polished citizens and grand hotels, Callie wished she hadn't rushed to invite Ashe over to dinner tonight. *Had I been wiser, I would have waited. And I must hire some proper servants. Ashe knows all about such things. It's embarrassing to have Weda and Jimmy serving like two hired kitchen helps.*

Weda with her fussing, and Samuel with his questioning, his doubts, his worried face, looking like an old suspicious hermit from his dugout on Sun Mountain. Not even the elaborate Halliday Mansion with all the silver decorations and rich furnishings did much to enhance either him or Weda among better society. Samuel's big old black Bible, sitting on a nearby table within easy reach, had been a worry to Callie all night. She was deathly afraid he'd reach over and open it up to read to Ashe before dinner. Once, she'd even managed to set it aside, pretending she was straightening the table, but when she looked again a few minutes later, it was back in prominent display.

"I believe he's a gentleman, sir," Ashe was saying, and unlike Callie, he didn't look the least upset by the barrage of questions that she'd encountered all evening.

"In fact," Ashe said, a smile in his voice, "I'm the one who introduced Callie to Hugh Ralston in San Francisco. So I suppose if there's some question about her becoming business partners with him, you could say I'm the responsible party."

"Now, I didn't say anyone was at fault," Samuel said. "I was just trying to find out where the truth lies in all this."

"Yes, I understand, sir. Naturally you'd want to know about these matters."

Callie tossed her napkin on the mahogany chair and stood with shoulders thrown back, the heat of indignation rising in her voice.

"The decision to go into business with Hugh was mine. There's no reason to quiz Ashe about it, Uncle. Furthermore I'm very proud to be owning half of the Stardust Theater, and I wouldn't change my mind if I had it all to do over again."

"Callie, shame on your manners," Weda said from the end of the table. "If Lilly were alive she'd not take your talking to Samuel like this."

Jimmy didn't look up from his second helping of cobbler.

Callie turned on her. "It's not my manners, Aunt Weda, that are in question."

"Callie!" Weda said, aghast, leaning back into her chair. "I declare!"

"I'm sorry, Aunt Weda, but it's so," and Callie looked over at Samuel. "You've been needling us ever since we arrived for supper."

Ashe cleared his throat. "I think it's been a perfectly delightful evening, sir, Miss Weda, but I fear I should be getting back to the International." He glanced at his pocket watch, scowled, and shook it. "Do you have the time, sir?"

Jimmy piped up, "Eight fourteen, Mr. Perry." The new silver watch from Switzerland gleamed under the lamplight.

Ashe turned to Callie who was still upset. "I've work to do tomorrow at the Stardust, making sure the other members of our acting group are ready for opening night."

Callie nodded agreement in stony silence, angry over how things had gone, yet admiring Ashe as he went to Samuel and extended his hand.

"I've enjoyed meeting you, Parson. I'm looking forward to more such visits. I hope you and Weda will be at the theater on opening night. You, too, Jimmy." Ashe smiled and went around to where he sat and offered his hand.

Jimmy looked surprised by the adult attention, and his olive-green eyes glinted. He shook Ashe's hand with a smile.

"My pleasure, Mr. Perry," came his practiced grown-up voice. "And I shall be at the Stardust to see your performance."

"Good," Samuel said. "We'll all be there. I wouldn't miss seeing little Callie. She's always had these dreams of being a star like her mama. You'll honor us with your presence tomorrow, Ashe?"

Tomorrow…Callie's gaze left Ashe and came to her uncle. *He wasn't really going to…*

"My presence, sir?" Ashe showed some bewilderment as to what he'd meant.

"At church in the morning. Tomorrow's Sunday."

"Oh…yes, Sunday, I see. Of course, you are a minister."

"Our service starts at nine o'clock sharp. Afterward we'll be picnicking in the back of the chapel. Weda here, and some of the ladies will be furnishing the food. We have this fellowship once a month. Helps us all draw closer together. It's important we know each other, don't you think, son? I mean, *really* get to know each other well? That way we can all chip in and help one another out when we need it."

Callie was tongue-tied. She stood there feeling an odd shame she couldn't have explained even to herself if her life depended on it.

"Nine o'clock?" Ashe repeated. "Well that sounds nice. I'll try to be there, Parson, I surely will. If at all possible with my busy schedule."

"Good. Callie will save you a seat in the pew."

She hadn't been attending church in San Francisco, nor was she anxious to rise early tomorrow and go. She was tired from the long stage trip and angry with Samuel.

Samuel turned to Weda. "You're going to bring some of your good biscuits, Weda?"

"Oh, tush, 'course I am. Arkansas goes plumb crazy over those things. 'Bout eats them all every time. Jimmy? You be sure to wash behind your ears before morning, understand?"

"Sure, Aunt Weda. May I have some more cobbler?"

Callie walked swiftly out the front door and waited for Ashe, then followed him onto the large front porch overlooking Virginia City.

The spring breeze touched and cooled her hot face. The same breeze blew her hair and skirts. She'd never been so humiliated.

Below, the lights shone like amber candles all over town. The echo of tinny music drifted on the wind. The same wind laid its cool fingers against her hot skin as if to soothe her humiliation.

"I need to explain," she said with a little laugh. "Uncle Samuel means well, and in many ways he's an old dear. I never noticed it much before, but he's quite old-fashioned. Too religious. And Aunt Weda is, well…" her laugh deepened as she glanced toward the house, "well, she's never had much schooling."

Ashe smiled and squeezed both her hands in his. "I gathered that. Don't let it burden you, my dear. We'll soon be married and leaving here." His smile vanished, and he glanced around Sun Mountain with a shake of his head. "I've never been much of a Western man myself. I don't see what the pioneers see in it. Give me the sensibilities of Eastern life anytime. But," and he smiled again, "we have our own lives to live…and we will. Just as soon as we play at the Stardust. Do you think Samuel will put up much of a struggle regarding us?"

She had no doubt now.

"Yes, but I won't let him win. I know what I want, and I intend to have it. There's only one thing I want to do before we go East, Ashe. I must see Annalee first."

Ashe looked a little concerned. "Yes, New Mexico Territory. Is she very ill, this older sister of yours?"

Annalee wrote her often telling her of the improvement in her health and how happy she and Brett were. Dr. Wilder, she had written, was an intelligent and gracious man. Annalee mentioned how anxious she was for Callie to come and see her and Brett.

"We're going to settle here," she had written. "Brett wants to name our ranch, the AB. I teased him saying we should add 'C' for Cimarron. The area of Cimarron, Pecos, and Mora is beautiful country. Wish you and Jimmy were here with us."

"Annalee's getting stronger," Callie told Ashe, "but once we marry and leave for New York there's no telling when I'll be able to spend time with her again. So I want to visit her first. You'll like her." She smiled a little nervously. "She's nothing like me. She puts me to shame, but it's not her intention. She's always been the saint." She frowned to herself.

"I like you just the way you are, dearest." Ashe took both of her hands into his and kissed her forehead. "Breakfast with me in the morning at the hotel?"

She felt tension over her divided mind. "I'd better not, Ashe. This is my first Sunday home in over a year. Not showing up at my uncle's new chapel will cause me more problems then if I simply just go—though I may fall asleep during his preaching."

He laughed.

She added, "He is long-winded and a loud speaker, so sleep will be difficult."

"Then come to the International afterward. We'll take in lunch. We've a lot to talk about. Good night, dearest."

She watched him leave the porch and go through the gate to where his horse was tied. She hadn't asked if he would be at the chapel, too. She'd noticed he had come short of promising Samuel by assuring him how he would enjoy coming, if at all possible—based upon his "busy schedule."

It had been a difficult evening, and she knew it hadn't ended yet.

Ashe mounted and rode toward town. Callie watched until he was out of sight, then she turned and went inside.

Jimmy had been hustled off to bed and Weda was in the kitchen busily cleaning the dishes and putting the food away.

"We need someone to come in and help Weda with the cooking and housekeeping," Callie said, making it clear she had no intention of doing so herself. She was positively done with such mundane things, having her fill of it in the difficult time she and Annalee had lived in the little cabin Brett and the other men had built for Annalee, on account of her illness. That winter had been one of the hardest that Callie could remember.

"Weda won't hear of any servant," Samuel said. "She takes pride in her homemaking. Some help would do her good, though. She's not well."

"I know, but if she digs in her heels in that stubborn way of hers there's little I can do to change her mind."

"Seems to run in the family."

She looked at him, and he stared back evenly. Then he grinned, and she did too, somewhat reluctantly.

"Oh, Uncle, did you need to be so picky tonight with Ashe?"

"Did I embarrass you, lass?" he asked quietly.

She flushed and turned away, walking over to the divan. "Well, yes. And I was afraid you'd start reading the Bible to him."

"Would that have been the end of the world—or your relationship with him?"

She looked at him startled and then angry. "No. Ashe is too sensible to let excessive zeal offend him. But I thought it was uncalled for. And all that probing about Hugh. Really, Uncle Samuel, was there a reason for that?"

He looked at her soberly. "Yes, Callie, there is cause for concern. I'd be negligent if I didn't face up to it. And you'll need to do the same before this is all over. You may want to run and hide from the truth, but God doesn't allow us to do that. Part of Christian maturity is facing up to our temptations and asking Him for the strength to overcome them. Sometimes it's wiser to flee youthful lusts."

"You mean marrying Ashe and going to New York is an evil thing?" she snapped. "How can you say that? That's so—so narrow."

"Lass, I didn't say it was always evil. And as for Ashe Perry, I don't yet know enough about the kind of man he is to make any good and wise judgment. Is he a believer in Christ? That's all important, you know. That's the foundation for any relationship. Without that, no matter how successful he is, or how handsome he is in his Eastern clothes, your house is doomed to crumble. Yes, I'm a plain spoken man, lass. But these questions need to be asked and answered."

The battle was beginning. She was weary...could she even stand up to it now?

"I'm worried about this Hugh Ralston, too," Samuel sank into the big chair and rested the side of his booted foot on the other knee. His fingers tapped the arm of the chair.

"Hugh Ralston may not be all he's supposed to be. It's important we know more about him."

For a moment she was speechless. "Why do you say that?"

"Sit down, little one, it's best we talk this over a bit. It's too important to let ride."

Reluctantly, she sat opposite him on a gold, velvet-upholstered chair of mahogany wood. Uncle Samuel watched her.

"There's no pleasure in my saying this, but there could be a mistake in teaming up with Hugh Ralston. He may be a friend of Maguire, but what worries me is that he was also a friend of Cousin Macklin and that lawyer partner of Mack's named Colefax. Remember him?"

Her eyes searched his. "Colefax? No, I don't think I ever met him. Macklin, of course I remember—" The man who murdered her mother and shot her father in the Virginia House Hotel. How could she forget?

Callie relived again that moment of gruesome horror when she'd been in the hall and heard the gunshots coming from Macklin's room. She'd been on her way downstairs to meet Gordon Barkly for dinner. Within a minute the hotel clerk came rushing up the stairs with the armed guard. Others had begun pouring into the hall from their rooms. "It came from Mr. Villier's room," someone had said. The clerk had rushed there with Callie and Gordon close behind. They'd entered Macklin's room and she had seen her father, Jack Halliday, sprawled on the floor with a bloodstained shirt. And Cousin Macklin was dead in his wheelchair, a chair that he'd used as a masquerade for his deception. She would never forget the emptiness, and later the pain, of seeing her father killed in such a horrible way, though he'd lived as a gambler and gunfighter from her earliest memories.

Callie hadn't missed the loss of a father as much as Annalee and Jimmy had. At least she told herself she hadn't. Rather than sadness and depression while growing up poor in the saintly shadow of her older sister, Annalee, Callie had been resentful and strong willed. Sometimes her feelings turned to anger if she fed them with reasons why she'd been treated unjustly by life. From her earliest days she'd wanted to become a star like her mother—to receive applause and roses, to believe in her worth and to feel good about herself. That desire still drove her forward. Now it was with Ashe and a new beginning in New York.

She realized she was gripping the armrests on the chair.

"I can't believe Hugh knew Macklin. You're certain about this?"

"Not certain. Rick Delance is asking."

At the name of Rick she stood to her feet, surprised. "How is he involved in this?"

"Rick met Gordon near the Stardust this morning. When Gordon told him about your business partner, Rick came hunting me at the chapel. He'd heard of Hugh Ralston, said that hired gunfighter of Macklin's—the one named Hoadly—had mentioned Hugh Ralston in Tucson when he'd gone there to hire some guns for Macklin. Hoadly seemed to think Hugh Ralston was friends with Macklin and Colefax. And that Hugh Ralston was dead."

Callie remained silent. So Rick Delance had been concerned about her and gone to Samuel. *Now why would he do that?* Her feminine pride was in a tug-of-war, both flattered and irritated. What had he said to her before? "You need a bodyguard." He'd only meant that in a teasing way, but those words had returned to haunt her—especially after two incidents in San Francisco. One of them, after a theater performance when she'd returned to her hotel room to find someone had managed to break in. Her arrival, escorted by Ashe, had scared the intruder out through the terrace. The second incident occurred just before leaving San Francisco for Virginia City. She'd gone for a stroll and someone had followed her. She hadn't noticed him at first, and when she tried to get a look at his face he ducked behind some trees. She was on her way back to the hotel when it seemed the same ruffian had tried to snatch her purse. The policeman on the corner heard her shout for help and came running with a billy club. The ruffian fled through the park.

And there was another time in which she hadn't been as fortunate. On the night her father was killed, Rody Villiers had been out of control trying to learn what happened to Macklin. He'd taken some of that fury out on her when she'd told him Macklin was a murderer—that he'd shot her father. Rody had reacted viciously by slapping her across the face. She remembered how Rick Delance had called him on that.

"Rick has no cause to mislead us," Samuel was saying. "He's a friend of Brett."

She noted how Uncle Samuel tempered Rick Delance's gunfighter reputation by linking him to Brett Wilder. Brett had been a deputy marshal in '59 and '60, sent from California to arrest her father, Jack Halliday. In the process Brett had fallen in love with Annalee.

"It sounds to me as if you like Rick Delance," she said with a trace of accusation.

"Rick's on the wild side at times. No denying that. But he's been working hard at Threesome Mine for the last year, minding his own affairs the way a man should. There's something eating at him, though, and I wish I had an inkling of what it was about. I've a notion it could destroy him, and I'd like to be used of the Lord to stop it from happening. He has potential, that one. The devil would like to get him and destroy him."

Restless, Callie remained silent. The devil...was he actually around, trying to ruin us? As though answering her question Samuel said: "The devil, as a roaring lion is prowling about to discover our weaknesses and set snares and traps to render men useless to God. May the Good Shepherd lead us into paths of righteousness for His name's sake."

She, too, wondered what could be troubling Rick. Whatever it was, she wasn't going to take the initiative to find out. There was a physical attraction there, but one she didn't have any use for. She was glad it was only physical because she could reject that, and time would turn it into a blurred memory. An emotional attraction would not be so easy to break. Rick Delance, while exciting, was the sort of man she should avoid.

"Delance won't talk about whatever it is," Samuel said thoughtfully. "I wish he would."

"Maybe if he did, it could get him hanged," she said wryly.

Samuel seemed to take her remark at face value. "I don't think so. He has a fast reputation to be sure. But he's not killed a man who didn't try to kill him first."

Her interest was baited. "How do you know?"

"Brett knows the lawman around Tucson. Says Rick's not a wanted man. He's been in gunfights, been seen riding with some mean hombres, but mostly he's known as a loner. There are witnesses to all the gunplay, and Rick comes off as a man acting in self-defense. Brett knows the commanding officer at Fort Craig near Santa Fe, too. According to the colonel, the Delance name was respected throughout New Mexico Territory."

Again, she was surprised. "He's from Santa Fe?"

"Cimarron region, and down around Pecos, or even Mora."

"Cimarron, isn't that where Annalee says she and Brett want to resettle with a new ranch?"

Samuel nodded thoughtfully. "It is."

She was surprised to learn that. "I'd taken Rick for a young, reckless drifter."

"You're not far wrong there, but it wasn't always so. Brett did say back in '60 that Rick came from a good family."

Unwilling to ask further questions about him she turned back to Hugh.

"About Hugh Ralston...so what if he did know Cousin Macklin? I suppose half the people in Virginia City knew him. San Francisco and Sacramento, too. Does that make him guilty of wrongdoing?"

"No. And you're right there, lass, about judging someone harshly without knowing all the facts of a matter. Each one of us is responsible for others' reputations."

Callie loathed thinking through all this ugliness about Macklin and the death of her father again. She wanted to get away from guns and violence and the men who resorted to them. She wanted a different breed of man—one she could stroll with down the civilized streets of Broadway in New York while she was dressed in stylish clothes...a sophisticated gentleman like Ashe Perry.

"I just don't see any reason for alarm because Hugh may have known Macklin at one time," she concluded with a smidgen of impatience. "Macklin's dead. Colefax, too. All that ugliness belongs in the past where I want to keep it buried. And besides, he may not even be the same Hugh Ralston. I'm certain he is not."

"I hope you're right, little one. But Rick doesn't think so and that's what worries me."

That Rick could get her uncle upset to the point of questioning her friends and business partners was bad enough, but the thought that it might lead to the disruption of her plans was even worse.

"There's no reason for Rick Delance to have come to you about Hugh. In fact," she said coolly, "if I ever run into Delance again, I'll tell him so myself."

"It might be a wise idea if you did talk to him. He went to Carson on some business or another and won't be back for a day or two. He'd like to talk to you, I'm sure of that much."

Callie wondered at Uncle Samuel's smile.

Did Rick want to see her? She felt herself drawn, yet reluctant. She had the notion the farther away from him she stayed, the safer she would be in her desired relationship with Ashe Perry. Outside influences to the contrary were not wanted.

Six

Rick Delance had left Carson City earlier that afternoon. As the day progressed and the low desert mountains became mantled in smoky-blue shadows, he selected a site in a canyon about six miles south of Virginia City to spend the night. The deepening hues at twilight faded to soft gray, and evening drifted across the hills surrounding the canyon as sagebrush, pinion pine, and rocks darkened into silhouettes. Soon the first stars were winking as a large moon edged up behind low, rounded hills that looked like camels lying down for the night. A distant coyote's lone cry echoed in the stillness, reminding Delance of his own solitary heart.

He picketed his horse a ways off where a smattering of grass grew by a winter water hole that had not yet turned dry. Rick built a small fire of fallen pinion pine branches. The wood was somewhat damp and sure to make a little smoke, but he wanted coffee. Perhaps he was getting lax he thought wryly. Life in Virginia City and partnering with Flint and Brett Wilder had softened him. He was wishing he had some of that warm bread from Lar's bakery near Sun Mountain. The big Norwegian sure could bake. Better than any bread he'd tasted in a long while.

One of the things he missed the most, since life on the ranch near Cimarron had ended so bitterly, was the fine meals in the large dining room followed by quiet evenings around the fireplace. There'd been nothing he'd enjoyed on cold, clear nights as much as reading while coyotes in the hills called out through the solitude. Contrary to most folks, he liked the sound of coyotes. He grinned at his thoughts, imagining what Callie would say to that.

Delance carried his father's Bible in his saddlebag, its edges charred, the lone survivor from his library. He'd like to have more books, but when a man lives from campfire to campfire in some of the roughest places around Tucson and Yuma with all he owns tied to a tired pack horse, well, he just couldn't tolerate the larger load.

Until recently, he'd not thought of his loss in dollar amounts—not until Callie Halliday O'Day had come along, stirring to life some unexpected longings for love, family, and the ranch. But Callie scorned him. He was probably a fool where she was concerned. Her visions were sparkling with vistas of Broadway—and men such as Ashe Perry.

Rick pulled his flat-crowned hat lower over his brown hair, and scowled into the coffeepot. That coffee looked mighty weak. He'd best let it boil a mite longer. Waiting, he became suddenly aware that the night had changed. Having lived in the wilderness for the last several years, it was now second-nature for him to recognize the various sounds—sounds from rustling grasses, insects, night birds, scampering night critters, and the steps of men. He listened…for what? *Sure seemed quiet out there.* Alert, he avoided staring at the flames. If anyone approached his camp from behind him, he knew that delayed vision could prove fatal as he turned his gaze in vain to search desperately into solid blackness.

His thoughts turned back to fine, fresh, yeasty warm bread, this time remembering it from Sal's oven on the Triple D, smeared with dripping butter an' clove honey… An unwelcome sound burdened the night. A stone had dislodged and rolled down the rocky incline to the water hole.

Somebody is out there. In an instant he drew one of his six-shooters and moved from the fire toward the nearest low brush, listening, his ears attuned to the sounds about him. Could it be an Indian? Back in 1860 there'd been trouble with the Paiutes out at Pyramid Lake, but he'd had too much experience with Apaches and Comanches in Arizona and New Mexico Territory to think of Paiute trouble as anything more than a disturbance. In his mind the Paiutes lacked the savagery and lust for torture and killing that he'd learned was true of Apache and Comanche. But the Paiutes—or Utes as some called them—had moved farther north toward Utah Territory, and the sound he'd just heard of falling pebbles seemed too clumsy for an Indian.

Delance slipped soundlessly through the cover of low pine trees, then behind jumbled rocks, aware of the risk of rattlers, but also remembering possible danger from the hired killers, Cesar and Johnny.

A mistake building that fire! He knew better. Though the small canyon he'd camped in would keep the flames from being seen outside the shallow hills, the evening was windy and the smell of smoke could travel for miles, picked up by any drifter accustomed to riding lonely trails and hitching himself to another's campfire.

When Delance had ridden from Carson he'd made sure to take a less traveled route, covering his trail by riding on rocky terrain whenever he could, but that evidently hadn't been enough. He was irritated with himself. He should have left Virginia City months ago, but his portion of the Threesome Mine and his interest in Callie had weighed him down…unwisely.

The night wind moved among a stand of elms that grew farther down along the incline near the water.

He moved away from the rocks to circle around his camp and come up behind whoever had been watching him. In the moonlight, he moved as silently as any Apache, toward some pinion pine, then Delance saw him—

His breath released with irritation. *Elmo Judd and his mule, Jenny!*

Rick shook his head and gritted as he holstered his Lawman. "Elmo! I told you once, I told you twice. Don't sneak up on me. It makes a body right edgy."

Elmo didn't look worried. He looked up, leading the mule. "Had to be sure no sidewinder trailed me 'fer I called out. So I come up nice and easy like."

"Chancey, old friend, mighty chancey."

"I'm comin' in," Elmo said. "I got news. You got plumb good reason to be fidgety. Trouble's abrewin'."

"I'm aware. Ran into one of them two days ago at the stage station. Calls himself Johnny."

Those who knew Delance considered him anything but fidgety. His cool confidence in a tight spot usually made an opponent edgy...and off guard.

Elmo, too, was a good man to have around. He could use a rifle when needed. The chuck-wagon "cookie" had made the rounds of many campfires on the Western trails, sharing coffee and news with whoever he met for more years than Delance had been alive. Many of those campfires had consoled dangerous men who'd just as soon shoot as bother to talk nice, and much of that news he'd passed on to Delance. Rick suspected old Elmo would have news worth the listening.

"All right, Cookie. Coffee's done and waiting. Watch that incline, Elmo. Those stones are loose."

"Knowin' you, you must'a dug 'em apurpose."

"Yep. Works well at night, one sliding stone and a prowler's lost his edge."

"You always was a canny one, even as a youngin'."

Delance had known Elmo even before the last Triple D cattle drive. He'd been a boy of around twelve back then, and he remembered the first time Elmo came riding up to the ranch looking for work. There'd been other cowhands with him—a seasoned crew from West Texas. Many of them had stayed on, riding for the brand. Elmo, too, settled in as permanent cookie on the drives through Texas to Kansas.

Elmo was tough when it came to the hardships of the desert. In his younger years he'd fought under Sam Houston for the independence of Texas. He'd been riding desert canyons, fighting "Injuns," as Elmo called them, for most of his life, and was now doing some placer mining along the Carson River.

As Delance watched, Elmo made his way up the slope where he used a slipknot to tie his mule to a mesquite. He gestured to the smoldering wood coals where the coffeepot simmered.

"Knew I weren't mistaken." His eyes twinkled as though he'd caught Rick in a blunder. "A body could smell that smoke a ways off."

"If this were Comanche country, I'd deserve a scalping," Delance commented dryly. "It's that girl. She's making me lax. If it weren't for her, I'd be gone by now."

Elmo chuckled as though the idea pleased him. "Miss Callie, sure as shootin'. About time some gal got her hook in ya, but you done picked a thorny blossom for a first try. I seen her comin' into Carson a few days ago." Elmo grinned. "Her and a bunch a them theater folks at the stage stop. Never saw such fancy duds. Mighty big star in Frisco—beautiful girl, too. You'll have a hard time winnin' that one," Elmo mused.

Delance cast him a dry glance. "I've a chance if she ever realizes a few things." But to himself, his thoughts went deeper. She would be next to impossible to win away from Ashe Perry in surroundings where he moved easily—surroundings that were very different from typical life in the rugged Western territories. The important question was, What kind of man did Callie really want? But that same question also applied to himself. What kind of woman did he want? He would find her disappointing if her requirements for choosing a man were a smooth tongue and a longing for slick society.

"Sit. Help yourself to coffee. There's jerked beef, too."

"Much obliged." Elmo sat himself on a smooth rock near the warm coals. His eyes were a whitish-blue beneath porcupine brows. Some teeth were missing so he had trouble pronouncing esses. He was a tough yet decent sort.

Delance believed Elmo had come to Virginia City in '59 because he'd gotten wind how Hoadly had met with Delance in Tucson about a job. He knew Elmo worried about the outlaw trail he'd ridden since leaving Santa Fe. Sometimes Delance thought Elmo felt a duty toward the memory of Lucien to try and keep him out of trouble.

They'd met frequently these past years "bumpin'" into each other on the trail from Santa Fe to Tucson, from Fort Yuma to Salt Lake. And when, for a period of time, Delance had ridden scout for the army at Fort Craig, Elmo had somehow shown up.

So Rick wasn't surprised when Elmo had shown up once at Strawberry Flat on the Sierra Pass. On that occasion, Elmo had avoided Delance, not wishing to draw Hoadly and Roc's attention. Later in Virginia City, Rick had gone to buy grub at Smitty's Dry Goods store, and when he came out, there was the old cookie with Jenny.

Delance had a warm affection for the old man. They'd been through a lot together, but now with his reputation as a gunfighter, he hadn't wanted to draw Elmo in, and so they'd exchanged few words in public. Sometimes Elmo would come to see him at Threesome Mine if he had news, but mostly late at night.

Now he had cause to worry about Elmo as never before. The man who'd killed Alex didn't realize anyone had survived that wicked night on the cattle drive near the Texas border. Elmo could identify the men called Bodene and Abner, and if they felt Elmo was a threat, they would come gunning for him. The fact that no one had troubled him these years showed they weren't aware he'd survived the stampede. But now Delance had run into Johnny at the Express Office, and he was worried.

Delance sat on his heels by the fire and picked up the coffeepot for Elmo. "You still have Old Betsy?"

Elmo patted a beat-up cup hanging from his belt. "Betsy here been with me since days a Sam Houston."

Delance grinned. One of the things he'd remembered about Elmo on the cattle drives was the way he always carried his personal tin cup. Sure enough, Elmo loosened a rawhide tie and removed an old dented cup into which Delance poured coffee.

Elmo sniffed the brew's aroma and waggled his brows, but after taking a swallow he stood and spat it out toward the mesquite, shaking his grizzled head with apparent disgust.

Delance frowned at him. "What's that all about?

"Bah, ya ain't never learnt to make good coffee, that's what. I done showed ya how, and showed ya how. More'n a hundred times on them cattle drives I showed ya how. Still tastes like watered-down chicory weed."

Delance grinned. He pulled a twig from the coals to light a thin, Mexican cigar.

"Them things er no good fer ya neither. You learned that foul smokin' on the border."

"Stop fussing," Rick said casually. "Anyway, you didn't show me how to boil coffee a hundred times, Cookie, maybe five times. Besides, at sixteen I had better things to do on a cattle drive than hang around the chuck wagon hearing your complaints. The only

time your chuck wagon was interesting was when you made those
shortening biscuits. I've been thinking a lot about hot bread and
biscuits all night. You see what civilization is doing to me? I
should've moved on from Virginia City months ago."

Elmo suddenly chuckled, as though he were remembering
something. "You had better things to do, all right. An' ya made a
heap o' trouble doin' 'em, too."

The sly humor in the old man's eyes brought a wry smile from
Delance. "Like trying to break the line-back dun?"

"You sure hit that New Mexico ground hard. It was a wonder
ya could walk straight after that one. But ya did, an' never hollered
neither. I saw you lookin' fer liniment in the chuck wagon come
nightfall. You didn't want Mr. Lucien to know how bad you was
really hurtin'." Elmo chuckled, remembering happier times, then
his grin faded and he looked at Rick quickly as if sorry he may
have stirred unhappy memories.

Delance remembered and put several small dry twigs into the
wood coals to keep them going.

"That was long ago, Elmo. There's no going back to happier
times. There's weeds a mile high growing on the gravesites of my
Pa and Alex."

Elmo glanced at him, all humor gone. "I doubt they mind a
few weeds. Both was believin' men. Especially I 'member Mr.
Lucien. God-fearin', he was. A right decent man. They got better
things to be lookin' at away up yonder." He looked up at the glittering stars in the black sky.

Rick was silent.

"It's you got me worried. Yer too good a young fellow to be
livin' like this. Your pa would be mighty upset—"

"Not now, Elmo. Don't want to hear it."

"When? You hear me out. I got forty years on ya. It's too late
to go back ya say, but not too late to keep huntin' them sidewinders."

"And I intend to keep hunting them till the last one's carried
to Boot Hill."

There was still snow on the Sierras and the wind blew chilly.
The desert had lost its warmth as soon as the sun set. The wood
snapped and crackled.

"Well, you was right about somethin'. Them was evil hombres that night." Elmo shook his head sadly and stared down at the coals. The breeze kicked up flames, and the wood sizzled and popped, spewing ash.

Rick remembered how, after three years of searching, he had ended the career of one of those evil hombres. Rick had run into him in Tucson by following the outlaw trail. Elmo had identified Clegg as one of the men who'd ridden with Bodene, and unfortunately for Clegg, Rick had seen him around Tom Hardy's ranch in better days. When Clegg showed up alone in Tucson, Rick had recognized him right away, but Clegg hadn't noticed Rick when he'd walked toward him on the dusty street outside the tavern.

"Are you sleeping well at night, Clegg?"

Clegg had turned his roosterlike head and looked at him with one unblinking eye. "Huh? You talkin' to me, boy?"

Rick smiled coolly. "That's right, pappy. I'm talking to you. Recognize me, Clegg?… Rick Delance."

Clegg had looked shocked, and then he paled.

"Remember that night Alex Delance was shot in the belly and left to die? Our cattle rustled? Sure you do. The others were murdered, too, shot through with lead in cold blood. Ten good men, ambushed. Where's Bodene and Abner?"

"Don't know what you're talking about. I'm just a cowhand drifting through."

"Well, no need to remain a drifter, I'm invitin' you to move up in society. You ready to come with me to meet the town judge? I aim to come to your hanging."

Clegg reached for his gun. Rick's bullet found its intended mark. Clegg was buried on Boot Hill in Tucson.

Word had gotten around quickly after that. Alex's kid brother, Rick Delance, was looking for the men in Bodene's outfit.

The others hadn't been located. He'd begun to think most of them had crossed the border into Mexico, living on the money from the rustled cattle. They may have taken Marita with them. He had looked for her to honor Sal's dying request, but hadn't found her. Only God knew where she was, or even if she was alive. By now she could be buried somewhere in Mexico, her blood crying out from the ground for justice.

After Clegg, the outlaw Hoadly showed up in Tucson asking him to work for an "important chief" in Virginia Town. Rick had thought the silver rush might lure a few outlaws. He'd hoped Hoadly and his kind would lead him to Bodene. Now it seemed that three men were in the area, likely sent by Zel Willard.

"You was deputized once by Wilder. Mebbe you oughtta get yourself a badge."

"You saw the trouble Wilder got himself into sporting that badge while hunting Annalee's father. Wilder nearly lost Annalee over it. And Wilder was able to set aside his personal revenge when hunting the man who shot and crippled his father. I can't."

"I'm knowin' the Good Book's familiar to you, same as to Wilder," Elmo countered quietly.

Rick stubbornly avoided his gaze across the fire. Not even Elmo knew he still read the Bible. Rick, however, had become disillusioned when the God he worshiped as all-powerful had permitted what to Rick seemed the senseless deaths of the two people who meant the most to him. He and Alex had been as close as any two brothers could, roaming the hills together as kids, learning to ride together, shoot together, only for one to be cut down by rustlers. And for what? Rick, seething with anger, had hardened his heart…a dangerous thing to do. Now and then he read his pa's old Bible, but he hadn't yet made any decision about whether to walk around his painful stumbling block and continue his journey. And having hardened his heart he couldn't lift himself all alone. He knew that only God could woo him back to Himself, but all he felt now was persistent anger.

Delance tightened his jaw. "This is a matter I've got to keep a settled mind about. This is between me and the men who killed Pa and Alex. It's personal—I want it that way, Elmo."

Elmo shrugged. "Just thinkin' of you is all. I'd shoot them skunks for ya if I could."

"You leave them to me, Elmo."

"Livin' on hate the way you been doin' these years could kill you, too. What about that woman you been thinkin' on? Miss Callie don't look like the kind to put up with such things. That's why she got a hankerin' for that Eastern theater star."

Delance was irritated. "I can't help it if she hasn't seen through him yet."

Elmo grinned, as though he knew how to get at him. "That pretty woman wants a live man, not one fulla bullet holes. Least that Ashe Perry will stay alive."

"While others protect him? Sure. He's not as innocent as he pretends. I noticed he had a sleeve gun usually worn by gamblers—easy to spot if you know where to look."

Elmo had grown sober-faced. Delance suspected why he had come. He had said trouble was brewing. Well, when wasn't it?

Elmo nodded. "Well, looks to me like that trouble with young Rody Villiers has riled some of his friends. The way you handled Rody Villiers back in '60, you beat him good and never even tried to kill him, though he'd have killed you for sure. You bein' able to shoot his gun hand like that did more to kill his pride than a burial out on Boot Hill. But if it ain't them who is out huntin' you, then word a what happened to Clegg must'a drifted to the scalawags with Bodene on that bad night in Cimarron."

The man at the Express Office... "Go on, Elmo. What do you know?"

"It ain't what I know but what I seen. An' my seein' ain't as pert as it used to be, but I saw a man ridin' other day, I'd swore was one of 'em on that night."

Delance looked at him sharply. "Where?"

"Carson. Same day the stage took Miss Callie and those theater folks away to Virginia City. That stage stopped at Carson, and I was in town gettin' supplies. That's when I seen him. This one feller that was with Bodene and Abner. I remembered him because of the scar. Some others that was riding with Bodene I'd not swear in a court a law to seeing, but this one hombre? He can't be mistaked for no one else. He's got that zig-zag scar cross his neck that I'd seen, same as I tole you about before." Elmo jutted out his bewiskered chin, and with his finger drew a Z on the side of his leathery brown neck. "Right about so. Looked like somebody branded him with a knife blade.

"I remember Alex asking him 'bout it an' he said a Comanche done it. Well now, that stuck with me. Because we know a mite about Comanches. An' if it were an Injun, then that feller wouldn't be sportin' a Z on his hide. He'd be plumb missin' his scalp."

Delance remembered what Elmo had told him five years ago. A man with the scar on his neck…left side, shape of a Z.

Rick's alert gaze seemed to prompt Elmo to squint while recalling. "I seen him. But I didn't remember where I seen him till he upped and rode off."

The small fire crackled and spurted in the wind.

The man at the Express Office hadn't sported a scar—or had he? It might have been covered with a bandana, or the left side of his neck may have been turned away. How many were there in town looking for him? Two, three? Johnny…Cesar, and now the man with the scar.

"You thinkin' what I am?" Elmo asked.

"That all three were sent here by Zel Willard? Maybe."

Elmo cocked an eye. "You have somethin' different on your mind?"

"The stage from Carson. Johnny sure was interested in who was on it. And now you say this man with the scar was also watchin' the stage. That worries me. They knew I wasn't on there for sure. So who were they interested in?"

Elmo rubbed his chin. "Hmm, didn't think of that."

Rick shook his head, thinking. Callie? Someone else? Ashe Perry? Someone in the Perry-Ralston Company? He'd thought of all those who'd gotten off the stage. There'd been quite a number of folks.

"I ain't leavin' Tom Hardy out of this, neither. He coulda sent the three of 'em. I'm thinkin' he'd wantta hide that murderin' son-in-law of his."

"Was the man you saw riding alone?"

"He was alone a'right. Asked some fellas about the stage from Frisco and when it was due in Carson City. He hung around over at Bill's saloon. Then when the stage come in, he came outta the saloon and stood a watchin'."

Delance didn't like the sound of this.

Elmo poured coffee and continued.

"He looked right at me, an' I eyeballed him back." Elmo took a slurp. "But he didn't remember me none because he paid me no mind. Looked right through me he did. I knew I seen him somewheres. So I just watched him 'cause I didn't like the look of him. Reminded me of some slinky coyote circling a chicken coop to figure an openin'. Then he asks one a them fellers standing 'round when that stage was due for Virginny Town."

That the gunfighter hadn't remembered Elmo was a great relief to Delance, but he wasn't willing to assume it would remain that way. As memory went, the man might later recall Elmo in a flash.

"It was only after I got to thinkin' how'd I seen that odd scar, that I remembered. Wish now it'd all come back to me then and there, so as I could a finished the murderin' scum off fer good."

"No, Elmo, you let me handle my own fights. It's bad enough he might still remember you and come gunning for you. You're the only living witness to what happened. Remember that. Only you can identify them. That includes Bodene and Abner. I need you alive."

"Sure, I know. I always known that, ain't scared none."

"I've been thinking," Delance said reflectively. "Since Billings got in touch with me about my father's will, things have picked up around here. Looks to me like our old friends around Cimarron are mighty nervous about me returning. That's made me do some thinking, Elmo. What if the men you know as Bodene and Abner go by other names? They could be in and around Santa Fe. Maybe they never left."

"Never thought of that. You thinkin' to return to Cimarron?"

"Sure, why not? I've searched the outlaw trail in vain for two men named Bodene and Abner. Now it's time to return to where it began."

Elmo scratched his chin again. "Never thought those rustlers would be in Cimarron. But mebbe…Anyhow, if what you say is so, looks to me like they already come here."

"True, but not all, Elmo. Not Zel. You can be sure if it's Zel Willard who first hired them five years ago, he isn't about to talk now. That leaves you, Elmo. You can point them out to me and to the authorities at Fort Craig."

"So's you think they're not usin' them names they gave your pa and Alex when they hired on the Triple D? And not wantin' you comin' back to stir things up none, they're comin' outta the shadows. Sure as shootin' sounds like it could be. That fella with the scar showin' up sounds like they're gettin' nervous. Wish I could remember Z-neck's name…but it wasn't Bodene or Abner. Some other strange soundin' name. It'll come to me in time."

"Just be careful, Elmo. They've nothing to lose. Stay away from me in public. The man sporting his scar isn't the only one in town."

Delance told him what the mail clerk, Helvey, said about the big man named Cesar, and also what had happened in Rick's meeting with the straw-haired gunslinger, Johnny.

"Ever hear of Cesar or Johnny?"

Elmo shook his head. "Not Johnny. But that Cesar fella sounds a mite familiar though. If I ever see the hombre I might be a knowin' him."

They were silent for a minute or two, and the wind rustled the pinion pine and stirred up the coals in the low-burning fire.

Rick's thoughts returned to the man with the scar. "Did he talk to anyone who got off the stage at Carson?"

Elmo set his empty tin cup down on the rock. "Didn't think so at the time. Now, learnin' what I have, I'm beginnin' to wonder. Maybe he did. First, I seen him ride off. That were that. But maybe not. 'Cause I saw that horse of his ag'in later behind the Nevada Hotel. If it weren't that exact same horse I'd wager Jenny over it. It was the horse, 'cause I recognized it had three white stockings. The back left was solid black. Purty horse, too. Well, I seen Ashe Perry come walkin' from the back of the Nevada Hotel."

"You're sure?"

"Yup. Aren't many handsome lookin' gents like that in Carson. I seen 'em when he got off the stage with Miss Callie. Oh, it were him. Well, I hung around after Ashe Perry went back to the Wells Fargo Stage eatery where the others were havin' a bite afore goin' on to Virginny Town. Then I went on with my business. Got my grub at Taylor's Dry Goods and went back to my placer minin' on the Carson. Then I got to thinkin' and worryin'." Elmo's voice slowed, as though his mind traveled long, dusty trails. "Well I got to thinkin' after Z-neck left Carson, an' it came to me I'd seen that no-good sidewinder that night at the Texas border. So I hightailed it over this direction, intendin' to go to Threesome Mine to have a powwow with you. Then I smelled that pinion pine smoke... nuthin' like it for fragrance."

"But you never actually saw him with Ashe?"

"No, but that horse...it had to be the same one."

But what would Ashe Perry be doing at the Nevada Hotel meeting with a hired gunman?

Ashe Perry. Coincidence...or was there more to this? If Callie's partners were mixed up in something dangerous, she wouldn't know of course, but should she be warned? Chances were she'd question his motives if he told her. Delance frowned and murmured his frustration to the cup of coffee he was staring at. A big moth had blundered into it and was struggling. Rick drew his dark brows together and flicked the bug into the sagebrush.

Delance was anxious to know whether Gordon Barkly uncovered anything about Ashe Perry and Hugh Ralston. Gordon's jealousy over Ashe would rouse him to dig deep into the man's past. He smiled to himself, satisfied that he'd put him onto the task.

"Look, Elmo, I've had to make a change in plans. As I said, looks like I'll be making a trip to Santa Fe to see Billings...and Wilder, too."

Rick told Elmo about the lawyer's letter and some of what his father had left him. Elmo tried to give a low whistle but his missing tooth made a hiss instead.

"So you think them hombres know yer comin' back to claim things?"

"What else? And it's more important than ever that you stay safe. I want you away from Carson River, Elmo. I want you staying out at Threesome. Will you do that?"

Elmo hesitated then shrugged his thin shoulders. "Sure, you could use a cook anyhow—to make coffee." He grinned. "I'd been thinkin' of Samuel's old dugout. He's not stayin' there now. He's at that Halliday Mansion. Fancy place—all Miss Callie's idea I'm hearin'. But look here, Delance, if yer goin' to make that long trip to New Mexico Territory, nuthin's keepin' me here."

"Don't worry. If we find the men we're looking for, I'll need you in Santa Fe to swear the truth to the colonel at Fort Craig. We'll be going there together."

"Now yer talkin'."

But first, thought Delance, *we'll both need to survive with killers roaming Virginia City.*

Delance narrowed his eyes and looked off toward the mesquite trees, thinking. *Ashe Perry and Hugh Ralston? Could their reasons for being involved with Callie be tied in with her share of the Halliday-Harkin Mine? Frank Harkin and Callie's father, Jack Halliday, were partners in the claim until Macklin Villiers hired Hoadly to kill Frank and blame it on Callie's father, hoping to make the mine a part of the Pelly-Jessup. But in the end, earthly justice had prevailed as far as Macklin Villiers and Hoadly were concerned. Frank and Jack Halliday were dead as well, and their coveted mine had reverted to their heirs. Jack's half went to his three children, and Frank's went to his younger brother, Dylan Harkin.*

When Delance had known Dylan in Tucson he'd been just another gunfighter drifting through the territories. He'd gotten wind that Jack Halliday shot his brother Frank in the back for the mine and had gone a little berserk. He'd come hunting Jack to even the score. But on that night in '60 when Wilder and himself had faced down the true killers, Dylan had disappeared—suddenly.

Delance frowned to himself. Dylan hadn't been seen or heard from in Virginia City since that night. Come to think of it, that struck him as a little odd.

Was Dylan collecting his portion of money from the mine? He must be, since Annalee, Callie, and Jimmy were getting theirs. A lawyer must be handling Dylan's share, which would be a heap more than what each of the three Halliday heirs were sharing between them. But what lawyer? Hadn't it been Colefax who managed the legal and financial ends of the Pelly-Jessup? Colefax and Macklin Villiers had been as thick as bean soup.

Dylan should be a mighty rich man about now, with no cause to be drifting saloons in rough Western towns, risking his life to a bullet from some crazed hombre out to enhance his reputation. Dylan could have most anything he wanted in this world. Maybe he went to Europe, or maybe he was having a plantation built somewhere in the South where he and Frank Harkin had come from?

Dylan had mentioned Mississippi once. Maybe he was all wrapped up in the war between the states?

It was time to ask around and find out who was sending the silver proceeds to Dylan. *Was Colefax still in control? And…just where was Colefax? Samuel might know since he ran the Halliday finances.*

Delance looked over at Elmo. "Seen Dylan Harkin anywhere recently?"

Elmo looked surprised. "Dylan Harkin?" he repeated. "That jackrabbit sped out of town over a year ago."

"I know, but he wouldn't put distance between himself and that silver unless someone he trusted managed his percentage, would he?"

Elmo pushed his hat back and his brows curled together. "You got me, there. No, he sure wouldn't, an' nobody else would neither. Not if he had an ounce of smarts. But then, that Dylan always did strike me as a nutty roadrunner."

Delance shook his head. "It just figures a little strange to me now that I think about it."

"I ain't thought none about Dylan much, either."

"I'll talk to Samuel. He may know something. Wish I'd thought of this before I talked to Bill Stewart. He may know about Dylan's lawyer."

Elmo shook the grounds from his tin cup and strapped it back onto his belt. "I'll be headin' back to Carson to pack my gear an' move to Threesome." He stood, rifle in hand, one light-blue eye cocked Rick's way like a wise old sage. "Wish you'd tell them good church-goin' folks in Virginny Town 'bout Mister Lucien bein' a gentleman an' all. The Delance family can match any I seen in these parts. Folks in town think yer nuthin' but a driftin' gunfighter."

Rick tightened his mouth. "There's a cost to everything a man does, Elmo. You just have to choose your way that's all. By trumpeting what Pa left me I'm also inviting folks to befriend me for what I have. Maybe I'm stubborn—"

"You be stubborn fer sure."

"—but if ever the woman I want, wants me too, it'll have to be for myself first. Any pleasant surprises will come afterward. Silence right now suits me."

"Well, it's yer call. But thems high stakes gamblin' if you ask me. I can tell you flat out most society folks in town ain't goin' to let you come a callin' on their nice daughters."

"Don't plan to," Rick drawled lazily.

"And that Callie O'Day's more fancy now than a preenin' bluebird with a new bonnet."

Rick laughed shortly—

A bullet whined past his ear, striking a boulder beside the camp, spraying chips of rock.

He hit the ground drawing his .44, squeezing off two shots toward the trees where he heard the shot come from, and then he rolled out of the way into the darker shadows of mesquite.

Bullets thudded, kicking up grit where a moment earlier he'd hit the ground on his belly. Another bullet blew the coffeepot from the wood coals with a clatter. Rifle shots zinged and ricocheted off the nearby rocks forcing him to keep his head down. *Where is Elmo?*

Seven

The small flame hovering over ruby coals flickered and died. All was silent now in the moonlight, where only minutes earlier the camp had been the site of chaos and danger as bullets had rained in upon them.

Rick remained in the shadow of a mesquite tree, waiting. He glanced toward the small rock where Elmo had sat by the campfire when the shooting started, afraid he'd see the old timer's body crumpled or dying in the dust. Elmo wasn't there, and relief swept Rick's heart. He must have managed to crawl off into the low rocks on the other side of the camp. If he knew Elmo, he was hunkered down with his rifle, watching alertly, just waiting to get off a shot.

Delance quietly loaded powder and balls into his six-shooter. He placed percussion caps in the back of the cylinder. He was ready. He listened. Time dragged on as the coals in the fire darkened. He wanted to move and search for the killer. He wondered who was out there, Cesar, Johnny, or the man with the scar? Rick decided he wasn't going to berate himself about how he'd given the gunman opportunity to get a jump on him. He needed to concentrate his efforts on one thing now—finding him.

He set his jaw and a coolness settled over his emotions. He'd faced these situations before. Now that he was no longer out in the open, he and the gunman were on a more equal footing. If he were in the other man's boots, what would he be thinking? The hired gunman knew he'd already gotten off his best shots and failed to eliminate his quarry, so he would start worrying. He'd be thinking of pulling out and disappearing as Apache-like as he'd crept in upon them. But first, he might try to reach Rick's horse.

If he ran off his horse, he would be a full day ahead of Delance on the trail.

Elmo's mule was in good stead, tied close-at-hand to a shrub near the campfire, and Elmo was sure to be watching her. But Rick's horse was unguarded. At least the gunman wouldn't know that Rick's horse didn't cotton to strangers; on a quiet night in the wilderness he could get mighty ornery if a stranger came poking around where he wasn't supposed to be. But that could be worrisome, too. If a bad hombre found that he couldn't control the horse, he might just shoot him.

The wind came up a mite stronger and rustled the taller grasses. Now was his opportunity. He was grateful to the Creator. Those rustling sounds, and the call of a night hawk circling above would cover any stealthy sounds he'd be making.

Rick eased from behind the sparse mesquite branches. Keeping flat, he crawled forward on arms and knees, his rifle across his forearms. There would be a view of the water hole where his horse was picketed if he could safely get beyond the rim of the slope.

He moved almost silently, using some of the tactics of Indian warriors. After the death of his father, Rick had ridden to Fort Craig to report the killing and rustling, but he'd ended up ill with a fever. A man named Pickering, who'd been at the fort when he arrived, befriended him. After his recovery he'd spent some months as Pickering's aide, learning to protect the fort from Comanche attacks. Pickering was a first-class scout for the army under Colonel Clark, and Pickering had taught him well. Rick might well have stayed on with Pickering and gone to West Point for an army career. He had liked the rugged, seasoned man who had tried to talk him into a military career, but it was not to be. Rick was still held captive by the past, and his overriding ambition was to find those responsible for the Triple D ambush. Pickering seemed to understand and, regretfully, had let him go.

Rick now moved through tall grass as carefully and softly as a cougar. The gunman might already be nearing the water hole where the stallion was tied.

He paused to listen for unnatural sounds. That man out there was no greenhorn or he wouldn't have gotten the jump on him.

Rick doubted the man would have much of a conscience. It must have been seared with a hot iron long ago. Rick felt a sudden unease. The man might not be wanting to hightail it out of here after all. He might be lying low up in those rocks to the left, just raring for Rick to show himself in the moonlight so he could let go with a close-range barrage—and this time he'd not be likely to miss.

Rick inched up to the rim of the slope. Just a few more feet and he'd see the water hole. The wind's drift brought the fragrance of dried sage. He edged over the top of the rim and crawled to the safety of a boulder on the downward slope. Lifting his head around the rock, he peered down at his horse and the glinting water.

Keeping flat, he eased his rifle into position. He wiped the sweat from his eyelids. His sharp gaze scoured the area below, just the way Pickering had taught him, the way a Comanche did, taking in everything within close range and moving outward very slowly, looking for any unnatural movement, anything that shouldn't be there, or that looked natural but moved when it shouldn't. He'd been with Scout Pickering when Comanches made it to the circumference of an army detail camped near Fort Yuma. They'd moved ever closer, camouflaged with sagebrush. One Comanche he'd fought had blanketed his body with grass, and Rick hadn't seen him until he was inside the camp and ready to take a soldier's scalp.

His vision scanned the tranquil gully, the water, the tall, over-wintered grasses, and scrub pine. He watched his horse as it cropped knee-length grass contentedly, its dark silhouette arched against the water that shimmered in the moonlight as the breeze rippled it gently. He raised his gaze across the water hole to the opposite slope, which was taller than the one he was on, where the moon climbing above it looked as big as a ripe Texas melon.

A pesky mosquito droned at Rick's ear. He waited. He had a good field of fire as long as the gunman wasn't up in the rocks to his left with a view of the area around his horse. If the gunman was foolish enough to show his silhouette now, his day of reckoning would come.

Rick, ever so lightly, turned his head to the side and glanced up at those ragged boulders. Moonlight fell like a mantle across the rock surfaces but there were shadows behind them, just right for a man to lay up with his rifle. There was stunted pine on the rocks clinging to a bit of soil, yet trying to send roots down through stone. He thought about that a moment. *When a man expected fruitfulness he'd best plant his roots in good soil. But then, this is no time to be preaching at myself. Or is it?*

Nothing seemed to be moving up among the rocks. Even so, he had half a mind to maneuver around and climb the backside. If there was anyone up there, Rick could come up behind him. He needed information, and he wanted to bring this man down with as little gunplay as possible. Who'd sent him, and who were the other hired guns recently trailing him? Taking him alive wouldn't be easy—it would require a good shot in the right place at night. Even with the moon growing brighter as it continued its climb—

Bullets blasted—two, three, four—but not from the rocks above or the water hole! How could the gunman have gotten around and behind him and back near the darkened campfire…in the pinion pine near Elmo.

A rifle shot answered the first barrage. That would be Elmo. It was followed by more shots pumped into the area by the hired killer, then Elmo's cry.

For a moment Rick listened, stunned.

Elmo is hit…Elmo bleeding, dying—

The thought of losing him brought a spasm of bitter pain. He'd been more attached to him than he'd admitted. Elmo, the feisty old cookie, Rick's last link to what had been, to what may never be again, dying, for no reason but the evil in men's hearts.

For a frantic moment Rick was just a boy again, alone and reliving the gut-wrenching loss and anger over the death of his father and Alex.

He had to get back to Elmo. He may still be alive.

The mesquite trees blocked the line of fire from the area near the campsite, and he raised himself from behind the boulder to run to the cover of a shrub until—a bullet came smashing into his back…from the direction of the water hole. His situation rushed through his mind: more than one gunfighter out here...he'd been right about the water—

Another bullet hissed past his ear. As he turned back toward the cover of the boulder, dropping to one knee, a third bullet struck near his collarbone and spun him half around. He fell as the fiery blaze of his wounds sent his brain into a spiral. He was going down the slope, rolling, bumping, landing in a stunned heap, lying somewhere near the bottom—

My rifle—

After what seemed like minutes, his blurred vision cleared enough to stare up at the black sky. For a moment he couldn't move. *Get up!* his mind ordered, but shock and pain tried to convince him otherwise. Quick! You can't stay here. He'll soon come to check on you, finish you off. You've got to be ready! You've got to live, to protect Callie!

Rick rolled over in the grass, surprised by his weakness. He looked about to gain some control over his situation. He was perhaps thirty yards from the water hole and his horse. He tried to crawl toward some dark clumps of pine shrub and a mound of rock. It should have taken only a minute to get there, but every movement seemed heavy and painful.

He began inching toward the scrubby pines.

It was no good. He'd gone but a few feet. His breath came ragged. His right arm felt numb. He sank against the ground. The front of his buckskin shirt was wet with blood.

The big yellow moon looked down at him. A soft breeze walked gently through the grass. Was this to be his grave?

Had he chosen the right path these last five years? His pa wouldn't have thought so. Maybe even Alex wouldn't have thought so. Driven by a passion to search for their killers...yet, if he hadn't tried, what then? They wouldn't have left him alone when he went back to reclaim the Triple D...and if he survived this time, there'd be more attacks like this one.

Rick crawled a few more feet through the tall grass, his breath coming in gasps. He didn't have much time. That hunter was close. God was closer. A breath away. Then death. Death, then Jesus' glorious face.

His horse warned him of someone's approach with a wary nicker as it pulled uneasily at its tether, trying to back away.

Rick rolled over on his side, grasped his knife from his belt and cut off a piece of cloth from his undershirt, stuffing it against the wound near his right collarbone. Blood had been running down the front of his buckskin shirt and onto his right sleeve. He thought the other wound was at his back or side. Lying on it would exert pressure to stop the bleeding. He was weak but needed all his senses. He mustn't pass out.

He managed to roll onto his back, then leaned his head up against a rock. He covered his right pistol with his buckskin shirt, relaxing his right arm. He reached with his left hand, loosening the ties on his left holster. He checked the loads. For years, at the Triple D, he'd made sport of practicing with his left. He eased the .44 Lawman back into its holster, then massaged the fingers on his left hand to keep them limber.

He paused, listening. Boots made a scuffing sound over the rock face as someone climbed down, loosening pebbles as he came. The man seemed haughty, sensing no need for caution.

He was reaching the bottom of the slope and coming. Rick's gaze found him. He stooped down near something…it was Rick's rifle. He paused a few steps to look at the trail of blood on the ground. Slowly he approached the grass where Rick had crawled.

In the bright moonlight a tall, formidable figure came from the rocks, his Spanish hat silhouetted against the midnight-blue sky. He was bold now, allowing a Spanish spur to jingle as he took a few steps in Rick's direction.

Rick saw the glint of a pistol barrel as it caught a beam of the moonlight. Arrogant and over-confident, the attacker appeared certain his swiftness with his gun would win him long life…eternal life? Foolish, all—

"Senor Ricardo, we meet," came the almost musical voice.

So this was Cesar. And Johnny must be back at camp with Elmo. Elmo! The memory, tasting like bitter gall brought a surge of indignation.

"Knew you'd come here…to run off or kill my horse…"

A flash of white teeth showed in the moonlight. "No, senor, no need now to kill good horse, I take. You, I kill. You do not need horse anymore. Adios, senor," Cesar mocked softly as he raised his gun hand.

"Wait…who sent you?"

Cesar pursed his lips. He shrugged his heavy shoulders a little, showing indifference. "Zel Willard."

"Were you there that night five years ago?"

Cesar's lips spread with mocking amusement. "Why you care now? Yes, we burn down Triple D hacienda."

Rick's anger surged. He must stay cool.

"Do you know who shot my father?"

Cesar's dark brows went up with wicked mirth. "No, senor, not me. I shot Salvador, and then I take Chiquita."

"Marita?"

"She is dead now. Buried between El Paso and Mexico."

"Your mouth condemns you, Cesar."

"It will not matter to you anymore!" Cesar was raising his six-shooter.

In a flash Delance's Lawman fired lead. Cesar's muzzle stabbed out flame, and a bullet splintered the rocks near Rick's head sending fragments against him. Rick fired a second time sending Cesar a step back on his spurred heels, his teeth bared in hatred and swearing. His hand shook as he tried to hold the six-shooter to fire at Rick again. Succumbing to shock, his knees became weak and he started sinking to the ground, one arm against his chest as his gun slipped from his hand into the dirt. He went down on both knees, his spurs jangling. He tried clawing at the ground for his gun. In the moonlight the whites of his eyes blazed. His expression was one of unbelief, as though it couldn't happen to him. Then he fell forward, face down in the dirt, silent and still at last.

The night wind turned colder and seemed to moan its disapproval to the world over which it flowed. Even the moon seemed to dim, or was it Rick's vision? Faintness tugged relentlessly at his brain, trying to drag him into darkness. He struggled to crawl to the water hole, to his horse nickering unhappily. Rick wanted to get away from Cesar. If he was to die, too, then he wanted to lie at the water hole near the innocent horse….

Sorry it turned out like this…Lord, sorry…but they killed Pa, they killed Alex, they killed me—

Rick Delance made it several inches farther before he collapsed facedown in the tall waving grass.

The wind rushed through the grass again, and the old mesquite tree shook its meager limbs. The silence deepened over the long, lonely hills. A coyote howled mournfully. From beneath a nearby rock a slithering form, sensing the stillness, cautiously emerged, its tongue smelling the air. The rattler slithered toward the water hole, turning its back on the dead and the dying.

Eight

"$\mathcal{A}$she, they're absolutely stunning." Callie couldn't keep the surprise from her voice as they sat at a dinner-for-two table in the fashionable dining room of the International Hotel.

She set down the ornate silver box and took out the blue sapphire pieces: a pendant, earbobs, and a gleaming gold ring with large sparkling blue jewels flashing in the lights of the chandelier.

The sapphires harmonized with the environment in the hotel dining room, which glittered with crystal and silver. Thick carpet and curtains also leant a tasteful elegance. Callie was gowned in blue satin and lace, and Ashe was the perfect example of handsome sophistication. She felt triumphant just to be seated in the dining room where so many other important and rich people were comfortably gathered.

She turned to him. "But, Ashe, they must be worth a small fortune." How had he come by this kind of money? And to spend it so lavishly on such a gift. Was he pressured into thinking he must give her jewels because she was a silver heiress?

Ashe, however, didn't appear worried as she looked at him. He laughed quietly, delighted with her response.

"For your opening night at the Stardust? Nothing is too good for you, my Callie. The good luck gift had to be sapphires to match your eyes."

Her eyes were actually an unusual violet blue, but she'd not be vain enough to mention that now.

"*Our* opening night," she corrected with a song in her voice. "They'll be coming to see you, the great Ashe Perry."

"I doubt most will even know who I am."

Callie wondered over the note of bitterness that had crept into his voice. She hadn't noticed that in him before. Something was bothering him. Was he disappointed in Virginia City?

"Granted, the people here aren't as refined as those from the rich background of the New York theater. But even those who aren't will flood the theaters. And many newcomers are quite sophisticated. Just look around us, Ashe, at how rich and elegant they all are."

She glanced about the large room. There were several mine owners here tonight, along with big investors, many of them mingling with others who were gathering their fortunes not from silver mining but by supplying the needs of the boomtown for lumber and luxury items. And she was now in the midst of them—as a silver heiress and half owner of the new Stardust Theater.

"Here, darling, try them on now."

"Ashe—people will stare."

He laughed. "Let them enjoy what they see. We're performers, remember?"

"But not now."

"No, of course not. Here, let me clasp the necklace..."

Callie put on the bracelet. The blue sparkled and danced in the light. She smiled at him.

"They'll all be coming to see my leading lady," Ashe said, inclining his golden head toward her.

He always included her in his success, and she warmed to this, rejecting the possibility that his response might be tainted. Her thoughts wandered.

Poor Annalee, how dreadful to be ill and missing so much in life! If I were in her place, I don't think I could stand it. How good it would be to see and visit with her again before moving to a full and busy life of drama in New York.

Callie decided a moment later, however, that she needn't feel too sorry for Annalee. Her sister had gained something valuable—she'd caught Brett Wilder. "Caught," because to Callie, it was always "catching" a man. She hadn't accepted Annalee's sanctified notion that meeting the right man was a "divine appointment." That was just Annalee. Her faith in God and her calm confidence in the face of trials and disappointments had often driven Callie to fits of frustration. Callie feared that if she ever worshiped God the way Annalee and Uncle Samuel did, God might not approve of her plans and she could be denied the best opportunities in life.

Yes, Callie believed in Jesus, the Son of God, who paid the penalty for all her sin. She prayed sometimes, too. But cultivating a relationship with her heavenly Father was something that eluded her. Perhaps she'd been affected by feelings about her own, mostly absentee father, whom she would not have trusted with her decisions. Regardless of the reason, Callie wasn't about to yield control to anyone who would spoil things for her.

Marrying Brett Wilder, however, certainly counted for something good, so she would give her sister applause for that. Callie, too, had found him attractive. Odd, there was something about Brett and Rick Delance that seemed to belong to a certain type of man. She had seen it sometimes in soldiers. Rick Delance reminded her a little of Brett. Not that they looked that much alike. Delance was even more—well, she wouldn't think about that. How he looked in a buckskin shirt and hat certainly paled compared with this wonderful moment with Ashe Perry at the International Hotel! And Rick Delance certainly would not fit in such an environment as the theater or this fine dining room.

She glanced at Ashe, "the Golden Lad," as he was called in the theater world. Then she glanced at the sapphires again. They sparkled a deep, turbulent blue.

She petted them. "Oh, Ashe, I just don't know what to say. How utterly sweet of you. I'll wear them with pride and keep them dear to my heart always." She hesitated, glancing at him sideways, still curious as any woman would be. "They must have cost you a pretty penny, I mean, sapphires, and so many of them, too. Are you sure you want me to have them?"

His wide smile was one she'd often seen on stage, and she'd come to depend on it when confronting personal doubts. That dazzling smile came naturally to him. It was one of the reasons for his success as an actor. He could turn emotion and charm on and off as easily as a jackrabbit could sprint. She'd seen some people so uncomfortable before an audience they couldn't smile. But not

Ashe Perry. Not that his manner lacked sincerity. Why, Ashe was genuine through and through.

"What's this?" came his teasing voice. "Am I sure I want you to have them? Question a man's gift and you question his good intentions, Callie dearest."

Callie's hand was on the white linen tablecloth, and he covered it with his own. His smile could only be described as tender.

"Well, if you put it that way," she said with a laugh, "I could hardly refuse them."

"No, nor should you. And that's the way I want it. And seriously, dear, I want you to know they are worth a tremendous amount on the European market. But it's not their value that means so much to me, as the history of the sapphires themselves."

A pause followed. Her curiosity aroused, she looked at him for explanation.

"You see, they belonged to my mother, and her mother before her. They go back to Great-grandmother Giselle Devonshire Perry, who came from the family of the Duchess of York."

Duchess. Callie Halliday now owned the jewels worn by a duchess? Awed, Callie felt her throat cramp with emotion.

"Ashe." She contemplated softly, looking at them, touching them. "How precious. To think I—I mean so much to you that—" her voice faltered and tears came to her eyes. Her own importance seemed to brighten like the desert stars. "That you'd entrust me with such prized family heirlooms."

"Callie, darling…" he grew grave, leaning closer toward her across the sparkling table for two. He took her hand into his and covered it between his palms. "I trust you with more than jewels. I've entrusted you with my heart."

Oooh. She looked searchingly and saw his intense emotion. Those words, those beautiful words, it was as if she'd heard them before somewhere, but Ashe had that kind of effect on her, and others, too. He seemed to walk off the stage, still bringing all of "the Golden Lad" with him into any situation. What mattered now was that it was genuine and expressly dedicated to her.

"On opening night I want you wearing those sapphires for good luck," he said softly. "This will be your night, Callie, not mine. Your starring debut. I want people to come to their feet in applause, moved to tears by your great abilities. Then, we're off to New York. It must be soon, Callie. We don't want to waste time. Life is too short for that. We must think of tomorrow. I want to introduce you to my friends there. You'll soon be up in lights, darling."

Her heart soared giddily. Such sweet words...words she longed to hear. And now Ashe Perry, of all people, was the one speaking them.

"If we could leave Virginia City in a few weeks..." his earnest voice trailed, and he looked toward a window as if seeing the streets of New York.

Callie followed his gaze and saw nothing except a lone table to one side of the window where a slim man sat. He had a black beard and was dressed all in black. He looked very tall for his legs showed under the table. He wore a black hat and spectacles while he ate, and he reminded her of a rabbi. He was preoccupied with his dinner.

"But, we can't leave that soon, can we?" Ashe turned a questioning gaze on her. "We promised your uncle—a good man we can't disappoint. Though I've received the impression that he can be domineering. If it's a choice between your career on Broadway and your uncle—" he left the final words for her.

Callie's fears of losing what she wanted most leaped into action. Uncle Samuel's meddling shouldn't be permitted to rob her of the best life had to offer. That would be too much to bear!

"I've made up my mind, Ashe, as I've told you. No one—not even Samuel—is going to interfere in my future."

"Wonderful." The encouraging eagerness in his eyes told her she'd made the right decision—the bold one, the one that pleased him.

He squeezed her hand. "Callie, I've news to share. I received a letter today from Foster Williams, an old friend in New York. Foster wants me to play the leading role in a new play he's written. And that's not all. He's willing to have you as my leading lady!"

Too good to be true! "Ashe, you mean that? But he's not even seen me perform!"

"Foster trusts my judgment. I believe in you, that's good enough for him. He knows you starred with me in San Francisco."

"But how did he know we were here in Virginia City?"

"I sent him a wire before we left San Francisco, hoping something like this would turn up. I said nothing to you because I didn't want to disappoint you with big promises should I not hear from him."

Ashe exuded excitement. "This play could be a new beginning for me, for both of us. Think of it! A Foster Williams play! Both of us with starring roles. I tell you, it's a chance of a lifetime. Think of the adventures we two shall have! Think of the possibilities."

Callie's heart beat faster just listening to him, watching the excitement grow in his eyes until, convinced too, she was cheering their imminent success. Ashe affected her that way. "Oh, Ashe, it sounds so wonderful."

He caught up her hand so tightly it hurt. "It *is* wonderful! There's only one problem."

His eyes were searching hers, and she heard a gong of doom as his face turned sober.

"We need to get your business matters concluded here sooner than planned. We need to leave in three weeks."

Three weeks. Was it possible? But she saw enthusiasm begin to glow in his eyes again, and the spark lit her own. He radiated the same driving emotion as when playing opposite her on stage, only now—it was real.

"What about the Stardust?"

"We'll have three weeks in Virginia City. That's long enough for anyone with greater opportunities."

"But there's the Company players." Her voice hesitated. She didn't want to think about obligations to the other actors and actresses, but their faces popped up anyway. Well, she'd just need to disappoint them. Maybe she could give them some extra pay—that ought to make them satisfied.

"The Company will do just fine," Ashe consoled. "Hugh will take over the management of the Stardust. They'll be working for him. He'll have the place humming."

Yes, of course he would. She'd forgotten about Hugh Ralston. He would oversee the success of the Stardust for his own benefit, as well as for the players'.

Ashe looked at her long and hard. "Don't you want to free yourself from the constraints that your family impose upon you? Don't you like to be yourself?"

She could feel her desire for independence pushing her forward. She laid her hand on his, determined not to allow Samuel and Weda's worries to spoil her visions of the life she wanted. "And we'll let no one deter us."

"If we could just take care of the business here so we can leave on schedule." He looked at her. "Are you still serious about selling your third of the Halliday-Harkin Mine?"

They'd discussed the matter on several occasions.

"Of course. I should get a good price. And there's plenty of mine owners in town who'd snap up my shares in a hurry if they knew I was selling."

"Naturally you'll need a lawyer to handle everything. Hugh knows a good man in San Francisco."

She trusted Hugh. Why shouldn't she? But Samuel's doubts muddied the water.

"Samuel has some concerns about Hugh Ralston," she admitted.

"Hugh is a respected man with many important friends and associates both in San Francisco and in the East. Your uncle is just being cautious. There's really nothing to worry about."

Callie agreed. Her irritation with her uncle grew. It seemed that every time she wanted to make a decision for her future happiness he was there in the shadows throwing obstacles before her path.

"Except first, I simply must stop at Santa Fe, Ashe. It may be the last time I'm able to see Annalee for many years."

"Then we'll do it. It shouldn't be too hard to arrange. Does the stage go there?"

"Yes, I'm sure. Though I don't know how Brett was ever able to bring her there to his father, Dr. Jim Wilder. It's not an easy trip, I'm told." She thought of the many miles across hard country. Annalee had written of the journey as "difficult, yet exciting."

"It can't be that bad," Ashe said carelessly. "Some of these Western men and gunfighters seem to think too highly of themselves. That Rick Delance for one."

She looked at him. Had they met? Probably in town during the few days since their arrival.

"He seems to think that men out here are more apt to succeed in the harsh elements than those of us from the East. Well, he's wrong. They have their pride, you know. I'll go with you, dearest. We'll conquer this together."

She smiled her happiness. She felt better. He made her feel as though nothing were impossible, that she was right in her decisions.

"The sapphires will be just the beginning, Callie. You'll wear them, and more, in New York."

She looked at the jewels. "I'd be honored to wear them on opening night, but really Ashe, they're heirlooms, do you think it wise?"

He laughed quietly. "In Virginia City? Yes, it's wise. You delight and amuse me! This is one town in which the rich can show off their possessions and no one worries. Look at John McLaughlin and his wife at their table over there. Silver on his carriage and his horses' bridles. Why even his mansion's doorknobs are made of silver I hear." He laughed shortly.

It all seemed so absurdly delightful that she laughed along with him, and several heads turned in their direction.

"And you, dearest, are among the elite. You are a silver heiress. Look, there's no need to worry," and he touched the necklace in the box. "They are insured, and have been since great-grandmother's time. Just the way McLaughlin's silver doorknobs probably are. Everyone does it that way, darling! What good are riches if you don't show them off?"

Callie was still smiling. Yes, what good was her wealth if she couldn't use it to live her life the way she wanted?

"And, now," he said, ending the subject and lifting his glass that sparkled beneath the glittering chandelier. "To us! To our future in New York! To our marriage!" He took the gold ring with its sapphire setting and slipped it on her finger. "There, you see? It fits perfectly. It was meant for you, sweet."

"Oh, Ashe…"

"Let's get married now! Before we leave for Santa Fe."

"I'd rather we waited and marry in Santa Fe so my sister can attend."

"Whatever makes you happiest."

Their crystal glasses touched and tinkled.

At that moment Callie was sure of Ashe. She gave herself willingly into his care and plans, accepting all of his preparations, trying not to envision Samuel and Weda's disappointment. She pushed aside her own questions because they only raised doubts where she needed confidence. She gazed instead on blue fire from the sapphire ring—the ring of an English duchess, and now her own engagement ring, an open door to a new life with Ashe in the New York theater.

Nine

As Callie stepped out on the boardwalk with Ashe, the moon, which was just beginning to rise over the eastern horizon when she entered the International Hotel, was now high above the hills in a clear, wind-swept sky. The wind swirled down C Street kicking up some dust. She turned her head until it settled again, thinking that if she wanted to ride out to the Halliday-Harkin Mine Works she would take C Street down toward Gold Canyon. She remembered that the Threesome Mine was also in Gold Canyon. Rick Delance was said to own a third of the mine. Was it producing good ore?

It was at least ten o'clock. The silver mines were being run continuously on three shifts, men were coming off duty from somewhere and fresh miners were arriving. Farther down the street it looked to her as though the Savage Mine Works was changing shifts.

C Street was crowded; buildings were cropping up like dandelions. Callie noticed some she hadn't seen before: the Nevada Bank of San Francisco near the Wells Fargo Building and a new hotel. The stamp mills and compressors were continuously pounding away. The unpleasant drumming of progress competed with vigor against the tinny piano music that drifted to her on the wind from every saloon and faro game parlor in town.

Callie and Ashe stopped on the boardwalk and turned to look down the street where a horse came galloping in from Gold Canyon. The rider came to a jerking halt and voices rose. Someone shouted, and men began gathering around the rider.

Now what? Callie wondered.

Gordon Barkly appeared from his office near the *Territorial Enterprise* building—probably sensing a story—and ran toward the group near the horseman. Gordon had called on her Sunday after church at Uncle Samuel's chapel, and she knew he was hoping to revive interest between them. There was no chance of that now, and he had not taken her refusal graciously. Afterward, he started asking questions about Ashe.

"Why, that's Elmo on that horse," she told Ashe. "What's he doing here this time of night? He usually rides a mule. He's not much interested in saloons. Samuel said he was staying out along the Carson River doing placer mining. There's something wrong, Ashe."

He took her arm. "Maybe there's more news about the war. Let's see what it's all about."

Elmo was still seated on the horse when she came up. Gordon Barkly was pressing him with questions.

"Did you see who shot him, Elmo?"

"All I want is Doc McMannis. Where can I find him?"

Shot him. Callie came swiftly alert and pressed forward toward the street where Elmo slumped in the saddle looking older and more tired than she'd ever seen him. Ashe came up behind her, and she felt his hand on her arm. She looked at him, showing her concern.

"Someone's been shot. Elmo is Rick Delance's friend. I wonder...?"

Ashe cocked a golden brow. "A gunfighter? His days are short regardless of how you look at it. Come, let's get out of here. I'll walk you to the buggy. This is no place for us."

"Wait, Ashe." She looked up at Elmo, straining to hear what he was telling Gordon.

"You tellin' me Doc ain't here? I tell you I be needin' him bad out at Threesome."

"McMannis rode to the Gilford's place way up at Summit Station," another man said. "Nellie's having a baby, and Jeb came ridin' in town this mornin' beggin' him to come. She was in a bad way."

"Is Delance hit badly?" Gordon asked.

So he had been shot! Callie looked earnestly at Elmo. "Where is Rick now, Elmo?"

At the sound of a woman's voice, the men turned and looked at her. They slowly stepped away, making room as she edged up, her gown glittering in the light coming from the Wells Fargo Building.

Elmo doffed his grubby old hat when he saw her. "Evenin', Miss Callie. He be hit aright, twice, an' if I don't get some help with them wounds he'll be bad up come mornin'."

Ashe watched Callie with a stiffening lip and a thoughtful glint in his eyes. "Don't think of going out there. It's too dangerous."

"What happened?" she asked Elmo.

"Best not to talk now, Miss Callie. One of 'em got away, and I wouldn't want him feelin' good tonight, but by now I got a mind he ain't nowheres 'round town."

"There's Eilley Orrum," Gordon Barkly said. "She's been treating the injured since before Ol' Virginny discovered the Ophir."

Callie interrupted, surprised at herself, "She wouldn't know how to treat gunshot wounds, Gordon. Look, Elmo, if Doctor McMannis is away then Samuel's the one to go to for help. He'll know what to do until the doctor can come. Samuel's treated scores of men with injuries, including bullet wounds. He even has a medical satchel at the house that he always took with him on his circuit-riding tours."

"You're plumb right, Miss Callie. Samuel's the best hope for gettin' help now. You know if he's up at the mansion or at the church this hour?"

"He'll be at the house. I'll tell him. I'm going there now. Can you wait at Flowery Street?"

"How did he get shot?" Ashe spoke up.

Elmo looked at him. "Mister, he were dry-gulched, that's what."

"Dry-gulched?"

Callie quickly turned to Ashe a little embarrassed. "It means he was ambushed."

"Then the men got away?"

Elmo's eyes flashed over Ashe's calm question. "One of 'em got away. The skunk shootin' at me and ol' Jenny. The shifty coyote facin' Delance is dead. Musta been some fight 'cause readin' sign tells me Delance was already bad hurt when this hombre thinks he has him and walks up proud as Lucifer."

Callie thought back to the showdown between Rick and Rody Villiers and felt a chill. The sooner she could get away from this savage land, the better. She glanced at Ashe to see his response, but he showed nothing. Something glittered in his eyes...grudging admiration for Rick Delance? This surprised her.

Ashe spoke up, "Who was this man he killed—do you know his name?"

Elmo looked more angry and pugnacious than she had ever seen him. His face was flushed, and he was talkative.

"Sure, I'm knowin'. I'm knowin' lots of things goin' on 'round here, an' in New Mexico Territory!"

"What's that, Elmo?" Gordon Barkly asked, alert.

"That coyote—a hired gun sent here to kill him, that's what, but Delance got him good. His name was Cesar."

Callie wondered at the hush that fell over the crowd of men.

Ashe lapsed into silence. But Gordon pressed closer, his amber eyes fixed on Elmo with apparent eagerness. Callie knew Gordon well enough to tell that he was narrowing in on a story. She, too, was alert.

"What about New Mexico Territory?" Gordon pressed.

Elmo scowled and stirred in the saddle as though realizing he'd said more than he intended. But his reluctance only made Gordon more persistent.

"Come on, Elmo, what do you know about Rick Delance you're not telling us?" Gordon asked with a hungry smile. "Come on, old timer, out with it. We're all friends of Delance here, aren't we, boys?" and he glanced about at the silent but growing crowd standing near the hitching rail. "And don't forget the lady," Gordon said with a somewhat wry smile toward Callie. "Delance once drew on Rody Villiers on your account, didn't he?"

Callie felt her embarrassment, and it angered her that Gordon would single her out now in front of Ashe, implying she had some sort of relationship with Rick. It was deliberate, she knew.

"You were there, Mr. Barkly, don't you remember? I believe that when my *dear* Cousin Rody dared to slap me across the mouth you just stood there for the longest period of time until Rick Delance intervened."

Gordon turned an unbecoming red, and his mouth tightened. "I didn't have a six-shooter strapped to my hip, and this cousin of yours was a killer."

Heads turned in her direction and feet shuffled as bodies moved back, but whether out of deference to her as a lady or in support of Gordon wasn't clear. Her heart beat faster. At that moment she could have shown her kinship with Rody by slapping Gordon Barkly.

"Never mind all that," Ashe's calm voice took command. "Miss Halliday has enough to concern her without bringing up a no-account gunfighter. Whoever Rody was, he's not here to trouble her now. And I intend to see it stays that way."

Callie looked at him, warm satisfaction replacing the tension in her heart. Ashe stood cool and disciplined in the lamplight, and she looked on him with a hint of surprise. Ashe was equal to any of them. When she turned back to Elmo, he appeared to have recovered and acted as though he had no intention of answering any more of Gordon's questions.

"You say Samuel's home, Miss Callie?"

"He's probably asleep now. I'll need to wake him. Ashe? Will you drive the buggy for me?" Without another glance at Gordon she turned toward the street.

"I'll wait near Flowery Street, Miss Callie," Elmo called, and turned the line-back dun to ride down C Street toward the Savage Mansion and the Halliday Mansion.

For a moment Callie paused as a wary chill went up her back. She turned again and looked back at Elmo, who was riding away on the handsome horse. Now why would she suddenly feel this way?

The men were all melting away into the darkened street and onto the boardwalks. Her eyes scanned the faces in the crowd but few of them were familiar. It seemed that they'd stood talking while keeping mostly in the shadows.

"What is it?" Ashe was looking down at her with a quizzical frown.

She didn't really know. She shook her head and walked on toward the buggy. "We'd better hurry."

A minute later, seated beside him on the leather seat, she knew there had been something about Elmo that disturbed her, but she couldn't make sense of what had sent that chill through her spine.

Ashe was quiet and thoughtful as he drove the buggy down C Street and turned onto Flowery, but Callie paid scant attention. Cesar…who had he been? Why would two gunmen be out to kill Rick Delance? Perhaps Rody Villiers? Rody had been furious that night, and his pride had been shattered. Perhaps that hurt pride had cultivated more hate for Rick than his physical loss? By now his wrist would have healed, but he'd probably never be quick with a gun again. Brooding over his disgrace he could have hired fast guns to kill Rick.

How badly is Rick injured? Elmo said he was at Threesome Mine. Rick looked to be a compact six feet and one hundred ninety pounds. Though Elmo was wiry, he wouldn't have been able to lift Rick onto the back of a horse and move him. At least Rick wasn't still out there in the Gold Canyon hills lying in an exposed area. But what if the gunfighter who escaped came back and trailed him to the mine? Even now Rick could be in danger.

"You seem terribly worried about a hot-headed gunfighter," Ashe noted sourly.

Her head turned quickly. Ashe stared straight ahead, but she could tell that he was unsmiling, his lean jaw showing a stubbornness she hadn't noticed before. This was one of the few times she was seeing him without his dashing theater smile, and it wasn't the Ashe Perry she knew.

She tightened her mouth. If there was anything she didn't need now it was a disagreement over Rick Delance.

Terribly worried, fiddlesticks! I'm simply doing my Christian duty in sending medical help to an injured man. So she told herself.

"I was concerned you'd resort to thinking something like that. I'm not unduly worried about him. I'm doing what Elmo asked of me is all. Sending medical aid to a man who's shot and in need of help. I'd do the same for anyone in that situation."

Ashe did not immediately agree. "Yes, I suppose I shouldn't have suggested otherwise." He flicked the reins, then turned his head to glance at her. "You never told me, though, that you and Delance were acquainted."

Gordon Barkly! She could box his ears right now. Always stirring things up and causing trouble. He'd tried the same thing with Brett Wilder and Annalee, telling her how Brett was engaged to a girl in Grass Valley and that Brett had gotten his land unfairly. Now he was trying to cause trouble between her and Ashe.

"I hardly know Rick Delance. I intend to keep it that way. Oh, Ashe, let's not argue. Gordon's a newspaperman, bent on digging up unpleasant things to benefit his old paper. I'm furious with him."

Ashe turned and started the horse up the narrow lane to the Halliday Mansion.

"Yes, you're right. Forgive me for being jealous?"

She hesitated, then suddenly dimpled, and laid her gloved hand on his arm. "It was nothing. I shouldn't have snapped at you."

"You don't intend to go with Samuel and that old geezer, Elmo, do you?"

"Of course not." She settled her hat…though she had thought of doing so. "Delance might get the wrong impression if I went running out to Threesome Mine to help out." She thought of that provocative wink he'd given her. She didn't dare mention it to Ashe.

"He would," Ashe said dryly, "and so would I. I told you, I'm the jealous type."

She smiled at him. "You need not be jealous of a gunfighter. Delance is everything I want to get away from—and soon."

"Good. Then soon it shall be. I will arrange matters, darling."

Yes, he was always wishing to arrange things….

The triple-story house with its terraces and gingerbread decorative trim came into view. Aunt Weda had left some lamps burning to welcome Callie home.

She entered the parlor with Ashe and handed him her wrap and handbag, surprised to find Uncle Samuel still up and reading his Bible in the big chair near the terrace.

"Hello, Uncle. I'm afraid there's been some trouble. Elmo's arrived seeking medical help."

Samuel looked up quickly, his greenish eyes worried. "Elmo's in trouble, you say?"

"No, but Doctor McMannis is away delivering a baby, and Rick Delance was in a gunfight—with two men. Elmo claims they were sent from Santa Fe to kill him."

Samuel was on his feet, moving quickly for a big man. He went for his medical satchel in the hall on a high shelf. She followed him.

"I've been afraid of something like this," Samuel said half to himself...or so she thought. He looked at her, black brows pulled together. "Where's Elmo?"

"Waiting down the lane on Flowery, I told him you'd come right away."

What had Samuel meant, "he'd been expecting something like this?" That Rick was a gunfighter so he naturally expected trouble? Yet she was inclined to think Samuel had meant something more. She was almost sure his response had been provoked by the mention of Santa Fe.

Callie suddenly recalled that Elmo, too, had become closed-mouthed after Gordon began questioning him about New Mexico. She wondered why Rick's trouble should come from there. Uncle Samuel didn't explain, nor would she pursue answers to her concerns before Ashe. He was already, as he'd said, "jealous," and she'd be foolish to nurture his suspicions.

"He's been shot twice," she warned. "Please hurry."

Samuel shook his head and grabbed his hat and frock coat from the wooden hat tree on a silver base.

"No telling how those bullets went in. Where is he now, somewhere in town?"

"No, he's out at Threesome. Elmo came riding in from Gold Canyon."

Ashe appeared from the parlor. "Is there anything I can do to help, sir?"

At his smooth voice Samuel paused, turned, and looked at him thoughtfully.

Callie expected her uncle to decline. She thought Ashe looked surprised when he did not.

"A mite of help, lad, would be appreciated. You got a horse bridled and ready to ride?"

"Not really, it's hitched to my buggy."

"We can take your buggy and go together. Come along, lad. You can do the drivin'."

Ashe didn't seem particularly pleased as he looked over at her. She wondered at Samuel's behavior. He certainly didn't need Ashe to help him. She decided Samuel wanted time alone with Ashe on the drive to learn more about him. This irritated her. She had a notion her uncle didn't like her beau and was just looking for reasons to reject him. She hoped he didn't start preaching at Ashe.

She stood stiffly as Samuel turned to her and smiled kindly, patting her shoulder. "You get yourself some much needed rest, lass. Ashe and I should be back in the morning."

He strode out the front door to the buggy, and Ashe stopped to look at her before following. "I think I'm in for an inquisition."

"Now's your chance to tell Uncle we're engaged," she said in a low voice. She held up her left hand where the sapphires shimmered.

He took her hand in his and brushed a cool kiss against her forehead. He appeared preoccupied.

"Tomorrow I'll begin looking into our traveling plans to Santa Fe," he said.

She walked with him onto the porch and stood as he climbed up into the buggy beside Samuel. Ashe took up the reins, and the horse trotted down the narrow lane. She watched the buggy taking the lane toward Flowery Street.

Callie went back inside and then stepped out onto the quiet terrace, enjoying the wind against her. *Will Rick be all right?*

From where she stood she could see the Savage Mansion and Mine Office, and closer at hand, the Mackay Mansion. The lights were on in both residences. She had thought when insisting on buying this piece of property and having the house built here that being neighbors with some of the richest and most powerful silver mine owners in Virginia City would give her a prestige few others enjoyed. While she had already received an invitation to the

Mackay Mansion for a dinner party, she wondered that it hadn't given her the thrill it would have a year ago.

She heard a step behind her and turned quickly. It was Elmira. She wore a faded brown dressing gown and her hair was braided into two long, black pigtails. The deep-set dark eyes stared at her and then blinked.

"Oh, I didn't know you were here. I came to lock the door. I heard the buggy leave."

"That was Samuel. He may not be back tonight. He's gone to treat Rick Delance. He was shot tonight in an ambush."

Elmira grimaced. "One killer attracts another. Shall I lock the front door?"

"Yes—"

The crack of a gunshot blistered the air.

Callie sucked in her breath and whirled, looking at Elmira. The woman stared back. "A rifle shot."

"I think you're right." Callie was surprised Elmira was able to tell a rifle from a pistol. Callie whipped around and rushed to the terrace rail, trying to see down the lane toward Flowery Street.

She remembered how she'd felt when she left the men gathering on the boardwalk, that odd premonition of danger. Then she thought of Elmo's remark—he'd be waiting at Flowery Street! Someone in that group of men had also overheard Elmo say something about New Mexico. She wished now she'd paid closer attention to who had been in that throng.

New Mexico again—what was it about that territory that put Rick and Elmo in danger?

Without a moment's hesitation she picked up her skirts and sped to the front door.

"Shall I awaken Miss Weda?"

"No."

Callie fled down the porch steps, across the yard, and ran down the lane—

Minutes later she was out of breath and walking, rounding past the big pepper tree off to one side when she saw the buggy. Uncle Samuel and Ashe had climbed out and were beside the lane, stooping near some low bushes. They were alive, at least.

The bright moonlight struck the scene, and she saw Samuel bending over Elmo.

She hurried near, catching her breath, expecting the worst, but Elmo was alive and sitting propped against a rock. Samuel was examining his ear.

"Blown a hole clear through it. An inch more and you'd be seeing Jesus welcoming you, that is—if you're one of His children. The angels were looking after you, Elmo."

"Second time tonight—ouch! What's that snake oil yer usin'? Be worse than that bullet!"

"Did you see who shot you, Elmo?"

"No, Miss Callie, I sure didn't. But I got me a mind of who it were, a no-good low-down yellow-bellied sidewinder."

"Now, just a smidgen more on that bloody ear—just so—there!" Samuel's voice was triumphant.

"Ever tell you the story of Peter and how he cut off the ear of the high priest's servant? Peter was going for the fella's head, but he missed and swiped off his ear. Soldiers came to arrest the Lord in the Garden of Gethsemane. Well, you know what the Lord did with that bloody old cut-off ear?"

"I'm thinkin' somethin' good," Elmo said and winced again as Samuel fussed with a bandage that wouldn't stay in place.

"Scripture says He touched his ear and healed it. Just reached over and put it back is what I'm thinking. Makes you wonder if the fella ever believed in Jesus after his ear was made just like new. Goes to show He's the God of all flesh. There's nothing too hard for Him—even dying and coming back again from the dead. 'No man takes my life from Me,' Jesus said. 'I have power to lay it down and I have power to take it again.' And you know why He did it, Elmo? So sinners like you and me can have our sins forgiven!"

Ashe was pacing. Callie thought Samuel's words were upsetting him. She touched the lace on her bodice nervously.

"Hadn't we best report this shooting?" Ashe stood beside Samuel looking grave.

"No one to report it to, lad, except the law-abiding folk in town. Well, Elmo, still some bleeding here, just a little more bandage."

"Say, that sneakin' sidewinder who tried to kill me just now, reckon Jesus would forgive him, too?"

Samuel attempted to tie a knot in the bandage. "Same as any other sinner—if he was to repent and have honest faith that Jesus Christ died for his sins. What's that verse I'm tryin' to remember?"

"You askin' me?"

"Ah…now I got it. 'Though your sins be as scarlet, they shall be as white as snow; though they be red like crimson, they shall be as wool.' That's Isaiah chapter one, verse eighteen. Remember that thief crucified beside Jesus? Well, that hombre sure enough didn't have much time to do any good works to get forgiven, couldn't anyway 'cause of no way to use his hands. He just said, 'Lord, remember me when You come into Your kingdom!'"

Ashe spoke up, his voice filled with tension: "Listen here, gentlemen, all this preaching is fine behind a pulpit on Sunday morning. But if this talk continues, and we're just going to be hearing sermons all evening, I've meaningful business to attend to at the hotel!"

Callie had never seen Ashe lose control of his emotions like this before. He had always kept them guarded, as though he were speaking memorized lines on a stage. The emotion in his voice, coming as it did with his breathlessness, unnerved her.

"Well, lad, I'm about done patchin'—and preachin'. We're gonna move out quickly now—if there's no more shootin'. Elmo you're almost as good as new. You ride in the buggy with Ashe. I'll ride Rick's horse."

"Ha! You get near that stubborn horse, and he'll buck ya soon as look at ya. He's toleratin' me 'cause he's seen me with Delance so much. That ornery horse knows Rick's hurt bad and wanted to come fer help." He struggled to his boots, resettling his hat. "I'm feelin' plenty fit now. We best get."

Callie watched Elmo cautiously mount the fine-looking horse. So the animal belonged to Rick.

"Will you be all right, Callie?" Ashe called stiffly from the buggy.

Samuel climbed up into the seat. "You can come with us, lass, if you want."

"I'll stay. I've my lines to go over. Be careful, all of you."

Elmo lifted his floppy hat in her direction and rode quickly toward C Street and the cut-off toward Gold Canyon. The buggy followed with Ashe driving.

When they'd gone from sight she stood there a moment, frowning. She could understand Ashe's impatience, though Samuel's stories had only taken a few minutes while he was busy doctoring Elmo. It wouldn't have occurred at all if Elmo hadn't nearly gotten killed. There would have been no talking about the servant's ear or forgiveness. Samuel used every opportunity to preach the gospel, and Callie was used to him, though Ashe was not. She was sure it offended her friend's higher sensibilities. She had also tended not to discuss spiritual things around his friends, since it made her ill at ease, too. Ashe was right! Such talk belonged in church on Sunday mornings with ladies in fine dresses, children with freshly scrubbed faces, and gentlemen dressed in decorum, and everyone on their best behavior. But preaching out on the reckless streets of Virginia City with gunfighters roaming, and taverns filled with whiskey and laughter?

Things probably weren't progressing well between Uncle Samuel and Ashe. Soon Samuel might take her aside and advise her to not marry him. Then she would need to take her stand. It was her life, and she was going to live it her own way. Her decision would cause a break between her and Uncle Samuel…and Aunt Weda, too.

She turned away unhappily, for she loved them both. Then frustration took hold of her. Why couldn't everybody just leave her and Ashe alone? Why did Samuel need to irritate her so?

She began walking up the lane toward the house. She went past the pepper tree and saw the moon getting lower. Whoever fired that shot at Elmo must have been hiding back behind this tree with a rifle, knowing where Elmo would be waiting. She had said nothing, but she didn't think it could be the same gunfighter who'd shot at Rick and Elmo earlier in the evening. That man wasn't likely to want to walk up and stand in the group of men who'd heard him calling for Dr. McMannis. This latest gunfighter was probably already in Virginia City when Elmo rode in. He may have been anxious to learn if his two friends had succeeded in killing Rick.

One of those hired guns was dead, and two more men were still after Rick and Elmo. But why Elmo? Why bother with a harmless old man whom most people felt a simple affection for? Elmo and his mule, Jenny, were a common sight on Sun Mountain.

As she felt a shiver, she drew her arms around her, turned away, and walked more briskly back to the mansion. She was remembering the uncanny notion of being followed in San Francisco and of the time when a burglar had been frightened from her hotel room.

If I can just get through the next three weeks until Ashe and I leave, everything will be all right. More than ever she wished to get away. To leave this wild, silver-crazed boomtown for civility in the East. Poor Ashe! What must his more refined nature think of all this?

Ten

*T*here were voices coming from outside the cabin near Three-some. Rick was awake, with swelling and soreness bothering his right side and shoulder. In spite of his discomfort, he was getting mighty restless from doing nothing but lying in bed for what now seemed like weeks. How long since the gunfight out in the canyon? Yesterday he'd been told ten days. He felt the handle of his pistol under the blanket beside him. Hearing voices, he glanced toward the small window Elmo had left open. He recognized Elmo's scratchy voice. He must be with Fanshaw and Everett, the two trusty young men working the mine.

Rick struggled to roll himself off his bunk and slowly straighten to his feet. He was stiff and bandaged. His wounds, although healing, were still draining some. He waited while dizziness ebbed, and keeping his balance, reached for his buckskin shirt from off the nail. Elmo had washed it. He looked at the three bullet holes, noticing an exit hole in the right side waist. Samuel, thankfully, had been able to remove the other bullet near his collarbone. Samuel had returned three days later with Doc McMannis to check on his progress, and they had stayed for more than an hour.

"The Lord's showed you kindness, young man," Doc McMannis had said sternly. "That first bullet made a clean pass through your side, hopefully leaving no damage that won't heal. The other bullet didn't shatter any bone, either. You're a tough young man, Delance. Except for the pain you're going through now, I expect you'll recover well enough. You'll be weak a few days from loss of blood, but as long as those wounds are kept clean and no infection sets in, you should come out of this well enough."

Infections? With the pints of those burning concoctions Samuel had been pouring on him? It wasn't likely any infections could survive.

When Samuel had first arrived, he remembered becoming conscious and seeing Ashe Perry in the room. Rick frowned, remembering. He didn't like the man. *Was it jealousy? Why had Samuel even brought him?*

Rick winced in silence as he carefully shrugged into his shirt. He had better get strong fast. Elmo had told him two gunmen were still about. But Elmo's safety worried Rick even more. He had to keep him under guard. Rick also needed to learn from Elmo the identities of the other two gunmen. He was sure the man he'd met in the Express Office wasn't named Johnny. And the man with the Z scar...well, maybe Elmo would eventually remember.

Rick strapped on his gunbelt, using his normal flip about his waist, that now wasn't so easy. Next came his boots. He stamped his feet to settle into them. He glanced into the cracked, smoked mirror and shook his head. He needed a shave and his curling hair fell awry across his tanned forehead. He looked ornery and reckless. No wonder Callie was afraid of him. Yes, she was definitely afraid of him. He could tell that from the moment he'd spoken to her out in front of Ma Higgins' eatery at Carson when she'd first arrived with Flint.

Flint—where was he? Rick scowled. Last time he'd seen him at the Express Office, Flint had said someone broke into his cabin. Rick had Miller go with Flint on that trip to deliver Threesome ore, and he should have been back by now. Maybe Elmo had heard from him.

Feeling weak, Rick edged up to the cabin window and looked out. Elmo stood talking to two miners. The gunfighter picked up his black hat and settled it before going to the door and stepping out on the porch. They turned to look at him.

A grin spread across Elmo's face. "Shucks. Will you look at that, fellers? Better'n new."

"Sure," Rick commented wryly. He leaned his shoulder against the wooden post across from Fanshaw and Everett. "I need coffee, Elmo. Anything to help jar me awake."

"Comin' up." Elmo hurried inside, arms swinging loosely at his sides. He was back in a wink with a steaming cup.

"Strong as aces," Elmo said proudly.

Flint had first recommended Fanshaw and Everett to Rick almost a year ago, and they'd proven themselves good men. He was thankful he had them to keep their eyes and ears open for trouble around the cabin.

"Mornin', boss," Fanshaw said. "Boys'll be happy to know you're up again."

Fanshaw was a Yankee who'd come from the coal mines of Pennsylvania. He was also a fair hand with a pistol.

"Thanks. Any trouble since I've been recovering?"

"No, been quiet." Fanshaw looked dubiously at young Everett. "All except for Ev. He's got some wild notion of pulling out for Texas."

Rick knew Everett came from the region across from Cimarron. He saw Everett frowning at his friend.

"War's started, suh," Everett said to Rick. "I've family in Texas. Lots of 'em. Seems to me it's my duty to fight for the Confederacy." He squared his shoulders.

Rick sighed quietly to himself.

Fanshaw muttered something. Everett cast him a sober look. "Well, don't it seem right?"

"Don't seem so to me, Ev. Time you get there, it'll all be over."

"If you're saying them Yanks will run, well, you're probably right, but—"

"Hogwash, we won't run!"

"Threesome's neutral," Delance interrupted calmly. "You have anything more to say, Everett?"

"Well, suh, yes I do. I surely do."

Fanshaw shook his head wearily, as if to say he had to endure so much from being friends with Everett.

"I'm joining up with the CS volunteers from Texas, suh. Well, someone sort of mentioned you came from the Cimarron region of New Mexico, and so I thought you'd understand the cause. There's a few more Texans in Virginia City expecting to come with me soon as they tell the mine bosses and get their pay. We'll be going to El Paso to Colonel Scurry."

Rick looked over at Elmo. He looked guilty, and Rick suspected that the mention about Cimarron had come from him. Elmo, a proud Texan, could never sit still in time of war without declaring his loyalties.

Rick had heard that the Fourth, Fifth, and Seventh Texas Cavalry Regiments, along with a company of independent volunteers, would likely commit to the Confederacy, at least in trying to gain control of New Mexico for the South. Brett Wilder had mentioned the upcoming trouble in his last communication with Rick.

"Thought, since you were from the area, you'd write me a word or two of recommendation and character reference that I can give to Colonel Scurry."

Fanshaw was shaking his head. "You're making the worst mistake of your life, Ev. You'll get yourself killed is all. No good can come of this. Isn't that right, Delance?"

"Probably." Delance could see that Everett was determined. "I'll write you that recommendation, though, if that's what you want. Which way are you traveling to Texas?"

"Through Tucson, suh, then Santa Fe, El Paso. Why?"

"Because I'm going that way myself soon as I can travel. Thought we could go together. We'll do better to form a company. Bill Stewart reports Indian trouble between here and Santa Fe."

Fanshaw looked shocked, as though he hadn't expected Rick to side with the Confederacy.

Everett's young face broke into a grin. "Yes, suh! Can't think of anyone I'd feel better about riding with." He looked at Fanshaw hopefully.

Fanshaw showed disappointment. "Not me. I'm not joining no Texas rebels to fight Northerners."

"Didn't ask you," Everett said soberly. "Texans don't need no Northerners anyway." Turning toward Rick he touched his hat and strode back to his lookout.

"You joinin' the Confederate Army, Delance?" Fanshaw asked in amazement.

"I've some business to attend to in Santa Fe," was all he would say.

When Fanshaw drifted to his place on guard, Rick came slowly down the steps and Elmo walked up.

Elmo, too, was glum. "Some mighty good boys is goin' to get all shot-up and killed befer this war's over. It's a sad thin'. What about you now, how are those wounds a doin'?"

"They're starting to feel less painful than the empty feeling in my stomach."

"Hungry now? I got coffee and scrambled eggs in the kitchen."

"I'm hungry enough to make up for what I missed in the last week or so. I want a gallon of coffee, too."

Rick went inside the cabin and got himself seated at the table and waited as Elmo served up a half-dozen eggs, a half-pound of bacon, some biscuits, and the dark, rich brew of his special Texas coffee. As Rick quietly ate, he started making plans.

"When we leavin'?" Elmo asked.

"Not long. I'm anxious to see Billings in Santa Fe. Brett, too. I think Zel Willard ordered that attack on us the other night, Elmo. It's time I face down Zel and demand the truth."

"Never cottoned to Zel myself. Seemed too sneaky to me. Marryin' that Miss Tina the way he did, seemin' fer to get the Hardy Ranch when her pappy dies. You think Tom knows what Zel's doin'?"

Rick set his fork down and looked at him. "I'm not sure about Tom Hardy. But Cesar talked plenty. He thought he had me and didn't mind boasting before filling me full of lead. He admitted shooting Sal and taking Marita—she's dead, by the way. He helped burn the hacienda, too. And he said he was working for Zel."

"Didn't want to tell you yet till you was a mite stronger, but when I rode to Virginny Town for Doc McMannis, someone took another shot at me agin. That's where this business with my ear came from. Sneakin' varmint. I was waitin' fer Samuel near Flowery Street when a rifle shot nearly took my head off. Like I tole ya' befer, I don't think the shot was fired by the other gunman at the campsite. He took off mighty fast after those gunshots blasted 'tween you and Cesar. I'm thinkin' he figured Cesar had got it. 'Cause sudden like it got really quiet where I was. Jenny had been hit, and I thought we was both goners. But he just upped and faded into the night.

"That's when I went down to the water hole and found you and Cesar. I did what I could to stop yer bleedin', covered you with brush, and took that line-back of yers and taken off. Went to Threesome and got help—led Fanshaw and Everett back down to show 'em where I hid ya. I tole 'em to bring you back here. I went straight to town for Doc, and 'fer I left with Samuel at Flowery Street, got shot through the ear. By the time we all got here with Samuel, and that Eastern gent, I didn't know if I was comin' or a-goin'."

Rick had heard most of this the first time he'd awakened in the cabin. He recalled how Samuel had stayed the night, and that Ashe was discontented about not being able to go back to his suite at the International. Why Samuel had brought Ashe was bewildering. Ashe was the last man Rick would have chosen to bring along.

Elmo poured the sizzling bacon drippings over a big bowl of mush. "Fer Jenny," he said when he saw Rick's quizzical brow. "That mule has gone plumb crazy over drippin's since I felt sorry fer her and gave her some. That bullet grazed her rump purty bad. Ricocheted right into her. That was when you musta heard me call out. I thought Jenny and me was both history. Mule's fit now. Must be the drippin's. Already rarin' to go adventurin' again. No adventurin' now, though, after that bullet just missed my skull. You suppose Zel wants me dead 'cause I can point out that murderin' varmint who shot Alex?"

"What else would it be, Elmo? You're the only witness. They thought you weren't around to talk; now they know otherwise. Even if they get rid of me and claim the Triple D, they'd still be worried about you. They don't want to be identified, and that's why I couldn't find any sign of Bodene or Abner among their kind. They can't be going by those names."

Elmo nodded his head and refilled Rick's cup. He put the dirty dishes into the washtub.

"That's why I want you lying low. You'll be safer here until I'm ready to leave for Santa Fe."

Elmo looked worried. Rick could see him eying the bandages near his collarbone.

"Them two hombres will try'n kill ya befer you even leave for Santa Fe."

"I'll be ready this time. Don't worry. It's you I've got to keep safe."

The sound of horse hooves on dirt neared the cabin. Rick got up and looked out the window. "It's Flint. Miller is with him, too." Miller was the mining foreman, and both he and Flint thought well of him. He was a family man with a young wife in Virginia City. Like Fanshaw, he had come from Pennsylvania and knew most everything about mining.

Rick walked to the door of the cabin and out to the porch, coffee cup in hand. Miller had ridden on, but Flint dismounted.

"When did you and Miller get back?"

"Late last night. Miller went home to his wife, so I stayed in town."

"How'd the ore shipment do?" They'd been getting lower grade ore the last two months, and Rick seriously considered whether or not the mine might have run its course.

"Fair. Nothing like the early stuff. I'm beginning to think we're tapering off. We can scrape out a living, but unless we hit some new lode, Threesome won't be any bonanza. Miller's the only one that still thinks it can happen."

Flint walked up, and Rick noticed he was carrying a rifle. For him, that was unusual.

"Just left Samuel. He told me there's been trouble. Also talked with Doc McMannis. He wants you to come and see him next time you're in town. You all right?"

"Surviving."

"That coffee smells mighty good now."

Flint followed him inside to the stove. Rick threw him a tin cup. Flint caught it, and Elmo filled it with coffee. Flint removed his dusty hat, showing sandy hair. He was a nice-looking young man and a dependable friend. He was also a fair hand with a rifle, although he was slow with a pistol. Not that Rick wanted him involved in any of his personal struggles. He liked him too much for that. Flint attended Sunday morning worship with Samuel at his chapel on Sun Mountain, unless he was out of town. There was a steadiness in Flint's character that Rick appreciated but never commented on—mostly because he wasn't ready to appraise his own faith in Christ.

Flint frowned. "I'm selling the mule train."

Rick was surprised since Flint had set high hopes on his business.

"Do you need a loan?"

Flint looked at him. "Why? You offering?"

"If I can help you, sure." He thought of the unexpected bounty Mr. Billings had told him about. "It may take awhile to get my hands on it, though. How much would you need?"

Flint's amber eyes showed gratitude and surprise. He smiled. "Thanks, but it isn't 'cause I'm busted so much as I'm thinking it's time to move on to something else. But if things go as I plan, I may come around reminding you of your offer. Anyhow, I could have made this move months ago, with that road over the Sierras improving all the time. A man's got to keep up with the times. Mules are giving way to other kinds of transportation."

Elmo set some bacon and eggs on a big plate in front of Flint.

"Thanks, Elmo. Say, what happened to your ear?"

"Shot, that's what."

Flint exchanged glances with Rick as if wondering why anyone would be after Elmo.

Rick believed the time had come to tell Flint about that night on the Triple D. With Elmo listening and nodding in agreement now and then as the tale unfolded, Rick laid out the events on the cattle drive near the Texas border, the burning of the hacienda, as well as the many deaths.

"Zel Willard is behind it. Cesar admitted it the other night."

Flint was quiet, shaking his head in disbelief and sympathy but saying little until Rick had finished.

"So that's what's been driving you these five years," he said thoughtfully. "Thought it was something bad. Somehow I thought you might have lost a wife and a baby. Does Samuel know all this?"

"Not all of it. I think he knows more than he's letting on, though."

"Think Brett may have told him then?"

"Maybe. I didn't want to talk about it, and Brett didn't know all the story while he was in Virginia City. He's learned most of it from Mr. Billings is my guess. Billings could have explained it. And it would have been easy for Brett to write Samuel about it…and he probably did."

"Then you're going back to New Mexico to face Zel Willard?"

"That's the idea." He told Flint about the properties his father had left him in his will. He also said he intended to return and settle down on the Triple D.

"Don't blame you for wanting to settle there." Flint was quiet a long moment, drinking his coffee and looking into the cup. He asked unexpectedly, "Callie know you got a ranch and other property?"

Rick showed no expression. "No reason she should." He looked away from Flint. He knew how his friend felt about her. He changed the subject.

"So you're selling the mules?" he asked, getting back to Flint's earlier news.

"Wagons can be used now."

Most of the ore was no longer shipped all the way to San Francisco, as Rick knew, but was being milled seven miles away on the Carson River.

"Money is in timber right now," Rick agreed. "Wagons are needed to bring it from the Reno area. And someday one of those railroad barons will want to build a rail line to haul timber to Virginia City. Once that happens, even wagons will be out. One day they'll lay track over the Sierras. It's bound to happen."

"I've been doing some serious thinking about ranching. If you're going to Cimarron, and Wilder's buying land thereabouts too, I might as well consider being among friends as staying here alone. Especially with the Threesome not producing much. What about you, Elmo? You thinking of heading out with us?" Flint looked over at him.

"Sure as shootin'. So is Everett."

Flint looked at Rick for explanation. Rick finished his coffee. "Everett's going to join the Texas Confederates. He's asked me for a letter of recommendation to a Colonel Scurry."

Flint said nothing, but nodded.

"If you're serious about cattle, Flint, I'll need men on the Triple D for sure. So will Brett. Either of us would consider ourselves fortunate to have you around."

"That's all I needed to hear. I'm going with you and Elmo. When you leavin'?"

"Soon. A week or two. No longer. Can you sell the mules by then?"

"I've got a buyer over at Dayton who wants 'em. But there's the Threesome to think about, too. We'll either need to sell to one of the big ones like Mackay or Consolidated, or lease it out."

"I've an idea I wanted to get your take on. What if we made a deal with Miller? He believes in it and he's honest—a steady worker with a good wife."

"Sure, but he has no money, and who would lend it to him?"

Rick smiled. "I would, for one."

For a moment Flint looked confused. So Rick explained. He would loan Miller enough so he could manage the Threesome and keep it going until he was paid for his first ore shipments. Miller would keep eighty-five percent of the profits and give Rick fifteen percent. He would increase Miller's percentage to ninety percent as soon as he paid back the loan. If the mine went bust, then he wouldn't have to repay the loan. If he struck rich lode, he would want to pay off the loan so he and Sally could keep the ninety percent.

"You could do the same with your third," he told Flint. "I don't know what Brett wants to do. He hasn't paid much attention to the mine in the last five months. Maybe he's taken up with cattle."

"Sounds fair to me. I'm sure Miller will jump at the opportunity. And if anyone deserves a break it's Mil. Sally's expecting, too. The news will come at a good time. Shall I talk to him or should you?"

"We both will. But he'll need to hang on with slim pickings for awhile. I can't do much until I meet with Billings and draw up papers."

"Knowing Miller, he'll hang on like a bulldog. All that boy needs is a big dream an' a hope of making it work."

After a moment, Flint frowned as though his thoughts took a different path. He paused, with a thick slice of bacon in mid-air, and looked at Rick.

"I ran into the boy Jimmy this morning. He was up early and hanging around Gordon's newspaper office. Told me Callie's told Samuel and her aunt that she's engaged to Ashe. According to Jimmy, she's sporting the biggest bunch of sapphires you ever saw—one of 'em an engagement ring."

Delance played the moment as detached as he could. He knew Flint had been mighty taken with Callie, but he could see Flint was eying him, wondering how Rick would take the news.

Sapphires. "Oh?" he said casually. "A big mistake on her part."

There was a look of worry on Flint's face. "That girl's heading into quicksand, if you ask me. Won't listen to Samuel, either. I knew a filly like that once, stubborn as all get out. Never could tame her right." He shook his head.

Rick couldn't help but smile. "If you expect to win her away from that smooth-talking actor, then you'd better not compare her to a filly. That girl's got pride and mountain-high dreams."

Elmo chuckled and looked from one young man to the other, as though enjoying himself. "If'n you both try to woo Miss Callie, I'm goin' to enjoy watchin'."

"She wouldn't be seen walking down the street with the likes of me," Flint said, finishing his breakfast and stretching his booted legs out before him. "I always did think my mules embarrassed her."

"Then maybe you're not missing much," Rick commented, feeling irritated. "You're worth two of that actor with his phony British accent. The way I see it, a woman should want a man for a whole lot of other reasons besides slick etiquette and wealth."

"Maybe it's just as well," Flint said. "Callie's sure onto what she wants."

"Is she? Most women are till a man changes her mind."

Flint laughed, but sobered quickly enough. "Not Callie. She's got her mind set on marrying a gentleman. The kind of gent that can move around the parlors of the fancy society folks in Frisco and New York."

Delance knew that. He also suspected Callie would have some difficult lessons to learn about men.

"If she has good sense, she'll nab hold of you and settle down, whether you use your knife and fork according to the latest social convention or not," Delance commented. "Those things can be learned easy enough, but a man who lacks character isn't going to have good manners toward his wife in the long run. That's even if she walks beside him down Broadway in the most expensive New York suit she can hang on him."

Elmo chuckled. "Sure as shootin'."

Delance finished his breakfast and dropped the tin plate into the dish pan. He poured more coffee.

He could feel Flint watching him with a mild look of curiosity.

"There's something about you, Delance. Makes me think you was raised proper. Even had some finer learning. Yet you don't want to talk about it."

"You're right—on both accounts." He smiled to soften the bluntness.

Delance reminded himself he'd not get roped in by falling too hard for Callie as Flint had.

Flint suddenly grinned at him. "Didn't know you were so worried about my succeeding with Callie, though. Mighty generous of you for saying I'm the right man for her."

Rick stared at his empty coffee cup, embarrassed. Flint had pretty well figured out that he had a certain feeling for Callie, too, and that some of Rick's irritation was directed at the way she'd been scorning him.

Elmo chuckled again. "Don't know about that. Both you fellas could be pretty slick if you decided to polish up a bit. Seen you at the Triple D equal to ol' Ashe when Mister Lucien insisted on it," he said to Rick. "Seen you and Alex put on quite a show around those two Hardy girls, Miss Tina and Miss Sue."

"Say, were we ever wrong about those two!" Rick said, running his fingers through his hair. "But they were the only girls around for miles."

Flint looked curious and Rick explained. "Those two were mean and ornery. Compared to them, Callie would seem like another Annalee. Alex was going to marry Sue. Tina is married to

Zel Willard—the man who's behind the trouble Elmo and I faced the other night."

Flint gave a low whistle. "Aren't you glad the Lord closed the door to that one?"

Rick had no answer. Least not one he wanted to discuss now.

"Anyhow," Flint said soberly, "Callie needs a real friend, one who will tell her the truth. Flattery is the last thing she needs. Somebody to talk straight and tell her she's all wrong and headed for quicksand."

Rick laughed wryly. "Don't look at me. You're the one to do it. In her eyes I'm a hot-headed gunfighter. Hardly the man to lecture her on the wrongs of marrying the Eastern tenderfoot."

Flint mused. Then he shook his head. "Don't know if I am or not." He eyed Rick thoughtfully. "She thinks that about you, but you're still the only man she noticed when the stage came in a few days ago. I didn't exist, and poor old Gordon wouldn't have mattered either, except he hustled his way through the crowd and forced it. Funny thing about Gordon, he used to be after Annalee till Brett took her from him. True love didn't seem to stay with Gordon very long."

Rick said nothing, wondering about what kind of man Gordon really was. Flint went on. "Jimmy said Callie's leaving town sooner than anyone thought. In three weeks, maybe less. She's selling her third of the Halliday-Harkin, turning the Stardust over to Hugh Ralston to manage, and taking off with Ashe for New York."

"Santa Fe first," Elmo spoke up while mixing biscuit dough for lunch. "She planned on that 'fore she ever took that engagement ring from the Perry fella. They're goin' to visit Miss Annalee…nice girl, that one. Fed me 'n' Jenny once or twice when Jenny's ribs were showin'. Not many gals that sweet."

Rick looked over at him. "They're going to Santa Fe?"

Elmo grinned and his eyes twinkled. "Yup. 'Bout the time we're pullin' outta here. Now ain't that interestin'? Why, shucks, mebbe we could all just go together?" he looked innocently from Flint to Rick.

Flint had straightened in his chair and exchanged alert glances with Rick.

Elmo continued, "Might fill her ear with a thing or two about that Perry fella befer you get to Santa Fe. Might even get her to give him them sapphires back." Then he grinned. "Then it'll be 'tween you two, who wins her."

"Never mind that," Rick said. "Do you think Samuel's just going to let her sell and take out with Ashe and all that money?"

Flint shrugged. "He can talk to her, but if she doesn't have a mind to listen, there's not much even he can do. Seems her mind's made up. Just like the prodigal son who decided to spend his money with fair-weather friends all lined up for a good time—till he showed up one day with empty pockets. So the important thing I'm thinking, is what do we know about Ashe?"

"More importantly, what does *she* know about him? Like I said at the Express Office, Gordon's checking into his past. But you mentioned some talk, too, about his career on stage coming to an end."

"Yeah, from Neil down at the Virginia Opry. Said he'd heard by way of theater folks in Frisco that Ashe Perry was all washed up in New York. But you know, we could be as wrong as all get-out about him."

"Maybe," Rick agreed. "Neil's theater is in competition with the Stardust. He'd naturally want to tarnish Ashe's reputation a bit to keep people from flocking there."

Flint nodded. But while Rick said this in caution, he knew little of Neil's character. Maybe he'd pay him a visit next time he was in Virginia City. Trouble was, even if he uncovered something, would Callie listen to him? Trying to convince her would be impossible unless she wanted to hear the truth.

The truth, though, seemed obscure at the moment, even to Rick. What were his own motives for trying to discredit Ashe Perry? Was he being fair?

Flint stood and walked toward the cabin door. "I'll see you later, Rick. I've got to close things down at this end. I'm lookin' forward to a change of scene in New Mexico."

When he'd ridden off toward his own small cabin in Virginia City on D Street, Rick pondered what he'd heard. He wondered what Samuel thought about Callie running off to Santa Fe with Ashe. He knew how he felt about it, and he was pretty riled.

Eleven

The morning was bright and sunny when Callie left the house with Jimmy and Elmira to take Aunt Weda's buggy down to the Stardust Theater. Callie was anxious to see how things were progressing. Ashe had delivered her a wire from Hugh Ralston saying he was on his way to Virginia City, and she wanted everything in order for his taking over as manager before she and Ashe departed.

The theater would open in a week. She wanted to see if the foreman had added the finishing touches she had asked for in her new dressing room. It seemed to her he was awfully relaxed about doing as she asked.

Callie turned to Elmira who was driving, unsmiling as usual.

"Did you tell the foreman I wanted red curtains instead of blue?"

"Yes, I told him."

"I also want to make sure Ashe's room has everything he needs. Lots of mirrors and comfortable, yet stylish furnishings."

"Yes, I talked to the foreman," came the toneless voice.

Callie felt irritated toward the woman. Everything seemed to be an exercise in misery for Elmira. Callie sometimes felt hesitant to ask her to do anything for fear the woman would feel persecuted.

"Did you make sure to tell him to order green velvet for Ashe instead of the ruby like mine? You know how he doesn't like red."

"Yes. I talked to Mr. Cummings yesterday. He said he would try."

"Try my foot. I'm paying him to work for me! Oh, I do hope that room I wanted for Mama is going to be big enough for the theater posters I've collected. The Lilly O'Day memorial should be a big hit. Did you send down the trunk I gave you yesterday?"

"Yes, I sent it."

"Then it should be there," Callie said, letting her know she could be held responsible.

Jimmy leaned forward. "Why do you keep saying 'Yes' all the time, Elmira? It sounds boring."

"Jimmy," Callie scolded, turning in her seat to look back at him. "It's rude to speak that way to Mrs. Jennings."

Jimmy cast his eyes down. "Sorry, Elmira. I didn't mean anything by it."

Elmira pulled up before the Stardust, and Callie's eyes endeavored to take in everything. The building was mostly brick, and one of the nicest ones on C Street. The sight gave her a sense of pride. *This is my theater. I had it built.* There weren't as many workmen around as there'd been even a few days ago, and this gave her hope that they were almost done. She saw just a few men coming and going, carrying odds and ends to wagons pulled by mules.

"Looks like everything will be ready for opening night, Callie," Jimmy said brightly. "May I go inside and tour the whole building?"

"Yes, if you stay with Elmira."

"I cannot walk far," Elmira reminded her quickly. "My stiff knee causes trouble and pain when climbing."

"That's right, I'd forgotten—"

"But I will do my best," Elmira said plaintively.

If it weren't for Ashe, I'd have gotten rid of this dour woman long ago, Callie thought once again, irritated by the problems she made for her. *Before we go to New York, I'm getting rid of her. That's all there is to it. Ashe will just have to accept it.* She'd send her back to San Francisco before leaving with Ashe for Santa Fe. Since Ashe's mother cared so much for Elmira, then *she* could see to it that Elmira had a "safe and secure position" in her own home!

"Jimmy, I'll show you everything on opening night. It'll be better then. The lights will be glimmering. For now you can have a sarsaparilla with Miss Elmira while I'm busy inside. Then we three will have a fun lunch afterward at the Chinese eatery. You said you like chop suey."

Jimmy forgot his disappointment and let out a whoop that caused Elmira to grimace.

"Ooh, can we?"

"Yes, if you don't tire Miss Elmira out."

Jimmy looked as though the trade-off might not be worth it, but after a moment his eyes sparkled and he smiled. "I promise."

"Good. Then I'll run along, and you two can proceed at Elmira's pace."

Callie walked along the boardwalk toward the impressive Stardust Theater. She stopped long enough to let her gaze feast upon it. There was a narrow porch and wide double doors stood open. When Mr. Cummings saw her and removed his hat, she stepped inside.

"Morning, Miss O'Day." He limped toward her, smiling amiably. "Come to see your theater? A fine one she is, too, and everything ready for next week just as I promised."

"Well done, Mr. Cummings. At first glance, everything certainly looks beautiful."

He chuckled as though she had said something profound. "Isn't that the way most things in life are, Miss O'Day? Most things look real fine at first glance."

She resented the implication invoked upon her casual assessment, and she cooled, lifting her chin.

"Did the designer locate the green velvet for Ashe Perry's dressing room?"

"They'll be working late to finish that, Miss, but your room's ready if you care to take a look."

"Thank you, I will. I'll just roam around on my own until I join others for lunch."

"Yes, ma'am. We shouldn't get in your way none."

As she moved on slowly, looking about, she saw that the foyer was done as she'd requested with gold plush divans, Queen Anne pedestal tables, and carpet throughout the theater that displayed large cabbage roses in a pleasant pattern. There were dark-red velvet draperies at every long window with silver ropes that tied them back. On the wall there were Albert Bierstadt paintings and drawings of theater costumes, tastefully done.

A room opened off the lobby, and she saw a long mahogany bar. She felt her brows come together. She hadn't wanted the bar but Hugh Ralston had insisted, and she'd been powerless to thwart him. She had conceded, but perhaps too quickly. There were two silver spittoons at each end. Small tables were set about the room, with a background of mirrors and bottle-filled shelves. She had no liking for it; it reminded her of the misery her father's drinking had brought. Jack Halliday had effectively loved alcohol and gambling above his wife and three children—if not intentionally, then through his weakness. The clutch of sin had been too strong for him. Strange, he'd been her own father, and yet she had no idea if he'd believed in Christ. She remembered how Uncle Samuel had lapsed into silence when Annalee asked him about that after their father's funeral. Callie pushed it from her mind. "I am sick to death of such ugly, unpleasant, predicaments."

"Callie?"

She turned, surprised by a voice from the front double doors. A figure walked toward her in an easy, quick stride. She recognized the energetic drive of Gordon Barkly.

"Hello, Gordon, come to see the new theater? Isn't it beautiful? I hope you give us a good write-up in your paper."

"Of course I will. But I need to talk with you about something else now." He glanced about alertly. "Ashe Perry with you?"

He looked about as though he hoped not.

"No. What do you want to talk about?"

He looked eager, and amusement showed in his amber eyes. "Where can we talk?"

His behavior had become offensive as of late. He seemed to always show up at awkward moments...like the night Elmo had ridden in for Doctor McMannis. And his first concern had not been about being helpful, but rather about getting information that he could use for his newspaper.

"We can talk here," she said a bit shortly. "Have a seat. You can try out its comfort while we're 'gossiping.'"

He didn't like her comment, and she could see a spark of something unpleasant leap into his eyes. *I'm glad Annalee didn't marry you,* she thought coldly. *And what a dunce I was to ever think you were charming.*

She sat down, spreading her crinolines about her, showing a bit of lace at her ankles.

"Well?" she asked with a theater smile. "How are things going with you, Gordon?"

"Oh fine, fine. I've gotten a number of scoops into the *Barkly Press* before the *Territorial Enterprise* even knew about them. Those reporters over there are so lax."

"Perhaps, but they do have Mark Twain." She couldn't resist a bit of a goad.

He waved an airy hand. "Oh, him—I don't know why anyone thinks his cynical comments are amusing."

"What is it you came to discuss?" she asked. "I'm quite busy. I want to tour the theater before meeting Jimmy and Elmira for lunch."

"Elmira?" he looked cagey.

"Yes, she's a friend of Ashe's mother. I've taken her on as a secretary to do Ashe and Elmira a favor."

"I see. Elmira, is it? Elmira Jennings?"

"Why, yes," she said a little curiously, wondering that Elmira of all people would snag his attention.

"A friend of Ashe Perry's widowed mother? His mother lives in San Francisco?"

Again, her annoyance grew. He took so long to get on with anything. "Yes, why?"

"Oh…" and with a wave of his hand again. "Do you mind, my dear?" he took out a pipe and a small, stylish pouch of tobacco.

"I suppose not."

"Elmira's a widow, too, isn't she?"

"Yes, she's a widow." She couldn't help herself: "Gordon, if you find her so irresistible I could perhaps arrange for you to meet her over dinner?" She dimpled.

Gordon looked taken aback, then laughed as though she were amusing. "No, nothing like that, I assure you. I just noticed her about, is all. A bit curious that she doesn't seem to do much work. So I wondered."

"The newspaperman's curious mind, yes…well, you're right, she doesn't." *And I'll be getting rid of her soon,* she thought.

"I hear you're leaving for Santa Fe faster than expected, and then on to New York. Marriage is in the offing I suppose?"

She deliberately kept silent, looking at him evenly.

"How does Annalee feel about your selling your third of the mine? That makes it difficult for her, doesn't it? Not to mention Jimmy."

"I don't see why it should," she said stiffly.

"Well, perhaps not. Though the new owner might want to buy them out as well. Owning a third isn't likely to satisfy someone with bigger plans, like say, owning all the Halliday-Harkin Mine for himself?"

What was he suggesting? The way his amber eyes watched her so intently made her uncomfortable. She said quickly, "Whether or not Annalee sells is up to her, and Brett of course. I haven't a notion of what they're going to do. Brett is into cattle. And Jimmy won't come into his own for years; Samuel is his guardian."

"And yet, if Dylan Harkin bought you out it would make sense that he'd wish to buy out Annalee and settle with Samuel for Jimmy's portion."

Dylan Harkin! Now why did he bring him up? Dylan was the younger brother of the man who, along with her father, had first set claim to the mine.

"I haven't even seen that gunfighter since Pa—since my father was killed by Macklin."

"Yes, no one else has either. Very odd, isn't it?"

"Is it? Perhaps."

"Ashe Perry, however, knows Dylan Harkin." His eyes took on an odd glow like a cat in a dark room.

Callie just looked at him thunderstruck. "How would you know that?"

He shrugged. "My father is a senator. He has friends in various important positions—like lawyers, sheriffs, bigger newspapers like in Chicago, New York, and San Francisco."

She tightened her lips. His look of satisfaction angered her. It was as if he wanted to dig up something foul on Ashe.

She stood with an abrupt motion that sent her skirts rustling. "What are you trying to suggest, Gordon? That Ashe Perry cannot be trusted? Is that it? Because if that's what you're trying to hint—"

"Now, now. I just thought you'd like to know is all."

"It seems to me you're meddling where you have no right. Just the way you meddled with Brett Wilder when Annalee turned from you to him."

"Now look here—"

"*No!* And I don't need the lies you're trying to spread about Ashe—"

He leaped to his feet, offended. "Every word I told Annalee about Wilder was backed by evidence."

"It was nothing but nasty rumors. Probably spread by some sour reporter around Grass Valley who was jealous of Brett's success!"

His eyes flashed. "You, my dear, are a most unbecoming woman, sometimes highly deficient in manners…and proper sense."

"If you don't remove yourself from my premises, Mr. Barkly, I shall need to call Mr. Cummings and have you thrown out!"

He drew in an indignant breath and glared defiantly. "No lady talks to me like that."

"Well this one does. Are you going? Or should I call for assistance?"

"I'm going. But you'll be sorry. You always were impulsive and hotheaded. Your lack of graces will see you in big trouble one of these days, Miss Halliday. You are," he said loftily, "so much more like Jack Halliday than Annalee or Jimmy."

"Why you—"

Her palm made contact with his cheek with a wallop.

Gordon gasped, stepped back, then stood rigid. His face went white, then flamed. "I hope you do marry him. Then you'll learn your lesson the hard and bitter way!" He turned on his polished heel and strode down the aisle toward the front doors, his figure fading into the shadows as he disappeared. She turned her back upon the scene.

She breathed heavily, her hands in fists. *That busybody! How could I have ever thought him a gentleman, or a man I wished to marry?* she shuddered. *Scoundrel! Cad!*

She shook with emotion, his words echoing and reechoing in her heart. *Lies. All of them lies.* It was like Gordon to try to turn something good and decent into something detestable. She was beginning to think he lived to unmask people, as though he enjoyed embarrassing and ruining those he was secretly jealous of. *I won't entertain his lies for even a moment.*

She unclenched her hands and took in several deep breaths, trying to calm herself. *Think about the theater,* she told herself, *just think of how wonderful it is and how beautiful it looks. Ashe and I will shine like desert stars on Saturday night. Everyone will think us wonderful and appreciate our contribution to their lives.*

She swallowed, her throat dry. She'd gotten so upset with Gordon that now her head was beginning to ache. She began walking about, touching the velvet, the polished wood, the seats, the drapes…

Mama would be proud of me. That room I'm going to dedicate to her memory will be full of her posters, newspaper articles, maybe that last dress, although it was shabby—Hmm…could I get by with using one of my own?

At the end of the room was the stage she and Hugh Ralston had both set their hearts on. She remembered sitting with Hugh and Ashe in San Francisco and going over the drawings with him. She walked there, head high, trying to rid herself of all emotion other than the effect the theater had upon her.

The stage curtains, a rich ruby color, were drawn apart and hanging in soft, draping folds. The stage looked so complete that she could practically see Ashe walking out and giving his graceful bow while people stood and cheered. And that was exactly what would happen next week when they gave their first performance in Virginia City.

She stood with the chandelier sparkling overhead as well as many lights shaped like flowers glowing along the side walls. The orchestra pit, though there'd only be a piano and violin player from the Perry-Ralston Company, looked straight up at the stage. The stage before her, looking empty, was waiting for life to begin.

She walked back to the chandelier and tried to gauge how the light would be reflected up in the gallery and the tiered boxes on either side of the stage. Everything was in ruby velvet and silver. The silver rails would gleam.

She walked down the aisle to the edge of the stage. Here there was a wooden gallery that could be reached by stairs backstage. A catwalk ran above ropes and pulleys that often were used to control stage scenery. The dressing rooms in the loft were smaller and more inconvenient than she had anticipated and a flood of disappointment swept over her. She had wanted a large dressing room for herself, and one for Ashe with their names in silver beside a bright star made of silver from the Halliday mine. Maybe it wasn't too late to have an annex added on, but later—and those stairs seemed a bit too steep and would be difficult to go down quickly. Even so, they were wonderfully made, and she ran her hand along the polished mahogany. She interrupted her musings.

Whatever was wrong with her? She and Ashe would only be playing here for two weeks before leaving for New York. She may never play this stage again, so what did it matter? Why was she so involved? For all it would impact her, the furnishings might as well be unfinished pine, and the dressing rooms the size of closets.

She sighed, knowing her mind was overburdened. But what was the reason behind it? She was tired, that was all. Tired and apprehensive over the unpleasant way things were progressing. First, the shooting of Rick, then the growing trouble with Uncle Samuel and Aunt Weda over selling her third of the mine and marrying Ashe, and now Gordon's lies.

She went up the steps holding the banister and suddenly felt aware of an awesome silence surrounding her. She stopped. Had the men all disappeared? And Mr. Cummings, too, seemed to have vanished. Where was everyone? Not even the sounds from the busy street drifted to her through the open front doors—

That was it. The front double doors had been shut, enclosing the theater in a cloister of silence and shadow. But Gordon hadn't shut them when he stalked out. Now why had Mr. Cummings done so? He knows I'm here and would appreciate the extra light from the sunny morning.

She heard a creak from somewhere amid the rows of seats—or had it come from the gallery? She looked up, but which gallery? All was shadowy and she could see no one standing there. Was there another way to reach the upper gallery than the stairs? Probably there was a door in the back.

If this were an old theater, I might think it a ghost, she thought cynically, but there was no excuse her imaginative mind could think of for that creaky sound. Someone else was in here and did not wish to be seen. Perhaps Mr. Cummings hadn't closed the front doors—but someone else—after he and the workers had left for lunch.

A shiver touched her skin as she looked carefully around, her hand tightening on the rail. She refused to go up there.

"Who's there?" she called.

Not a sound answered.

She edged back down the steps and stood another moment, listening intently. She supposed even new buildings creaked. *Why not?* Just then another creak sounded from the catwalk or thereabouts and she looked up. She couldn't see the area well, so she walked into the middle of the theater and stared upward. Her eyes widened as unexpectedly the chandelier swayed and broke away from the ceiling.

Her cry froze in her throat. In a moment she saw it beginning to fall, coming straight down from above her, her efforts to move away seemed to happen too slowly—

Her mind told her, *Run!* She threw herself to one side and fell as the magnificent crystal chandelier came crashing down beside her with a terrifying smashing sound. She felt a spray of broken glass. She lay there in shock.

When the broken glass finally settled, it became quiet again except for the sound of her beating heart. She opened her eyes and stared. The beautiful Viennese glass lay shattered in thousands of pieces scattered all over the floor…and over her.

The front doors flew open letting in sunlight and the broken glass sparkled like diamonds. Several workmen rushed in.

"Miss O'Day? What happened—look at that will you!" one man exclaimed.

Callie, stunned, just lay there, then slowly, shakily, managed to sit up.

She was helped to one of the plush red seats and sank into it, trying to quiet her pounding heart.

Mr. Cummings and two other workmen gathered around where she sat. They stared at her, then at the broken chandelier, then they craned their necks to look up at the ceiling.

"Impossible—yet there it is, in smithereens! Miss O'Day, are you hurt?"

"I—don't think so—just—" her mind was blank. She sat staring at the glittering diamonds all around her, and her mind kept repeating, *But they're not real diamonds. They're only glass. Just pieces of broken glass.*

"Frank, better go for the doc. Make it fast."

Twelve

Rick Delance left Doc McMannis' office on B Street, and walked down to Gordon Barkly's newspaper office. He entered and quietly closed the door behind him. Gordon looked up with a flushed face and furrowed brows. Rick gave him a measured glance. He'd never seen him looking this agitated. Something had him mighty riled.

Gordon stood abruptly and his hand brushed against a stack of papers on his desk, scattering some. Stooping to gather them, he dropped his writing pen. He straightened, his angry amber eyes meeting Delance's.

Rick's brow shot up. "Looks like I've come at a bad time."

"No, no, just busy is all. Have a seat, Delance. How are you doing? Looks like you're recovering from that ambush. Any idea yet who the other one is that got away?"

Rick noted the breathy rush of Gordon's voice that failed to conceal the tenseness in his chest.

"I've an idea who it might be. Have you seen two men around town recently, one with a scar on his neck, shape of a Z, the other a straw-haired hombre with a big gray horse with three white stockings?"

Gordon was wiping his forehead with a handkerchief, frowning. Glancing toward a window facing the street, he went there and stood looking toward the Stardust Theater.

"Texas Johnny, I think is what the straw-haired man calls himself. The other one, no, I don't think I've seen him around. A scar you say? Should be easy to spot. You might check with Will at the saloon. Drifters tend to stop there when they ride in."

162

"I've talked to Will. He hasn't seen either of them." *Why is he staring at the Stardust? Hmm…is Callie there?*

Casually, Rick walked over to the other window and glanced down the street. He saw nothing of particular interest except a small group of people gathered outside the Stardust. He saw Jimmy Halliday, alone, running down the boardwalk.

Gordon turned with a grim look and faced him. "You think it was one of those two who shot Elmo in the ear?"

"Most likely."

Rick turned from the window. Apparently neither man had returned to Virginia City. They could be hiding out anywhere, even in Carson City. He wasn't going to be deceived though. Just because they hadn't shown themselves didn't mean they wouldn't try to kill him and Elmo again. He was glad he'd left Elmo with Flint and the boys at the Threesome cabin.

"You think Rody Villiers sent them? He would be nursing a grudge after you demolished his pride. If he can't come after you himself, maybe he hired them."

Rick wondered how much to tell him. With a newspaperman it was always a risk. You never knew how much would end up in print, and he felt that Gordon Barkly would exaggerate the story.

"Then again, with Rody Villiers humiliated, you may never hear from him again. If he returned to New Orleans as most folks say, he'll be wrapped up in the war by now." Gordon's mouth curved. "His kind just fade into the woodwork like roaches when their bullying days are over. He probably even changed his name. Maybe Tom Hardy hired him."

Rick's gaze shot across the small office at Gordon.

He apparently recognized Rick's surprise and shrugged indifferently. He pulled out his chair and sank into it, leaning back, hands interlaced in front of him as he studied Rick.

"It's a newspaperman's business to know things. You wanted me to check into Ashe Perry's background, so I did. I also checked into yours. Now, now, don't get all riled about it. I was very discreet."

"I'm sure you were. Newspapermen usually are."

Gordon's cynical smile showed for a moment. "I see you haven't much liking for our breed."

"Depends."

"Well, anyway, as soon as I knew you were from the Santa Fe region I was curious. I recalled, from past conversations my father had with Colonel Winthrop at Fort Craig, mention of a strong cattle family with the Delance name around Cimarron. After that, it was simple to delve into matters."

Rick told himself he should have expected this.

"Colonel Winthrop related the ugly business about your father's ranch. I'm told the Hardys have become a rough bunch."

"They always were. They had dreams of owning all that land around Cimarron for the Hardy brand. His son-in-law, Zel Willard, will inherit when Tom dies. So he has reason to be interested in my plans."

"Will you return?"

Gordon looked especially curious, and Rick wondered why.

"Thinking about it."

"Going back to face down the Hardys or to reclaim the Triple D?"

"Probably both."

"Zel Willard has a boy around five. He's not going to like his plans spoiled by your riding into Santa Fe."

Rick already knew about Zel's ambitions. He switched the topic to Callie, and saw Gordon's eyes snap with immediate anger.

"I've no more interest in that woman," he said shortly, and straightened in his chair, snatching up a pencil and shuffling his stack of papers. "What she does now is no longer my concern."

Whatever had occurred between those two must have ended with burning bridges.

"I thought you two were old friends from Sacramento? What happened?"

"What happened? That girl refuses to accept the truth, that's what. The innocent messenger of bad news, in this case me, was treated as the enemy. If she had a gun, I'd bet she would have used it on me!"

Rick kept a straight face. It couldn't have worked out better—for him. Callie knew the truth now, but she'd learned it from Gordon rather than himself.

"Sounds like trouble over Ashe Perry?" Rick inquired smoothly. Gordon was almost unaware of him now and simply wanted to vent his frustration.

"To put it mildly. What if I told you, as I did Callie, that Ashe knows Dylan Harkin? Ah! I see you're surprised, as was I. I thought Callie would appreciate the information. But not that woman! I didn't dare try to tell her that Ashe is in business with Dylan. She'll lie to herself to defend him—and her own dreams."

Ashe in business with Dylan? Rick stared at him.

"That's undoubtedly why Ashe came to California, hoping for a new start." Gordon's wide mouth formed a rigid line. "I could put all that in my paper and ruin him if I wanted to."

Rick's thoughts raced back to how Elmo had seen Ashe leave the Nevada Hotel at Carson by the back way. Since the stage merely stopped for a quick break before going on to Virginia City, Ashe wouldn't have gone there to ask about a room. Even more curious was that Elmo said he'd seen the horse ridden by the man with the scar tied behind that same hotel. And he'd seen Ashe. Was there some connection between Ashe Perry, Dylan Harkin, and the man with the scar?

But neither Ashe nor Dylan had any connection to the trouble in New Mexico. Rick had met Dylan once or twice in Tucson, and it didn't seem likely Dylan would hire the man with the scar.

"What about Ashe being in business with Dylan?"

Gordon was brooding, as though his meeting with Callie still had him smarting.

"It was Dylan's finances from the Harkin half of the mine that sponsored the Perry-Ralston Company in San Francisco, enhancing Ashe's comeback on stage. In fact, Dylan leant money to Hugh to stake his half of the Stardust. Callie certainly doesn't know that—and she doesn't want to hear it, either. I've learned that the transactions were done through the San Francisco-Nevada Bank in town."

Rick just stared at him. The image of the erratic young gunfighter interested enough in the world of theater to sponsor a loan for the Perry-Ralston Company and half the Stardust, left Rick puzzled. It didn't make sense.

"Who told you this?"

"Clark Simmons. He works at the bank. He's involved with handling money for the Halliday-Harkin Mine. He's not a top man at the bank, mind you, but Simmons knows a thing or two. And you can talk to Neil Howard over at the Virginia Opry. He worked with Ashe years ago in Chicago."

"Thanks." Rick opened the door to leave, but looked back. "If I were you, I wouldn't put that scandal about Ashe Perry knowing Dylan in your paper."

"Why not? He deserves it."

"Because it would likely turn most folks in Virginia City against you, rather than Perry."

Rick left the newspaper office and walked down to the Virginia Opry House.

Neil Howard was down front when Rick came in and sat in one of the worn theater seats. The place was much smaller than the Stardust and smelled of stale tobacco smoke. The Stardust would have little trouble competing with the Virginia Opry House. It might even put it out of business.

Neil looked over, saw him, and walked up breathing hard. He was a pudgy man with florid features and a heavy, drooping mustache. He sat opposite Rick, and taking out a skinny cigar, offered him one, but Rick declined. Neil struck a match to light his cigar. Blowing smoke, he rolled it over to the other side of his mouth, his eyes bright and inquisitive.

"Heard you took some lead."

"I'm doing all right. Have you seen a big man, new to Virginia City, with a scar on his neck the shape of a Z?"

He shook his head. "But I'll keep an eye open. How's Elmo?"

"As feisty as ever."

Neil grinned. "What can I do for ya, Delance?"

"I just left Gordon Barkly's office. He mentioned you knew Ashe Perry in Chicago some years back. Thought you might be able to tell me about it."

Neil looked at him a long moment, then nodded.

"Ashe is a fair enough actor. Not as great as he puts on, or as Miss Callie's trying to make him. She's star-struck; I think he's pulled a hood over her eyes. I've worked with Ashe for awhile. He convinces the audience well enough. I knew him when he just started out, before he made it to Broadway. Later, Ashe moved to St. Louis, then on to New Orleans, finally New York. Now it's the mining camps out here in the West."

"Did he know Dylan Harkin in the past?"

He paused, puffing his cigar, and squinting. "Dylan? Now that's a curious thing…I wonder. You got me there, Delance. It's been too many years since Chicago. I saw Ashe, of course. I was the stage manager. Then he made a fool of himself, was hauled off the stage for showing up drunk to play his part. He was fired. After Ashe's blunder in New York, we split up.

"Ashe is a big social man. Loves attention, the best of food, clothes, wine, wants to travel throughout Europe, you know the type. Hates mediocrity, poverty…gambles when he's moody. Was the same way with his past drinking. I say past because he's not doing it now or he wouldn't be with Miss Callie. I was surprised when he showed up here, working with her. From the looks of things, they're doing all right. They seem to have lots of money. Did you see those sapphires he gave to her? They're worth plenty. Wonder where he got the dough to buy 'em?"

Rick was lounging back in the theater chair stroking his chin thoughtfully, listening to all Neil said while trying to read beyond the words.

Neil watched him alertly. "Why are you so interested in Ashe?"

"Gordon claims Ashe knows Dylan Harkin. Sure you've not heard anything about that?"

Neil puffed thoughtfully. He shook his head, as if bewildered. "Don't know why he would know him, or Frank Harkin, either. Ashe and his crowd belong to another world."

"That's what I thought. But Gordon seems to think Dylan is the financial source for both Ashe and Hugh."

"Dylan Harkin?" Neil asked incredulously.

"Dylan's lent money to Ashe to start his theater company, and also to Hugh Ralston to pay for half the Stardust."

Neil squinted over his cigar, then shook his head. "Got me, Delance. Barkly's gotta be wrong."

"Wrong, why?"

Neil shrugged his heavy shoulders. "Why would a fella like Dylan even meet up with Ashe and this Hugh Ralston fellow? And another thing…when Dylan left town the night you and Wilder faced down Mac and Rody Villiers, I'd never seen him so worried—and it wasn't about Wilder or you because he thought that neither of you boys would draw on him unless he provoked it. More I think of it, somebody had Dylan really scared."

This Rick had not heard before. He sat up straight, staring at Neil. "Scared of what?"

"He didn't say, but he was plenty frightened. Looked like the furies was on his trail."

"You mean you saw Dylan just before he left that night?"

"Yep. I stepped out of the theater here just to see how you and the marshal were doing against Rody and Hoadly. That's when Dylan comes down the back alley behind my place heading round to Beebe's livery stable. When I first saw him I thought he was helping you and Wilder out because of the way he was sneaking around and looking behind him. So I called out to him.

"'Hey, Dylan, I hear you'll inherit Frank's half of the mine,' I said, then he whirled in a crouch, hand at his holster till he saw it was just me. Then he said something like, 'Yeah, as long as I keep him outsmarted.' Something like that, anyway."

Rick scowled. "I've not heard this before. Brett hasn't either."

Neil shrugged again. "Didn't think too much about it after things calmed down. You think Dylan ever met up with trouble, like someone wantin' to kill him?"

"Don't know, just wish I knew who he was afraid of. Whoever it was, the message got to him quick-like. He got out of town before Rody left."

Neil nodded thoughtfully. "Something scared him all right."

"But he's not scared now."

"He's not? What do you mean?"

"If Dylan's lending money to Ashe and Hugh Ralston, then he's probably been taking it nice and easy in San Francisco."

Neil removed the cigar from between his teeth and narrowed his eyes. "How do you figure Frisco?"

"Where else would Dylan have met Ashe and Hugh recently to give them a loan except the theater world of San Francisco? So it figures Dylan could be living there. And that's also where Ashe and Hugh first met Callie and arranged for her to buy into the Perry-Ralston Theater Company…and evidently the Stardust. It would seem Dylan should have been there to protect his interest when backing them."

Neil chewed the end of his cigar and just looked at him. "It figures, Delance. But also sounds a little strange, doesn't it?"

"Sounds mighty strange. I think I'll have a talk with Callie about how she met Hugh Ralston in Frisco."

"You going to talk to her Uncle Samuel first?"

The doors opened, and one of Neil's actors came hurrying in from the street.

"Hey, there's a big rumpus over at the Stardust. Awhile ago Miss O'Day came close to having a fatal accident."

Rick stood and turned his head sharply. "How's that?"

"Miss O'Day," he repeated, as he approached in the aisle. "She was touring her theater when the new chandelier came loose. Nearly fell on her. Don't ask me how. The builder is denying it could happen. One chance in a thousand maybe, yet it happened. It was a close one for her. Said she threw herself out of the way just in the crack of time. Pretty dramatic, eh? Maybe it's all a stunt. She has her opening on Saturday night, but she seems pretty frightened about it—"

Rick went past him and rushed out the door.

Thirteen

ঌ

$\mathcal{R}$ick entered the Stardust and saw some of the Perry-Ralston theater people gathered around the shattered chandelier in a robust discussion of what could have gone wrong. Their voices drifted to him.

"Of course it was an accident. Come on, Mary. What else could it be?"

"But why did it happen? How could it have happened?"

"We can speculate all day," Callie's surprisingly calm voice said. "Let's forget it, Mary. I think Smiley is right. It was an accident. Mr. Cummings just thought he had everything fully secured."

"Well, it doesn't make a bit of sense to me," the woman named Mary persisted.

"If it wasn't an accident, then what was it?" Smiley asked.

The voices ebbed into uncomfortable silence.

"Enough of this," Callie stated, and Rick found himself admiring her steady voice and unwillingness to panic. Yes, there was sand in this girl all right. He had thought so all along, and this proved it.

"Jimmy?" she was saying, changing the subject, "would you go out on the boardwalk and see if Uncle Samuel's coming yet?"

"I just did," Jimmy said. "I ran all the way to the house and told Aunt Weda, so's she can worry even more."

Someone chuckled.

"She says Uncle Samuel left early this morning to visit a bad hombre in jail over at Carson. The man might hang. Uncle will be back tomorrow."

Rick realized no one had noticed him yet. So he walked the perimeter of the theater studying the catwalks and the various ropes and pulleys. There were at least two places where someone could have crouched in the shadows high up near the roof and not be noticed easily. If what happened wasn't accidental, then someone wanted Callie dead. What would anybody have gained by that? Ashe could gain nothing until he married her.

Though Rick didn't think much of Ashe Perry, he couldn't imagine him as a murderer, hiding up there on the catwalk, waiting to cut loose the chandelier over the woman he wanted to marry.

Rick frowned and looked over to the theater group, still discussing what had happened. Just then a man in the group turned and saw him and announced: "Someone's just come in," then he walked toward Rick.

"No visitors are permitted, mister."

Rick turned to the medium-sized man with a city pallor, and took him at once for the man called Smiley.

"I'd like to speak with Miss Halliday."

"She doesn't want to see anyone now."

But Jimmy had spotted Rick and came running up.

"Hi, Rick! Look at the chandelier!" He pointed, obviously excited by the commotion, not fully aware of what might have happened.

"I am looking. Now why don't you go tell your sister I'd like to talk to her."

Smiley now looked uncertain as he eyed Rick. "Are you a friend of Miss O'Day?"

"It's okay, Mr. Smiley, Rick is *my* friend."

"That won't do, Jimmy." He turned to Rick. "No offense, mister, but she's asked not to see anyone right now." He turned and called to someone: "John! Get somebody watching the front doors till the doctor gets here, will you?"

Jimmy ran over to where Callie must have been seated with the theatrical crew surrounding her.

Smiley eyed him again. Then he put out his hand. "My name's Tom Smiley. I'm Callie and Ashe's stage manager."

"Rick Delance."

Evidently his name as a gunfighter was not known to Smiley, for he showed no response.

"We're opening on Saturday, but with this happening, it's rotten publicity." He shook his head. "Hugh isn't going to like this."

Rick came alert. "Is Hugh Ralston showing up for opening night?"

"He's coming all the way from San Francisco."

Rick hadn't expected the fortunate break. He would attempt to meet Ralston and find out what he knew about Dylan Harkin and the loan on the Stardust.

"Anybody know how the chandelier came loose?"

Smiley shook his head. "Just has to be an accident. I suspect Cummings and his builders were in a hurry. We've been putting them under pressure to get everything up and ready by Saturday morning. Cummings denies any of his workers were careless, but what else could it be?"

"Has anyone been up there to check on things?" Rick asked.

"I went up soon as I got here. Nothing was disturbed as far as I can tell."

Smiley looked toward the doors where a worker stood guard. "That doctor ought to be here by now."

"Is she hurt?"

"Not that I know of. She was lucky. She got out of the way just in time. She said she 'threw herself aside.'"

"Then something made her look up toward the chandelier just as it was beginning to fall?"

Smiley must have understood because he looked up at the ceiling for a thoughtful moment, remaining silent. He breathed something to himself and, seeming to forget about Rick, walked toward the door, calling out again: "John, who was watching things while Cummings' builders were out to lunch?"

"Watching?" came a surprised voice. "Why, no one stayed. Miss O'Day was here looking things over."

As the two men stood talking, Jimmy came toward Delance looking pleased with himself and bringing Callie. She stopped when she looked at Rick. Had Jimmy not told her who was asking to see her?

She was, in Rick's viewpoint, a beautiful young woman, who would have been just as lovely in a faded calico dress with an apron tied around her waist. He thought he might like her even better that way. However, he was smart enough to know there'd be no kitchen apron on this girl if she could help it.

Her wardrobe, he decided, must have cost her plenty. She seemed inclined that way. He guessed that her appearance, her new stardom, and becoming an heiress, were things that she felt compensated for the hardship she'd experienced in her early years. He doubted, though, that they would satisfy her for long—Ashe included. Her drive for self-worth by seeking the world's applause was leading her on a path to real pain in the future. *Samuel,* Rick thought, *ought to have a long talk with her.*

Her dress had, what looked to Rick, more yards of green velvet than he'd seen in his life—enough to make three dresses. Her thick, dark hair was slightly mussed and coming down from a set of curls in back. Her cheeks were tinted with emotion, yet despite the accident she appeared in control of herself.

Rick felt a stir of admiration. Young, she was. Yet finding herself in a spot of danger, she'd rallied herself to a moment of calm. That told him something more about what might lie deeper in her soul.

She walked toward him with Jimmy leading the way. Jimmy's small shoulders were thrown back, a look of grown-up severity was on his face, but his eyes glowed with boyish exuberance.

"Here she is, Rick," he said with gravity, as though he'd delivered on an important promise. "Callie, this is my friend, Rick. Rick, this is my sister Callie."

Rick smiled over Jimmy's formal behavior, and then he looked at Callie. She looked back evenly, a little flushed.

"We've already met," she told Jimmy.

"Oh, I know you have," Jimmy said. "But it was on that night when Cousin Rody started bad trouble with you."

"Yes, I remember," she said too quickly.

Rick thought she might be heading-off Jimmy from one of his favorite stories. "We've met more than once," he said with affected sobriety. "I remember each and every occasion."

Her chin lifted and her blush deepened. "Jimmy tells me you wanted to speak with me," she said with too much dignity.

"Yes," he said, his tone deliberately humble, as though unworthy of the courtesy. "If you will, ma'am, alone."

She studied his face a moment, and he kept any amusement from showing. He saw her glancing at his gunbelt, which he'd discreetly tried to conceal as best he could beneath his buckskin jacket.

He thought for a moment that she would decline, but she must have decided that his request was important since he'd not asked before.

"I'm expecting Doctor McMannis any moment. If you can wait...I'll see you afterward."

He looked at her. "I'll wait."

She swerved her gaze down to Jimmy. "Where's Elmira?"

He shrugged. "I haven't seen her in ages. I think she's the one who took the buggy to get Doc McMannis."

"I really don't need a doctor. All this fuss over nothing."

Did she really think that the concern over the chandelier incident was a "fuss over nothing"? He credited her with more intelligence than that; she must be putting on a theatrical show of indifference. Was it for his sake? Or for someone else present? He was prompted to pay closer attention to those in the theater, and he took them all in casually. The faces were all strangers. He wouldn't have known one actor from another. He assumed they all were from San Francisco. Where was Ashe?

"How did it happen?"

She looked in the direction of the twisted chandelier and shattered glass, and he saw a slight repulsion when she tensed.

She shook her head. "I don't know. I asked Mr. Cummings— he's the builder here from San Francisco. He insists it was well supported and safe. One moment I was standing there and the next—"

"Mind if I look around?"

Her gaze darted to his. He could see that his reasons for wanting to look around were not lost on her. She looked quickly at Jimmy.

"No, of course not."

"I want to go up on the catwalk."

"The builders have been working up there, and I've been told some of the boards are loose and unreliable."

"Who contracted Mr. Cummings?"

She looked surprised. "To do the building?"

"Yes, ma'am."

"Hugh Ralston. I didn't know much about builders and neither did Ashe."

Rick kept silent. He looked up at the catwalk.

"Are you sure you ought to go up there?" She took a quick look at the bandage visible near his shirt collar. "Maybe you shouldn't tax yourself. You are…improving?"

"Getting better. I'll have a look. It's no problem."

"Jimmy," she said, "why don't you go back to the house and console Aunt Weda. Let her know everything is all right."

"Okay, but I was thinking I'd go on up the catwalk with Rick."

"'Mr. Delance,'" she corrected.

"Just Rick," he said smoothly.

"You shouldn't go up there, Jimmy," she said swiftly. "And you're likely to get in Mr. Delance's way."

"Oh, but—"

"She's right, Jimmy," Rick drawled. "Better go up to the house and wait for her, will you?"

Jimmy sighed laboriously. "All right."

She, too, turned to leave.

"Before you go, may I ask a question? What alerted you to get out of the way of that falling chandelier?"

Her eyes came back to his, searching.

"Why do you ask?"

"Seems a good question."

"It is. But no one else has asked me that."

She looks a little nervous, he thought.

"I heard a sound up there on the catwalk," she admitted.

"What kind of a sound?"

She hesitated. "I thought I heard a noise. But there couldn't have been anyone up there."

The determination in her voice told him more than her words. "Are you trying to convince yourself or me?"

The violet-blue eyes hardened like gems. "What do you mean by that?"

"I'm wondering if you're determined to convince yourself that you just imagined a noise up there."

Her chin came up and two spots of red colored her cheeks. "Why would I do that?"

"Only you know the answer to that, ma'am."

She turned, back straight, and started toward the steps to the dressing rooms, but stopped when her ankle seemed to give.

Rick reached a swift hand and caught her. "Looks like you might have twisted that ankle earlier. May I help you up those steps?"

"*No!* I'll make it on my own."

She tried to pull her arm free, but by now Rick had noticed the blue sapphires sparkling on her left hand.

This must be the engagement ring Flint Harper had mentioned. He was staring at it, considering, when she pulled her hand away beside her swaying skirts and glared at him.

His brow shot up. "Nice sapphires," he murmured.

"I'm surprised you'd know," she quipped fiercely, and gathering up her yards of velvet flounced away, dutifully enduring the pain in her ankle.

Rick narrowed his eyes as he looked after her. For a raw moment he had half a mind to go after her and tell her a thing or two about what he did know about jewels...and it was probably much more than she knew. That Lucien Delance had left a family of nobility in France, and what a great lady his mother had been— far more refined than Callie. Rick put a quick rein on his emotions. That would gain him nothing in the end except broadening the wedge between them.

So, little Miss Callie can also be a real brat? He frowned to himself. *What do I even see in her?*

But he knew the answer to that. There was more to her than her immature behavior, and he was a patient man. He intended to win in the end.

Rick watched as the man named Smiley came quickly to her aid as she held to the banister and led her slowly up to her dressing room to wait for the doctor.

Rick went up a ladder to check out the catwalk.

Now why did I say that? Callie wondered, rebuking herself. There was no call for her to feel so prickly toward Rick Delance. So far, every contact she'd had with him had been helpful. Even his willingness to have a look around now showed his interest in her. She was flattered, and yet—She closed her eyes, placing her palm against her forehead. *I won't even think about him. He upsets me.*

A half-hour later, after Doctor McMannis left, Callie was seated on a plush velvet chair facing Elmira. The woman stood discreetly to one side of the small dressing room, her hands neatly folded in front of her. Her dark eyes looked on sleepily as Callie stood and fussed in her stocking feet. She had slightly twisted her ankle, and though it didn't hurt very much, it was swollen enough that she couldn't get her slipper on.

"I don't know what's keeping Ashe. Are you sure you left a message at the International, Elmira?"

"Left it with the clerk, yes. Ashe is expected back any time now."

"Did the clerk say why he'd been called to Carson?"

"No."

Ashe could at least have left me a note about when he'd be returning! She limped over to the chair again and sank into it. *Elmira was useless!*

"Are you sure there's no container to heat water in so I can soak my foot?"

"We'll have to go back to the house for that, Miss Callie. Maybe we should go now. It doesn't look as if Parson Samuel is coming, either." Elmira looked at her wearied. "Is there any reason why you wish to stay here longer?"

There was, and Elmira already knew the reason but had shown disapproval, though she'd actually said nothing when Callie mentioned she would be talking to Rick Delance.

"Why don't you go down and rest in the buggy, Elmira. I shall be down soon," Callie told her. Anything to be rid of this woman watching her with sleepy but steady eyes.

When Elmira didn't answer, Callie glanced at her through the wall mirror and saw a disdainful scowl. It shocked Callie, but when she turned to look at the woman's face, it had been washed into her normal stoic expression.

I've got to get rid of her! Callie thought again. *She doesn't think much of me, and the feeling is mutual. Just as soon as I see Ashe next.*

"As you wish," Elmira said, and walking to the door, she went out, her black skirts rustling stiffly.

Callie looked after her, frowning. She didn't understand the woman. She opened the door a crack just to see if Elmira had really gone and saw her exiting the bottom steps. Elmira glanced back just as Rick Delance appeared from exploring the catwalk. He walked up toward Callie's dressing room. As he approached she slowly pulled the door closed and waited. There came a knock.

"May I come in?"

Rick's face was sober as his gaze held hers.

Callie stepped back uneasily, and he entered, setting down his black, flat-crowned hat.

Fourteen

☙

*C*allie closed the door after Rick Delance, noting how his masculine presence contrasted with the small room done in red velvet with cream-and-rosebud wallpaper. She denied that she felt even a hint of fear, but it was there nonetheless. A new bandage peeped from his shirt collar, and she thought he must have had a recent visit with Doctor McMannis. Samuel had told her that Rick had been shot twice. She couldn't imagine anyone still being on his feet after that, but he was, and mostly with Samuel's help. Delance looked as ready as ever to pursue his enemies.

He didn't look the least intimidated from their earlier clash.

Callie portrayed dignity, noticing all the while his dark, robust eyes.

"I don't know what Cummings told you, ma'am, but someone fooled with that chandelier. The support chain was unbolted and was replaced with a temporary rope. I know a few things about rope failure. I'd say someone deliberately cut that one. Whoever it was waited for just the right moment and wanted—at the very least—to frighten you...but maybe much worse. Any idea who might want to do that?"

Callie sank heavily into the velvet chair and stared up at him.

"You've got to be mistaken." But even as she said it, the incidents in San Francisco emerged like menacing shadows from the past.

"I wish I was. I don't think so."

He was strongly opinionated, but even so, she feared he might be right, and she didn't like thinking about it. Although she knew she was trying to dispel the fearful thoughts she'd had just before the chandelier fell, she could at least say she had not been sure about the cause of those noises.

The calmness in Rick's eyes mollified her fears. His interest and concern helped to steady her. He was right about wanting to face the incident squarely.

"And yet it might be better if you didn't say anything just yet," she told him quietly.

He pondered, as though trying to understand her. "Is that wise?"

"I want to talk to Ashe Perry first."

She turned and looked at him to find that there was no challenge in his eyes, just a sober gaze that seemed to take in information.

"Do you know where Samuel is? I think it would be unwise of me to keep my concerns from him. He ought to be told," Rick said.

She shook her head. "I'm not sure, but Jimmy learned from Aunt Weda that he went to Carson to preach at the jail. I've a notion he had another reason as well." She stood suddenly, convinced she knew why he'd gone there. A spark of determination shot through her—Samuel wanted Mr. Stewart's judgment on the lawyer Ashe would hire to sell her third of the mine. A lawyer by the name of Burl O'Brien.

"I'd rather you didn't share your suspicions with my uncle, Mr. Delance," she repeated firmly.

"Is there a reason I shouldn't?"

She hesitated. "In my way of looking at things, yes. You see, you're not alone in your unfair distrust of Ashe. Anything Ashe Perry wants to do is questioned by Uncle Samuel."

"Let's try to stay objective, Miss Halliday. I haven't yet said anything, good or bad, about Ashe Perry."

She looked away. Mentioning distrust of Ashe when they had merely been discussing the unusual circumstances surrounding the chandelier had been too hasty. She still felt, however, that she was right in being defensive about Ashe.

"Samuel invited Ashe to come with him to the Threesome cabin the night I needed medical care. If he was so untrusting, why did he bring Ashe along?"

"I really can't say why he asked Ashe to go. What I can tell you is that ever since that night, Samuel's resistance to my going with Ashe to New York has become intolerable."

"Maybe he has some wise reasons."

She shot him a cool look, and his smile annoyed her.

"Samuel has no legitimate reason to oppose me and Ashe except he's narrow-minded and judgmental."

She thought of Samuel's unhappy face when he'd told her that Ashe was not a Christian and therefore an unsuitable choice. He'd even gone so far as to say that she would never know the harmony God intended for marriage if she forged ahead stubbornly. Callie knew Samuel had come to that conclusion after the conversation he'd had with Elmo the night he'd been shot in the ear.

"Ashe had shown his 'true colors'," as Samuel had put it. *"I had more discussion with him on the way out to Threesome,"* he'd said, *"and I can tell you, lass, the young man, talented and handsome though he be, is not one of the Lord's children. If you marry him, you'll not only experience a life of discord, but you'll be in outright disobedience to God's clear instruction: 'Be not unequally yoked together with unbelievers.'"*

Callie had been thinking this when she looked over at Rick Delance and found him watching her with a deep, pondering gaze.

"Samuel treats me like a child still needing parental guidance. So does Aunt Weda. It's most aggravating." She sank to the chair again with a swirl of green skirt and petticoats and looked at him, with eyes narrowed and arms folded.

"Samuel's a great man. You should be proud of him. He's served God faithfully all these years in a hard and difficult land, mostly unappreciated."

That he defended Samuel nettled her. "Yes, he's a good man," she admitted. "I've no argument with that. But he's too old-fashioned. I won't have him running my life for me." She looked at him. "Your defense of Samuel's Christian convictions seems a little odd, especially coming from a man I thought would not have cared much about that."

She expected a retort but none came. He frowned to himself and his thoughts appeared to wander far away to some distant trail. His reaction wasn't what she would have expected from a gunfighter.

"I'll need to accept your charge, Miss Halliday. If it seems odd, it's not because Samuel's wrong. If anyone is wrong, it's you and me. Samuel's a man to glean wisdom from. He's had more experience with bad hombres than we've had birthdays. Just maybe he has reasons to be cautious where you're concerned. I know he thinks a good deal of you."

His endorsement of Samuel's faith goaded her more than he knew because she could see Rick was sincere in what he said.

Another lecture, and this one from Rick Delance. She smiled sweetly, then frowned revealing her true emotions. "I'm leaving town. The sooner, the better. And I'm leaving behind all these 'bad hombres' you've mentioned, hopefully, once and for all."

He laughed softly, his arms folded, as he leaned against the door.

She hadn't expected that response and felt her temper rising with the afternoon zephyrs that rattled her window and moved the red velvet drapery.

"Do I amuse you, Mr. Delance?" she asked coolly.

His dark eyes sparkled. "Yes, ma'am, but I admit that you irritate me, too."

Her brows lifted.

"You seem ungrateful," he said easily. "You don't realize that if it wasn't for the God-given silver lode, and men like your good uncle and other industrious people like Flint Harper, you wouldn't be in the privileged place you're in that allows you to scorn them. It was men like them who built Virginia City, and built the roads so people and commerce could get across the Sierras. Ashe Perry and those like him show up when it's all over, with specks in their eyes the size of pinion pines, parading themselves as superior."

Instead of a burst of temper she seemed thoughtful. "I must have said something that touched a raw nerve, Mr. Delance, and do remember that you said you were not going to speak good or bad about Ashe."

His eyes narrowed as he looked at her, and then he smiled suddenly. "Not exactly. I meant that 'I hadn't yet spoken good or bad,' but as long as we're now discussing Ashe, do you intend to go against your uncle's wishes and marry him?"

She leaned forward snatching her fan from the low table at the side of her chair. "That's none of your affair."

"True enough, and it's unfortunate for you, ma'am. Because if I had anything to say about it…"

She felt the heat surge into her cheeks, and she snapped her fan shut. Coming quickly to her feet she winced from her mild sprain and sank back into the chair.

He affected gravity. "Better have your maid soak that little foot, ma'am. When you walk across that stage at the end of the play on Saturday night to kiss Ashe Perry, you'll want to fly into his arms."

That did it! "I can see you have nothing more to contribute but ill-mannered barbs. You may leave now, Mr. Delance!" She pointed to the door.

"I'm going—in a minute or two." He smiled. "First, though, I need to ask you a few more questions about that chandelier."

"I don't see why it should concern you, really."

With arms still folded he just looked at her, unhurried. "Well, now, ma'am, it's Samuel's feelings I'm worried about. I'd hate to see anything happen to you that would add to his unhappiness."

Samuel, again! It's not me but Samuel who prompted his interest in the matter. Maybe he just wants to sprinkle salt on my pride and see me smart!

"Well, Mr. Delance, I certainly wouldn't want to see you become overly worried that some of my adversity might add to my uncle's unhappiness."

"Thank you. You can start, ma'am, by trying to think of someone who would wish to frighten you out of Virginia City. Any ideas?"

Now why would he say that? "Frighten me into leaving? But whatever for?"

"I don't pretend to know, but that's my next question…and something for you to ponder. Could it be that someone wants to spur your discontent with Virginia City? Upset you enough to get you to quickly leave for New York?"

Unwillingly, his words sparked her memory. Ashe had wanted to help her sell the mine quickly so that they could leave at once. She understood his reasons, however, and was in agreement. They were both motivated by the opportunity to star on Broadway in the new play. She wouldn't mention this now, knowing Rick would jump to a wrong conclusion about Ashe.

As her gaze caught his, she saw a genuine flicker of sympathy and concern, and she relaxed her defenses a little. Maybe Rick wasn't so callous after all. One thing about a man like Rick Delance, if she kept him at a safe emotional distance and avoided mentioning her plans, he could prove useful for protection. Callie looked him over when he didn't notice. *He is,* she thought, *a remarkably good-looking young man.*

"There was an incident in San Francisco," she confided unexpectedly. "Someone broke into my hotel room. Fortunately, though, Ashe was with me at the time. We'd just left the theater, and he brought me to my hotel when something inside my room alerted us. By the time we hailed the guard, the burglar escaped by the terrace."

Rick frowned. "Did you see him?"

"No. He ran through the garden, and it was too dark."

"Did he steal anything?"

"No. Perhaps he was frightened away before he had the chance. There was another incident, as well."

"In San Francisco again?"

"Yes. I'd gone for an afternoon walk before my performance that night at the theater. I sensed someone following me, but when I turned around and tried to see his face, he'd gone behind some trees. Later, on the way back to the hotel, it seemed the same man had tried to snatch my purse. The policeman on the corner heard my shout and came running, but the thief fled through the park."

As she saw Rick's sober gaze she said quickly, "It couldn't have been my imagination."

"No, and the noise by the chandelier wasn't either. When you thought someone was following you, was it before or after the hotel room incident?"

"About a week later."

"But it hasn't happened since?"

"Well, there was an incident at the stage depot in Carson City."

She had caught his immediate interest.

"Carson? Someone following you?"

"He didn't follow me. But he seemed an odd character and rather frightening, too. He came out of the Dry Goods Store and stared at me."

She could see Rick was listening intently to her every word. *Was he remembering something?*

"What did he look like?"

"He was a big man, with a broad, leering face and blondish hair. He seemed interested in who was getting off the stage."

"Did you notice any scars?"

She was surprised. "Why, yes. There was one on his neck."

He looked down at her a long moment, and she wondered what was running through his mind.

"How long did the stage hold over before leaving for Virginia City?"

"Maybe twenty minutes. But he never came inside. He rode away down the street."

"Toward the Nevada Hotel?"

"Yes, there was a hotel. Perhaps he went there, but it appeared as though he'd left town. I thought he might be following our stage. Do you know who he is?"

"Yes and no. That sounds strange, I realize. I believe he's a hired killer out to stop me and Elmo. But I don't know his name. I have strong reason to believe he came here with the two other hired guns that jumped us out near Gold Canyon."

She knew that one of those hired guns was dead, someone named Cesar. She could understand gunfighters pursuing Rick, but the idea that they would want to shoot Elmo certainly changed things in her mind.

"Why is that man with the scar after you?"

"It's a long story—too long for now. Someday, if you're still interested, I'll tell you about it. Were you ever separated from Ashe at Carson, even for a few minutes?"

She sensed his thoughts leading down an unpleasant path that she didn't want to visit.

"I suppose we were. For just a very few minutes. Why is it important?" she asked warily.

Rick studied her face, then, just as she thought he was about to tell her something, he seemed to step back and decide against it.

"I'll need to talk to Samuel," he said.

"Please leave Samuel out of this. It will only give him a reason to try to rein me in even tighter."

"And you want your freedom, no matter what. I'm sorry, Miss Halliday, but I'll have to talk to him when he gets back."

She had the notion Rick knew something he was reluctant to tell her, which was troubling since it seemed he preferred to trust Samuel with it. She wondered if it had anything to do with Ashe.

Changing the direction of their conversation, he asked, "Was Cummings and his workmen here in the theater when you arrived?"

"Well, yes, they were, but they soon left for their lunch. Then there was no one else. I'd sent Jimmy and Elmira off together and intended to meet them for lunch around one o'clock, after I toured the theater."

"Then you didn't come here today with Ashe Perry?"

"No. Why should it matter? I come and go as I please. Ashe is in Carson on business," she said stiffly. Though she hadn't known his whereabouts until Elmira told her earlier.

"Carson, again," he said thoughtfully. "When I once told you of your need for a bodyguard, I meant it. I suggest you consider hiring one."

She remembered well enough what he'd told her on two other occasions. One, when that odious man called Big Birdie had been watching her after she'd first arrived with Flint Harper. She'd been staying a few days at Ma Higgins' while waiting for Annalee to arrive with Brett Wilder. Big Birdie worked for a disgraceful Chinese man who ran a dive in what was known as the Barberry Coast District. Big Birdie had been watching her from across the street when Rick had walked up to her as bold as day and told her she needed a better bodyguard than Flint Harper. Since then, however, Rick and Flint had become friends.

The other incident had taken place outside the Virginia House Hotel after Macklin's death. Cousin Rody had showed himself a proud and ruthless cad, and Rick stepped in and challenged him, then soundly defeated him. After that she had quietly admired Rick's tough ability to survive in the raw West.

"Even so," she said loftily, "thank you but I have Ashe Perry."

"But he wasn't here today when you could have used some help, was he? And pardon my saying so, but he's likely to prove less a man than you presently need."

"Well, indeed!" She crossed her arms and scanned him. "You do think a lot of yourself, don't you, Mr. Delance?"

His smile was faint. "No, ma'am, but I know what I can and can't do. I've experience out here. It's my opinion, if you go depending on Ashe Perry, you're likely to come up short."

Oh how he rankled her! She couldn't resist: "Then are you offering yourself, Mr. Delance?" she asked with a pleasant theater smile.

His dark eyes smiled. "Maybe. Except I'm not in much condition presently to take on a gang of thieves."

"Oh, I'm sure you'll improve," she said dryly.

He smiled. "I imagine so."

Then she grew sober, wondering. *I'd better not dismiss him too lightly. I might need Rick Delance later on.*

"I'll think about your suggestion," she said casually. "I'll discuss it with Ashe."

"He'll never agree."

She shrugged. "Maybe not, but I still want to discuss it with him."

"As you wish."

Suddenly, in the midst of their conversation, he abruptly turned away, took hold of the doorknob, and opened the door so quickly that Callie drew in a breath. This was one man who utterly confused her.

But she wasn't the only one who'd been surprised. Elmira gasped and would have lost her balance and almost fallen into the room had he not been prepared to catch her.

Why that woman had been standing out there with an ear to the door. Callie's dislike of her reached its summit.

"Oh!" Elmira said breathlessly, hands flying to her heart. She looked warily from Rick Delance's noncommittal expression to Callie's open glare.

"I'm sorry if I'm interrupting, Miss Callie, but I just saw Mr. Perry ride in. He's at the International."

Ashe was back. Thank goodness! She must see him right away. She wanted the image of Delance swept freely from her mind.

Callie's gaze left Elmira's waxen face to fix on Rick. He'd turned toward Callie, his eyes reflecting confidence as he reached for his hat and nodded goodbye.

"Pardon me, ma'am, I was just leaving," he told Elmira.

Callie watched as he went past Elmira, his boots sounding confidently down the steps. Callie brushed past her through the door to see which way he was leaving the theater. She saw him approach the side exit that opened onto a quieter side street. He looked back for a moment while she was still on the steps watching. He lifted a hand and was gone as quietly as he'd come.

Aware of Elmira moving about in her dressing room, Callie left the steps and came inside, closing the door. She sensed her frustration welling up inside her as she faced the woman with hands on hips.

"You were eavesdropping, Elmira."

"How dare you insult me so, madam!"

"You deny it? You were just caught listening with your ear to my door."

"I was doing no such thing. I had my hand raised to knock when that gunfighter threw the door open and scared me. Really, Miss Callie, your ill treatment of me—and your hobnobbing with that—that killer, grieves my heart. Why, for your own good, I should perhaps tell Mr. Perry about this."

"You just go right ahead and talk to Ashe. Because I'm going to talk to him, too."

Her pupils dilated. "What do you mean?"

"Just what you heard me say. It's obvious our feelings toward each other are best described as mutual dislike. If Ashe wishes your employment because you're a friend of his mother, then *he* can employ you as his secretary. I no longer wish you working for me."

Elmira gasped. "Oh, Miss Callie, please! Please! Give me another chance! I promise I'll do you better."

Her response so surprised Callie that she gaped. Was this the same stoic woman who one breath ago was denying and accusing, but now practically begging? Elmira's look of consternation over the possibility of being dismissed was so genuine that Callie now felt she had been too harsh. After all, Elmira was a poor widow, and maybe she should have another chance.

"I'll do better," Elmira repeated. "Wait and see, please. At least allow me to go with you and Mr. Perry to New York. You see, I— I have a brother there. He's just emigrated from Europe, and he and I will be renting a flat there and working together to start a new life. We're thinking of opening a meat shop."

Callie's frustration with her ebbed toward feelings of sympathy. Perhaps Elmira's troubles were so deep that they produced her dour disposition.

"Very well," Callie said quietly. "You can stay with me and Ashe until New York. After that…"

"Oh, thank you, Miss Callie. You won't regret your decision."

Callie wondered.

"Shall I—shall I go down to the International for Mr. Perry now?" Elmira asked.

"I think not. We'll let Ashe rest until dinner."

"Then shall I call the hotel to send over some hot tea?"

Impressed by her sudden thoughtfulness, Callie hesitated. "Yes, Elmira, that sounds wonderful. We'll both have some tea. You look like you could use a cup, too."

"Why, thank you." She turned and hurried away.

Callie sank into a chair. How complicated life was!

Her thoughts returned to Rick Delance. After meeting him she now realized he was more complex than she first thought. He wasn't an uneducated, crude gunfighter. Quite the contrary, he had shown character and intelligence, and she found his dynamic presence difficult to dispel from her mind.

Fifteen

Rick left the Stardust and paused just outside the door on the boardwalk, settling his hat on his head while he glanced easily up and down the street. While he affected coolness, he knew clearly that the hired guns were still out there. The border between Texas and New Mexico was crawling with gunmen who could be bought by Zel. There was only one thing to do as he saw it. Return and settle it with Zel himself.

Time…he didn't have a lot of it. He saw no one suspicious, but that didn't mean they weren't there, behind buildings, second-story windows, or lying low on a roof. What he did see was just a busy, growing town with prosperous folks going about their everyday business.

He thought of Elmira again. She had been eavesdropping on him and Callie. An odd woman. Was she merely the prickly busy-body she looked? Those dark eyes were as cold as any he'd seen facing him across the muzzle of a gun. Who was she?

He saw Jimmy running toward him on the boardwalk. *Nice boy,* he thought. *Fortunately, he has Samuel in Jack Halliday's absence.* He remembered that while looking out the window in Gordon's newspaper office he'd seen Jimmy running toward the Stardust around the time of the accident. Callie had said she'd sent him and Elmira off somewhere together and had planned to meet them for lunch. Yet, when he'd seen Jimmy he'd been alone. Rick couldn't recall seeing Elmira around.

Jimmy spotted him and was running from the direction of the Halliday Mansion waving his hat to get his attention.

"Rick, wait for me!"

Rick smiled and stopped to oblige him.

Jimmy ran up breathless "News!" he cried.

"Again?" Rick teased. "Don't you ever run out of news?"

"No, sir!"

"You're a born newspaperman, Jimmy. But didn't Callie ask you to go keep your aunt company?"

"Aunt Weda don't need no company," he scoffed.

"*Doesn't* need *any* company."

"That's what I said, Rick. She don't need any. She's busy with Keeper. She does most of the looking after her now. Keeper's got five mouths to feed. And that's a mighty big family. So Aunt Weda's busy."

Rick gave him a slanted look. "Keeper? Five mouths to feed?"

Jimmy grinned. "My cat. I brought her all the way from Sacramento. Annalee let me. She's got five babies now—not Annalee—Keeper does. Know what I'm namin' 'em?"

"No, why don't you tell me."

"I'm using some names of the silver mines: "Ophir, Yellow Jacket, Savage, Confidence, and Union," and he puckered his brow. "Except I think I'm going to change that last one to the Kentuck mine."

Rick smiled. "Those are all good names…even Union. I've been wondering, Jimmy. Where were you when you found out the chandelier fell?"

Jimmy pushed his hat back, and stood the way Delance did, one hand on his hip and narrowed eyes. Then turning, he pointed back down the street. "Parkers. I was aiming to buy a sarsaparilla. Callie told Miss Elmira I could have one. But there was a big ginger cookie there, too. I could only have one of 'em, so I was thinking hard."

"Don't blame you."

"That's when I saw Smiley run by the window. He looked upset some. So I figured he was headed for the Stardust. I looked out Parker's window. That's when I saw the other theater folks standing around down by the door. One lady, the one with red hair, I think she's Mary. She was raising both hands in the air. It looked like something exciting happened. So I ran there to see."

"So you left Miss Elmira inside Parker's place?"

Jimmy shook his head. "No, she wasn't there."

"Where was she?"

"Next door at Wilson's Dry Goods. Said she wanted to talk to Mrs. Wilson about buying cloth for a new bonnet or something." Jimmy's eyes took on a curious glow. "Why?"

The boy was alert and too smart for his own good. If Rick wasn't careful, he'd soon have Jimmy spying on Elmira—not a good idea.

"I suppose you took a long time deciding between the sarsaparilla and the ginger cookie."

"How did you know that?"

"I sort of remember what boys are like."

"Girls, too. Even old ladies like Miss Elmira. She took a long time, too. That's why I wasn't hurrying on my decision."

"I sort of figured that. She probably never got that cloth, did she?"

"Nope," Jimmy looked at him, "I know because there wasn't any package in the buggy. She's up at the house now waiting for Uncle Samuel."

Rick said nothing. Jimmy grabbed his hat off his head. "I never got the sarsaparilla or the cookie. Miss Elmira had the money Callie gave her to buy me something... Now I remember what I was supposed to tell you, Rick. Uncle Samuel just rode in from Carson, but he's not at the house where Elmira can find him. I told him what happened, so he wants to see you right away."

"Where is he?"

"Flint's cabin."

"Here, go get that sarsaparilla and the ginger cookie." He handed him a coin.

Jimmy grinned. "Thanks, Rick!"

Flint Harper's cabin was back from F Street near the site of the Ophir Mine Works and Boot Hill, a fact Elmo liked to rib him about.

"Never you mind, Elmo. A fella's got to get a square foot of property wherever he can get it," was Flint's usual comment.

Smoke was coming from the cabin's chimney. Rick saw the spotted mule Samuel always rode tied to a hitching-rail outside the crooked porch, but Flint's horse and mule weren't there. Why had Samuel come here?

He pulled up, swung down, and tied his stallion. The door was ajar. Even though he had no reason to think anything suspicious, Delance was cautious. He loosed the thong on his six-shooter then walked a half circle to reach the door. He eased it open with his boot.

"That you, Delance?" Samuel called out.

Rick stepped inside and saw Samuel making coffee on a stone hearth with a small fire. Samuel looked at him over a broad shoulder.

"Where's Flint?" Rick asked.

"Dayton. He went there yesterday to sell his mules. Should be back any time now. Don't worry. All's well, far as I know. I just thought this was a better place to discuss our problems than the house."

Rick shut the door and removed his hat, eying him curiously. "Were you thinking of Elmira?"

Samuel's bushy black brows climbed with obvious surprise. "You met her?"

"I just left the Stardust." He told him of Elmira listening outside Callie's dressing room.

"It was Ashe who wanted Callie to hire her," Samuel said.

Rick didn't appreciate the news.

"Maybe I'd better talk to Callie about her. Here, have a seat, Rick, and have some coffee. I had my meeting with Stewart in Carson about the lawyer Ashe recommended—that O'Brien. There's a few things I thought you should know." Samuel pulled back his chair and sat down as Rick filled a cup with hot coffee.

"What did Bill Stewart say?"

"First, better read this. He took a folded paper from his black frock coat and handed it to him across the small table with a checkered cloth cover. "Stewart said to give this to you. It's a wire from Brett."

Rick took it and spread it open.

Delance,

An attempt was made to kill your father's lawyer, Clay Billings. He was shot while riding from Santa Fe to talk to Tom

Hardy. Two riders from Dan Ferguson's ranch found him on the trail half dead and brought him in. I think he's a marked man on his own. I brought him to the house, and my father has him recovering. Billings is anxious to talk to you about your father's will. I advise you to come to Santa Fe as soon as you can.

B. Wilder

Samuel must have noticed his concern for he watched him alertly.

"Anything I should know about, lad?"

"Clay Billings was shot. He's recovering at Brett's place."

He told Samuel for the first time about the Triple D and what had happened there and on the cattle drive five years earlier. When he finished he felt better.

"So that's the gist of it, is it? Brett told me some of it—it's worse than I heard. Both your pa and your brother…that's a bitter pill to swallow." He shook his large dark head smattered with hair of silver-gray and stroked his drooping mustache.

"I wonder about that sudden sickness you say struck the Triple D's cowhands. Seems to me it might have been easy enough to put something in the chuck-wagon grub to bring it on."

"Elmo would be a mite upset if I hinted someone got by him to his stew, but you're right. I'd thought before that someone could've done it, and so did my father. But by then, Alex had taken Bodene's crew out of Texas. The doc sure didn't have a clue what was wrong with any of them."

He decided to tell Samuel about the other property that his father had left him.

After he was done, Samuel looked at him carefully. "You still have your best years, lad. You're wise to go back and claim what's yours. Begin a new life. I'll be praying for you, too. Evil must not triumph. But neither must man's revenge."

Rick drank his coffee. Would he even make it to Santa Fe?

"You were but a lad back then, and probably didn't pay much attention to what your pa owned or his background. Came from France, you say, and a God-fearing man?"

"I have his Bible," Rick said. "He was much like you, except—" he stopped.

Samuel's eyes shone with good humor. He chuckled.

"Except he had some French refinement?"

Rick smiled. "I could use a little myself. These last five years I've left a lot behind."

"Time to find it again. Time go home, lad. Everything has its time the Good Book says. 'A time to be born, and a time to die; a time to plant, and a time to pluck up that which is planted; a time to kill, and a time to heal.' I'd say for you it was God's time to heal, to plant, and to love."

"A time of war, and a time of peace," Rick added from the first chapter of Ecclesiastes. "For me it's been mostly war, but I'd take peace—if it came after justice."

"You're right, lad. There's no compromising with evil and calling it peace. Men will say, 'Peace, peace,' when there is no peace. You can't have peace by surrendering righteous principles. Billings is a respected man in Santa Fe. This attempt on his life will alert other good men thereabouts, including Wilder. That helps your cause. You'll want to take the Triple D back and turn it into something wholesome. A place you can be proud of rebuilding and raising a new generation on. God is a God of mercy and grace, but also of justice and holiness. You do what's right under the law, and leave the outcome to God. Vengeance belongs to Him alone. The wicked He will surely judge."

Rick stared into his coffee mug and was silent for a while. Outside the cabin, the wind stirred restlessly.

"I've been feeling God calling me to Him for a long time, and mostly since I met you and Wilder. I guess He brought us together. Though I sure wouldn't have thought so when Hoadly wanted me to come to Virginia Town as a hired gun. Flint's helped, too. Even Elmo. He's stayed faithful to me all these years."

"I know Elmo's got a Texas-sized place in his heart for you, lad."

"Something's awakened in me that's been long asleep—asleep since I left the Triple D. I thought my heart had become too hardened to have the faith I had as a boy, looking up at the New

Mexico stars on a clear night...but that faith in Christ...is still there."

Samuel leaned across the table, his eyes earnest. "The Lord never gives up on His own. Remember how God told Israel through Isaiah: 'Can a woman forget her sucking child, that she should not have compassion on the son of her womb? Yea, they may forget, yet will I not forget thee. Behold, I have graven thee upon the palms of my hands.' Now, think of those nail prints in Christ's palms while He is ever living up yonder at the Father's right hand to make intercession for us."

The sound of an approaching horse broke off their discussion. Rick stood and walked to the window.

"It's all right. It's Flint."

Flint Harper dismounted and walked briskly toward the cabin door.

"Howdy. Stage came in a short while ago. Thought you'd like to know Callie's Stardust partner is in town."

Rick glanced at Samuel and saw the concern.

"It's Hugh Ralston," Samuel stated.

"Ashe and Smiley, the stage manager, met him at the depot. Took him to the International."

"I'll introduce myself to him tomorrow," Samuel said.

"Recognize him, Flint?" Rick asked. "I'm growing mighty curious about Hugh Ralston."

Flint poured coffee, and tasted it too thoughtfully. He rubbed his brow. "I've been in these parts a long while. Long before Ol' Virginny and Comstock discovered the Mother Lode, but can't say I recognized him."

"Okay," Rick commented. It was time to let Samuel know what he'd learned from Mr. Simmons, the banker, and Neil Howard. He knew it would add to his concerns.

"Gordon Barkly's dug up information on both Ashe and Hugh that may be enough to turn Callie around, but you're the best one to tell her, Samuel."

Rick explained about Dylan Harkin lending money to Ashe and Ralston. "It's really Dylan who holds the deed on half the Stardust. If it came to it, and Ralston couldn't pay what he owes, half the Stardust would become Dylan's."

Samuel looked dismayed.

"Now if that don't take all," Flint said.

Samuel paced the small cabin, rubbing his whiskered chin and shaking his head.

"Neil Howard was a stage manager in Chicago years ago," Rick continued. "He claims Ashe was fired in New York for showing up on stage drunk. He gambled, as well. You can understand why I didn't tell this to Callie today. Coming from me, she'd not likely accept it."

Samuel sank into his chair. All the energy that made him such a vibrant minister seemed to be drained from him by disappointment.

"This is a matter for earnest prayer. There must be something the Lord would have me say to get through to her."

Rick casually picked up his cup and refilled it. "I don't think she's really in love with Ashe."

Rick was aware that Flint was looking at him.

"She's enamored with his stardom and the idea of going to Broadway."

"The world, the flesh, and the devil," Samuel murmured to himself. "Satan doesn't need to come up with new lies to deceive us with. The old ones work in every generation. All he has to do is change their style. Broadway! Fame! The adulation of fickle crowds." He shook his head sadly. "You're probably right about how she feels about Ashe. I've thought for some time she's searching for something that's missing in how she feels about herself. I guessed that were the case when she sank so much money in having the house built out near the Savage place. There was better property for building farther out of town, but her house had to be next door to the Savage family, one of the wealthiest in Virginia City."

"Don't see that it matters much now," Flint spoke up. "She's not going to live there. She's going to New York."

"Not if I can help it," Samuel said. "And not if the Lord does something to open her eyes."

"I've been wondering about Dylan Harkin," Rick said. "No one has seen him since that night over a year ago."

He told them of Neil's strange encounter with Dylan the night he left town.

"Wasn't Colefax interested in the theater?" Flint asked Samuel.

Samuel's frown deepened. "I think you're right. Colefax is a slippery eel, always in the shadows. Even when Macklin was alive and running things, Colefax spent most of his time in Frisco."

Odd, Rick thought again. "He was never here in Virginia City?"

"He was supposed to be from time to time. Even had an office—or so Macklin implied. Yet after Macklin came to town Colefax wasn't heard of again. And once the tragic shootings over at the Virginia House Hotel took place, even the name of Colefax dropped from my hearing. Least nobody seems to know where he is."

"Just like Dylan Harkin," Rick commented, still puzzling over things.

"Maybe they're both in Frisco," Flint suggested.

"Colefax is doing a fair job of keeping undercover," Samuel said. "The law couldn't find him after Macklin's death. Brett looked for him after he and Annalee went to Grass Valley for a spell. No one could say where he was. His house was empty. The house servants told Brett they hadn't seen Colefax in six or seven months. A mysterious fellow."

"Meaning, he could've lit out of here," Flint said. "He might've turned on Macklin before the showdown with Jack and gone back to where he came from, somewhere in the East, wasn't it, Samuel?"

"Chicago, I think it was."

Rick looked up. *Chicago?*

"Maybe Macklin did Colefax in?" Flint said.

"To gain full control of the Pelly-Jessup Mine?" Rick asked thoughtfully. He turned to Samuel. "Between the two of them they own the majority of shares don't they?"

"They do. And scheming all the while, too," Samuel said. "Macklin and Colefax both knew the Pelly-Jessup was busted, and they were the first to start selling their stock. When the news got out, the investors quickly dumped their stock for pennies. But Macklin and Colefax had something up their sleeve. They bought the stock up cheap. Macklin's plan was to also gain control of the adjacent mine, the Halliday-Harkin, then claim the Pelly-Jessup had struck a bonanza and resell their stock sky-high. But Frank Harkin wouldn't sell. So he hired Hoadly to kill him. Colefax was the false witness, saying he'd seen Jack shoot Frank in the back."

The Pelly-Jessup... Rick hadn't given the mine much thought recently, nor had anyone else as far as he knew.

"Who owns the mine now?" Rick asked Samuel.

"I think Colefax still owns his shares. But the mine is closed down now. There's no excavating at all.

"Let me tell you what I learned in Carson," Samuel said. "Stewart tells me he's never heard of a lawyer named O'Brien. If Callie won't take my word for things, I've a mind to let Bill Stewart talk to her."

"Maybe you ought to question Ashe Perry as well."

"I've thought of that. If Callie finds out I went over her head though, she'll harden her attitude. I should tread softly where that lass is concerned."

Rick noticed the sadness in Samuel's eyes.

Samuel caught up his big black hat from the peg and went to the door. "I'll talk to Callie tonight," he told Rick soberly and left the cabin.

After the sound of Samuel's mule faded, Flint spun the chair around and straddled it, resting his arms on the backrest, coffee mug in hand.

Rick leaned back in his chair with his hands clasped behind his dark head, musing.

"Wait till Callie finds out Ashe is partners with Dylan Harkin," Flint said. "She ain't going to appreciate that. Say, Saturday night's the big opening at the Stardust. You going?"

Rick hadn't decided. Though he was curious to see how good Callie actually was. "Don't know if I will."

"Might as well come with me and Gordon. He's got a box in the theater and invited us both to join him. If you wear a coat right, no one's going to notice your bandage. Do you some good to get out and away from your own trouble for awhile. Let's take Gordon up on that invitation. I'm anxious to see Callie on stage. This is the first time she's played Virginia City since she left here a year ago."

Rick remembered, but he hadn't gone to see her back then either. Truth was, he didn't like the idea of her on the stage with every male in town noticing how beautiful she was. That was another difference between himself and Ashe, who must want her under the spotlight.

"What time?"

"Around eight. Meet me out front of the Stardust."

Rick wanted to get back to Threesome to see how Elmo was doing. He stood, and taking his hat, drifted to the door. "See you on Saturday." Rick lifted a hand, and went out. He mounted his dun and rode off toward Gold Canyon.

The wind had come up in the canyon, blowing dust devils and tumbleweeds. He pondered the twists and turns of all that was happening as he rode. There was much to think about, and it was getting difficult to separate speculation from suspicion.

Sixteen

☙

*C*allie scowled down at her new gilded slippers, chosen for Saturday night, and wondered crossly how she would ever manage to get her swollen foot inside. Of all the times an accident had to happen, why just a few days before her crowning moment at the Stardust? She heaved a sigh and dropped the shoe on the carpeted floor.

"It won't do, Aunt Weda. Unless the swelling goes down soon I'll never be able to get it on."

"Balderdash, girl, who's going to see your slippers anyhow? Nothing shows under that hemline. And I still say that dress is too daring to wear in public."

Callie ignored the frail lady who stood with hands on hips looking down on Callie's four-poster bed where a grand, shimmering, turquoise watered-silk ball dress lay, its wide skirt covering most of the coverlet.

"Don't be so old-fashioned, Auntie. It's a perfectly gorgeous dress, and Ashe adores it."

"Ashe, Ashe. Fiddlesticks! That other young man makes two of him. Don't see why you don't realize it."

Callie raised her dark brows. "I admit he's very good-looking...dynamic, actually, but hardly a gentleman, Auntie. Anyway, I didn't think you liked Rick Delance." She turned to the mirror and smoothed her dark hair into place.

"Rick Delance my foot! That gunslinger? I wasn't talking about him. I was thinking of that nice young man, Flint Harper."

"Oh." Callie avoided her eyes in the mirror, knowing she'd give her real feelings away about Rick if she looked at Weda.

"Flint's all right. But I've no interest in mules."

"You silly girl. Is that all you can see in Flint is his mule train?"

Callie smiled. "Of course not. He's nice. But I think of him as a friend, not as...well, as someone I'd like to stroll in the moonlight with."

"Well you stay away from Delance or I'll—"

There was a knock on the door, and Weda went to answer it.

Uncle Samuel entered and stood, his face lined with care. Callie thought it must be due to the chandelier incident, so she smiled brightly.

"Hello, Uncle, I'm fine, so I hope Jimmy didn't bring you wild tales about the accident. How do you like my new ball gown for opening night?"

But was it just an accident? Certainly Rick didn't think so. The last thing she wanted though, was for Samuel to think otherwise.

"I told her it's too bold," Aunt Weda complained. "Look at it, Sammy. Land sakes, I never heard of Jenny Lind or Lottie Crabtree dressing like this."

"Very pretty dress, lass, I hear you got sapphires from Ashe to go with it."

Callie felt the heat start up in her cheeks. Now it was coming. She'd dreaded this moment. Now she had to tell him and Weda that she was wearing Ashe's engagement ring and would marry him in Santa Fe. *Drat that Jimmy!* He must have tattled to Samuel about the ring on her finger.

"Sapphires?" Aunt Weda looked with shock from Samuel to Callie and then back to Samuel again. "What on earth—?"

But Uncle Samuel remained grave, and said quietly to Weda, "Not now, Weda, if you will. I'd like to talk to Callie alone. Callie, can you come downstairs?"

Callie was surprised by his manner, and it sobered her.

"Of course, Uncle."

Even Aunt Weda looked puzzled and concerned, studying Samuel with a frown. "I hope everything's all right," she began, but Samuel patted the older lady on her silver head as though she were a little girl and smiled.

"Why don't you tell Mrs. Elmira to start thinking of setting dinner out?"

"Elmira? Serve supper? Huh! That woman couldn't find a teakettle from a frying pan if Paiutes surrounded the house. *I'll* stay in charge of my own kitchen, thank you. Now don't be late, neither of you. That roast beef will dry out if it sets too long. I'd better send Elmira to hunt down Jimmy. *That boy!* He can't stay put in one place any longer than a grasshopper." She fussed her way out of Callie's bedroom and went downstairs, calling for Elmira and Jimmy both. Samuel followed her.

Callie stood there, perplexed. Something told her things were not going to be pleasant with Uncle Samuel. She raised her left hand and looked at the glittering blue stones. She bit her lip. She had better be prepared to hold her ground. She hated disappointing him, but there was just no other way to get around this. She was going to New York to star on Broadway, and *nothing* was going to stop her.

A few minutes later, having changed into a sedate late-afternoon dress, hoping to make Samuel think she was meek and mild, she came down the winding staircase and walked into the parlor.

Samuel waited with hat and frock coat on. "It's a pretty evening out," he said, "I thought we'd go for a little walk while Weda sets dinner out."

"All right," she said casually. "But I can't walk far. My ankle is swollen."

"Oh, well, lass, I didn't know. Then we'll talk here so you'll be comfortable." He frowned. "Thank God He had you move out of the way of that heavy chandelier in time. It's written that the angel of the Lord encamps around those who trust in Him and delivers them."

"I can walk a little," she insisted, wanting to get out of the house. She still didn't fully trust Elmira to not be snooping. Anything spoken between her and Samuel would be done without Elmira hovering nearby. "There's a pink sunset over the mountains. Let's just walk to the pepper tree."

"All right, if you're sure, lass. You can take my arm for support. Besides, it's been a long while since I walked with my girl."

The pink was turning into lavender as they strolled through the gate onto the dirt road. Virginia City was still bustling, and she heard the familiar stamp mills and the sound of the ore wagons grating on the tracks as they were hauled from nearby Gould & Curry and the Savage Mine Works. She felt her tension mounting in the muscles behind her shoulders. What was Samuel going to say to thwart her plans now?

"This time together brings me no pleasure, Callie. I wish we were on more pleasant terms. I know you're impatient with me. You see me as domineering, trying to keep you from plans that will bring you fulfillment."

She kept her silence, but her breathing was uncomfortable.

"Yet it's my duty and my affection for you that prompts me to speak out now."

Still she kept silent.

He sighed. "Are you going to let me speak my mind?"

"I'm listening," she said, her tone defensive.

"You're as prickly as a cactus apple."

"Because I already know what you're going to tell me."

"I don't think you do know, not fully."

"It's about Ashe Perry. You don't like him."

"It's about Ashe—and Hugh Ralston. And you need to know and pray about them both before you go through with your plans to marry Ashe."

Her heart beat faster with a rise of temper.

"Gordon, again. He came to the Stardust this morning and hurled lies and insults about Ashe. I don't want to hear them again."

"It was Rick Delance who came to me about this, lass. Did you know Hugh Ralston got his money to partner with you in the Stardust from a loan from Dylan Harkin? Dylan loaned money to Ashe, as well, to begin the Perry-Ralston Theater Company. Did either man tell you this before you went into partnership with them? I can see by your face they didn't. Marriage is a lifetime commitment, Callie. You've got to know the man you're committing your loyalty to through and through before you go off with him to New York. No matter how bright the lights or how starry-eyed you feel for the short-haul, the long-haul can get you into the dark pit of unhappiness. But by then it'll be too late. With a child on the way, another life will be affected by your actions. Have you considered all this?"

That was the last thing she wanted to think about. It was stardom and bright lights, exciting dinner houses, beautiful clothes, and adventurous people that she was interested in.

"Who wants to think about marital squabbles, morning sickness, and diapers?" she said wearily.

"How would you like it if Ashe didn't come home until late at night on one of those long, tiring days that started out with morning sickness? And then when he came home to you after losing his wages in the gambling dens of New York, he was full of liquor to boot?"

She stopped and looked at him horrified and then indignant. *"Uncle Samuel!"*

He looked sheepish. "I'm sorry, lass, I hate talkin' like this, but I love you too much not to talk. You need to ask yourself and Ashe, why and how he and Ralston know Dylan. You need to ask him if he drinks—how often, how much, and why he needs it. Your pa had those same two weaknesses of drinking and gambling, and you don't want to marry the same kind of man like Lilly did. Later on she regretted it and grieved because despite it all, she loved him."

Callie stared at him, shaking her head, a cold feeling stealing over her and turning her stomach. *No. No not like Pa—*

Stunned, she could not answer. They had stopped on the road near the pepper tree, and her uncle was looking down at her with a worried face.

"I think you'd better explain those claims, Uncle. Do you know what you're saying?"

"I do. Ashe was fired from a theater in New York for showing up with too much liquor under his belt. And he's been known to gamble at times...like your pa."

Callie's emotions reeled from the blow of his words. Her eyes searched his, looking for the same faults she'd seen in Gordon— pride, anger—but they weren't there. The man before her could not be dismissed the way she'd dismissed Gordon. There was no doubt in her mind that her uncle was a decent and godly man who would not knowingly spread malicious rumors.

Then surely Samuel must be mistaken. Rick Delance had told him this. Rick was not the least like Gordon Barkly, but should she believe the gunfighter?

"Where did Rick get this damaging information? From Gordon?"

"He talked to Gordon, yes—"

"You see?" she cried jubilantly. "Lies, Uncle!"

"But Rick also talked to Neil Howard at the Virginia Opry Theater and Mr. Simmons at the San Francisco-Nevada Bank. Callie, I talked to Ashe in the buggy the night we drove out to take care of Rick after that gunfight out in the Canyon. I don't have any reason to think Ashe is a Christian. You saw the way he behaved that night when I spoke to Elmo. He didn't like the talk about our Savior one little bit."

"Yes, I saw, but it was because you were going on and on, and he had other things to worry about."

"I'm not taking credit for being the most flowery preacher around, and I'm sure my rough ways and speech might rub gents like Ashe the wrong way sometimes. But truth is truth. He could hardly be civil. If a man adores Jesus Christ, he's not going to get like an angry bull when the Lord's truths are explained—especially after Elmo nearly got a bullet through his head, but for the grace of God."

Callie shook her head in frustration. "Uncle, you're not being fair with Ashe or me. He does believe. He said so in San Francisco. He's just not vocal like you are."

"He's blessed with more vocal ability than me. Made a half dozen excuses, too, for not coming to worship on Sundays. It's clear, he's not comfortable talking to the Lord. How's he going to encourage you spiritually when you're down or afraid? Does he know enough Scripture to be a balm of Gilead?"

She closed her lips tightly. "I know enough for both of us."

"A man ought to know it for himself, in his own heart. It's God's way to direct his paths."

"Uncle, you can't just lay down the law for me and dictate my life. I don't *want* to live that old-fashioned way. I want to be free to do as I please."

"Without Jesus? Without His grace and mercy and strength guiding you, protecting you, forming you into the young woman He desires you to be?"

Callie felt her face turn hot. "That's totally unfair. You're trying to make me feel guilty."

"It's the last thing I want, lass."

"You want to shame me into submitting to your plans…and Aunt Weda's. You're ganging up on Ashe and spreading lies started by Gordon. Gordon is worse than a spy! Who is he to go around digging up dirt on everyone he doesn't like?"

"I don't know about Gordon. I'm not defending him. But if some of this is true, don't you want to know it before you pledge yourself to Ashe before God and man with your wedding vows?"

She refused to answer; it only would trap her. "Why should I trust what Rick Delance says? Rick's a gunfighter!" she accused. "He came to Virginia City to work for Cousin Macklin. Have you forgotten that? A hired gun, that's what Delance is."

"I haven't forgotten why he first came here," Samuel said. "But that's not the kind of man Delance is. He didn't draw a gun for Macklin. He stood beside Brett who was alone against several killers. That tells me what Delance is made of."

She knew that was true, nor did she even have a bone of contention to fight about Rick. She had only brought up his being a gunfighter because she needed something, anything, to hurl back in defense of Ashe and herself.

"I'll talk to Rick," she said stiffly. "Where is he?"

"Out at Threesome. But there's something else you should know about Delance—something I only learned today. He has a reason for carrying those guns, Callie."

"I know that. I'd be blind not to know men are trying to kill him and Elmo. But he's the one who chose to ride with gunfighters. You're always quick to say a man reaps what he sows. There's probably some personal quarrel between the whole passel of them, Rick included."

"You're right. But it's because he's tracking some cold-blooded killers who shot his pa and his brother, Alex, in New Mexico. Kidnapped a girl, too, and left her dead somewhere in the border country. They rustled the Delance cattle, and Elmo saw them kill Rick's older brother. Elmo barely escaped with his life. The crooks burned down the Delance ranch and shot all the hands in the bunkhouse. They would have killed Rick, a sixteen-year-old kid, if they could have found him. It's to his credit he's been able to escape them these five years. Cesar, the gunslinger who ambushed him was one of them. There's two others in town somewhere. And more back in Santa Fe. Yes, he swore vengeance. He's been tracking them ever since. He's killed two of them, but only after they drew on him.

"We had a talk today at Flint's cabin. And unlike Ashe Perry, I'm convinced Rick is not only a believer in Christ, but he's willing to trust God with his life now. He's tired of fighting. He's doing it now only because he has to—there's no other way when mad dogs are ready to spring and sink their teeth into you. You gotta defend yourself. You won't find a young man with an ounce more courage."

Callie digested all this in astute silence. Against her will her heart softened toward Rick, and that reaction worried her. Now he was more intriguing than ever, and she grudgingly admired him. Sixteen years old when all that had happened to him!

"I didn't know," she said after a minute.

"Nor did I. But Brett Wilder always had the idea that Rick was deserving a better reputation than he'd gotten on the trail he rode all these years."

She remembered Brett once saying he thought Rick Delance had come from a finer family than he bore witness to with his lifestyle. But no matter what Rick was or wasn't, she was going to New York with Ashe to star in a play on Broadway. It was her dream, her burning desire, to excel at what she wanted most in life—and no one was going to shut the door on her now. But she knew it would be wiser to not continue to argue with Uncle Samuel now.

"I've got to think about all this, Uncle. I want to talk to Rick, and I want to talk to Ashe about this, too. And that includes the loan you say he received from Dylan Harkin. There's some mistake. There has to be. And I won't let misunderstandings and lies ruin my plans or Ashe's reputation. I want the truth."

"That you can have, lass. You go ahead and talk to Delance and Ashe Perry. I hear Hugh Ralston's in town now, staying over at the International. You can have a chat with him, too. I wouldn't be tellin' you to ask around if I didn't want you to know the truth in this matter. But the most important truths are from God's Word, little one. It cannot be broken by our willful desires, it can only be disobeyed to our hurt. And that grieves God who loves you dearly and wants the best for your life. 'Be ye not unequally yoked together,' the Scripture tells us. That admonition is for our best good."

Callie said nothing, and felt the thud of her heart as his words echoed. She refused to meet his gaze, though she saw only love and grief in his eyes. She refused to respond to his affectionate hand on her shoulder. He stood there sadly, looking down at her, the evening wind tossing his frock coat and dark, silver-tipped hair. The cross someone had made for him out of a piece of silver hung on a chain around his neck, glinting upon his gray cotton shirt. Yet her spirit rebelled and yearned to break away.

She was tired of Uncle Samuel and Aunt Weda. She didn't want to hear words that battled her desires.

Samuel patted her shoulder. "We best go back. Weda's probably got dinner on the table by now."

"I'm no longer hungry, Uncle. I want to be alone for awhile."

"All right. Can you get back on that foot?"

She nodded.

"I'm sorry, lass, this conversation's brought me no pleasure. It's a grief to me as it is to you."

She kept silent. He turned and walked back to the house.

Callie stood there alone in the wind, her emotions like a corraled wild mustang anxious to leap the rails. There was an old tree stump near the side of the road, and she sat down on it glumly. She looked down at the sapphire engagement ring. Her feelings welled up like a volcano.

Was it Ashe Perry or was it a career on Broadway that she really wanted...and was Ashe just the ticket to get there?

Rick Delance...she would ride out to Threesome in the morning to confront him face to face. He was to blame for upsetting Samuel. If he'd minded his own business and not gone to him with tales about Ashe, this confrontation with Samuel wouldn't have happened.

But was it true about Dylan Harkin? She could go straight to Ashe and confront him, but why cause stress between them when the charges could be false? No, she'd confront Rick first.

Early the next morning Callie got up, changed into her blue riding habit, and saddled her dappled mare for the trip out to Gold Canyon. The golden daybreak showed streaks of orangy-yellow clouds. As usual, the wind was shaking the sagebrush against tan hills and whitish rock. If she wished to admit it, the West was, in some ways, a beautiful land, and this part of it she would miss.

Threesome Mine was three miles from the Halliday-Harkin and the Pelly-Jessup, though no one much bothered talking about the Pelly-Jessup anymore. It was closed down as far as she knew. It had also been a long while since she'd been out to the family mine, and she wondered how things were progressing there. The silver couldn't last forever, but how long the bonanza would run was anyone's guess. She was due to talk to Hugh Ralston about the lawyer he'd recommended to Ashe to handle the sale of her part of the mine. That must wait.

What Uncle Samuel had said yesterday evening about Dylan lending money to Hugh and Ashe just didn't make sense to her. She drew her brows together and leaned forward, urging her horse to go a little faster. She tried to remember the last time she'd seen Dylan Harkin but couldn't place him. He'd been a hot-headed troublemaker when he'd wanted to hunt down her father, wrongly thinking that he'd shot Dylan's brother Frank to get the mine. As far as she knew Dylan had left Virginia City the night Pa was killed. But he must be getting his money from the mine. No man would turn his back on such a fortune.

Her frown deepened. A sign read, "Threesome Mine." She turned off the main canyon road to a trail on a hill with rocky fragments at its base. The trail climbed as the wind tossed her hair beneath her stylish blue straw hat tied beneath her chin. As she rode around a small bend in the hill a voice surprised her: "You alone, miss?"

She drew rein and looked up to see a guard with a shotgun looking down at her.

"I've come to see Rick Delance. Is he here?"

The young man grinned and said something in a low voice to a second man, who came up beside him. They smiled at each other, then looked down at her. By this time Callie felt her face warming.

"On business," she said loftily.

"Yes, ma'am, he's here...fact is, he's *right* here. Hey, Delance. You got yourself company."

"Who is it?"

Callie recognized Rick's voice from just behind them.

"Better have a look for yourself," one of them said.

Callie stiffened as Rick came into view above her. He wore a poncho, hat, and leather jerkins, the way she'd first seen him in Virginia City, and he was loaded with weapons. He wore his gunbelt and held a rifle. He must have been surprised to see her, for a moment he didn't speak, then he simply nodded to her and turned back from the ledge of the hill and disappeared. For a short time she waited until she saw him riding around the hill on his horse. She sat with dignity while he maneuvered his horse beside hers.

She remembered that when she'd first met him, she had thought him a determined and ruthless young wolf; she could still sense it. He wanted something in life he did not yet possess, and it seemed he was at conflict with everything around him, including, perhaps, himself. But, she quickly realized, that could also be said about herself.

Now, after what Samuel had told her of his past, she thought she understood him better.

He smiled, somewhat rakishly, she thought, and his dark eyes showed appreciation.

"What a pleasant surprise. Or am I jumping to conclusions about the warmth in your eyes...?"

She met his gaze evenly, managing to hold her own. "When I told your two gunslingers up there that this was business, that's precisely what I meant."

He looked over his shoulder at the two young men farther back on the hill watching the surroundings. Rick lowered his hat a little.

"One's a Reb and the other a Yankee, but I don't think we could call 'em gunslingers, ma'am."

"Whatever you prefer," she said coolly, refusing to step back from confrontation.

"I see you're in a harmonious mood this morning. You must have talked with Samuel. Did he tell you about Dylan lending Ashe and Hugh money?"

"He told me. And it's a lie."

His gaze was steady. "Is it? You're sure?"

"Where can we talk?"

"You can come to the cabin—if you promise to be civil."

Her eyes narrowed over his amused gravity.

"I heard how you cuffed Gordon when you got mad at him," he drawled. "I'm defenseless and wouldn't want you to get overly riled with me."

"I would not step a foot into your cabin."

He smiled. "Elmo's there. Want some coffee?"

"No. And I don't care if Elmo's there or not. This is not a pleasant call."

"So I gather. All right. We'll ride." He turned his horse and rode past her to the path around the hill. She followed, and in a few minutes they came onto a trail that wound between some elm trees. The green leaves rippled in the wind and made a softly rushing sound that soothed her nerves. Rick turned his dun up into the trees and rode up following the slope to a mound where there was grass and a small creek trickling over smooth stones. He started to ride on.

"This is far enough," she called.

He obliged her and walked his horse beneath an elm.

She brought her horse toward him until they faced across from each other, holding their mounts.

He looked inquiringly at her. The silence between them lengthened until she dragged her eyes from his to look down at the creek.

"I'm listening," he said. "Go on. Tell me how wonderful Ashe Perry is. Tell me what a lowdown gunfighter I am, trying to make trouble for you and destroy your dreams."

Her eyes came quickly to his and for a moment she couldn't speak as a strange confusion fell over her. For at this moment it wasn't Ashe that she was aware of, but Rick Delance.

Seventeen

*C*allie faced Rick, hearing the elm leaves above their heads rustling in a windy dance.

"I'll come right to the point," Rick said. "Samuel would have told you by now how you're apt to be making a mistake about Ashe Perry. He's not the man you think he is."

"That, Rick Delance, should be of little concern to you. But I can see you've joined forces with Gordon Barkly to ruin a gentleman's reputation."

He narrowed his eyes. "I can understand your hesitancy in listening to me, or taking my advice, but when you shun even the counsel of a godly man like Samuel, that doesn't say much for that independent streak of yours. It could lead you straight into more trouble than you've a mind for."

"Oh, really?" She tilted her head.

He pushed his hat back. "Maybe you'd best do a little detective work on your own where Ashe Perry is concerned."

"That's what I'm attempting right now, and so far I've little reason to believe you. It would be a delight to prove both you and Samuel wrong. Yes, Samuel told me what you claimed to be true about Ashe. I suppose you got it from Gordon Barkly," she scoffed. "He already tried filling my mind with lies about Ashe. And now even Samuel's convinced. Gordon has his own inconsiderate motives. He's a newspaperman who's not out for the truth, a gossip writer who likes to get even with people whom he feels threaten him in some way. And that reminds me—it was you who set Gordon onto digging up nasty information about Ashe."

"Yes, ma'am, it was," came his unapologetic reply. "I wanted you to know what he's like under his theater makeup and fancy duds."

Callie was surprised he'd admit it to her and was grudging in her respect.

"I won't argue Gordon can be vicious in his own way," he said. "I've no particular liking for him. I can understand his distress in losing you to a theater star, though. That's twice he's lost out."

"He didn't ever have me to lose." She hurried on. "If you'll recall, he also spread untrue stories about Brett Wilder's land in Grass Valley. Gordon's so-called facts about Ashe getting a loan from Dylan Harkin is absurd. That kind of tale isn't going to change my mind."

"You underrate me, Miss Halliday. I'm not one to accept tales till I do some investigating."

"And have you?" she asked coolly.

"In this case, I have. Gordon's more right than wrong. I have it from a respected source at the San Francisco-Nevada Bank that both Ashe Perry and Hugh Ralston are in a partnership of sorts with Dylan Harkin. I passed that on to your uncle, and he was wise to warn you."

"I'll tell you what I told Samuel. Ashe has been in London and performed before royalty!" She said this with profound dignity in her voice. "He would never move socially among gunfighters."

He looked at her a long moment until his dark gaze caused her to look away.

"I reckon I know well enough your low opinion of men who carry guns."

If she were fair, she'd admit that a reputation with a gun didn't prove Rick Delance to be on the level of Rody Villiers or Dylan Harkin—not after what Samuel told her about the Triple D and his father and brother. She also knew that if Rick and Elmo hadn't been armed when they were attacked near Gold Canyon, both of them would be dead, and men like Cesar would have ridden off, likely to kill again.

She backed off a little. "I don't condemn *every* man who wears a gun. But I think even you'll admit that you have a reputation that is feared among other gunfighters. That speaks for itself." She flipped her reins. "Rody was afraid of you that night."

"Not afraid enough. Rody was overconfident."

"And even Dylan was afraid of you."

"Dylan was afraid of something else that night. He left town by way of a back alley. As far as I know he hasn't been back since. That's what bothers me about Ashe and Hugh Ralston getting big loans from him."

"You still insist on that fabrication? I've told you—"

"I keep wondering what would motivate Dylan to help them out financially. It doesn't make proper sense to me. And if Ashe is so socially above anyone with a gunfighter's reputation, why did he seek finances from somebody as mean and low-down as Dylan Harkin?"

"I tell you there is no reason Ashe would make friends with someone like Dylan."

"Because Ashe Perry is a cultured gentleman."

Callie wondered how so much cynicism could be packed into the word "gentleman."

"But you're forgetting something," he said. "Remember that Dylan owns three times as much of the Halliday-Harkin Mine as you. He can buy a lofty title with his wealth. He should now be able to don the gentleman's pose very effectively."

She thought about Dylan's wealth for the first time in months, and found herself irked by her forgetfulness. Yes, Dylan was heir to all that had belonged to his brother Frank.

"Well, I suppose Dylan might have become a gentleman by now—"

"And there you have a reason why Ashe Perry could suddenly find Dylan to be acceptable company." He smirked. "Not only that," he added, "even I could become a gentleman. All I need is adequate wealth, like a cache of silver. Then if Threesome suddenly hits a bonanza, you would have to change your mind about me."

She knew he only meant to infuriate her by unmasking flaws in her thinking.

"It takes more than money," she insisted defensively, "and I'm sure you know that."

"Yes, and I'm pleased you're beginning to remember, Miss Halliday. Samuel taught you that much after all."

"Never mind Samuel. It's Ashe we're talking about...and Dylan. Ashe doesn't know him. Nor does Hugh."

"You're sure of that?"

"Yes," she said impulsively, then was immediately aware she may have fallen into a trap.

"What if there's proof of that loan I mentioned? Since you won't take my word about this, go down to the San Francisco-Nevada Bank and talk to a man named Simmons. Another thing, Neil Howard got his start in the theater working as stage manager in Chicago. Ashe was working for Neil at the time. It's Neil who says Ashe's character is lacking. "

She saw sobriety in Rick's eyes and grew quiet. She knew Neil Howard, who owned the Virginia Opry Theater. She had gotten her first acting role there when Mr. Hill had worked as Neil's manager.

"The question that I'd like answered is how either of 'em met Dylan. Don't you find it strange he's not shown up in town to check on the progress of his own mine?"

Now that Rick mentioned it, yes. She must admit—to herself anyway—that she'd not given Dylan a second thought since that night her father was shot by Macklin. If Rick and Samuel hadn't brought him up now, she wouldn't be thinking of him at all, though he owned half of the same mine that was now filling her bank account and enabling her to be independent.

She pushed the nettlesome thought of Dylan aside.

"Even if that were the case, if there was proof that Ashe knew Dylan and received a loan...well, there would probably still be a respectable explanation."

"Anything to exonerate Ashe," Rick stated. "Your mind's already made up that things must be the way you want them to be. I'd say you won't let the facts interrupt your plans no matter how they stack up against him."

Callie grew mute. He was too close to the truth, and she felt like a glaring light was shining on her.

"I'll tell you what I think of you!"

"I can hardly wait, ma'am." Rick smiled.

"You—you," she sputtered, "are just like all the others of your kind."

"My kind, ma'am?"

"Yes! Your kind—gunslingers! All you know is fighting and killing to settle disputes. But Ashe uses his honor and his intelligence."

"Honor? Then Samuel hasn't brought himself to break your heart and tell you Ashe is a gambler and was fired from a New York theater on Broadway for showing up drunk?"

She snatched her horsewhip, and if she'd been within striking distance she might have tried to smack him with it.

"Your temper needs reining-in, ma'am. You cuffed poor Gordon, and now you threaten me with a horsewhip. Will Ashe be able to control you, using only honor and intelligence?"

"Mock me, will you? At least Ashe doesn't go around mocking… or solving every unpleasant issue he comes up against with guns and violence."

"You don't believe in violence? How about a pretty palm striking like a viper or using a horsewhip?"

Rebuked and frustrated with her short temper, she lowered her hand and let the whip settle against her leg. How ashamed her mother would have been of her recently! She could imagine Lilly's serene face looking at her sadly. It was easy to fault Uncle Samuel and Aunt Weda, but Callie knew well enough that her mother, if she were alive, would be more disappointed in her than anyone else. And she would undoubtedly side with them. Callie hadn't written Annalee yet, either. Her sister, too, with her strong faith in Jesus, would be questioning her as vigorously as Samuel and Rick.

Callie felt her defenses beginning to crumble.

Rick noticed her change in demeanor and turned his horse to ride up beside her.

"I heard about the Triple D and your father and brother," she stated tensely, still affected by her frustration. "Samuel told me yesterday. He thinks well of you."

He smiled. "Maybe Samuel thinks a rancher could handle you a little better than an actor."

She looked at him long and hard, and somehow his boldness and his suggestion did not seem so preposterous. She drew on her acting skills to keep her poise. She smiled.

"Are you proposing to me, Rick Delance?"

He looked at her long and hard. "Maybe."

She drew in a breath and her gloved hand tightened on the pommel. "Maybe?" she repeated in her shock.

"Yes. I've been thinking about it for a long time."

"Have you?" To her infuriation her voice shook.

"I think I'd like to settle down. Go back to Cimarron. Not that I ever planned it in the past, mind you—not until I saw you." His voice softened, as did his gaze. "Why do you think I've been hanging around all this time?"

She was speechless, and suddenly afraid...afraid of the strange emotions stirring unbidden in her heart. He was serious. She could tell he wasn't teasing her. His determination and gravity did more to unnerve her than anything he'd said up till now.

Again, she drew on her acting skills. "How do I know if you'd actually settle down? You're too occupied with your gunslinging. Killing is wrong. The law should handle injustice and murder. Ashe would have let the law deal with the unpleasant issues that happened at the Triple D. But you've taken it upon yourself to hunt the criminals down these years. You'll never settle down and go back to Cimarron—never."

"Is that a challenge?"

Was it? "Maybe."

His eyes warmed her. "You're convinced Ashe wouldn't settle unpleasant issues himself, is that right? What nice words to use to frame the cold-blooded murder of my father, brother, and the hired hands. And I'll wager you're wrong about him in that area as well. Ask him why he carries a sleeve gun. Gamblers carry them. Rody did. Jack Halliday did."

Her energy paled at the mention of her father. She knew he had implied a similarity in the character of her father and Ashe. Jack Halliday, a slick gambler and a gunslinger, represented the very things she now scorned. Her father's addiction to gambling and drink had left her mother with a heavy heart. And her mother had to act in the noisy melodeons of San Francisco to pay the bills and support her children's education. Remembering brought a chill to Callie's skin. It was true about Jack, and perhaps that was the reason she rejected others of similar reputation. But to hang those sinful weaknesses around Ashe's neck was cruel.

"Ask Mr. Perry if he's gambled his assets away in the past," Rick challenged. "Ask him why he left New York in shame. Ask him, Callie, if you really want the truth—and if you can handle it. Because if you don't ask him now, you'll be asking later when it's too late to make a difference in your life." He reached over and took hold of her left hand and slipped off the riding glove. He held her hand so that the blue sapphires twinkled. "Ask him before you exchange these for a diamond wedding ring."

She let out a small cry of anger and tore her glove from his hand. She turned her horse and used the whip on its flank and galloped back down the gently sloping hill toward the trail. She didn't slow her mare until she was back on the road toward Virginia City. She looked back over her shoulder, but the gunman hadn't followed.

Her heart burned. Why did she struggle so hard to defend Ashe when her emotions were also pulling toward Rick with a force too strong to control? Two men, two ways, two very different futures....

As she rode into town it was still early. People were about their daily business along the street—miners were at work, huge wagons were hauling ore from the mines to the mills. She saw the San Francisco-Nevada Bank, and slowed her mare to a walk, her eyes fixed on the brick building.

Is it true about Ashe?

She rested her hand on the saddle horn. What did she have to fear? The truth couldn't destroy her plans for New York. She'd accept Rick's challenge and talk to Mr. Simmons and Neil Howard. She wasn't afraid. She'd prove to Rick she could face anything—even him.

Callie left her horse at the livery stable. First she'd pay a visit to the bank, and then she'd talk to Neil.

She walked outside and looked along the boardwalk to the main part of town toward the bank, and walked there slowly. The sky was blue with few clouds. Her shoes echoed on the board-walk.

When she reached the door she hesitated, her hand on the knob. Then drawing in a deep breath, she entered. If there was anything at all to what Rick and Samuel said, then she'd go to Ashe about it…and maybe even Hugh Ralston. She was to meet Hugh that afternoon, anyway, to discuss turning the Stardust over to him while she and Ashe were in New York. She would also need to discuss the lawyer Hugh had recommended to handle the sale of her portion of the mine. Before the day was over, she would have the facts for herself.

Eighteen

*I*t was noon when Callie left Neil at the Virginia Opry Theater and walked slowly toward the International Hotel, her spirits grim. Mr. Simmons at the bank had backed up what Rick said about Dylan's loan to Ashe. And Neil Howard said he'd known Ashe in Chicago. Even so, she was aware of the fact that the Stardust was in competition with Neil's Virginia Opry Theater. Though Neil seemed like a pleasant enough man, could he be fully trusted?

Stories are often exaggerated, she thought again. *Even what I read in the newspapers has the journalist's own opinions mixed in, as Gordon Barkly demonstrated!* she thought crossly. *Stories can even become embellished and altered.*

She would certainly reserve judgment until she had actually spoken with Ashe. There was no need to do anything too hastily that would threaten her starring role on Broadway. She was to have lunch with Ashe, then meet Hugh, but should she raise these burdensome issues now?

She entered the International Hotel lobby and went into the opulent dining room where Ashe was waiting for her. He saw her at once and stood, smiling, his blue eyes showing pleasure.

"Callie, darling, I was beginning to think you'd forgotten we were to have lunch together." He pulled out her chair of dark mahogany, and when he leaned over her shoulder he whispered in her ear. "You look wonderful in that blue riding habit. By the way, sweet, Hugh is joining us a little later. Hope you don't mind."

"Of course not, I've been wanting to talk to him since he arrived. Where's he been keeping himself?"

"You know Hugh. He comes and goes like a phantom. What will you have?"

"Just something light. I'm not very hungry."

"Nervous about tomorrow night?" he smiled. "Don't be. I've heard you going over your lines. You have them down perfectly." He reached over and took her hand, squeezing it. "Darling, something has come up. We've got to leave for Santa Fe next week. Do you think it's possible?"

She looked at him. He seemed excited...or was it concern?

"News from your playwright friend, Foster Williams?"

"Yes, Foster needs us there as quickly as possible. The play will open weeks sooner than he thought. I've received another wire from him yesterday. I told Hugh about this, and he's all for it. He tells me not to worry about things here in Virginia City. He'll take care of everything. That includes you, too. He has wonderful plans for the Stardust. Wait till he shares them with you. It's going to boom, Callie. I wish we could be here to see it happen, to perform for a month or two, but..."

The waiter came and Ashe ordered roast beef and, for Callie, chicken soup.

"When will Hugh join us?" She glanced toward the dining room doorway and the stairway that went up to the rooms.

"He said not to wait for him. He'll be down for coffee and dessert." He glanced her over. "You went riding this morning? Why didn't you tell me? We could have gone together."

She put her spoon down and looked at him. "You wouldn't have liked where I went." How much to tell him now? Would it be wise to start asking him questions about Dylan Harkin and Chicago, or wait until after opening night? Nothing must threaten her opening night on stage. It was too important.

He laughed. "Well, where did you ride to? Let me guess. The mine? You know, it might be entertaining to have a tour before we go. I've never been inside a mine before. Maybe an old ghost mine would be interesting as well. I hear the Pelly-Jessup is shut down now. Maybe we could ride there on Sunday morning. The pressure of opening night will be over; we'll be able to relax and take satisfaction in our success. A pleasant ride to a ghost mine will be our entertainment."

She wrinkled her nose. "To see the Pelly-Jessup? Whatever for, Ashe? It's just a dirty old abandoned mine."

He shrugged. "I've heard a lot about it. I find mining fascinating."

"Do you? You never mentioned it before."

"Well, we had too many other things on our minds, I suppose."

"Anyway, the Pelly-Jessup was never very successful. Not like the Mackay Mine for instance or even the Halliday-Harkin."

"That's not what I heard." He took a bite of his roast beef.

She was curious now and surprised. "What did you hear?"

"That the original owners, John Pelly and Hubert Jessup hit a bonanza but were cheated out of their find by a neighboring claim. That's when Macklin Villiers came in and bought up a lot of their shares and turned it into a successful producer. Macklin even kept the Pelly-Jessup name because he knew they'd been treated badly."

She gave a laugh. "Macklin didn't have a generous or sympathetic bone in his body. If he bought Pelly and Jessup out, he did it for his own gain."

"You don't sound very kindly toward a relative. He was your mother's cousin, wasn't he?"

"No," she said flatly. "He was my father's relative. And you're right. I've no positive feelings for the man who murdered my mother in the Sierras and shot my father."

Ashe looked stricken. He stared at her, then quickly reached over and laid his hand over hers. "Callie, how brutish of me. I didn't realize…"

She said nothing for a moment. "It's all right. Of course, you didn't know. I've never talked much about how my parents died. And if you don't mind, I'd really prefer to not discuss it now. It's something I want to forget."

He nodded and calmly changed the subject.

"From what I heard around town, John Pelly had originally staked a larger claim than the Pelly-Jessup. He had the footage of what was the Harkin claim. But Pelly's claim on those feet disappeared from the mining ledger, and the next thing he knew Frank

Harkin owned it. Then Jack Halliday bought in, and they became partners."

"This is the first I've heard about it. I doubt that it's true. You'd be surprised how the stories become exaggerated with time."

"I suppose you're right. But I'd still like to ride out there and have a look around."

The white-coated waiter brought a message to Ashe on a small silver plate.

"For you, Mr. Perry."

"Thank you. I wonder…oh, it's from Hugh. Says to have coffee and dessert without him. He's going to be meeting with Burl O'Brien this afternoon."

The lawyer who will handle the sale of my shares in the mine. Her interest pricked up.

"Isn't it time *I* talked with Mr. O'Brien?"

"Past time, in my opinion. Hugh wants us all to have dinner with O'Brien here tonight. Why don't we ride out to the mines on Sunday? The Pelly and Halliday must be just feet apart."

"They are. As Uncle Samuel puts it, 'They rub noses.'"

She remembered the trouble with Macklin and Colefax over their scheme to take over the Halliday section, but thought better of explaining the ugly matter now. She had more than enough to discuss with Ashe. Maybe a quiet ride out to Gold Canyon on Sunday to the mines would be the best place to discuss Dylan as well. And it was a way to delay an unpleasant subject that could threaten her future.

"All right, Sunday morning," she said quickly.

"Ah, here comes our coffee and praline pie."

As the waiter served them and left again, Ashe said, "By the way, you never told me about where you rode this morning."

Another opportunity to bring up Rick's charges—now confirmed by Mr. Simmons and Neil. The opportunity came…and went. She looked down at her china cup filled with creamy coffee and said casually, "Oh, nowhere in particular."

When she raised her eyes again, something caught her attention at one of the tables across the dining room. She noticed the same man she'd seen once before on the night when Ashe had given her the sapphires. The tall, slim man in black with a heavy beard, hat, and spectacles, sat alone, having his lunch.

She set her cup down with a clatter and stood. Ashe did the same, pulling her chair back and showing curiosity.

"Everything all right, Callie?"

She wore her fixed, attractive smile like a mask, but she noticed he watched her carefully.

"Yes, just fine. Thank you for luncheon. I'll see you tonight for dinner."

She left the International and hurried to the livery stable where the hostler, Beebe, led her mare out. She mounted quickly and rode up the street, turning toward her mansion on Flowery.

Odd, how that man, a stranger, made her feel as though he were watching her—or was he watching Ashe?

Was it her imagination or was Ashe unusually tense today? She thought he might be anxious about the play, but it wasn't like him to be worried. She wondered if something were bothering him. Could he have gotten wind of her visit to Rick Delance, or even to the bank, or Neil Howard? Maybe of the talk about a loan from Dylan Harkin?

It was a windy night, and because the appointment for dinner with Hugh and O'Brien was earlier than usual, she could see a dust devil kicking up in the street as she drove her buggy toward the International Hotel. Purple twilight lingered solemnly above Sun Mountain.

Ashe met her in the lobby, and they walked into the gilded dining room and took their places at the reserved table by the window facing the street.

Ashe appeared sullen, despite tomorrow being the crowning day for the opening of the grand Stardust Theater. He was quiet and preoccupied. Callie noticed he looked out the window several times. Neither Hugh nor Mr. O'Brien, the lawyer, had yet shown.

Ashe's behavior intensified her own misgivings, and she glanced about the dining area for the tall, slim man with the long beard who looked rather like a rabbi. He probably hadn't come down from his room to eat dinner yet.

"What's keeping Hugh and Mr. O'Brien?" she asked.

"I wonder." He turned his head toward the door. "Perhaps I should go up to the room and remind them." He pushed back his chair and got to his feet. "I'll only be a few minutes."

She nodded and turned her attention back out the window.

There was a coach with two horses parked along the street, and she wondered to whom it belonged. She'd noticed it there when she and Ashe entered the dining room and took their table facing the window. Most likely the owner was inside the dining room having supper, but the driver was absent, and that sparked her interest.

It was a handsome coach, shiny and black, and the horses were well-groomed.

Ashe returned ten minutes later with a frown. "No one answers the door. I'm afraid they've gotten busy somewhere and forgotten the dinner date. It now looks like we'll need to wait until after opening night to meet O'Brien." He scowled. "I don't like this delay, Callie. We need to leave for Santa Fe before Samuel tries to stop us."

For the first time she didn't rush to reaffirm her decision to leave Virginia City. She wanted to get back to the house, and when he mentioned ordering dinner she suddenly shook her head.

"Let's forget dinner, Ashe. All I want is to go home. I need to be rested for tomorrow."

He looked displeased and worried. "Is anything wrong between us, Callie? You seem withdrawn, as if something's upsetting you."

"No, nothing is wrong."

His mouth stiffened. "It isn't that gunfighter, is it? Has he been annoying you? He's dangerous."

She gathered her handbag. "I don't want to talk about him. Shall we go?"

They walked outside onto the boardwalk and were struck by the strong wind. It loosened her hat and before she could hold it in place, the wind lifted it from her head and blew it across the boardwalk. Her hat tumbled into the wheel spokes of the shiny new coach and stopped there.

Ashe hurried to snatch it up, and as he straightened she saw him look into the window of the coach. He stood still, then his shoulders appeared to jerk, and he stepped back losing his hold on her hat so that it blew again across the dusty street and jammed against the opposite boardwalk.

Rick Delance stooped down and picked it up and looked across the street at her.

Callie stepped back out of the wind and waited in the doorway of the International. *What was he doing in town? What if he confronts Ashe?* She felt unreasonable anger. He was ruining everything for her.

As Rick stepped down from the boardwalk, his poncho blew in the wind and the spurs on his boots made a sound that ran along her nerves. She had to avoid him. The attraction between them was putting her on edge. Quickly she looked at Ashe.

Ashe hadn't moved. He was still staring into the coach window. Then, suddenly, he flung the coach door open and leaned in saying something the wind took away from her hearing.

What is going on?

Delance stepped up on the boardwalk, dusted off her hat, and handed it to her. His dark gaze captured hers, but he must have noticed something disturbing in her face, because he sobered quickly and turned toward Ashe and the open door of the coach. He walked up beside Ashe.

Callie found her feet at last and hurried up between them, trying to look inside the coach at what held their interest. A small cry died on her throat as she saw a man's booted feet and legs sticking out in a most unnatural position. Then she saw a clawed hand reaching out as though grasping—

Rick took hold of her arm and quickly drew her aside and back toward the hotel.

"You don't want to look," was all he said in a calm but decisive voice. "Why don't you go inside and sit down, Callie?"

His voice was gentle, and it made her worry even more.

"Who is it?" she whispered.

"I don't know. I never saw him before. But it looks like Ashe recognizes him."

She noticed the thoughtful interest in Rick's voice when he said that, and she looked from him back toward Ashe. He was still leaning inside the doorway, bracing himself with one hand on the coach door.

"Is the man dead?" she asked Rick.

"No doubt. Somebody killed him. And not in a very nice way."

"Miss Callie? Have you seen Jimmy—"

Callie turned her head, as did Rick, and Elmira came hurrying toward them down the boardwalk, her dark skirts and shawl whipping in the wind. "He didn't come to dinner and Miss Weda and your uncle are worried—"

Elmira stopped when she saw Ashe by the open door of the coach. Before anyone could move fast enough to stop her, she came up beside him, said something, looking inside. A screech came from her throat, and her hands flew to her chest.

"It's Hugh Ralston—"

Callie felt Rick's fingers tighten on her arm as he turned swiftly toward the coach. "Hugh Ralston?" his hand dropped from her arm and in a few strides he was at the coach door again beside Ashe and looking in attentively. He turned to Ashe and spoke, but Ashe didn't answer and stood as if in shock. Then Ashe turned away, almost bumping into Elmira as he came over to Callie.

Ashe's face was dazed, and she saw a glazed look over his eyes. "Somebody killed Hugh," he whispered.

"A robbery?" she choked.

"No, no…" he jammed his hands into his coat pockets and looked to be in a trance. "This is murder; he was choked." His eyes came to hers. He stared at her. She was taken aback by the sudden look of fear that spread over his features.

A crowd had gathered by now, and several prominent men were talking to Rick. But his voice was so low that she couldn't hear what he was saying. The men seemed to take charge. They began clearing the crowd away and one of them—Mr. Myers, a friend of the governor—walked up to Ashe and spoke with him, then gestured inside the hotel. Ashe went with him and several others, and Rick shut the coach door and gestured to several men to guard the coach. Doctor McMannis came scurrying down the boardwalk with Mrs. McMannis who, upon seeing Elmira, must have realized the poor woman was in shock. Mrs. McMannis took her by the arm, and with another lady, led her inside the hotel.

Callie stood alone, hovering in the shadows of the hotel. Rick walked up to her, took one look at her face and frowned.

"I'll take you home."

"Ashe—" she began, but Rick took her arm and steered her down the boardwalk. "How did you come? Did you bring a buggy?"

She swallowed and nodded. "At the end of the street, behind the hotel."

"Wait here. I'll go get it and come back."

He walked away into the windy, dark night. Callie stood there shivering, but not from cold.

Hugh Ralston dead. And not just any death, but strangled in his own coach. What was the reason behind it? She'd never forget the look on Ashe's face.

Rick brought the buggy and got down to help her up onto the seat, then he went around and climbed up, taking up the reins. He drove away leaving the confused scene behind them.

"A robbery?" she asked, hoping for a different answer than she'd received from Ashe.

"I don't think that was the motive."

She shuddered, watching the side of his handsome face. "What motive, then, do you think?"

He looked at her from under his hat as the bright moonlight shone down on them, his gaze thoughtful. "Ashe was frightened. That's mighty curious. What would make him so afraid?"

She had noticed Ashe's reaction as well, but bristled hearing it come from Rick.

"If you think he's a coward, you're wrong."

"Calm your ruffled feathers; that's not what I meant."

She drew in a breath and sat stiffly. "Take me home, please."

"That's what I'm doing," he said dryly. "I'll have you there in a few minutes. Listen, Callie, what happened tonight? At the International, I mean, before he discovered Ralston? You were having dinner with him," he urged, "then what? Were you expecting Ralston to join you? Did Ashe talk about him?"

Hugh had been murdered tonight, and Ashe had definitely been afraid when he discovered him in the coach. And that fear had been from more than the shock of finding an associate's body. She wasn't sure how deep their relationship had been. Ashe had not spoken of Hugh in terms of friendship, but mostly in terms of the business interests they'd shared.

"He did mention Hugh. They weren't close though, if that's what you mean. It was always business. Ashe had a respect for Hugh's theater savvy and ability to get things running smoothly. I'll admit something to you…" and she looked at him. He watched her, alert.

"Ashe is an exceptional performer on stage, but he's a puppy when it comes to managing things well. He doesn't have a head for the business angle of our work the way Hugh did. They complemented one another."

"Is that why Ashe turned to Ralston to find the right lawyer to sell your share of the mine?"

She wasn't sure what lay behind the question, but she took it at face value. "Yes. Hugh had many friends who were lawyers. He respected Mr. Burl O'Brien."

"Did Ashe tell you he'd met O'Brien?"

"No, but Hugh and O'Brien were to meet us at dinner tonight, and they never came down from their rooms. Earlier at lunch today Hugh sent another message down to Ashe saying we'd discuss things at dinner. O'Brien was to be with him tonight. Why do you ask about whether Ashe met Mr. O'Brien or not?"

"Because," he drawled, "Bill Stewart—without question one of the best lawyers in Nevada Territory—says he's never heard of a lawyer from Frisco named O'Brien."

She straightened her hat. "So? That proves nothing."

"Seems to me it's worth thinking about. If O'Brien is such a great lawyer, why doesn't Stewart know about him?"

"Really, Rick, all you're trying to do is discredit Ashe."

"Have it your way," he said easily. "But something's mighty wrong, isn't it? Ralston's dead, and Ashe looked like a mouse surrounded by a pack of hungry tomcats."

She made a frustrated sigh.

"Did Ashe say anything at dinner tonight about Ralston?"

"I can't recall anything. But Ashe did—" she stopped. Should she tell him? It would only give him more reason to find fault.

"Yes?"

She shrugged. "He was, well, preoccupied I thought. It seemed unusual for Ashe to be nervous before an opening night. He's usually pretty relaxed about it. So it seemed curious is all."

"But he didn't mention Ralston or that O'Brien fellow?"

"No."

"Did you see the note Ralston sent to your table at lunch?"

"No. Ashe did. It was just a message about Hugh not being able to meet us at lunch because he was meeting O'Brien."

"Do you know what Ashe did after lunch?"

She sighed. "No, but he wanted to see the Pelly-Jessup and Halliday-Harkin mines. He wanted me to ride out with him for a tour, since he'd never seen a real mine before, but," and she looked at him evenly, "after the ordeal I underwent at Threesome, I was in no mood for another dusty ride out to Gold Canyon."

"Wise decision," he murmured, as though deliberately misreading her wish not to be with Ashe. "So he wanted to see the mines," he said after a thoughtful minute.

She looked at him. "I see nothing so strange about that."

"Seems strange to me. Why would a fancy Easterner, who obviously scorns us wild Westerners want to admire our rough 'n' ready mines?"

Callie folded her arms and stared straight ahead.

"The Pelly-Jessup? Now, that's mighty strange," Rick said again. "It's all shut down, a bust. Not only that, the timbering's starting to decay. There could be a cave-in. For two novices poking around, it could be mighty dangerous."

She moved uneasily. Thoughts of being closed into tight spaces made her uncomfortable. She reached up and settled her hat again, though it was perfectly in place.

"Did he go out there alone?"

"No, I don't think so. He mentioned riding out there on Sunday. I told you, Ashe seemed a little bothered about something tonight. I'm sure," she said, suddenly cross, "that it has to do with all you and Uncle Samuel are doing to push him into a corner."

"Do you know how long that coach was sitting out front of the International?"

"It was there when we first took our table."

"So, it could've been there even longer," he mused, driving the horse at a slow pace. "Come to think of it, the body looked as if it was there a few hours."

She moved uneasily. "Would you mind hurrying, please?"

He flicked the reins and the horse began trotting.

"Sure has me mighty curious."

"You seem to be a *mighty curious* young man about too many things, Rick Delance."

"Guess I am." He looked at her and smiled.

Rick pulled the buggy into the yard and jumped down. He came around and helped her down. Before he released her, he asked, "When was the last time you saw Hugh Ralston?"

She raised her brows at him, aware that his hands rested on her arms. "I haven't seen Hugh since a month or so before I left San Francisco."

"Ashe saw him after he arrived in town?"

Now why was he emphasizing that?

"Well, yes, I think so. They were both staying at the International. We were to have met Hugh at lunch."

"But he didn't show."

"No. As I said earlier, he was going to meet with O'Brien, who'd just come in from San Francisco. Then they'd meet us later tonight for dinner."

"Except neither of them showed up. Do you mind telling me how you met Hugh Ralston and became partners in the theater?"

She hesitated. "Ashe introduced us. I was playing for Maguire in San Francisco, a small part, actually. Ashe happened to be in the audience one night, and he came backstage and asked if he could meet me for tea the next day. Aunt Weda was against it, but she finally relented, and I went. Ashe told me he thought I was a very good actress and wanted me to join his Perry-Ralston Theater Company. It was a wonderful break! One I've never regretted," she stated.

"He already had the Perry-Ralston Company?"

"Yes, they were having financial difficulties. He wanted me to meet Hugh to see if he agreed on a third partner. We met for dinner at my hotel. Hugh was very knowledgeable, and I was impressed. He comes from a family of theater people back East."

"Chicago?"

"Why yes, I think so."

"What about the Stardust?"

"That opportunity came later. Hugh reminded me of how mom wanted to open a theater here. That was what sent her over the Sierras in '59 with Cousin Macklin. They were going to partner and open a theater. Well, I'd wanted to do something that would commemorate her career on stage in the California gold fields, so it seemed a wonderful idea. "

"Wait—he reminded you? How did he know Lillian O'Day wanted to open a theater here in town?"

She looked at him a long moment. "I—I suppose Ashe told him."

"Then Ashe knew? You told him?"

No, she hadn't told Ashe...not back then in San Francisco. She looked away from Rick's dark, perceptive gaze.

"That's worrisome," he said pensively. "Because Samuel once mentioned to me that only Macklin Villiers and his lawyer Colefax knew your mother's plans to open a theater in town. So how did Ashe and Hugh Ralston find out?"

"You're not suggesting Hugh Ralston knew Macklin or Colefax?"

He looked thoughtful. "I wonder...."

"That's impossible, Rick," she said quickly.

"Not impossible at all. Samuel said the other evening that Colefax came from Chicago. I knew something bothered me about that statement. It's that Neil Howard told me about how he worked in Chicago. He was stage manager there for Ashe."

Rick looked at her soberly.

She narrowed her eyes defensively. "Macklin had a keen interest in the world of theater, too. I know that comes as a surprise. In fact, a short time before his death Macklin contacted friends of Colefax to help him open a theater in Virginia City. He talked about it to Annalee when she went to see him in his hotel room, and later he also contacted me. Brett once told Annalee that Macklin was going to let me star there, building up my debut as the daughter of the beloved Lillian O'Day. He had plans to involve me with his nephew, Rody Villiers."

"The mine, naturally. If Rody married you, Macklin would have access to the Halliday-Harkin, which was what his plans were all along. And if Ralston turns out to have known Colefax, then that explains a whole lot of things. Including him wanting to provide the attorney to handle selling your share of the mine."

"You haven't even proven Hugh knew Colefax, and already you're leaping to conclusions he's trying to steal the mine. You could be very wrong," she insisted stubbornly

"Could be. I could be right, too. If I am, Ashe has much to explain. Have you talked with him about that loan from Dylan?"

"No."

She wasn't ready yet to tell him that she'd spoken with Neil and Mr. Simmons.

"You still aim to leave for New York in a few weeks?"

She didn't care to admit that, either. Right now she wanted to put off even thinking about things requiring hard decisions and conflicting desires.

The wind rattled coarse leaves on some bushes nearby, and the stars were clearly visible, shimmering like jewels in the soft black sky above. She became aware of Rick's nearness, of how his hands were still holding her. Quickly she pulled away and turned toward the house. "Are you coming in to talk to Samuel? I'm sure," she said dryly, "that he'll be only too willing to conclude Ashe, Hugh, and Colefax are partners in crime." She turned and walked quickly toward the front steps, leaving Rick to look after her.

Samuel must have heard the buggy because he was waiting at the door when she came up the steps. He took one look at her, then at Rick, who had followed her, and stepped aside.

"Something happen?"

Callie shook her head in helpless dismay and went past him to the winding staircase. She climbed, anxious to get away to her room. Halfway up, she turned and looked back, and saw Rick watching her. She looked at him a long moment, then hurried upstairs.

Nineteen

ॐ

Rick filled Samuel in on the details of Hugh Ralston's murder as they stood outside the big house with gusts of wind pummeling them.

"What I noticed was that Ashe was not just shocked over Ralston's death, he was afraid of something."

"Question is, afraid of what?" Samuel queried.

"Or of whom, maybe?"

Samuel looked at him sharply. "Was that fear genuine?"

Rick tilted his head. "What do you mean, Samuel?"

"I'm not sure. He's an actor, and a good one they say. Ah, well… Do you think Ashe has a hunch who did this dark deed?"

"He had two or three minutes alone with Hugh's body before I crossed the street to Callie. He may have seen something inside the coach before I got there."

"What was he doing all that time?"

"He looked like he was in a trance, unless he was just acting, like you suggest. Could be."

"Could he have picked up something from inside the coach?"

"Possible. And someone needs to question Elmira when she calms down. She appeared on the verge of hysterics. Not a normal reaction…unless she was close to him."

"There's some strange things going on, Rick. It would be good to get to the bottom of it."

"I wasn't aware Elmira knew Hugh that well."

"Why don't I talk to her in the morning, and you pay a call on Ashe?"

"I thought I'd walk over to the International tonight before he has time to settle his nerves."

Samuel nodded his staunch approval. "You go ahead. I'll take care of the horse and buggy."

Rick started down the road to C Street. The moonlight was bright and showered down on the dusty road. He purposely kept to the edge in the shadows, ever aware that an assassin had tried to pick Elmo off the night he'd waited here for Samuel. That, too, bothered Rick. He was used to challengers who drew on a man face to face, but whoever killed Hugh Ralston had acted as a hired assassin with no concern for fairness. He'd been able to trick Ralston into allowing him to board that coach where he'd strangled him. This was no ordinary hired gun like Cesar. Rick didn't think it was Johnny, either, though he could be wrong. The man with the scar? Maybe. So far, that man had managed to keep out of sight, behaving more in line with a hired gun. What about his own trouble, was it connected in any way? Yet Rick didn't think it had anything to do with Santa Fe.

Just as she had thought…she couldn't sleep. Callie paced the carpeted floor of her lavish bedroom, wide awake. She went out on the terrace connected to her bedroom and leaned against the rail. The moon glowed a cool white in a clear sky, and the wind in the bushes and from the more distant fields of sagebrush and mesquite, had a soothing effect on her frayed nerves.

"Lord, whatever am I to do?"

But the dullness in her heart remained. As though her heavenly Father reminded her that disobedience to His will had turned the ministry of His indwelling Spirit to one of grief and conviction.

Callie dropped her head into her hands feeling miserable. But still, she would not yield her will.

The pungent aroma of sage drifted to her.

Rick's questions persisted in her mind, hammering away at her resolve regardless of the determination she pretended to have in his presence. She was reluctant to let him know just how effective his efforts had been. And Uncle Samuel, too, had reached deep within her heart.

Do I want the truth? Even if it dissolves my plans and leaves them in rubble? Can I rebuild again?

Hugh is dead. She shivered in the warm wind. The awful image of that claw-like hand stiffly reaching out to grasp...at what? His murderer perhaps...by the throat? Or in pleading petition to God for His help? *Hardly that. Not Hugh.*

Why would someone want to kill Hugh Ralston?

And what of the events surrounding me? That chandelier, for instance. Had the timing of its fall been a mere coincidence, or was Rick right when he'd insisted the rope had been cut?

And why was Ashe so afraid?

And those incidents in San Francisco—more coincidence or related?

She returned to her room. "I must sleep. I've got to be rested for tomorrow's opening night." *Will Ashe be calm enough to do his best on stage? What if they both blundered?*

Rick...

He'd showed strength tonight in taking control of an ugly situation. He'd troubled to bring her home, and though she'd shrugged it off in his presence, his small acts of kindness and masculine leadership in putting her safety before his were not lost on her, including the retrieval of her hat. He'd even knocked the dust off for her.

He was concerned too, about what had happened to Hugh. True, he didn't trust Ashe's motives, and that upset her because she was sure he was wrong about that. But Rick had been there for her in a moment of crisis while Ashe had nearly gone to pieces and forgotten about her as he had simply walked into the hotel. After a few years of marriage, when the glamor had worn thin, what then? What would Ashe be like? How would he treat her? Uncle Samuel's questions burned in her soul. Be wise. Be careful. Wait...wait and see. A verse of Scripture from Psalms came to mind: "Wait on the LORD, and keep his way, and he shall exalt thee to inherit the land."

She looked toward town and saw the lights still glowing warmly. She'd seen Rick and Uncle Samuel talking on the porch. They must have discussed her as well as Hugh. A short time later Rick had walked back toward town. That hadn't been lost on her, either. He had to walk back because he'd used her buggy to bring her home. He was a gunfighter, but there was the unmistakable flavor of a gentleman under his buckskin. Strength and tenderness when mingled together made a man difficult to resist. Just what had life been like for him on the Triple D Ranch? What had his father been like?

Callie pushed the bolt on her terrace door into place, then she checked the other windows making sure they too, were secured.

The crowd had dispersed from the hotel by the time Rick arrived. Hugh Ralston's murder had become just another death in a long list of deaths and shootings around the noisy saloons.

Rick saw Dr. and Mrs. McMannis leading Elmira to their own buggy to bring her up to the house.

Rick entered the hotel and went up to the desk.

"Mr. Perry?" the clerk repeated Rick's question. "He has room 15."

Rick turned from the desk and hurried up the carpeted steps. As he turned into the hall on the second floor, the door to room 15 was just being pushed closed from within. Rick reached it as the lock clicked shut. He knocked twice. It opened, and Rick faced an agitated Ashe Perry with his sleeve gun pointed straight at Rick's heart.

"What the devil do you want?" Ashe demanded.

"Name's Delance. I want to talk with you."

Ashe measured him coolly, as if Rick's confidence troubled him.

"I've heard the talk. I know about you. I saw you with Callie tonight, too, and I must say I didn't like it. I want you to stay away from my fiancée."

"I reckon you would."

Ashe turned an unbecoming ruddy color. "You're an arrogant man. What do you want?"

"Talk, like I said." Rick gestured to the unconcealed gun. "Miss Halliday doesn't think her fiancé should own a gun. You're too polished for that, Mr. Perry."

Ashe's blue eyes hardened with cool dislike. "There was a murder tonight. The man was a friend and a business partner. I'd be a fool not to carry a weapon to protect myself."

"You'll get no objection from me. I just believe in being honest about it is all. She doesn't think you carry a weapon…and you do. And from the way you had it ready so quickly, I'd guess you have some experience with it, as well as a reason to carry it."

Ashe's mouth tightened. "What business is it of yours? Does a gunfighter with your reputation come here to lecture me on ethics, or do you have something else on your mind?"

"We'll talk inside."

Ashe's mouth twisted. He bowed with exaggerated decorum and waved him into the room. "Please come in. By all means."

Rick entered, making sure he didn't turn his back on the actor. Ashe noticed, and there was a glimmer of respect in his eyes.

"A man of some experience yourself, I see."

"It pays to be careful." Rick gestured to the private bar with mirrors, bottles, and glasses. "Another surprise for Callie?"

"What gives you the right to call my fiancée by her first name?" Ashe's voice was cold. He pushed the door shut and clicked the bolt, all the while watching Rick's every move. The actor hesitated, then shoved his gun into his belt behind his jacket.

"You're wise to be careful after tonight's murder. I'm mighty surprised Ralston didn't have a bodyguard."

Ashe's expression changed to one of wariness. He looked Rick over as though he were more clever than he'd given him credit for.

"Hugh?" he said as though stalling for time to think. "He did have one, yes…in San Francisco."

"But not here in this wild boomtown?" Rick lifted a brow. "He'd come here unprotected, but reserve his bodyguard for Nob Hill?"

Ashe shrugged impatiently, obviously upset that Rick seemed to be gaining ground.

"Why ask me? I was just one of his partners in the theater company. How should I know if his bodyguard came with him?"

"Just asking. Seems like he would have."

"Perhaps he did."

"But you never met him back in Frisco? You wouldn't know his name?"

"No. Look, I appreciate your concern for Hugh, but it comes a little too late, does it not? You've come here uninvited, and I am a busy man. Tomorrow is my opening night at the Stardust. I've just discovered the body of a business associate and friend violently murdered, and you barge into my room asking questions like a New York policeman. I ask you, Mr. Delance, to remove your presence from my room."

"You say you're only one of Hugh Ralston's partners. Is Walt Colefax the other?"

A wary look came to Ashe's eyes. He glanced over at the bar then his eyes slanted away.

"Colefax? I don't recall. His name doesn't come to mind from anything Hugh's ever mentioned to me. Who is he?"

"I thought for sure you'd know who Colefax is. Callie didn't tell her fiancé how Colefax was partners with Macklin Villiers? It was Colefax who swore falsely that he'd seen her father Jack Halliday shoot Frank Harkin in the back."

Rick could see Ashe had trouble retaining his composure, and yet the actor's talent was coming through to rescue him.

"Ah...yes, now I recall something unpleasant. Callie's father...yes, she has mentioned that tragic affair. Like I've said, however, I don't know Colefax, and I don't think Hugh did, either."

Rick let it pass. Whatever had frightened Ashe so badly earlier tonight, he now seemed back under control.

"Hugh was probably murdered by some cheap thief. The town is full of violence and gunfighters," Ashe said with disdain. The insinuation was not lost on Rick.

"I'm taking Miss O'Day away from here as quickly as I can arrange matters for safe travel to Santa Fe."

"I don't think so."

Ashe looked at him with a rise of color in his face, indignation showing in the straightening of his shoulders.

"You don't think so!" came the challenge, but with a measuring appraisal.

"I don't think a petty thief killed him. I don't think you do, either."

"Now, what gives you the audacity to tell me what I do or don't think?"

Ashe's superior manner riled Rick, but he remained cool. "You were mighty scared when you looked into that coach tonight. What was it that got to you? There needed to be something more than finding Ralston's body."

"Are you mad? A friend and business partner dead? Strangled? What reaction can you expect? Someone like yourself who looks upon life cheaply may find the murder of a good and decent man insignificant, but in the East we're not used to barbarianism."

"You can save your theatrical speeches for someone else. They're wasted on me. You were shaking in your boots. It was either real or it was an act. It wasn't from grief over the death of Ralston. As for his being a 'good and decent' man, I'd say that's hogwash. And you were as frightened as a jackrabbit because you were thinking of your own neck. I'll say something else, too. I think you know who you're frightened of—I think you have a notion why Ralston was murdered."

"Keep talking, Delance. You're only making a fool of yourself. If I knew who killed Hugh, I'd be the first to make it known."

Rick didn't believe him. "Perhaps, but keeping quiet about what you know isn't going to save your skin. Your best chance is to talk. I think you know plenty. Who had it in for Ralston? Was it Colefax?"

Ashe stared at him. A muscle twitched near his mouth but his eyes never left Rick.

"My dear fellow, I haven't the foggiest notion what you're talking about. There was trouble—lots of it over the Halliday-Harkin Mine. That's all I know. And all I care to know about such rubbish. And now, you can get out of my room before I call the clerk and order an armed guard up here to throw you out."

"Hugh Ralston was to introduce Callie to an attorney named O'Brien. O'Brien's as phony as your lines will be on stage tomorrow night. Bill Stewart will testify to that."

"Keep talking, Delance. Maybe you should have been a lawyer."

"That's what you have in mind, isn't it? Gain control of Callie's share of the mine?"

"You're jealous over Callie, so you want to cheapen my reputation in the hopes of frightening her into delaying our marriage. It won't work. We're leaving here, and we won't be back."

Ashe was angry now, but Rick kept pushing.

"You had two or three minutes before Elmira screamed and I walked up to the coach. You had time enough to remove something from Hugh Ralston's jacket—what was it?"

Ashe stared at him coldly.

Rick could see Ashe had in his acting repertoire enough masquerades from which to draw from and hide behind. Only after that first shock of finding Hugh Ralston dead did he crack.

Rick upbraided himself. He should have been wiser and quicker to seize that moment by the coach.

Ashe smiled. "It looks as if you've run out of ideas." He walked over to the door, slid the bolt back, and drew it open. He stood with an even stare.

"Get out!"

Rick walked to the door and then paused to look at him. "One last thing, Ashe. If any harm comes to Callie, I'm holding you responsible. You'll live to regret it. I'll hunt you down if it's the last thing I do. Not even Broadway will keep you from justice. Remember that."

Ashe clenched his jaw. "Nothing's going to happen to Callie. She will soon be my wife. Nothing's going to happen to either of us."

"That chandelier was tampered with. Someone replaced the chain with a rope and cut it just as Callie walked underneath. He may have meant to scare her…or to kill her. Keep what I said in mind. Anything happens to her, and I'm coming after you, Ashe."

Ashe looked frightened for the first time in their conversation. "If anyone tampered with it, it may have been the same insane person who murdered Hugh tonight. Instead of bombarding me with questions you'd do well to find the killer."

Rick measured him. "Who is he?"

He flushed angrily. "I don't know."

"That evening in Frisco when someone broke into Callie's hotel room, any idea who it may have been?"

Again that wary look. "So she told you? No, no idea. By the time I got up to her room, whoever it was, male or female, had gone out the window and over the terrace."

"Why did you mention a woman?"

"I didn't say it was a woman. I don't know."

"What relationship does Elmira have with you?"

His face went blank. "Elmira?"

"That's right. I'd guess she's a plant to spy on Callie and report back to you—or to Ralston, before he was killed."

"Elmira is a friend of my mother who lives in San Francisco. That can be checked quite easily. I asked Callie to give her a job. If she's snooping on Callie, it's because of a weakness in her character, not because I need someone to keep an eye on my fiancée. Any more questions?"

"Yes." Rick had saved the important question for last. "Where did you meet Dylan Harkin?"

For a small moment it looked as though Ashe tottered emotionally. A flicker of alarm widened his eyes.

"I've heard of Frank Harkin, but I've never heard of a Dylan."

He was lying of course. They both knew it.

Rick offered a brief smile. "No? Well, I suspect you will."

He walked out into the hall.

Ashe shut the door. Rick heard the bolt slide through the lock.

Rick stood there a moment, thinking, then he left the hotel by the back way.

The night was still windy and the sky washed free of clouds. Piano music was coming from down the street, and men were loitering on the boardwalk.

Rick walked to the livery stable for his horse, then he suddenly decided to change his plans. He wouldn't leave town for Threesome tonight. Tomorrow was Saturday…the opening night at the Stardust. If anything else was stirring in the wind, he wanted to be near should Callie need help.

He turned around and walked into Marten's Emporium, bought the dress clothes he'd need for the theater, then checked into the Virginia House Hotel.

He was given a pleasant room with a bath, but he hardly noticed the luxury. Restless of spirit, he paced the floor wondering how close to the truth he'd come in trying to get Ashe to talk. Ashe had turned out to have tougher hide than he had thought. He was polished, all right. A real smooth talker. No wonder Callie had been taken in by him. He must seem the epitome of contrast with all she wanted to escape from in the wild boomtowns of the West.

What was it Callie had said about Macklin? That he'd been committed to opening a theater here in town? Macklin had theatrical "friends" he could call on to help him organize things. That could fit Colefax, all right. Colefax, alias Hugh Ralston, maybe? But it also could fit Ashe Perry.

Rick removed his gunbelt and draped it over the back of a chair.

That loan from Dylan Harkin. How did it fit into the scheme of things?

For a moment Rick wondered if Ashe could be right after all—that Hugh Ralston was just who everyone claimed. Suddenly disgusted with everything, including his plans to win Callie for himself, he threw off his poncho, removed his faded cotton shirt, and struggled out of his boots. He dropped them with a disgruntled thud. Then, scowling to himself, he checked the round bathtub. Naturally it was too small. The hotel boy had brought up jugs of hot water but dipping his finger into one, he found it already lukewarm. He muttered his frustration.

He ought to forget everything. He ought to find Flint and Elmo and ride out of Nevada Territory for New Mexico, confront Tom Hardy and Zel, and rebuild the Triple D. He ought to find another woman and one that wasn't so contrary!

But he knew he wouldn't. Because try as he might, he didn't want another woman. Irritated, he poured the buckets of water into the round tub. He sensed that things were coming to a head and, one way or another, matters would soon be settled. In the meantime he'd better watch out for murderers and that cold-blooded rattler, Johnny. They were around somewhere, and they'd been quiet for too long. If he didn't start worrying about his own neck instead of proving Ashe and Ralston low-down thieves, the townsfolk might soon be burying him, too.

Twenty

Elmo stood out back of the cabin in the shade of a tree kneading bread dough and singing off-key.

"Well, I be wishin' I be in Dixie, hoo-ray, hoo-ray. In Dixie-land I'll be takin' me stand, to live er die in Dix—eee!" It was a warm Saturday afternoon, and he preferred to bake his bread outdoors.

He swatted at a few bugs. "It'd be perfect out here 'cept fer those durn flies that keep abuzzin'." *Now where is Delance? He shoulda been back last night from Virginny Town. The boys are all down at the mine except for Everett and Fanshaw who are keepin' watch. And Fanshaw sure is bein' quiet.*

Elmo stopped kneading the dough and looked off down the road to the big boulder. Fanshaw was thereabouts keeping an eye on things. Elmo rubbed his chin and squinted afar off. "Come to think of it, Fanshaw shoulda come up fer coffee 'bout an hour ago. It ain't like him to miss his coffee," he muttered to himself.

Elmo looked around growing more uneasy by the moment. His eyes scanned the hills around him. He felt hair bristle on the back of his neck. He untied his soiled apron and dried his floured hands on it. Catching up his rifle, he moved back against the side of the cabin. *Somethin' is wrong, all right.* He could smell it as sure as he could whiff an Apache creeping round the bushes.

He went around the cabin, keeping to the mesquite, the rocks, the brush. He wound his way in the direction of the big gray boulder where Fanshaw was stationed. But before he got there he saw him. Not Fanshaw, but another man, the big man he'd seen at Carson outside the dry good's store. This was the hombre he'd seen at the campfire when Alex was killed. The man with the Z on his neck. He couldn't see the scar now, but he recognized him.

"Ow! Durn that weed—" he'd stuck his thumb. Suddenly the hombre's name sprang to his mind. "By golly, that were it! That's the feller's name, Thorne, it was…Thorne Wiley."

Thorne was astride his horse sizing up Threesome like he was looking for somebody, and Elmo had little doubt about who that was.

Elmo ducked behind a shrub as Thorne maneuvered his horse down the rocky hillside and turned onto the dusty road. He sat his horse like a pro, that one did. His gloved hand rested on his thigh where his holster was within easy reach, but he had a rifle, too, like he preferred to keep his distance and shoot somebody from afar. Thorne's gaze was searching the grounds around the cabin like he could see through shrubs and rocks. That gave Elmo a funny feeling in his belly.

Slowly Thorne turned his horse and walked toward some cottonwoods farther up on the ridge.

I got t'warn Delance. I gotta warn him right away 'fore he rides into a trap. But how can I ride off down the road without that hombre up yonder seein' me?

Jenny was grazing in the gully on the other side of the hill, and if he could get there and ride the longer route to Virginny Town he could be there by dark. Only thing was, if Delance was already on his way back from town he'd miss him.

That be part of the gamble. I'll risk it. "I'm bettin' Delance will stay in town 'cause this is Callie's opening night at the Stardust," he whispered to himself.

Slowly Elmo inched away from his concealment and crawled through the dried brush until he was able to come up around the other side of the hill. He saw his mule standing out black against the grasses and carefully made his way to her.

A few minutes later he had her bridled and was heading her off toward the old Indian trail that would take him to Virginny Town.

The Stardust was crowded when Rick Delance arrived with Flint Harper and Gordon Barkly. He got along with Gordon mostly because they shared a common distrust of Ashe Perry. Rick was a little surprised the play would go on tonight after Hugh Ralston's death. But with so much riding on a successful opening tonight, Ashe and Callie didn't want to postpone it.

All the seats were taken as Rick followed Flint and Gordon to an upper box suitable for six chairs at one side of the theater.

He saw Samuel come in with Jimmy, who was tugging at the arm of a reluctant Weda. Delance smiled to himself. *That sweet, gray-haired granny doesn't like me at all,* he thought. He'd missed growing up without a mother and grandmother. There'd been no woman's touch in his life. *Someday I'll need to win her to my side.*

Weda was all fancied up in a tasteful dress with high collar and cuffs, and she wore jewels. Callie must have gotten them for her. Weda didn't look the sort of practical woman to douse herself with jewels. She also appeared as though Callie and Jimmy may have had to do some strong arguing to get her here tonight.

Samuel, Weda, and Jimmy sat in a box across the theater, and Samuel nodded when he saw him with Flint and Gordon. Weda looked surprised as she looked him over. It must have been his fancy clothes, but then she scowled at him. Jimmy waved exuberantly until he was slapped on the wrist by Weda. Jimmy took out something silver and shiny and waved it toward Delance trying to show him what it was. It looked like a silver chain. Delance gave a nod of his head to show he understood and that it was a nice present. Again, probably from Callie.

The curtain went up and the play, *The Visitor,* began. It opened as expected with Ashe Perry, debonair and polished, playing the part of Sir Richard arriving to make an appeal to Lady Katherine's father for her hand in marriage. Callie was beautiful as Katherine—no surprise there. What did win Rick's respect was her real talent for acting. Ashe seemed showy and exaggerated, while Callie's emotion seemed believable.

The first act ended, and during intermission several waiters walked about carrying trays of refreshments. One waiter came to their box and offered them coffee.

"Sure, I'll have some," Flint responded. Then he turned to Gordon and Rick. "That girl's better than I would have thought."

"Yes," Gordon said, looking disgruntled. "She'll do well in New York."

"Does that mean a good review in your newspaper?" Rick asked him mildly.

"She deserves a good review, but I'm not much impressed with Ashe Perry," Gordon said stiffly. "By the way, what do you think of the murder of Hugh Ralston last night? Very odd, don't you think? Right out in front of the International!"

Rick wondered how much Gordon suspected.

"How could someone enter the coach and kill him without his yelling for help? There must have been fifty people coming and going during the dinner hour. Even Callie and Ashe Perry sat by the hotel window close enough to the coach to have heard an argument. Odd, don't you think?"

Rick had spent most of last night going over those same questions in his mind. He had his own idea, but that's all it was.

"Maybe he was already dead when the coach pulled up in front of the hotel," Flint suggested.

"That doesn't make sense," Gordon protested.

"It does," Rick said, "if you consider the driver may have been the killer who brought the coach to the hotel where he left it parked. If not, he could have been involved in some way. After he left, maybe someone else came up alongside the door facing opposite to the International, entered quickly and killed Ralston."

Gordon looked at him sharply. "Well, now, that's interesting."

"I've got an uneasy feeling whoever killed Ralston had mighty easy access inside that coach. The murder took place there, and I don't think Ralston had any notion the man was dangerous when he entered," Rick continued.

"The person Ralston was to meet may have killed him. O'Brien, the lawyer?"

"I don't think so, Gordon."

"Why do you say that?" Gordon quizzed. "You just said Ralston trusted this person and was caught off guard."

"Well, that part could be true. But it seems more likely to me that if the driver brought him someplace for a meeting and the man he expected showed up and killed Ralston, then why didn't the driver stop him?"

'Look here," Flint said, "I think Delance is onto something. That driver wouldn't be worth his salt if he'd just sit there and let it happen, now would he?"

"Where is the driver? Ever ask yourself that?" Rick said. "Makes a whole lot more sense to think the man Ralston expected never showed up. The driver killed him, drove the coach to the International where he parked it, and then walked away leaving Ralston's body to be discovered. Or, after the driver left someone else showed up."

Gordon pursed his lips and his amber eyes gleamed. "You may have something there, both of you. I'll put that in the paper and get some questions stirring. Yes, yes, and who would have paid much attention to the driver walking away?"

"Most folks wouldn't look twice to notice his face," Flint agreed. "Even if he wore some fancy uniform like those drivers do in Frisco. And Ralston was from there and was used to such things. Ralston wouldn't think nuthin' of rentin' himself a shiny coach an' not checking out a driver who's all dressed up."

"Masquerading as the driver you mean. Yes, good point, yes." Gordon tapped his fingers and looked at his watch. "I'll have that in the paper first thing tomorrow."

"I wonder who would have it in for Ralston?" Flint asked.

Gordon looked at Rick. "He had a lot of money. He took out that big loan from Dylan Harkin don't forget."

Rick wasn't forgetting.

Flint frowned over his coffee. "Maybe someone followed him here from Frisco."

"Or," Rick said quietly, "whoever killed Hugh was already here waiting for him."

"Hmm…" Gordon lapsed into his thoughts.

Elmo rode Jenny down C Street, stopping outside the Stardust.

Lights are a glowin' ever'where and there are buggies and coaches more'n I've seen in many a moon. He ducked inside and looked around. *Looks like Miss Callie is a big success. The place is filled with folks.*

Elmo never went to plays, but down at Neil Howard's old theater they would go on sometime till after ten o'clock. Then all the folks would pour out and go to the fancy hotels for refreshments and what the rich folks called "get-togethers." He had never been invited to a get-together, but he didn't have a fancy for going anyhow.

Look at all them black suits and white frilled shirts! Looked like a feller was put in mummy clothes. He noticed that even Delance had gotten him one of them suits and shirts to wear. Flint, too. *Those fellers look mighty handsome all fancied up like that. But if Miss Callie had some sense and went for any of 'em, it would be Delance.*

The old man left and crossed the street. *Mebbe I'd better wait till the play is over. Flint's cabin's a fine spot to hunker down till they come back. Then I'll tell Delance what I saw at Threesome. He'll be mighty pleased to learn that no-good feller's name is Thorne Wiley.*

Mounting his mule, Elmo tapped her sides with his heels. "Let's get movin', Jenny."

Across the street a lanky straw-haired man watched Elmo. Abner, alias "Johnny," spat his tobacco juice. Zel was right about the old geezer. The cookie was there that night on that cattle drive with Delance's brother. He recognized him now.

Must a hid somewhere, an' neither me nor Bodene saw him. If I'd a seen him, I'd a stomped him…along with that kid. How was we to know he'd grow up to be worse with a six-shooter than even Alex?

But Zel was right. That fussy old cookie had to be quieted…and then Delance.

Abner shifted his holster, feeling a little uneasy as he thought about Rick Delance. *That smooth hombre won't be as easy as the old cookie. Delance was a cool one, him. Cool and calm as you please.* Abner worried, *I don't like a gunfighter that don't sweat. Delance even smiled some when he faced someone. That means he's as hard as nails. The boy has been huntin' me an' Bodene for five years. Ruthless that one.* He'd seen it in Delance's eyes when they'd met in that Express Office when the stage came from Carson. Delance even had him buffaloed.

Abner was still mad about that. *Fate, that's what it were. A bad card draw. Delance weren't supposed to be there gettin' his mail that day.* Abner had been there to watch that woman and Ashe Perry get off the stage. Thorne had asked him to watch Ashe 'cause he didn't trust him. So Abner just walked in as the stage was comin' and who was there? Rick Delance.

"I shoulda killed him then and there. I shoulda drawed on him. It woulda worked 'cause he didn't expect it with all them folks around."

But Delance unnerved him comin' straight at him like that, crowding him, with eyes warnin' he wasn't going to back down an inch. He got Cesar, too. That was really worrisome. Cesar had been good. Cesar's going had bothered him so much he'd even left town awhile to recoup and get his nerve up. He'd even done a little more practicing with his draw. *Yes, Cesar had been good. Not as good as me and Bodene and Thorne, but good.*

Abner watched Elmo turn off toward D Street. That was where Flint Harper had a cabin. Abner knew because he was more careful this time. He'd been watching Delance—and Flint—from afar. He couldn't get near Elmo since he'd been out at Threesome—until now. The old rascal had made his first and last mistake. He'd left Delance's outfit to come here alone. Now, he had him. Why'd he come? Maybe he'd seen Thorne thereabouts waiting for Delance?

Well, he wouldn't be warning Delance.

Abner glanced around warily. Then pushing away from the building, he followed Elmo slowly and careful like. He couldn't have asked for a better time with all the townsfolk, including Delance and Flint, in the theater.

This time he wouldn't miss.

The second act was soon to begin. Callie and Ashe came onto the stage with two others in the cast of players.

Rick took a moment to look around at the crowd, recognizing some faces, but many were unfamiliar since the town kept growing. A man entered late, spied Rick up in the box and walked around the back of the theater and up the steps. It was Bill Stewart—a man respected by many as a supporter of President

Lincoln and the Union. He was a big man with a shock of red hair. He came over to Rick's seat and stooped beside him, speaking in a low voice.

"Hello, Rick. Sorry to be troubling you at a time like this, but Dr. Jim Wilder's a friend of mine who wired me from Santa Fe with a request. He and Brett asked me to deliver an urgent message to you promptly." He reached into his jacket and handed Rick a folded message. "If there's anything I can do, call on me. By the by, Clay Billings sent the papers for you to sign. They should arrive any day now. I'll let you know when." He straightened.

Rick took the wire. "Thanks, Bill."

Heads turned in their direction, for Stewart was liked. They noticed he'd gone straight to Rick. Even Callie appeared to have noticed as she glanced over at Gordon's box where Rick sat leaning against the wall.

Rick opened the wire and in the dimness could just make out Brett's message.

> *Urgent. Tom Hardy and Zel Willard on their way to Virginia City. They have three or four gunmen with them. Don't know when they left here. No one at Hardy Ranch wants to talk. I'm guessing it's been several weeks ago. My advice, choose your own time and place for a showdown.*
>
> *B.W.*

Rick looked up from the wire and down to the stage. Callie and Ashe were vowing their eternal love despite "her" father's disapproval of the visitor.

Choose my own time and place for a showdown with Tom Hardy and Zel? Can I afford that luxury?

They may have left Cimarron weeks ago…that was dark news considering that Johnny and the man with the scar were still around somewhere committed to carrying out Zel Willard's orders. What had happened to make Tom Hardy decide to come here? Could they have found out he'd killed Cesar? Perhaps one of the two men here had wired Zel in Santa Fe.

Rick slowly folded the message and placed it into his inside jacket pocket.

Rick was restless about more than Zel. He looked at Callie. He would need, at least, to face down Zel, maybe more. He should find Zel first. He thought about the possible reaction from Callie if he hunted Zel down and shot it out. What would she think? Most likely she wouldn't understand. It could reinforce her convictions that he was nothing but a gunfighter.

Flint glanced at him and said in a low voice, "Trouble?"

"Plenty."

The play ended, and they filed out onto the street. Rick paused on the boardwalk, looking around. Should he go backstage? He decided against it.

Gordon walked quickly away toward his newspaper office to do some work, and for a minute Rick debated what to do next.

"Come on over to the cabin for coffee," Flint suggested.

Rick was considering the offer when Samuel strode toward them, leaving Weda to usher a reluctant Jimmy off to the buggy.

Callie was still wearing her stylish ball gown as she readjusted her hair and listened to Elmira commend her.

"You were a big hit tonight. Ashe has brought you stardom. He did exceptionally well tonight, too."

Callie looked at her in the dressing mirror while unclasping the sapphire necklace and laying it inside the ornate box. Next came the earbobs and bracelet. She was used to Elmira complimenting Ashe, and because she was satisfied with her own performance she could smile.

"Yes, he was grand, wasn't he?"

"If only Mr. Ralston could have seen the success of the Stardust tonight. Poor Mr. Ralston," Elmira said as she removed her handkerchief from her sleeve and shed tears into it.

"I didn't know you felt so strongly about Hugh. I didn't even know you knew him." Callie watched her while removing excess makeup.

"It's not that I knew Mr. Ralston so well. It's the tragedy of it, the horror of it. Strangled like that—"

Callie shuddered. "Please, Elmira, not now. I want to relish my success tonight, if you don't mind."

"Yes, of course, I shouldn't have brought it up. It's just your uncle was asking me so many questions this morning that my mind is absorbed with trouble....Miss, have you any idea who would have, could have, done such a thing to Mr. Ralston?"

So Uncle Samuel has been asking Elmira questions? Well, it was no wonder. The woman behaves oddly at times. Callie still didn't know quite how to take her, although they were getting on better now after she'd caught her eavesdropping...or rather after Rick had caught her.

Rick Delance. How positively dashing he looked tonight in that black suit and white frilled shirt! He could certainly hold his own in a crowd. Not even Ashe looked better.

"Then you've no ideas?" Elmira asked again.

Callie felt a wave of impatience. "No, I've no idea. Why should I? Get my dress from the wardrobe, would you please? And those matching slippers—no, the green ones, Elmira. And Elmira," she said too casually, "when you've done that, go down and see if Mr. Delance is around. He may have already left, but he might still be in the theater. Tell him I wish to talk to him."

Elmira's dark eyes honed in on her until Callie blushed. She set her brush down.

"Yes, miss, I'll see if he's still here. I saw him in Gordon Barkly's box with that other young man, Flint Harper. Delance looked quite different, didn't he? Very handsome."

Callie shrugged theatrical indifference. "Oh?" But she had again seen them sitting in the box when going out on stage to acknowledge the audience with smiles and curtsies.

"Yes, naturally you'd have no idea who would have done such a dreadful thing to Mr. Ralston. I wondered whether you or Ashe had seen anyone around the coach while you sat at your dinner table by the window is all."

Callie turned her head and looked at Elmira. She looked so long and curiously that Elmira quickly snapped out of her inquisitive mood and walked around the dressing cubicle to the wardrobe where Callie kept some of her costumes and street dresses.

That woman is so intensely curious about people and situations that she ought to work for Gordon Barkly. Callie was reminded that she'd told Ashe how Elmira had agreed to find work in New York with her brother. Things had gone well. Ashe had agreed. Apart from their lines in the play and a brief embrace and "good luck" before they'd stepped out on stage, she hadn't spoken to him since last night. He'd appeared tired, and she'd noticed lines about his eyes as if he hadn't slept well last night. Well who did? There was time enough to—

"*Oh!*"

Callie turned toward the dressing cubicle. A splintering crash reverberated as something toppled to the floor. It sounded like it might have been the large blue vase of yellow daisies that Ashe had sent over before the play. *Now what? That woman!*

"Elmira? What now?"

There was no answer. Callie looked toward the divider, and her eyes slid down to the floor where a woman's shoe poked out.

"Elmira—"

Callie hurried around the cubicle and saw the woman sprawled face down on the floor, the blue vase shattered, the yellow daisies scattered across her shoulders, water running down her head and neck—

Callie gasped. Elmira had been struck from behind with the vase! Hearing a creak of wood, Callie whirled around as a dark blanket came down over her, wrapping her tightly within, smothering her in darkness. Rough hands shoved her into something—the wardrobe?—and the door slammed shut.

Callie struggled to free herself from the blanket. It took several horror-filled minutes and by then she was gasping for air. She finally pushed it aside and in the darkness pressed against the door. The wardrobe didn't have a lock. She shoved against it again, and it opened roughly. Something was piled against it. A table and a chair—

"*Elmira!*"

The woman was sitting up, looking dazed, rubbing the back of her head. Her dark eyes widened when she glanced up and saw Callie.

"S–someone hit me," Elmira cried. "He came right out of the wardrobe!"

Callie clambered out of the wardrobe. She looked at Elmira's head, but there was no blood. She helped her to her feet and into a chair.

"*Dreadful!*" Elmira kept saying, "Dreadful town…thieves, murders, gunslingers—oh my head, my head…"

"I'll get Ashe." Callie left Elmira in the chair and hurried past her dressing table to the door. She stopped.

The ornate box with the sapphires… It's gone!

So that was it. Someone had seen her with them on stage and was somehow able to get into her dressing room and hide.

Or is it that simple? Her mind rushed back to the other incidents. *Are they connected? But how could they be?*

As she stepped out of her door, Smiley was coming toward her. "Things couldn't have gone better," he called. "You'll have good reviews in the paper tomorrow. Even Gordon Barkly was enthused."

Quickly she told him what had just happened.

"Get Ashe, will you?"

"He's not in his dressing room. He's in a meeting. You want me to haul him out?"

"No, not yet." She thought for a moment. "Smiley, do you know who Rick Delance is?"

"Delance? He was here tonight. He may still be here. You want me to try to find him?"

"Yes, and I'll get Mary to help with Elmira. Please find Doctor McMannis, too."

"Will do." Smiley hurried off.

Callie found Mary, but she didn't mention the sapphires. While Mary attended Elmira, Callie waited in the narrow railed walkway on the steps above the main theater. She felt cold and frightened. The thief could have killed both her and Elmira.

Where is Rick?

The minutes dragged by and then she heard voices below and saw Smiley with Rick coming through the side door and across the theater. She took several steps down the stairs to meet them.

"Mary's with her," she told Smiley.

Smiley rushed past her. "I couldn't find the doc. I'll see if she wants me to take her to his house."

Callie hardly recognized Rick in the black broadcloth suit that he wore so well. She knew he'd be carrying his guns. Here in the theater where the elite of Virginia City's society met, those who wore weapons kept them out of sight.

"Trouble again?" he asked.

"Thank goodness you're still here! Rick, the sapphires are gone—stolen."

"The sapphires?" for a moment he appeared baffled.

Quickly she explained, keeping her voice low, and glancing over her shoulder toward her dressing room.

"No one else knows, not even Elmira." She told him the details of what she'd heard and how, when she'd gone to the cubicle Elmira was on the floor unconscious.

"You didn't get a glimpse of him?"

"I turned, but he was too quick with the blanket."

He frowned, and his dark eyes held hers. "I've warned you before of the danger you're in."

"Yes, a bodyguard…" her eyes drifted over him. "I, um, thought you might—well, that's why I wanted to talk to you. I want to hire you."

He looked at her. For a moment no one spoke and then she realized her hand rested comfortably on his arm. She felt his warm fingers touch hers. She used all her willpower to draw her hand from his and dropped her gaze from the warmth in his eyes.

"We'll talk about it," was his simple reply.

She looked back to her dressing room. "Not here, Rick. Elmira—well, you know how she is already."

"I do. How about something to eat over at the International? I haven't had dinner yet, and you probably haven't, either. You were very good tonight. I enjoyed the play."

"Thank you. I'm afraid I'm still a little shaky. That was a very frightening experience."

"I need a moment or two to look around your dressing room, do you mind?"

"Of course not. If you want to know where the sapphires were, I'm afraid I wasn't very careful. I had so much on my mind.

And Elmira kept talking and talking about Hugh's horrid death. I was taking them off and setting them down in the box they came in, intending to lock them away when Elmira cried out. One thing led to another and—well, the thief has them now. Oh! What will I tell Ashe?"

A brief smile touched his mouth. "You could tell him you're able to return the sapphire engagement ring, for a start."

She looked away from his penetrating gaze. "I'll see how Elmira is doing while you have a look about."

She went back up into her room. Rick followed. Her heart was pounding. *If you don't watch yourself...*

Smiley looked over at them. "She won't need a doc. A headache powder and early to bed should do her fine. So says Mary."

"Mary, could you stay with her awhile and see she gets to the house?" Callie asked.

"Oh, sure, honey, me and Smiley will take care of things. You go ahead and run along with the gentleman." Mary looked over at Rick who was casually surveying the dressing room. She rolled her eyes. Callie gave her a rueful smile and went to get her cape. As she did, she shuddered when she looked at the blanket the thief had covered her with before shoving her into the wardrobe.

She joined Rick who was in the hall talking to Smiley. Mary had gone to her dressing room to get a few things, and Elmira was lying on a damask-covered divan. Her face was sullen, and her eyes were closed.

"Elmira, did you get a glimpse of him?"

She shook her head no. "I want to go to New York," she said in a stiff voice. "I've had enough of the West."

"Your having come here to work for me was all Ashe's idea, remember?"

Elmira didn't reply, and Callie walked out to where Rick waited alone on the steps. She came up and they started down the steps into the now dim theater that an hour ago had been packed with applauding townsfolk.

"Are you all right?" he asked.

She managed a brief smile. "Considering what's happened, yes."

They were walking down the boardwalk toward the International when Flint came riding toward them, his jacket open and flying behind him. He was down from his horse in a moment.

"I was over with Pastor Jones and his niece Becky having a bite at the Virginia House when Mel come burstin' in. Says my cabin's being shot up. Elmo's there, Mel saw his mule—"

Elmo! Rick let go of Callie's arm and grabbed the horse's reins from Flint. Mounting, he rode swiftly the few blocks to the far side of D Street.

"Oh, no!" Callie said, fear lurching through her heart.

"It's Delance's fight, Miss Callie. Goes all the way back to Cimarron and what was done to his pa and brother. The outlaws burned the Triple D and rustled the cattle, too."

"Who's out at the cabin, do you know? The man with the scar?"

"Don't know. But this is just the beginning. Bill Stewart brought him a wire tonight from Wilder. Rick says trouble aplenty's on the way. Fellas that started the whole thing are back in New Mexico. But let's get you up to the house to Samuel. There's nothing we can do here. Come along, now. Is your buggy parked in back? Good, we'll be home in a few minutes."

"Flint?" she asked quietly.

He turned and looked at her. She smiled gently. "Thanks. Thanks for everything. I—I haven't forgotten how kind you were to me when I first came over the Sierras with Annalee and Jimmy."

Flint looked surprised, and then he smiled. "Shucks, there's no need to say that, Miss Callie. C'mon, let's get you to Samuel."

Callie looked back over her shoulder in the direction of D Street as they walked away from the Stardust.

"Callie?"

She stopped and turned around. Ashe walked out of the theater and came toward her. She saw Flint's stoic expression. Flint turned, tipping his hat. "Good evenin', Miss Callie. Looks like Ashe will take over. I'm going after Rick and Elmo."

Callie kept silent and watched Flint cross the street and head rapidly for the livery stable where he'd find another horse.

Ashe came up, taking her arm. "Darling, I've been looking all over for you. Where have you been?"

She mentioned the trouble out at Flint's cabin. "Rick's gone there. There'll be more shooting, Ashe. Things have turned horrible."

"Cheer up. We'll soon be out of Virginia City for good. Come along, I've got to talk to you at the hotel. I'll buy us some dinner."

Rick had been about to take me to dinner. And now...

With a last glance behind her, she saw Flint mounting a horse from the livery and riding off. Callie felt Ashe's hand on her arm leading her away. They walked together the few blocks to the International.

Twenty-One

*R*ick saw smoke coming from the cabin. Flames were spurting from one of the windows. The whine of a bullet told him Elmo may have gotten out. If so, he'd likely try to make it to his mule.

Leaving the horse a ways back, he unloosed the leather thongs on his holsters and ran through the brush, from boulder to boulder to circle around the backside of the cabin.

He worked his way toward the corral and a makeshift stable where Flint had once kept some of his mules.

He came up behind the building and glanced around. Elmo's mule was still in the corral. Outside the enclosure, he spotted Elmo sprawled on the dusty ground as though he'd been hit. Rick couldn't see if he had his rifle, or even if he were alive. There was no sign that the gunman was still here. He may have pulled out knowing the cabin fire could draw some townsfolk, or…was he still out there waiting?

The flames danced cruelly against the horizon, bringing with it the memory of another night…long ago.

He saw Elmo move in the dust, inching his way toward the corral. It looked as though he'd made a run for his mule, got shot, and went down, dropping his rifle. If Rick wanted to reach him, he would need to leave the safety of the stable and move out into open ground toward the corral. How badly was Elmo shot? Could he get to him?

A hired murderer was still out there somewhere. His every sense told him so.

Rick stepped out from behind the stable. Still, there was nothing. His gaze sought any movement other than Elmo and the mule in the corral. He moved past the corner to merge with a big shade tree, its leaves rustling. A few more steps and he'd be in the open approaching the corral. Dare he call out to Elmo?

Just as he thought this he heard a cold voice behind him.

"Been watchin' for you, Delance."

Elmo must have also heard, for he moved his head.

Rick turned toward the voice, his hands near his holsters.

He stared at the straw-haired stranger he'd met in the Express Office weeks ago. Johnny stepped out from among dense stalks with a pistol. He was a tall, lank figure in heeled boots and Texas spurs. He stood about thirty feet away, beside Flint's stand of corn, several rows deep, rustling in the breeze.

Elmo was now drawn up on an elbow, his rifle still out of reach.

"That's him, Rick! That's the one they called Abner."

"Maybe you think so, old man, but this is the last time you're goin' to talk about it 'cause I'm sendin' you to Hades. But first I'm goin' to kill Alex's kid brother."

Abner! Rick went cold and still. *At last!* He stood, his boots well grounded.

"Glad to see you here, Delance," Abner's voice was low and cold.

"We meet again. Who ambushed my father on his way to Fort Craig?" Rick demanded.

"I guess I can oblige you that before you die, Delance. Zel or Bodene. Don't know for sure."

"Did Tom Hardy know Zel's plans to kill Alex and take the herd?"

"Don't know. Just that Zel hated Alex 'cause Tina liked him."

Elmo called out, "Abner, you yeller-bellied cockroach. If'n I hadn't dropped my rifle when I fell with this bullet in my leg, I'd a shot ya by now."

"Shut up, Elmo," Abner said coldly.

"Nope, I ain't shuttin' up, you varmint. An' you got no choice now 'cept to listen. He come prowlin' roun' here tonight an' almost blew my head off, Rick. Him an' Zel's likely gettin' worried. This here's the evil feller who killed Alex. I saw him shoot yer brother sure as I be a lyin' here."

Rick stood with his head lowered just a little. He looked across the yard at Abner.

"Yeah, I was there on that cattle drive. Mebbe I killed Alex, mebbe I didn't. That night the lead was flyin' so fast with more'n one of us shootin', who can tell who shot him?"

"You killed him a'right, Abner, 'cause I saw ya do it."

Samuel's voice roared through Rick's mind, *Vengeance belongs to the Lord.* Yet they were not merely Samuel's words, but those of his Lord.

"God can answer whether that's true, Abner," Rick said.

Abner looked taken aback. "God? God, you say!"

Abner laughed with a sarcasm that cracked the stillness. "An' all this time I've been worried about who they called the Kid Gunfighter! Why, you had them all fooled! I'll wager it wasn't even you who got Clegg."

· "I got Clegg. He was fool enough to draw on me. But you don't have to play the fool. You may get me, Abner, but you'll die, too. If you're smart and want to see tomorrow, you'll put the gun down. I'll see that you get a fair trial in Santa Fe."

"You plain crazy? Yer outta your mind, Delance! I've already got the draw on you, so you ain't gonna get me, and you ain't gonna get Bodene. And there's gonna be no trial neither, 'cause no judge in Santa Fe's willing to stand up against Zel. In another couple a years he'll own that town. And he's got big plans for the land that belonged to your old man. He's got Hardy cattle feedin' there, an' he's bringin' in a thousand head more from Texas. You don't stand a chance. Even Tom's afraid of him."

Tom Hardy? Afraid of his son-in-law?

"Is he afraid Zel will shoot him in the back and take over?" Rick suggested with scorn.

"That there's somethin' you won't need to worry about. You ain't leavin' this town."

"Did you know Zel is on his way here?"

"Sure, I know it. An' with you an' that crazy old cookie both dead when they ride in, me and Thorne will have us five hundred dollars a piece."

"Thorne?"

Elmo was crawling now…moving toward his rifle. "No you ain't, Abner. I was mighty scared to get my rifle knowin' you be a watchin' me befer, but I ain't scared now."

"Get away from that rifle, Elmo, or you'll be dead where you lay."

"I'm gonna get ya, Abner," Elmo called, "an' I'm gonna aim 'er right at yer heart. Go ahead, Abner, shoot me, I dare ya!"

Rick was watching Abner's eyes. He was starting to get nervous now, giving away his next move, shifting his head with darting glances to the side as Elmo was crawling within reach of his rifle. Abner was running out of time…Elmo had grasped the barrel…only seconds left. Rick waited, alert. Abner's gaze and his six-gun suddenly jerked aside.

Rick's hands flashed for their guns. The blurring movement that produced the twin Lawmans blasted before Abner could steady his six-gun at Elmo.

Abner got off a bullet that struck wildly into the stable rail, splintering wood. He looked back at Delance, shocked, then he staggered and fell, clutching his pistol to his heart.

Rick walked up. Abner was still alive. He pulled the gun from the outlaw's grip and shoved it behind his belt.

Abner didn't have long before his journey into the fearsome darkness without the Savior.

"You've been a fool, Abner. You never looked at life beyond the end of your nose. Do you think this is what life's all about? Carrying a gun for hire, getting a little money for drink and cheap women?"

"S'pose you think you're better than me," Abner said with difficulty, the sneer still in his voice.

"I'm not your judge, Abner. You haven't much time. You'd be wise to use it to make peace with the Judge of all men. There's still time if you're smart."

"Shut up, Delance! I'll see ya in hell!"

"No, that's one thing you won't see, Abner. You won't see me—or Alex. But you're likely to see the rest of your friends. But there's not a one of 'em who will be able to deliver you. There is only One who can do that. *Jesus* can make the vilest clean…even you."

Abner scoffed and spat blood. "Ya don't mean that. Ya gotta hate me—you want to see me burn."

Rick stood and looked down at him, aware that Flint had ridden up and stood a short distance away with a rifle in his arms.

"There was a man in the Bible with your name, Abner. He stayed safe from an avenger as long as he stayed in the city of refuge. But he was lured out and killed. When King David heard how Abner died he said, "Died Abner as a fool dieth?" Why? Because he could have stayed in the place of refuge and lived. My pa once told me that the city of refuge was a symbol of Christ. Any man who dies, refusing the true Refuge, who is Christ, dies as a fool dies. You share Abner's name. Don't share his folly."

"Delance—you can take yer preachin' an' you—"

Abner gasped, choked, then rasped into a final silence, his head lolling to one side.

In the moonlight the whites of his eyes shone in the firelight, looking startled and terrified.

Rick left Abner and walked over beside Elmo and stooped down.

"How bad are you injured, old friend?"

"Bullet creased my leg." Elmo wiped tears from his eyes on his dirty sleeve. "If I hadn't dropped that rifle, I coulda shot him myself an' saved you a lotta trouble. But he were hidin' behind that corral, an' I didn't see him till he skinned me. I think Samuel's right. The good Lord's been lookin' after me aplenty."

"Yes, Elmo, I think so, too," Flint said. "Let's see that leg."

"Somethin' I gotta tell ya," said Elmo. "That fella with the scar was nosyin' round Threesome. 'Membered his name, too. Thorne Wiley. Funny name. Come to me when I stuck my thumb."

Thorne—another of Zel's hired guns. Rick had never heard of Thorne Wiley.

Twenty-Two

*T*he dining room in the International was almost empty as Callie and Ashe entered. Only a few late patrons were seated about the room, and none close to the table Ashe selected. He pulled out a chair for her, then seated himself across from her.

"We were a success tonight, Callie."

He smiled, but she noted that his mouth was tense. He must not have gotten over Hugh's sudden and violent death. She, too, was shaken...but over what happened in her dressing room.

The waiter came and they ordered. Callie looked at Ashe across the table.

"I was robbed tonight, Ashe! The sapphires have been stolen! All except the ring." She tightened her hand in her lap. His face became taut.

"Callie, you can't mean someone broke into your dressing room tonight?"

She told him how it happened, while he listened with a growing frown.

"Was Elmira hurt?"

"Not badly, but she wants to leave here. Remember I told you that she has a brother in New York and she has plans to join him."

Some of the fear she'd seen in Ashe last night was back, and it fed her own insecurity, especially after tonight. First the chandelier and now this. She could still feel those rough hands pressing that blanket down over her and pushing her into the wardrobe. Whoever it was might have killed her and Elmira.

"Those sapphires were worth a good deal of money, Ashe. We need to report this to the law."

"What law!" he scoffed. "A group of citizens who take it upon themselves to keep the order?"

"We'll soon have a governor, I'm told. Someone to stand up to that man named Terry who's planning trouble in favor of the Confederacy. It'll probably be Bill Stewart."

"I've no time to concern myself with emerging local governments for or against the Union. Sapphires or no sapphires, we've got to leave town. We can't stay." He leaned over and took her hand. "Our lives, darling, are certainly worth more to us than anything else."

"Ashe...is someone trying to kill us?"

"I'm sure of it. First the chandelier, then Hugh's murder, now the attack upon you tonight. Not only that, I found this in my dressing room tonight.

She looked at a piece of paper he handed her. She read it under the lamplight.

Your life will be worth nothing if at this time tomorrow you and the girl are still in Virginny Town.

She looked up, searching Ashe's sober face. "This was in your room after the performance?"

"On my dressing table. Whoever left it could have gone directly to your room and waited in the wardrobe until—well, you know," he said gravely.

"You think it could be the same man who killed Hugh?"

"Of course! Who else? I tell you we've got to leave here, Callie!"

She almost told him how she'd contacted Rick and asked to hire him as a bodyguard, but Ashe looked so unhappy tonight that she couldn't bring herself to disturb him further.

"What about the Stardust?" she asked. "Without Hugh..."

"Smiley can take care of things. He's talented. We can arrange things with a lawyer."

"That reminds me, I've been told there's no such lawyer as Mr. O'Brien. Do you think Hugh may have given you the wrong name?"

"Possibly a mistake, but it doesn't matter now. We can find a lawyer in Santa Fe."

The waiter delivered their food, but Callie wasn't feeling very hungry.

She shook her head. "I realize what a blow Hugh's murder is to you, but how can we leave now, Ashe? If we're both in danger, as it appears, there's got to be a reason for all this. What do they want?"

"They?" he shrugged. "I have no idea."

"Stealing the sapphires hardly seems related to the falling chandelier, even if it wasn't an accident. Rick believes it was planned."

"Rick? First he addresses you as Callie when he came to my room, and now you call him by his first name."

"Rick Delance came to see you?"

Ashe's features tightened. "In my hotel room, here, last night. Delance is more dangerous than even Gordon Barkly. Instead of being a cheap reporter digging up dirt on people, Delance is a gunfighter, a killer. He's killed ten men. Did he tell you that?"

Ten men? Her throat went dry. "Is that what Gordon said? Because if he did, I have my doubts about it."

"I've heard it from more than just Gordon."

She thought nervously of the shooting out at Flint's cabin. *How had things gone?* She looked toward the window but there was nothing astir on the street. She wanted to get home. Samuel was likely to be the first to hear what really happened since Rick would talk to him about it.

"What did Rick Delance want?" she asked.

"He came storming into my room last night after he left you. I had to endure his threats and insults. He accused me of some nefarious plan to murder Hugh Ralston and gain control of your wealth. I nearly hit him on the chin. I would have," he said firmly, "except I feared for my life—he was looking for a reason to draw his gun. I'm worried about you, darling. About both of us. He's determined to have you even if it means getting rid of me in any way he can. He said he'd hunt me down if I married you."

Callie could hardly believe this, but Ashe looked so upset, she couldn't imagine why he'd say such outlandish things if there wasn't something to them.

"He couldn't have meant it, Ashe." She tried to keep her expression from giving away the feeling that she was tempted to be flattered over Delance wanting her for his own. "He isn't the settling-down kind. Even though Samuel says he has a ranch in New Mexico, I can't see him staying there for long."

He shrugged. "At any rate, he worries me. Wouldn't surprise me if it wasn't him playing all these tricks on us."

The idea was ludicrous. She didn't know a lot about Rick Delance, but she was certain he wasn't an immature troublemaker.

She shook her head. "I don't think so. What reason would he have? No, I can't believe that about him. He's dangerous, yes, but in another way."

She didn't want to compare Ashe with Rick Delance at this moment, but she was beginning to notice great contrasts between the two men. Delance was rugged and unafraid of an opponent. He was also confident in his masculinity and in what he believed.

Ashe didn't appear to like her comments about Rick, but he voiced no objection.

"Whoever killed Hugh is after me, too. You saw the note. If I don't leave here tomorrow, I could end up like Hugh. The question is, Will you come with me? The dream still awaits us in New York, darling." He took her hands into his, looking at her earnestly. "Will we take advantage of it and seize the opportunity for a new start? Or will we stay in Virginia City and worry about some crazed madman who is threatening our lives for some unknown reason? If I stay here, I take the chance of a bullet finding me!"

"Ashe, you must have some idea who is behind this."

"I wish I did. It makes no sense."

She drew in a breath, coming to a decision. "Ashe, there's something I need to mention to you. It's about Dylan Harkin."

His gaze came swiftly to hers. She looked back evenly. If she were to leave with Ashe, then she wanted all the facts to come out now.

"Dylan?" he repeated, nothing in his voice.

"Yes," was all she said, waiting.

He sighed, and laid his knife and fork down, watching her with a disappointed look.

"So, then, you do know. I thought Gordon might come to you about it."

She didn't want to mention that Rick had told her more than Gordon had.

"How did you know it was Gordon Barkly?" she asked.

"Because he came to see me yesterday before Delance barged in. He tried to blackmail me into leaving Virginia City without you. He wanted me to sneak away like a coward. I refused. Well, I see he did what he threatened. He came and spoke to you about Dylan Harkin."

"Gordon threatened to blackmail you?"

"Yes, in his own way. He didn't want money, but he wanted me to give you up and leave town. That's why I was in such a low mood when we met in the dining room waiting for Hugh. And all that time Hugh was in the coach...not far from this window... while we sat waiting."

She shuddered. "Don't bring that up again." She glanced toward the window, half expecting to see the coach parked there. The incident in the dressing room still preyed upon her nerves.

The information about Gordon coming to see Ashe at least explained his anxious manner last night when he kept looking out the window.

"Gordon threatened to release information on Hugh that would have damaged us."

She looked at him, alert. Information on Hugh? What about on Ashe himself?

"Hugh had a gambling problem. He had enemies. In the past he'd been a heavy drinker. There was some scandal." He shook his head, troubled. "I don't know all the facts. But Hugh had met your cousin Macklin somewhere along the way, and they teamed up together in a lot of ventures. Some of them not within the bounds of the law."

She hesitated. "Did he get a loan from Dylan Harkin?"

"Yes, he did. A business associate in San Francisco arranged the whole thing. Personally, I never met Harkin, nor do I want to. I've heard he's full of revenge, and that he came to town to kill your father for something he didn't do—something about shooting Dylan's brother in the back."

"I don't even know if Dylan realizes that it was a man named Hoadly who killed his brother, or that Macklin's lawyer, Mr. Colefax blamed it on my father."

Ashe looked miserable. "All I want is for us to leave here as soon as possible."

"Ashe, Neil Howard—you know him? Neil said some disturbing things about you…about when you were in New York. I didn't want to bring it up, but I feel I must after what's happened."

"So that's who it was. Neil. Yes, I knew Neil in Chicago years ago. He was stage manager at the time. Well, there's nothing to the talk. I told you why Rick, Gordon, and even Neil, are trying to ruin me. It's jealousy. I'll explain about New York…it had to do with Hugh. I told you how Hugh gambled and drank. That's why he needed a loan to start the Stardust. I first met Hugh in Chicago. He gave me a big start, and I felt I owed him. But our relationship didn't come without penalties. He gambled our successes away, time and time again."

Our successes? She looked at him carefully.

"It was a sickness with Hugh, but he managed to cover it up. Sometimes he used me as his cover. He did that when he was drinking. That's why Neil thought it was me who drank and gambled. Well, it wasn't. Hugh would never have blamed me, either, when he was sober. He'd blame the gambling debts on me, and it would get into the newspapers. My reputation has suffered these last few years because of him. That's why I left New York. Things will be different this time. It was Hugh who showed up that night a few years ago in New York drunk and causing trouble. I took the blame."

"You took the blame? But why, Ashe, whatever for?"

His jaw tensed. "Well, when I saw the news article about me being drunk, I immediately went to him and complained. He was apologetic, and has never, over the past years, done that again. It was too late, however, to undo the effect of the article. And, unfortunately, at that time my acting career still depended upon him."

She shook her head and stared at him.

"Since then we had become friends and worked together well for years. Now can you understand why I was so affected by seeing him unexpectedly strangled? What happened last night was murder, plain and simple. He was murdered—and his debts and his enemies could come back upon me. He'd also known Macklin. There'd been a plan in place for Macklin to start a theater here."

"So that's how you both knew. I wondered. Rick asked about that, too, last night."

His eyes hardened. "Did he? Macklin had already contacted Hugh about managing it. Then when I met you…Hugh knew I'd fallen for you. Coming here seemed a new chance for us all."

But someone had been waiting here for him.

"Who might have set him up, Ashe?"

He reached over and took hold of her hand. "I don't know who killed him, Callie. But I know we'd be wiser to leave Virginia City, sell your share of the Halliday-Harkin, and start over in New York."

Between the threatening message, the stolen sapphires, and the chandelier, it all forecasted something dark and deadly. She hadn't wanted to live in the West anyway. She'd wanted to get away. And now was their opportunity. They could open their own theater after starring in Foster Williams' new play on Broadway.

"I love you, Callie. With a new start in New York, we can be truly free."

She squeezed his hand and met his gaze. "All right, Ashe, I'll go with you."

He swooped up her hand and pressed her palm to his lips. "You won't be sorry, darling."

No, she wouldn't be sorry. She would refuse to embrace the lively eyes of Rick Delance in her mind and heart. She'd made her decision. She wanted to be an actress. Ashe shared the same interest and passion for success.

Though Rick Delance set her emotions fluttering, how long could it last? A ranch in Cimarron surrounded by beautiful mountains, blue sky, and roaming cattle, all sounded peaceful, and she would have been near Annalee…but Delance had a reputation with a gun. There would always be men looking for him, trying to prove themselves better.

"We should leave tomorrow," Ashe said urgently. "That message…"

"I can leave a letter for Samuel and Weda, and promise Jimmy he can come visit us in New York. He'd like that. I'll tell them we're going to Santa Fe to see Annalee and marry there." *That way, Uncle Samuel won't worry about me as much.* "I'll promise to wire Samuel as soon as we get to Annalee's. And what about Elmira? I promised her we'd bring her to New York to stay with her brother."

"She'll need to come with us."

"We will make it, Ashe. *We* will make it," but there was little cheer in her voice.

Twenty-Three

*T*he next morning, still reeling from the dreadful events of the last two days as well as the news of the gunfight at Flint's cabin, Callie arose while it was yet dark and started quietly packing a portmanteau with necessities for the journey to Santa Fe. The greater part of her belongings would need to be sent to her once she was in New York.

Leaving now didn't bring her the happiness she'd anticipated. She had wanted everything to be perfect, but it was becoming clear that her plans and dreams would not realize the glittering success she desired when so many things were wrong.

She had written three letters—to Samuel, Weda, and Jimmy. They were lying on her bureau. By the time they were discovered she, Ashe, and Elmira would have been gone several hours.

The amber dawn was now reaching the horizon. She went to the terrace to make sure the buggy she'd brought up to the side of the house last night was still there.

The day would be warm. Mauve clouds drifted high above, and a lone bird swept over the distant mesquite and sagebrush. Somewhere, a cock crowed.

Callie returned to her shadowy room and stood for one last moment glancing around. She walked over to the bureau and ran her fingers along Aunt Weda's crocheted scarf, as though by touching it she could keep from breaking the family thread that still bound them together. Aunt Weda would never make the long journey to New York. Even a trip to Santa Fe was out of the question from her aunt's viewpoint. Callie felt a prick to her conscience. She had not been alone with Weda for a chat in several days. When she'd come home last night after the dinner in the

International with Ashe, she'd been too upset to want to talk. She'd not even spent much time with Jimmy recently.

What would the three of them say when they realized she'd left town with Ashe? In fact, what would Annalee say to her when she arrived in Santa Fe on the arm of Ashe Perry?

Callie refused to sink deeper into the quagmire of emotions reaching to take hold of her. Quickly now, she picked up her handbag and her suitcase and left her room for the last time, climbing down by way of the terrace steps.

The buggy waited under the awning on the side of the house without windows, assuring her that Weda, who often got up at dawn to start the coffee and hotcakes, would not see her. She put her bag in the buggy and started to climb in.

Hurrying footsteps from behind brought a start to her breath. She turned toward the backyard and was shocked to see Jimmy.

"Did you find the note?"

"Note?" her voice came a little breathless from the tension and guilt of sneaking off. She was afraid Jimmy would notice her bag on the floorboard of the buggy. "And whatever are you doing up this early?" she asked, anxious to change the subject.

"Oh, Callie! Have you forgotten what today is?" his brown eyes looked at her, and there was an excited smile on his face.

Oh, no! "It's your birthday, Jimmy!"

"Yep! Look, Delance left a note on the buggy seat."

Somewhat bewildered she turned. There was indeed a note sitting on the seat, held there against the wind with a clean, round stone. She retrieved it while Jimmy looked on attentively. Obviously, he'd already taken the liberty of reading it despite his innocent look.

Callie hesitated. What could Rick possibly want after that horrible shootout at Flint's place? She'd heard from Samuel late last night before she'd gone up to her room that someone had tried to kill him and Elmo. The hired gunfighter was dead; he was a man from New Mexico. Rick was unhurt, and Elmo had a minor injury.

"How did you know this was here?" she asked, unfolding the paper.

"I had to go to the barn to check on Keeper and the kittens. I'd plumb forgot about 'em last night with the shooting and all. Aunt Weda has a fit every time I bring 'em into the kitchen. So she put 'em out last night. That's when I saw the buggy with Tipper here. Tipper's usually in the stable at night," he said somewhat accusingly. "I wondered why you left him here hitched to the buggy. So I came to see, and that's when I saw that piece of paper with the rock. I could tell it was a note."

Tipper, the buggy horse, was another of Jimmy's beloved creatures, and woe to anyone who didn't make sure his creatures were well cared for during the night. She felt relieved he didn't ask why she was up so early and what she intended to do with Tipper and the buggy. Evidently he thought it had something to do with his birthday celebration. Her conscience smarted. She would leave for New York on his birthday without telling him goodbye, without a birthday present, and without even a hug and a promise to have him visit sometime. The hurt would long be remembered.

"Oh, Jimmy—" she sighed, frustrated with herself, events, and Ashe.

"What's the matter, Callie? Don't you wanna go on the picnic?"

She looked at him, then at the note, realizing what must be written in it. She read:

> *Don't seem like the right time after last night, but a promise ought not to be broken jes because of a bit of gunplay. I promised your brother a picnic at the mine. Even Ashe is coming. Bring Jim and meet us there.*
>
> *Delance*

Callie reread the message. She frowned, then looked at Jimmy. She didn't want to see Rick. She loathed admitting it, but the idea of never seeing him again left her more troubled than she would admit. If she refused to think about it, burying conflicting feelings, she was sure she would forget about him once she was in New York. But Rick Delance wasn't a man anyone could forget easily. Perhaps in later years when looking back to her youth she would always remember him. Remember and wonder if things might have been different between them if...

"Callie, you're going, aren't you?"

The heartbreak in Jimmy's voice decided for her.

"Of course, silly. It's your birthday. But isn't it too early for a picnic?"

He laughed. "Come on, Callie. We're not going to eat *now*. We're just going to explore and things like that. Then when we get mighty hungry we'll eat."

"Well, who's supposed to bring all the food?"

He shrugged. "Delance and Elmo, I guess."

"Elmo's coming too? I thought he was injured last night."

"Sure he was, but they put a bandage on his leg. Bet he's got some big stories to tell us now."

She had little doubt about that. Perhaps Ashe would take advantage of one of Elmo's long stories as a convenient distraction for the two of them to slip away.

"Wait, I gotta do one thing first," Jimmy said, and ran around the house to the kitchen door. Callie's frown deepened as she climbed up into the buggy seat and put her gloves on. She pushed her portmanteau neatly out of sight and picked up the reins.

Something wasn't right. What was it? She read the note again. She ignored her unease, blaming it on the decisions facing her, and their effect on others. Ashe would be there, too, she reminded herself, and felt a little better.

Jimmy was back in a few minutes wearing a poncho and a black hat. She smiled ruefully. "Are you trying to mimic someone we both know?"

He grinned. "Uh-huh," he drawled, and drew his hat a little lower over his eyes. "All I need is a pair of ivory-handled Colt 1860 Lawmans."

"You're not getting them," she said coolly.

"Someday I will," he said, and when she looked at him, he smiled.

"Rick won't like that," she said. "Both he and Uncle Samuel want you to grow up and go to college. Become a doctor, a lawyer, or a—minister."

"How come you said it like that?"

"Like what?"

"A—minister, like maybe you didn't think it was as good as being a doctor or a lawyer?"

"I meant nothing of the sort. I suppose it's just because Uncle and I aren't getting along too well at present."

"Yeah, he doesn't like Ashe none. I heard him telling Rick he'd rather trust a polecat." Jimmy climbed into the buggy.

She bristled. The idea that Samuel trusted Rick Delance but not Ashe Perry was curious. And yet, didn't she trust Rick, too? She had wanted him as a bodyguard. Now, that was out of the question. Strange that Samuel and Rick Delance got on with one another. Delance, a gunfighter, and Samuel, a minister. Yet Samuel liked him. So did Brett. Why was that? Did they see something in his heart despite the impression he gave? She was sure they did. She did, too. *Careful, Callie,* she told herself.

Callie drove the buggy toward Gold Canyon. *But...*

She pressed her lips together. If she yielded her life to the Lord the way Annalee had, it would likely mean the end of everything she wanted—including Ashe. *Maybe I'm like that man—Jonah— that Samuel preached on. Jonah knew God's assignment but he didn't want to do it. God told him to go one way, and Jonah went and bought a ticket for the farthest town in the opposite direction.*

Callie moved uneasily on the buggy seat and glanced toward the sky. It was clear. No storm clouds in sight—and no big fish to swallow her!

Callie resisted the worrisome thoughts that raced through her mind as she drove the buggy down Gold Canyon. She tried to enjoy the beauty of the Nevada hills and desert around her and that massive spread of blue sky overhead glowing like a sapphire.

Sapphire...who had stolen the sapphires? Forget that now. You have enough problems to make your peace with now without stirring up more.

Tipper carried her and Jimmy along at a good pace, and now and then Callie gazed off toward the high ridge of the hills where the trail led toward the old Pelly-Jessup and the Halliday-Harkin mines.

"Look! I bet that's Delance now," Jimmy said. "Waiting up there for us."

Callie looked where he pointed to a small figure on the shoulder of a hill. She squinted against the bright sunlight at a man on horseback silhouetted against the horizon. He seemed to watch her progress up Gold Canyon. He was too far off to iden-tify.

After the events of the last two days, the man worried her, but she didn't want to turn back. Maybe Jimmy knew more than she and could identify the horse. Was it Rick's line-back dun?

Driving on she allowed Jimmy to indulge in his constant chatter. When next she looked up at the hill, the man was gone. Was he riding down the trail to meet them?

She was not particularly nervous about coming here. Even though the sapphires had been stolen and Ashe had received a threatening message last night, she couldn't believe anyone truly wished to harm her. A thief stole because he wanted the goods, and if Ashe had an enemy who wanted him out of Virginia City, well, that too was understandable after what she'd learned about Hugh.

But someone out to kill her? Rick had thought so, but that chandelier was a quirk. Rick didn't like Ashe, and his dislike col-ored his judgment. Surely that rope must have frayed under the weight of the heavy chandelier—or Mr. Cummings had used an old rope to begin with. It seemed her mind was too full of ques-tions and denials over all the recent puzzling incidents.

Tipper's pace slowed, and Callie flicked the reins as the buggy started its trek up a hill, the horse's hooves clattering on small rock. She heard the wind in the brush and around the boulders.

"There won't be anyone at the Halliday-Harkin today," Jimmy said. "And the Pelly-Jessup's been abandoned for ages now."

Complete solitude wasn't what she had expected. "I thought the mines operated seven days a week, on all shifts?"

"The other mines operate that way, but Uncle Samuel didn't think it was right to have the miners working on Sunday."

This was Sunday! Why hadn't she remembered? "Jimmy, you're supposed to be in Sunday school this morning. Doesn't Rick know that?"

"Well, sure he does, but…" he squirmed uneasily on the seat and lowered his hat. "I guess I plumb forgot."

"Well, I don't think Rick would." She frowned and slowed the horse. A picnic on Sunday morning that would interfere with Samuel's preaching? Somehow Rick paid more respect to that than Ashe or even she would. Another prick to her conscience heightened her awareness of something wrong, not only in coming here, but in her heart and life.

"Jimmy, I'm turning back—"

"Oh, Callie, no, no! It'll be all right. Oh, please! We'll go to church this evening. Uncle Samuel won't care—"

"Oh, he won't, won't he? We both know better than that. And taking you away from church this morning will get me in even deeper disfavor with Uncle Samuel and Aunt Weda than I already am."

"Don't matter does it?" Jimmy asked, glancing at her sideways. "You're leaving with Ashe anyway. Everyone knows it. Even Delance."

She looked straight ahead. "You should still go to church."

"But you usually don't," he said quietly, plucking at his poncho.

She knew she'd only gone to worship services a few times since she'd been back. She hadn't thought about how her actions would influence Jimmy.

"I saw Delance readin' the Bible."

She looked at him alert and interested. "You did? When was that?"

"The other day when he was waitin' for Flint. It sure looked like an old Bible, though. Wonder why he don't buy a new one. It looked like he'd gotten it from a fire or something."

She was quiet a moment. The thought of Rick reading Scripture moved her. It had been a very long time since she had taken out her Bible and read anything.

"Maybe he did get it from a fire. You've heard how outlaws burned his father's ranch in Cimarron?"

"Flint told me. They killed his pa, too, and even his brother, Alex. I guess Rick's pa was like Samuel, except he was French and wore fancy clothes—even on the Triple D."

"He did? How interesting."

"His name was Lucien Delance. He taught Rick and Alex, too. Flint says that Rick is pretty educated."

Callie looked at him. "That's something about him you could mimic."

"Did you know his pa was sending him to law school?"

She lifted her brows. *Rick a lawyer!* No, she hadn't known that, and it was hard to imagine—or was it? Dressed up like last night he could fit in anywhere. The truth was, though, she rather liked him in buckskin. She was curious about what life had been like for Rick growing up with a French father. That must be why she had noticed things about him that hinted of a finer background than she'd first thought.

"To get back to this picnic—"

"Callie, let's talk to Delance first. Maybe he forgot, too, like us. And maybe he'll decide to come to church with us. We still have time."

She sighed. "Well—"

"Look, we're almost at the mine now. C'mon, Callie, hurry."

She flicked the reins, and Tipper speeded up.

"Anyhow," Jimmy said, "Uncle Samuel got the foreman at our mine to close down on the Lord's Day. An' there's nobody on guard at the Pelly-Jessup. The door's padlocked. I seen it once when I came here with Uncle."

They rode on seeing no one in the area. The only signs of life were some prairie dogs that darted away as the buggy approached.

She drove the buggy past the curve of the hill and by some old wooden buildings that still bore the names "Villiers" and "Colefax."

Tipper slowed and picked his way gingerly along the slope.

Now, as Callie neared the entrance to the old Pelly-Jessup, Jimmy pointed with surprise in his voice.

"Look, the door to the mine's open."

The entrance was a heavy timber frame in the side of the hill, with the wooden door hanging open on its hinges, the padlock dangling loose. She felt her stomach curdle.

"I don't see Rick anywhere. If Rick was the man you saw on the ridge, he'd know we're here and be waiting." She twisted on the buggy seat and looked all around. Some dried grasses rustled and the wind moaned.

"This is no place for a picnic, Jimmy."

He laughed at her. "We're not going to eat inside. But in that shady spot yonder." He pointed off in the direction of a sloping hill with some scraggly pinion pine. C'mon, Callie! Hurry! Get down. Let's go find Delance. Today I'm goin' to look for butterflies and grasshoppers."

"Jimmy, wait!" her voice came more sharply than she intended.

He looked at her, a little startled.

She tried to smile. "Don't run off, do you hear? And don't go dashing inside—there." She looked at the door standing open. "It's dangerous."

He looked tolerant of his big sister's fears. "Oh, I'm not that silly. Some of them timbers could be rotten by now and could break. An' if they did nobody'd find us for a hundred years."

At least he understood. She nodded and tried to smile.

"All right, then. Go find Rick and Elmo, but don't wander far."

"Maybe he's not here yet. Maybe that fella we saw was a guard. Uncle said they were going to hire a guard to watch the place day and night. I'll look around and see."

Callie watched as he jumped down full of boyish enthusiasm. He ran off toward the mine, picking up some loose rocks and tossing them as he skirted the opening and headed for the old wooden buildings.

Callie flicked the reins and drove the buggy up the pathway toward the pinion pines. She parked in some partial shade and looked about with distaste. Ants crawled everywhere—big red ants that would make a picnic lunch on a blanket nearly impossible. Insects dived and buzzed adding their warning of no trespassing. *This is going to be a miserable picnic,* she thought, feeling cross. Why couldn't Rick have picked something more pleasant and somewhere near a stream?

She climbed down, making sure the hem of her skirt didn't touch the ground where ants crawled busily. She snatched her cloak, adjusted her hat, settled the bow under her chin and turned to glance back toward the Pelly-Jessup entrance. She also looked over toward her own family mine, the Halliday-Harkin.

Where is Ashe?

She walked down the sloping path, feeling dirt inching into her shoes. Her stockings would soon be ruined.

Wind spoke its lonely language around the nooks and crannies of the rocks, kicking up dust and making things unpleasant. Was this in keeping with Rick's personality?

If it hadn't been for the guilt she felt over slipping away from Virginia City without telling anyone, added to the shame of missing Jimmy's birthday, she would never have come here.

On an impulse she took the note from her handbag and read it through again while the dry wind whipped it in her hand. The writing was rather bad, the grammar poor. Did that fit what Jimmy had just told her about Rick having been accepted into law school? No. Could Elmo have written it for Rick? She'd never seen Rick's or Elmo's handwriting before. Maybe she'd been an utter fool coming like this. Between her guilt and Jimmy's pleading, she hadn't shown common sense. She shouldn't have given into Jimmy, not while feeling this uncertain.

She sighed, then continued on her way. Frowning, she stuffed the message back inside her handbag. Her fingers touched her loaded derringer.

If you were smart, Callie Halliday, you'd call Jimmy right now and get out of here—

Jimmy's shout of alarm took her breath away. The shout was followed by a scream that sent her heart thumping.

The scream! Which direction? The mine? The old buildings?

She picked up her skirts and ran to where she thought it had come from.

"Oh, heavenly Father, take care of Jimmy," she prayed. "I'm sorry, God! Sorry, sorry I came here—I've been so unwise—"

She had to slow down as her shoes slipped on stones half-buried in the earth. Again, Jimmy shouted. She heard her name...and also an echo.

She stopped, breathing hard, clutching the derringer.

"Oh, Lord, help me," she prayed.

She approached the mine opening, and stopped, looking into the shadowy cavern. This was one time she wouldn't run away from whatever waited. Not with Jimmy in there.

The wind whipped her skirts. She heard a man coming from inside the mine. He emerged from the shadows and saw her and stopped short. He took off his hat and waved it.

"Ho, ma'am, you got a boy?"

She cautiously held the derringer beneath the folds of her skirt and waited.

He came toward her, a tall man, wiry-looking, wearing old mining clothes. He had a gunbelt strapped on, and he was smiling foolishly.

Callie's eyes narrowed. She stood still. "That's far enough, mister."

He stopped. "That your boy, ma'am?" he gestured his head toward the mine. "Sorry, ma'am, to sceer you like that. That boy was callin' fer a feller named Delance, somethin' like that. Then when I called out to him he came runnin' to me like he thought I was him. Craziest thing I done ever see. I think his foot went through a rotten piece of wood, ma'am. He fell down a hole, but don't you worry none, 'cause me and some other miners can get him out."

Jimmy had fallen. Her greatest fear had been realized.

The man's face was thin, and there was something odd about it. His cheeks and forehead were brown from the sun, but his upper lip and chin looked pale. His nose was thin and hawklike, his eyes were deep-set under black eyebrows.

Had she seen him before? He seemed vaguely familiar…perhaps she'd seen him around town.

"Can you talk to him? Does he answer?" she cried.

"He seems to be okay. He said to go fer somebody named Samuel, I think it was. You know somebody named Samuel, ma'am?"

"Yes, he's our uncle. Who are you?"

"Andrew Jackson, ma'am. Named after that good president, yes, indeed. Ma'am, better let me go straight into town and get Samuel and some miners out here right away."

She relaxed a little. He seemed genuinely concerned and helpful.

"Thank you. I'm expecting several gentleman to arrive any minute, but perhaps we should have Doc McMannis out here just the same."

"You're surely right, ma'am. I'll go fer them both. Maybe you could jes' go inside the door a short spell and call down to that boy. Tell him help's on the way."

"Yes, he'll need me. Thank you. Please hurry."

"Yes, ma'am. I'll jes' walk you over to the openin' and make sure you got a safe place to stand—"

"No. You just go get your horse, Mr. Jackson, and be on your way for help, thank you."

She watched him hurry away to where she assumed his horse was tied.

She strained her hearing to pick up the sound of hooves but all she heard was blowing wind. She waited a minute longer then, with derringer in hand, she cautiously neared the mine opening. Though fearing to step inside, her concern for Jimmy pushed her forward.

There were some miner's candles, oil lamps, and matches resting on a ledge near the opening. She picked up a lamp, but there was no oil. She checked the others. All dry. She took a candle, struck a match a few times on a dry rocky wall and a flame sparked. Carrying the candle in her left hand, the derringer in her right, she prayed, then stepped precariously into the dark cavern.

Twenty-Four

*A*she Perry sat at breakfast at the International Hotel dining room reading both Gordon Barkly's newspaper and the *Territorial Enterprise*. The waiter approached with a silver tray.

"Good morning, Mr. Perry. A message for you, sir."

Ashe opened the envelope. He was worried. He hoped it wasn't from Callie, informing him of a sudden change in her decision to leave. Despite her portrayal of independence and of being quite grown up, she was young in many ways. He drew his golden brows together as he read:

> *Mitey important. Come to the Pelly-Jessup at ten o'clock this mornin.*
>
> *Callie*

What in the world had gotten into Callie? "Mitey" important?

Ashe set his coffee cup down and glanced about the dining room. There weren't too many guests eating breakfast this early, just three men in business suits reading the newspapers.

Why would Callie leave for the old Pelly-Jessup mine this early? Had something gone wrong? Maybe her uncle had learned she was leaving and planned to stop her. But why hadn't she simply come straight here to the International and told him?

Maybe she was being overly cautious. She was wise about that, at least. She didn't want anyone to see them together when they left town.

Ashe drummed his fingers and stared thoughtfully at the note. Was it in Callie's handwriting? For the life of him he couldn't recall ever paying attention to her writing before. One of the words was misspelled, but there were times when she drifted back to her poor upbringing at Weda's farm in Sacramento. She'd gone to a fine school in San Francisco, so she'd told him. Ah, well, none of that really mattered. She was a beautiful and rich young woman. And right now she held the key to inheriting those riches. He wanted his own theater in New York more than he wanted anything else. A theater where he could produce plays rather than act. Not that he disliked acting, but he would be getting up in years and would not always be the handsome male lead that women theater-goers appreciated. Producing his own plays, owning his own theater on Broadway—Callie could bring him this.

His jaw set tightly as he folded the message and put it inside his white linen shirt pocket. Besides, he had as much right to the silver from the Halliday-Harkin mine as she, even more. Ashe was a Pelly. His father had owned the Pelly-Jessup before that foul Macklin Villiers destroyed his father and cheated him out of the claim.

No one knew that Walt Colefax had come to town under the name of Hugh Ralston. Now, Colefax—"Hugh"—was dead. Ashe smiled to himself. He had put on a good show of fear the night he'd found Colefax in the coach. He laughed to himself.

Ashe, who'd changed "Pelly" to "Perry" felt his heart quicken. Murdered in the coach—strangled. Colefax had many enemies—that was the story.

He looked up quickly as someone approached his table.

Elmira Jennings, actually Elmira Pelly, stood with worried lines on her brow. Her dark eyes were troubled and her black hair was drawn severely back from her pale face, making her look much like a stern Spanish senora in an outrage over a mistreated daughter. She wore a severe black taffeta dress that rustled as she stopped before him. Her breathing came rapidly.

"So you thought to run out on me."

"Don't be foolish, Aunt Elmira. Callie expects you to come with us as far as New York."

"You bought tickets last night. How do I know you didn't just buy tickets for two? I think something is wrong, and if I'm smart enough to know it, so does that uncle of hers. And don't underestimate that gunfighter, Delance."

"I'm underestimating no one, least of all Rick Delance. Sit down. You'll draw attention to yourself."

Elmira sat down, glancing over her shoulder.

Ashe glanced, too, saw no one watching them, then looked back at his aunt. She'd been working with him ever since San Francisco. She was the sister of Charles Pelly, who'd been killed by Macklin Villiers. Hank Jessup was dead, too. But no one knew how or why. His body had been found face down in alkali dust along the Forty Mile area. Someone said he'd run out of water. Maybe. Afterward, though, Macklin Villiers and Walt Colefax had bought up the Pelly-Jessup, or rather, they claimed they bought it. They had proof of purchase, but nothing had been paid to either the Pelly family or Hank Jessup's daughter. She had eventually married, turned her back on the whole affair, and moved with her husband to Oregon.

But he and his Aunt Elmira wanted what they believed was theirs, and they intended to get it—through marriage to Callie Halliday.

What would happen when Callie learned his true identity? He wouldn't think about it now, and there was no reason for her to know yet. Elmira would get her share, and she would leave to join her brother in New York to buy into his business. And he and Callie would proceed with their own theater. All would turn out well in the end.

"As we'd planned, I bought three tickets for Santa Fe," Ashe said. Reaching into his spotless jacket he produced them and pushed one toward her. "If it will make you feel any better, take it now and keep it on you…and don't lose it. We need to leave on schedule. As I told you last night, we'll go to the mine first, then ride to Carson on horseback. We'll catch the stage there and be gone before anyone realizes what's happened."

Elmira still looked doubtful and suspicious. "Callie left early this morning with the boy. I saw her. Jimmy came back into the house and went up to his room for something, and I caught him on the way out of the kitchen. He told me they were going out to the mine for his birthday. Something's all wrong. I don't like this, Ashe."

That disturbed him as well. Why had she brought the boy with her? It just meant added difficulty. Now they'd need to come up with some excuse to send him back to town alone before they rode on to Carson. Whatever had gotten into her?

"She's just sent me a message saying she was riding out there. Stop fussing, Aunt Elmira. We can pull this off without anyone knowing."

"I'm staying with you. I don't trust her or that gunfighter. Do you have everything packed? The sapphires?"

"I told you not to even say that word," he snapped. He felt his face flush with embarrassment and anger. It had been necessary to retrieve them from Callie's dressing room since he'd promised Elmira she could sell them in New York and keep the money. He had carefully arranged the incident with Elmira, who had let him into Callie's room to hide in the wardrobe. Elmira had broken the vase on the edge of the table, tossed a handful of water and shards on her head and back, then fallen to the floor, pretending unconsciousness. As soon as Callie emerged from her dressing divider to stare down at the woman, Ashe had covered her with the blanket and pushed her into the wardrobe. He hadn't liked roughing her up, but he'd make it all up to her later. He had slid furniture against the door before leaving her dressing room carrying the ornate box holding the sapphires.

Callie had fallen for it. Giving her the sapphires had been a stroke of genius. They really convinced Callie that he'd come from a wealthy family and had a great-grandmother of nobility in London. Well, he was an actor. Playing the role of a rich, devoted, love-smitten man had come as easily to him as a tip of the hat.

"I just want to make sure you have them on you," Elmira snapped back. "Sometimes I think whoever killed Colefax thought he could take them from him."

"There was no reason for anyone to think that," he said stiffly. He avoided her piercing stare. For some reason he couldn't put on his theater face around Aunt Elmira.

"I'm not as sure about all this as you seem to be. Colefax was furious when he learned you'd stolen them from his room."

"Don't call him by that name."

"I think that was the reason he dared to come here and show his face in Virginia City. He'd meant to give them to that red-headed wench in San Francisco. He took a big chance of being recognized by someone who'd seen him here with Macklin Villiers."

A few more hotel guests had come down, but it was not crowded for a Sunday morning.

"Someone did recognize him," Ashe said, glancing around as he pretended to be enjoying his breakfast.

"Someone followed him to town and killed him. He had enemies. We both know that. It could have been any of several, so stop worrying....Did you have anything to do with his murder?" she hissed bluntly.

He felt a stab of fear. He looked at her and swallowed.

"You fool. We could have accomplished all this without murder."

"Are you crazy? I didn't kill him."

"You're certain?" her dark eyes bore through his soul.

"Yes, certain."

"Because the San Francisco authorities could become suspicious of us. Either of us had reason to want him dead."

"They'll never believe you could strangle a man the size of Colefax. No, there are others who had their reasons, too. They could have nothing against us...except the sapphires."

"If they trace them to you—"

"They won't. No one even knows they were taken from him. Colefax never reported it to the police. Once we leave town we'll be scot free."

"Maybe. But don't you leave without me."

"Of course not." *Elmira, I sure hope you'll understand about the sapphires,* he mused silently. *But I'll cross that bridge in New York. The money from the Halliday-Harkin should more than make up for what I've done.* His thoughts moved on. "I've an idea about the boy. You can bring him back to town. Say his uncle isn't well and wants to see him. Then bring him home and ride directly to Carson. We'll meet you there at the stage depot."

She looked displeased. "So you and the girl can slip away with the sapphires?"

"Don't be absurd."

She didn't argue further, but watched him.

"By the way," he said warily, "did Callie convey any hint of suspicion about you being knocked unconscious?"

"No, she thought I was nervous and worried. It worked."

Ashe smiled grimly. "Just don't ever tell her you once played the New York theater."

"Once I get my share of the money I won't be anywhere around."

"Then let's go." He looked at his pocket watch. "We'll ride out together. It will look better that way."

He stood, as did Elmira, and they walked out the front door of the hotel.

The sun was climbing in a clear sky over the brown hills of Nevada, and the town was coming alive. Ore wagons were rumbling down the street toward the mills, and the stores and shops were opening for business.

A short time later Ashe and Elmira left the livery on horseback and started riding down C Street through Gold Canyon to the Pelly-Jessup and Halliday-Harkin mines.

Her prayer finished, Callie moved precariously into the dark cavern. Holding the candle in front of her, there was nothing but rough earthen walls and dark support timbers. A cold musty odor came from the depths of the mountainside.

"Jimmy?" she called, cupping her hand by her mouth. "Can you hear me?"

Jimmy was somewhere in here, helplessly trapped. From behind her the wind moaned past the opening and around the slope of the mountain. A footstep crunched behind her; her skin prickled. She turned, raising her derringer, but someone grabbed her arm, knocking the gun from her grasp. She heard it fall.

"No you don't, you little varmint!"

She stared. It was the man calling himself Andrew Jackson.

"Name's Dylan," he said with a leer. "Dylan Harkin. An' yer no-good pa killed my brother and stole the mine." He hit her, knocking her backward.

Callie, stunned, slipped to the cold ground, unable to think. The last thing she saw was a rope as Dylan bound her wrists and ankles.

"You'll have yer grave with the boy," she heard his words echo in her subconscious. "You think me and Frank were fools, huh? Colefax and Macklin, and Ashe Pelly, jes' like yer pa, were thieves. I'll get 'em all 'fore it's over."

Ashe Pelly? Her fogged brain struggled, grasping for consciousness. *Pelly?*

"Lord Jesus, help me, forgive me, help me and Jimmy—"

Like Jonah, I'm going down, down, down to the depths of the deep, being swallowed up in darkness, like the giant fish's belly. "Lord Jesus, save me!" she called, whether aloud or in her soul she did not know, but Dylan's grasp loosened and he backed away.

"Don't you be callin' out like that, you hear?"

"Jesus! Help me!"

"I said, don't say that, girl!" he stuffed a rag into her mouth, ripped off his bandana and tied it behind her neck, to hold the rag in place.

"There, that'll teach you."

Picking her up roughly and throwing her over his shoulder like a bag of potatoes, he moved forward with a miner's oil lamp. Callie's brain swam as she weaved in and out of consciousness. When she was able, she prayed, confessing her sins and crying for mercy while suspended in the dark.

Oh, Uncle Samuel, pray for me in church this morning. Pray for me and Jimmy.

Dylan chortled as he carried her deeper into the murky caverns. He finally put her down next to Jimmy. The boy lay in a heap, unconscious and tied. She glimpsed bruises on his forehead.

Dylan left them in the pitch-blackness and made his way back out toward the mine entrance. He climbed onto the rocks and sat down in the sunshine to wait.

Rick Delance had finished bathing in his room at the Virginia House Hotel and was putting on a shirt he'd had washed and pressed last night before he'd gone to bed. Coffee had been brought up, and he was pouring a second cup when a rap sounded on the door.

He doubted it meant any gun-wise trouble, but he wasn't taking chances after last night. He picked up his gunbelt from the back of the chair, threw it around his hips, and buckled it with one hand from years of such practice.

"Delance? It's me, Samuel."

Rick swiftly opened the door and stepped back. Samuel pushed in, looking more worried than he remembered seeing him.

"Callie's gone."

So. It had come to this. Rick's reaction was mostly disappointment. What had she seen in that weak-kneed Ashe Perry? Nothing except stardom. She had hitched her future to his just to play on Broadway. And that, despite all the signs surrounding him that spoke real trouble in New York.

"They would have headed for Carson," Rick stated flatly.

"Not yet. Jimmy's gone, too. Look at this." Samuel handed him a small piece of paper.

It was from Jimmy. Rick read quickly.

> *Uncle, don't forget to come to my birthday picnic out at the Pelly-Jessup. Callie's bringing me in the buggy. Rick left an invitation for Callie on her buggy seat this morning. We've gone to meet him there.*
>
> *Jimmy*

Rick looked at Samuel sharply. Without a moment's hesitation he grabbed his rifle, his hat, his poncho, and flung open the door. Samuel was right behind him.

"Who'd forge an invitation to get them there?" Samuel asked.

"I'll check the International to see if Ashe is still there."

"You think they're leaving town?"

"That was their plan all along. That's not new, but bringing Jimmy is. But why the Pelly-Jessup?" *And why would Callie ever believe he'd ask her to a picnic at an abandoned mine?* His temper flared. Someone had used his name to trap her, and he was furious.

Rick's boots sounded on the stairs. Samuel rushed after him.

"Is the trap for her or for you?" Samuel asked.

"Don't know. Guess I'll need to find out."

"Elmira's gone, too."

"I'm going out there, Samuel."

"I'll meet you there after I fulfill my duty behind the pulpit. We'll be praying for you. Be careful, Rick. Someone's been trying to kill you ever since you rode in."

After learning Ashe was not in his room, Rick left the International, alert for trouble. Seeing nothing amiss he made his way to Beebe's Livery Stable.

A minute later he was saddling his line-back dun. Beebe was talkative.

"That Mr. Perry and Miss Elmira rented horses a little while ago. They didn't say where they was headed, but I noted somethin'. That woman had a bag tied on the back of her saddle. For a woman who behaved like she didn't know anything about horses and such, she sure knew what she was doin'. Mounted easy and handled the horse well, too. I'd say she's been around West more than she cares to let folks know. Looked like there was clothes inside that bag, too. Sure been lots of trouble stirrin' around town lately."

Then she expected to board a stage with Callie and Ashe. But the question still remained, why meet at the Pelly-Jessup? Perhaps they weren't going there at all?

Rick paused, frowning. Maybe that letter from Jimmy was a false clue.

"Don't suppose they hinted where they were going?" he asked Beebe.

"Nope. But I spotted a Wells Fargo Stage ticket in that gal's bag."

"When did they leave here?"

"Not more'n ten minutes ago."

Ten minutes.

"Saw Miss Callie and Jimmy ride out earlier, too. They was in a buggy. Wondered where they was headed this early on a Sunday morning."

Then Jimmy really was with her. No trick there. And he didn't think she would allow Ashe to use Jimmy to trick Samuel. Then they must have gone to the Pelly-Jessup after all.

"If you see Flint around, tell him I went to the Pelly-Jessup."

"Will do. Expectin' more trouble are you?"

"Looks like it's hunting me. Check on Elmo later, will you, Beebe? He insisted on staying at Flint's cabin even though it's charred-up badly. His leg's injured, but he's all right."

"Sure. I'll go out at lunch."

Rick brought his horse out and glanced carefully down the street. All appeared quiet. He kept his horse in front of him, shielding himself, then mounted, keeping his gaze toward the upper windows across the street. Then he quickly rode out of town toward Gold Canyon.

Dylan Harkin saw two riders coming down Gold Canyon. He pulled out a hunk of tobacco, bit off a chew, and watched with greedy satisfaction.

Wind kicked up dust devils and whipped Dylan's long, black coat. From a shoulder of the mountain he watched them approaching the Pelly-Jessup. That was Pelly, all right, but who was with him?

He chuckled out loud. Why it was the old crow, his Aunt Elmira. Well, she'd sure made a mistake tagging along with him this time.

Dylan thought of his meeting with that murderin' thief Colefax. He'd sure been surprised to see him step inside that fancy coach. Bein' the coachman, Colefax hadn't suspected him at all. He chuckled again. Colefax had mistaken him to be that crooked lawyer callin' himself O'Brien. "Best part was when I took off my false beard. Colefax's eyes popped when he was knowin' who I really was," he murmured to the wind. "Ol' Frank would be proud of me." *What had Colefax said?* "*I didn't intend to cheat you, Dylan. I been meanin' to give it all back. Ever' last penny. Here, take this for a beginning.*" And Colefax had given him his gold watch, his ruby ring set in silver, and all the bills in his money belt. Dylan had enjoyed scaring him so much, he'd decided against killin' him after all. He'd enjoyed collecting some of what was due him, and he'd taken it and left the coach. "I'll be back ag'in, Colefax," he'd told him with a laugh, then closed the door and left.

Then who'd killed Colefax? Someone had strangled the old snake. Who? Dylan thought he had a good notion of who it was. *But I'm not sayin'. Not yet anyhow.*

Dylan Harkin giggled, then choked a little on the dusty wind blowing. *Ashe Pelly is goin' to die, too. They all are.*

Dylan leaned over and spat dust from his mouth. He tucked his black brows together in distaste.

"So that Halliday gal wants to marry Pelly an' turn over her shares in *my* mine to him, does she?" Dylan mumbled. "Well, she ain't. She's no good. A purty face and figur' who didn't deserve nuthin' of what Frank found. And that no good pappy of hers shot Frank in the back. Served her right when I sceerd her with that chan'leer. In Frisco, too. I was goin' to sceer her plenty in her room that night, but ol' Pelly interrupted."

Dylan spat again to relieve the hate that churned in his belly like bitter gall. Greed and hate had been eating at his innards for a mighty long time.

Oh sure, he'd heard about the excuse of how Hoadly went and killed Frank, but that was easy to say because Hoadly wasn't around to deny it anymore. Anyhow, even if Brett Wilder were telling it true, he didn't like Jack Halliday, regardless. His boy, too, was in the way. He'd grow up to inherit a fat hunk of Frank's silver.

I'm goin' to get 'em. I'm goin' to get 'em all. Ever'last one of 'em fer this is over. But first it's Pelly I'm gonna get rid of. Once I have Pelly and his aunt inside the mine, I'll light the fuses and blow 'em all to starry bits.

He chortled, slapping his thigh. It would be a fitting end to the Pelly-Jessup and the Halliday mines. It would all be his, then. He'd slip away and come back in maybe a year, and no one would be any wiser.

He sobered again. No one except maybe Rick Delance. Delance made him sweat. A cool one, him. And he had a thing for that girl, too. And he liked the boy, Jimmy. He was going to be plumb mad when he found out they were dead.

Well, I won't be 'round for him to find me. Pretty clever to lure 'em all here. Why, that birthday thing was the best thinkin' of all.

And all 'cause I heard that Halliday woman and Pelly talkin' 'bout visitin' the mine. There I was, sittin' right in the hotel with 'em jes' a few tables away listenin' to most ever'thing they said. That beard sure did fool 'em. And then on the street that time, when the kid told Flint it was goin' to be his birthday on Sunday. Why, there was jes' no end to all the things a man could overhear when he made himself disguised. That Halliday woman looked me over half a dozen times an' jes' looked away ag'in. Pelly, too, and that old biddy, Elmira.

Dylan Harkin pulled his hat down to keep the wind out of his eyes. Everything was ready. He'd been up all night laying explosives. And he didn't have any regrets. Not after all the misery they'd put him through these last two years.

Twenty-Five

*A*she and Elmira rode up to the Pelly-Jessup and sat looking around. The moaning wind and rustling sage filled their ears.

"I don't like this, Ashe. Something is wrong. Why would she come here with the boy and tell us to meet her? This is an awful place." She slapped at an insect.

"You read the message. You know as much as I do. Let's get down and give her a chance. There's got to be a reason."

Ashe dismounted. He was relying on his sleeve gun for protection if needed. No one knew he carried it. No one, that is, except Delance. How he'd guessed, Ashe didn't know, but Rick was too smart for his own good.

Elmira slowly stepped down from her saddle while looking around her.

Ashe walked up to the door of the mine and poked his head into the musty darkness. "Callie?"

"She's not foolish enough to go in there," Elmira snapped.

"No?" He sounded triumphant. "Then what's this?"

Ashe turned and held up Callie's hat.

Elmira's dark eyes looked cautiously about. "I tell you a woman wouldn't go in there on her own. It's a trap," she whispered. "Let's get out of here, Ashe."

Ashe looked at the hat and noticed the ribbon was dirty and coming loose. "Maybe you're right." He, too, was worried now. He had to find Callie! He looked up quickly, dropping the hat, and his head turned as his gaze searched the rocks and brush. *That message last night—it had to be Dylan Harkin...*

"Don't move, Pelly," came Dylan's voice from behind a boulder. "One move and yer meat for the vultures. Put your hands up behind yer head. You, too, Elmira. Get over beside him."

Ashe froze and broke into a sweat.

"Don't, Dylan! Don't shoot! I had nothing to do with your brother's death! It was Colefax."

"Keep quiet. I don't wanna hear any more actor's words from you. Lie down on your face and keep yer hands behind yer head. You, too, Elmira."

Ashe got down on his knees and lowered himself into the dust, just as he was told. If Dylan didn't check for the sleeve gun he might get a chance to use it.

Suddenly Elmira whirled and faced him, derringer in hand. Her teeth were bared in hate as she fired. The bullet struck Dylan in the arm. She was running toward her horse when Dylan's bullet struck her in the back and brought her down.

Dylan rushed up to Ashe. "Get up! Get in there! Go on, do as I say!"

As Ashe stumbled through the door into the darkness, glancing back with horror at Elmira, Dylan shoved the gun barrel into his back.

"Here, Pelly, you carry the lamp out front of ya, then keep movin'."

Ashe moved forward against his will as though entering a mythical monster waiting to swallow him alive. He'd be hidden here in the darkness that could become his grave. Perhaps this would be his entrance into hades—forever and ever. Ashe broke out in a terrified sweat.

"Let me go, Dylan. Let me go—" his voice rose higher in panic. "Let me go! Please!"

A sharp crack to the back of his head, and Ashe went down on his knees into darkness.

Dylan, breathing hard, his arm bleeding from the bullet wound, struggled to drag Ashe down the passage to where Callie and the boy were tied. He dumped him there, tied him and gagged him. "There, that'll do ya. Too bad 'bout yer Aunt Elmira!" He picked up the lantern and hurried outside.

He ran up to the woman and turned her over. She was dead. *Well…she done asked fer it, shootin' at me like that. Why, she tried to kill me!*

He dragged her into the mine and slid the body into one of the dark pits, and then he went back outside to lead the two horses farther away into the brush. He heard horse hooves coming in the canyon toward him. He cursed and clambered up onto the rocks to see who it was.

His heart went cold. *Delance.*

Dylan licked his dry lips. *Now what?*

He stood still, thinking. He became more aware of his arm bleeding from the bullet. He used his teeth and tore a piece of undershirt and stuffed it into the sleeve. As his eyes roved the area he got a daring idea.

Is it possible? Could I win this poker hand by getting Delance into that mine before lighting the fuses?

He almost chuckled aloud, but then sobered quickly. One thing about Delance made it easier. Delance wouldn't be afraid to enter the mine. And if he carefully planted the girl's derringer, which he'd knocked from her hand? He'd lay it next to her hat. Delance must have heard those gunshots. He'd be worried about her. Just maybe it would work.

He climbed down and reentered the mine, working swiftly to plant the bait.

When he came back out he used sagebrush to smooth out the ground where Elmira had fallen and bled. He climbed back up into the rocks to wait. *If Delance goes inside, he'll find the others tied up in the far end of the tunnel.* Dylan laughed quietly. Having lured his prey into the trap, he would then light his fuses and the whole thing would go up! He'd heard how a man named Zel and Tom Hardy were lookin' for Delance. It was all over Virginny Town now. Maybe he'd go to this Zel and collect money for doing a job the other hired guns had failed to do.

He heard Rick Delance's horse approaching and ducked his head below the rock. Of course, he could always just shoot him in the back. Save time that way. But his hands were shaking too much…he might miss. That Elmira had shown some spunk. If Pelly had been as feisty, they might have overcome him.

The sun was up; the day would be hot and dry. Rick didn't like riding the normal route to the mine when an assassin could just as easily ride ahead and be waiting with a rifle. But he didn't have time to spend on a back trail when Callie and Jimmy might be in trouble. What worried him most was why Ashe had apparently plotted to get Callie and Jimmy out to the Pelly-Jessup. Or was he assuming too much? Might it be someone else? The one who killed Hugh Ralston, maybe? If so, then Ashe and Miss Elmira were also riding into a trap.

Whoever wrote that note has a diabolical mind to use Jimmy's birthday to lure Callie out here. Rick's anger increased.

Elmo said the man with the scar was Thorne Wiley. Where is Thorne? Is he still prowling around Threesome, waiting for me to come back so he can use his rifle from a distance? Or has Thorne decided to use Callie and Jimmy to lure me into a trap?

But why had Ashe and Elmira come?

Rick rode up to the mine. He dismounted and left his horse on the shaded side of some boulders. He grabbed his canteen, and then saw the buggy and walked over there.

Callie's bag was under the seat. A quick look inside confirmed his suspicions. She had expected to ride out of town with Ashe, probably for Carson, then board a stage on the long trip to Santa Fe. Evidently Elmira intended to use her ticket and go along.

Rick held his rifle and looked toward the mine. Had the three of them already left for Carson? Maybe all his worry about a trap was wrong, but it was hardly likely that Callie would bring Jimmy with her to Santa Fe without telling Samuel and her aunt.

Rick pushed aside his feelings. There'd been a time or two when he'd even thought Callie cared for him against her will. Naturally she'd fight that, because falling for him hadn't been in her plans. *Well,* he thought dryly, *that goes both ways.* He opened the canteen and took a large swallow.

If, however, she'd been willing to leave town with Ashe...

The mine looked deserted under the warm sky. The few wooden shacks, built during the silver rush to Washoe a few years earlier, huddled together and had already begun to waste away. A few old ore wagons were parked to the side, starting to rust.

Rick's gaze skimmed the buildings as he slung the canteen over his shoulder. *Is anyone hiding in there with a rifle, waiting?*

The dust swirled, and a tinkling sound lingered in the air as gravel blew against the short boardwalk that ran to what once had been the Pelly-Jessup mine office. The wind crooned a mournful dirge. They were all dead now. Pelly and Jessup, Macklin Villiers and Jack Halliday, Frank Harkin and—Colefax? The lust that had driven them to steal, lie, and kill had consumed them. In the end, they left this world with nothing.

Staying close to the wooden buildings Rick moved with care toward the assay office. Cautiously he opened the door, keeping to one side. It was empty. Dust was everywhere. There was a row of lamps hanging on a rail. On the desk he saw a sun-faded layout of the mine-workings. He went in, bending over it. He studied the mine shafts, noticing how the Pelly-Jessup boundary was shared with the Halliday-Harkin.

Rick put some candles and a spiked candleholder in his pocket, and left the ghostly office.

His logic protested what seemed plain—that they had gone into the mine. Why? It would be dirty, dark, and damp. Callie wouldn't like that, especially if she expected to ride to Carson and board the stage. Nor would she want Jimmy down there.

He neared the open mine entrance. He kept back for a time just surveying the scene and learning from the ground what might have happened. Someone had tried to wipe away footprints. The broken sagebrush close at hand had been trampled, and he could still smell the poignant fragrance. The ground was kicked up in one spot as though a horse may have dug in a hoof in an anxious moment. Something had happened here all right.

His eyes lifted to the rocks around the mine. Again he noted where sagebrush was trampled in haste. There were new boot-prints below a boulder, as though someone had climbed it. All was silent; all looked deserted.

He didn't believe it for a moment.

He circled around the mine and found what he was looking for. Two horses hidden in the brush. Elmira's bag still tied to the back of her saddle.

They are still here...somewhere.

Rick followed the hoofprints and a few minutes later found a third horse. Then there was someone here other than Ashe, but it wasn't Thorne Wiley. Rick didn't recognize the horse. Thorne's had three white stockings.

He checked the saddlebag. There was nothing to identify the rider.

One unknown person, Ashe, Elmira, Callie, and Jimmy. What happened here?

He walked to the mine entrance. Stillness pervaded. And in that stillness, danger. He could sense it. It could be a trap, but he had little choice. He would enter the Pelly-Jessup. Who knew what this unknown man had in mind? He couldn't afford to wait, for fear that his friends and Ashe and Elmira would be murdered while he hesitated.

Rick entered the mine. It was dark and still. There was no sound but the distant drip, drip of water. He stood still, trying to hear any sound that might alert him to human presence. He could call out but it would also alert an enemy. He couldn't explain it, but he felt the enemy was close by.

He progressed until he couldn't see far enough ahead for his own safety. There were recesses in the sides or behind timbers where a man could lurk in the darkness. He struck a match and lit one of the candles. The flame caught and intensified, and then his heart lurched. There on the gravel floor lay a woman's hat—an expensive hat that was dirty and the ribbon torn. A few feet away lay a derringer such as a woman might carry for protection.

Did Callie have a derringer? She hadn't mentioned it. After all her fuss about guns being evil it didn't seem likely, but with Callie who knew? He smiled ruefully. *But might her indignation over guns and my reputation just be something she had conveniently used to keep me at bay so I couldn't reach her emotionally? Now why would her hat and the derringer have been left there? Even if Callie had wanted to drop the hat, neither she nor an enemy would want to leave the gun.*

It looked like a trap. The "plants" too carefully placed for him to see. He listened behind him toward the mine opening, but it was cold and silent. Standing here with this candle made him a sitting jackrabbit.

He moved ahead along the narrow track on which the old ore cars had traveled during the mine's brief success. Coming to a Y in the drift he spied a pick off to the side. He picked it up and carried it with him for a distance before setting it down. According to the chart in the assay office, he should be nearing the dead end of the section that connected to the Halliday-Harkin.

When he had taken a few more steps, he paused, stooped, and picked something up from the ground. *Odd. What is this doing here? It's been over a year since there'd been any blasting, and yet this was a piece of Bickford used for blasting rock—and from the looks of it, it's fresh.*

Suddenly it dawned on him what the enemy expected to do. Rick turned his head sharply toward the mine entrance just as a deafening explosion blasted from that direction. The ground shook and the powerful burst put out his candle as falling rock and debris closed off the way to the entrance. He raised his shirt to his mouth and nose to block the dust. He stood in total blackness, breathing through his shirt, smelling powder smoke.

He'd played right into the enemy's hands like a fool. Now he was trapped. Then a second explosion was muffled and farther away than the first, probably nearer the opening. Even if he could manage to dig through the first blast of rubble there would now be another! Whoever had done this had just lowered the odds of escape to almost zero.

Rick waited for the dust to settle, then relit his candle. He walked back along the track to the mine entrance, except there was no longer an opening. He lifted his candle. There was a pile of fallen rock and dirt along with splintered timbers. And behind that, another mountain of rubble.

Too much rubble to dig through. And that, of course, was the whole idea...and the reason for the note. It was—

He heard muffled sounds from behind him, farther back in the drift.

I'm not alone! Callie? Jimmy?

Rick held up the candle and walked toward the end of the passage. He saw them.

Callie was bound and gagged. Jimmy looked to be unconscious, and in the other corner he saw Ashe, also bound and lying
on his stomach.

Dylan Harkin chuckled as he stood well clear of the Pelly-
Jessup mine entrance having heard the successful explosions.
That's the end of them folks! he thought gleefully. He walked to
where the horses waited and was untying his own when a voice
stopped him dead in his tracks.

"Where's Pelly?"

Dylan slowly turned. He ran his tongue along his dry lips. A
big man had stepped from behind a rock and faced him with his
six-shooter pointed two inches above his belt buckle. The Z-
shaped scar showed visibly on his tanned throat. The gray eyes
were cold and hard as steel.

Dylan didn't answer. He couldn't.

"I heard an explosion, Harkin. Who was in there?"

"All of 'em," Dylan gloated, finding his voice. "The woman, the
boy, even Delance. You owe me, Thorne. You was supposed to kill
him for Zel, but I ended up doin' it fer you. That money Zel
promised you and Abner should be mine now."

Thorne Wiley looked at him long and hard.

"Is Zel in Virginny Town yet?" Dylan asked.

"He's in Carson. You killed Ashe Pelly?" he asked again, warily.

Dylan grinned. "He'll be dead soon. They're buried alive
down there."

Thorne Wiley's face turned an ugly red. "You killed Ashe? You
sidewinder! He owed me those sapphires for killin' Colefax."

Dylan swallowed. "You killed Colefax? I thought it was Ashe."

"It was me, you fool. Pelly hired me in Carson. He promised
to give me those sapphires he'd gotten from Colefax. Why do you
think I left that girl alone all the while she wore 'em? I knew he'd
take 'em back and give 'em to me. Those were my wages for doin'
his dirty work."

"Thorne, I'm s—sorry, I d—didn't know," Dylan said nervously.

"You stupid fool."

"No Thorne, no, no—don't shoot!"

The bullets struck him with such force that he staggered back. Dylan fell to his knees. A dust devil swirled around him. Dylan choked. The sagebrush shook as the wind moaned around the rocks.

Thorne Wiley turned and walked away. He mounted his horse and rode toward Carson to join forces with Zel Willard.

Dylan lay dying. He looked up at the hazy sky where a buzzard circled.

All for nuthin. And now what awaits me?

The last thing he saw was the black buzzard gliding lower with wide wings.

Twenty-Six

&

Rick pressed the spiked candleholder into the wall and went to Callie first. He removed the gag, and she gasped. He took his knife from his belt and cut the rope that bound her wrists, and then he freed her ankles. She sat up holding a palm to her forehead.

He stooped beside Jimmy. He removed the gag and cut the rope from his hands and feet. He massaged his wrists while Callie did his ankles. He removed Jimmy's poncho, folded it, and placed it under the boy's head. He brought the candle near and saw the bloody bruises. Rick's anger churned.

Callie tried to stand. He took hold of her, lifting her. "All right?"

She clutched him in unashamed relief, burying her face against him. "Rick—oh, thank God you're here!" Her voice shook. He held her tightly.

"Jimmy's hurt. Do something! Do something!" she began crying. "Get us out! Get us out of here!"

He stilled her fists with his hands as she pounded them against his chest and gave her a shake. "Take it easy, Callie." He tried to keep his voice calm. "Who did this?"

"Dylan Harkin," she sobbed.

"Dylan? You're sure?" he was shocked.

"At first I didn't recognize him. But he came back here accusing us of stealing the earnings from his half of the mine. Then he began to gloat over trapping us. He said he would blow us all up. I—I think he's insane."

"Anyone who'd do this to you and a boy is likely to be insane…or just given over to evil. I've wondered for some time if Dylan might not be dead."

"No, it was him all right. And taking diabolical glee over his ability to fool everyone. He said Hugh Ralston was actually Colefax. And—" she looked wide-eyed over at Ashe. "And—and that Ashe was a Pelly. Ashe Pelly, he called him. And Elmira Pelly was his aunt." She looked up at Rick, stunned.

"Was?"

"I think she's dead. I heard gunshots, and since she's not here with us….Elmira Pelly! I can hardly believe it. And Ashe…"

Rick held her in his arms as she sought comfort and strength. "It's all right, Callie. We've got to be strong." *Ashe and Elmira Pelly. So it had been Dylan.* The last man he'd suspected!

He released her gently and she backed away as though now embarrassed she'd allowed the affectionate time in his arms.

"Let's have a look at Jimmy," he said.

Rick lifted Jimmy's eyelids and studied his pupils in the candlelight. He put his ear to his small chest and counted his heartbeats.

Callie leaned toward him. "Will he be all right…do you think, Rick?"

"His heart's beating steadily. He's a strong boy. If anyone can survive this, Jimmy can." He took the canteen of water and Callie tore a piece of lacy cloth from one of her petticoats. He sopped it and cooled the boy's face, cleaning the bruises as best he could while she held the candle close, her hands shaking.

"Dylan was horrid. He's crazy," she repeated. "He kept chuckling…kept smiling." She looked at Rick. "That loud noise I heard. Was it—?"

He met her gaze, hoping to retain calm and confidence.

"An explosion. More than one. I don't believe in keeping the truth from you, Callie. We're trapped. And it looks like we're in a heap of trouble. There's a pick up the shaft a ways, but unless that mound of rock and rubble can be cleared in time there's no way out. We've a pocket of air in here and perhaps we can find water. I've got one canteen is all, and some more candles."

"You think we'll die in here?" she whispered.

In the light of the flame her eyes were luminous, like blue-violet jewels, and he felt his heart contract.

He tried to smile some hope to her. "Not if I can help it. And not if God wills otherwise. We need His help, Callie. We need to do some praying. Samuel knows we're here. When we don't show up, he'll get some of the miners and come dig us out. But we can't rely on Samuel alone. We've got to start digging our own way out before what air we have goes bad on us." He turned and looked over at Ashe.

From the corner came an angry muffled complaint as Ashe Pelly tried to get to his knees.

Rick stood and walked over to him, looking down at the handsome man, his fashionable jacket and trousers now disheveled.

"I hope you can do more than quote Shakespeare," Rick said with a bite of sarcasm in his voice. "Can you use a pick?" He stooped down and cut him free. "And, you've also a lot of explaining to do."

Ashe removed the gag from his mouth and threw it aside vehemently.

"Water!" he cried hoarsely, breathing hard.

Rick took the canteen he carried and unplugged it. Ashe grabbed at it, but Rick held it back.

"Hold on. This may need to last us unless we can find water here. One swallow."

Rick held it to Ashe's mouth and let him take a drink, then withdrew it as Ashe tried to take a second gulp.

"Selfish to the end," Rick said.

"Shut up!"

"If I didn't need you to help dig, you'd be wishing you hadn't said that." Rick shoved the stopper back into the canteen. "Get up. We've got work to do. Probably something you haven't done much of recently, if ever."

Ashe struggled to his feet, and swayed, balancing himself with one palm against the rock wall. "Ow, my head…"

Rick chuckled. Ashe glared at him.

"That was an explosion I heard."

"That's right. We're trapped in here."

"Trapped?" Fear leaped into Ashe's pale-blue eyes. "There's got to be a way out."

"If there is, we'll need to dig it."

Ashe brushed past him and went over to Callie. He took hold of her shoulders.

"Darling, about Elmira and I being from the Pelly family. I know this comes as a shock, but I can explain all this. I was going to tell you at Carson—"

"Sure you were," Rick interrupted dryly. "Just like you were going to tell her that Hugh Ralston was Colefax. That you were in the theater business together from your early days in Chicago. But there's more, isn't there, Ashe?"

Ashe turned, wariness drawn on his face. "More ranting and raving, Delance?"

"Cold hard facts, *Mister Pelly.*"

"Such as?" he challenged.

"You left the Wells Fargo Stage station in Carson when you first arrived with Callie from San Francisco. You secretly met a hired killer. His name is Thorne Wiley, and you arranged to meet with him behind the Nevada Hotel."

Ashe wore a startled look, then he shook his head as though the idea were preposterous.

"That's a fabrication. Don't listen to him, Callie!"

"What were you doing there, Pelly? What do you have in common with a hired gun?" Rick insisted.

Ashe's golden head turned sharply in rage. His hands dropped from Callie as he turned toward Rick.

"Don't look so indignant," Rick mocked. "Or is that a look of shock from the second act of one of your plays? You're mighty good at that, aren't you? I'm beginning to wonder when the *real* Mister Pelly steps from his masquerade. Callie must be wondering, too. Just who is this shining star she's willing to go away with to New York?"

Callie looked to Ashe with surprise. "You met that man with the scar? Thorne Wiley?"

"He's lying, darling. He's trying to make himself look good. Can't you see? I don't know the man he speaks of. I don't keep that sort of cheap company."

"No?" Rick's voice suggested otherwise. "You kept company with men equal to his caliber both in Chicago and New York. You also knew all along that Hugh Ralston was Colefax, a common thief and the man who bore false witness against Callie's father. It was Colefax who swore he saw Jack Halliday shoot Frank Harkin in the back. All the time you acted your way through your part of Mr. Innocent. Why did you meet with Thorne? Did you hire him to kill someone? Colefax?"

"You don't know what you're talking about. You can't prove a word of what you say."

"Looks like all your lies are unraveling, Ashe," Rick said. "Tell me, I'm mighty curious. What was it Thorne left you in the coach? Or did I imagine that?"

"Thorne? Dylan?"

But Rick noted a smug glitter in Ashe's eyes as he tore his gaze away, refusing further search. Callie seemed to have noticed that smugness as well. She watched Ashe.

"There was nothing in the coach. Absolutely nothing."

"Then you were just acting out your fear and grief. You knew Hugh Ralston was Colefax all along?" Rick repeated. He wanted the truth to sink deeply into Callie's heart.

Ashe shrugged, looking away from Callie. "Yes, I knew who he was. And he knew who I was. Somehow that didn't stop him from giving me my first break in the theater, though. And it didn't stop me from taking it, either."

"And you didn't dislike him after what you claim he did to your father and to the founders of this mine?"

"Yes, I disliked him! Probably as much as Dylan did. Like you just said, Colefax along with Macklin Villiers cheated my father out of this claim. My father died soon afterward. So did Jessup."

"And you hired Thorne to kill Colefax?"

"No. But I loved the theater. It was my life. It's all I have!" he finished, turning away as though drained of energy.

Ashe leaned against the rock face.

Rick didn't let up on him. "How did Colefax manage to lay his sticky fingers on Dylan's money?"

"How do I know?" he snarled. "I wasn't privy to all the inner workings. I do know that for the last year Colefax arranged banking operations, and his legal knowledge enabled him to tap into Dylan's account in the Halliday-Harkin. Colefax was the lawyer in charge of the Pelly-Jessup finances. He changed the books I suppose. Maybe even forged Dylan's signature."

"How did you find out he was cheating Dylan?"

Ashe looked more confident now. "Elmira. She worked for Colefax for awhile in San Francisco. She was able to search his office files when he was away. It was after we found out he was cheating Dylan Harkin that we met Callie in San Francisco. It wasn't planned that way, it just worked out. She was playing the theater. I was impressed with her acting—"

"And my share of the mine?" she remarked coldly.

Rick felt satisfied. She understood. The bubble she'd encased herself in all these months was beginning to break.

"*No!*" Ashe walked toward her. "I brought you to meet Colefax—Hugh—and one thing led to another. Remember, Callie, I didn't badger you. You were as much enamored with me as an actor as I was with you. You wanted to meet Hugh and form a partnership in the Stardust. You wanted to go with me to New York."

He was right. Rick looked at Callie. She seemed unintimidated by this. He felt his hopes rise.

"Yes, but I wouldn't have formed a partnership if I'd known Hugh was really Colefax. You kept the truth from me. You deliberately deceived me," she stated calmly. "And I allowed my desires to make a fool of me. I should have seen through all this a long time ago, Ashe, but I didn't want to see the truth. Uncle Samuel was right."

Rick felt her gaze and believed she was about to include him with Samuel, but she turned her head away.

Ashe wasn't giving up easily. "I was going to tell you everything once we were married. I swear I was. You've got to believe me. I was afraid to tell you, afraid you'd change your mind about marrying me."

"That's all you wanted, wasn't it? Marriage to me so you and Colefax and Elmira could claim my share of the mine. That's all it ever was! Rick warned me. I should have listened. You lied to me, and like a fool I fell for it. You were the great Ashe Perry."

Rick kept quiet now. Callie was doing all right on her own.

There was a moment of silence. The drip of water sounded loud.

Ashe stared at Rick. Then he turned quickly to Callie. "This conversation is meaningless. We ought to be deciding how we are going to survive and get out of here. Our lives are at stake. So if you're so clever, Delance, come up with a way to get us out of here. You've been a miner at the Threesome. You've been running things out there. How do we find a passage out?"

"You're right about getting out of here. We've a mountain of rubble to dig through. But I don't think we'll get out by trying to remove that pile. We'll need to break through from this end into the Halliday-Harkin. If my recollection serves me right, the two mines come close to joining. Whether we can do it or not is another thing."

Ashe's face looked pale and stricken in the feeble light. "Break through to the Halliday claim? Are you mad? We can't do that. This rock wall is solid."

"Yes, you're right about that. What other choice is there?"

"We can start removing the rubble that seals the mine entrance. If Samuel and others come that's where they'll start digging us out."

"Maybe not." He looked over at Callie. "Do you remember when Brett Wilder came here and discovered what Macklin and Colefax were up to in trying to gain access to the other mine?"

Callie looked bewildered. "Vaguely. I'm afraid I didn't pay much attention at the time. But I believe there was a section of the Pelly-Jessup that had gone over into the Halliday-Harkin boundary."

"That's right. I saw it on the mining chart in the assay office before. And if that chart's right, we've a chance to break through from that end. A small chance, but it's a possibility. We'll never make it if we try to work through the rubble. I heard two explosions, and I think Dylan made it impossible to get out before our air runs out."

"That doesn't make sense to me," Ashe argued. "We should try to reach the entrance where we came in."

"We'll be exhausted before we get there. There will be at least two big sections of fallen debris. Even if we get through the first, we'll be confronted by the second."

Ashe shook his head. "You don't know that for sure."

"No, but I've seen how much collapsed earth and rock the first explosion moved, and it makes sense that the second pile is just as large." He looked at Callie again. "But if we give that section of wall between here and the Halliday-Harkin everything we've got, we may have a chance.

"You're sure of that?" Ashe scoffed.

"As sure as I can be in these circumstances. We'll let Callie have the deciding vote." He looked at her. She was watching him with interest.

"Why Callie?" Ashe protested. "It's my neck, too."

"Callie decides," Rick said again quietly. "You heard the arguments," he told her. "We can try to get through two piles of rubble to the entrance or dig through that section of wall adjoining the Halliday-Harkin."

She straightened her shoulders and shook her dark hair away from her face and shoulders.

"I remember Brett mentioning Macklin's plan. According to Brett they'd come fairly close to crossing over. I'll go with your idea, Rick."

Ashe said nothing but from the hard look on his face he was angry.

"All right," he said coldly. "Go ahead and trust *him* instead of me. You'll be proven wrong. And when this is over you'll wish you'd done the logical thing. Maybe I should start on the pile of rubble—"

"*No.*" Rick's voice was so decisive that both Ashe and Callie looked at him. "You'll waste time and strength. If we have any chance at all, we need to work together attacking that one section of rock wall."

"What are we to use to dig with, our bare hands?" Ashe challenged.

"We'll use our hands, too. We'll use anything at our disposal. This pick will do for a start. We'll take turns. If I were you I'd take off that jacket and get comfortable."

Callie looked from one man to the other.

Rick removed his poncho, shirt, and unbuckled his gunbelt, watching Ashe as he did, knowing he had a sleeve gun.

"You can come clean with that sleeve gun. You won't be needing it in here." Rick gestured to Callie. "We'll leave our guns with her. You first."

Ashe smirked. "What do you think I'm going to do, shoot you when we need each other to get out of here alive?"

Ashe removed his dove gray jacket and unbuttoned his shirt sleeve then rolled it up to reveal a derringer that was held in place with straps. He avoided Callie's eyes. In the candlelight the metal glinted. Rick looked at her. He wondered if she was remembering what he'd told her about a sleeve gun in her dressing room. She must have, for her attention lifted from the gun to meet his gaze.

Ashe untied the straps and loosened the short pistol from his forearm. He hesitated, and then handed it over to Callie who placed it next to Jimmy. As she did, she laid a palm against Jimmy's pale cheek.

Rick left his gunbelt beside Callie and dropped his poncho and shirt on top of it.

Callie was kneeling beside Jimmy, taking his hands into hers. Rick heard her speaking softly but he couldn't tell if she was praying or crying. There was nothing he could say right now that could remove her fears.

Rick took the canteen of water and placed it beside her as well.

"Go easy on this. It's all we've got."

She nodded and then looked up at him, her eyes searching his, seeking the truth.

"What chance have we?"

"Not good. But we won't give up. You sit here and pray. Ashe and I will battle the mountain."

He turned to walk away when her voice stopped him.

"Rick? What made you come?"

He looked down at her. Their eyes held. "Samuel found a note Jimmy left at the house. He mentioned a birthday picnic that I knew I hadn't planned."

"Did you know we could be trapped here with a gunman when you entered the mine?"

"Yes, that's how it looked at the time."

"And you still risked your life to find us."

He lifted a brow. "Why should that surprise you?"

She looked at him a long moment in silence. He turned away and reached down for the pick. He pulled the candleholder from the wall and gestured for Ashe to follow him.

"The dead end section is through here."

Rick lifted the candle. The light shone onto the rock showing a rough arched section, like a ship's bow, between the two tunnels where they separated.

He walked through to the section that led near the Halliday-Harkin boundary. The area was still barred as it had been over a year ago. He remembered Flint talking about it, as well as Brett. There was still some ore that hadn't been touched.

Brett had mentioned that if one proceeded in this direction this tunnel would end up into the other claim. The Halliday-Harkin claim was not large, perhaps fifteen feet across, but it was in a coveted location near established mines producing rich silver ore.

"We'll never get through," Ashe complained.

Rick ignored his pessimistic tone. He placed the spiked candleholder into the rock wall and lifted the pick.

"It's impossible," Ashe said.

"We'll see," Rick replied. He gave a heavy whack that penetrated only an inch and knocked off a chunk. He gave another whack. This time a fair sized rock broke loose. That was a good sign. He continued smoothly and methodically, conserving his strength, cutting away at the wall, one whack at a time.

Twenty-Seven

ஐ

*I*n the blackness of the passage a single candle flickered. Callie stared at the flame. The air was still good, for the flame burned steadily—but for how long? She looked over at Rick. He was covered with dust and sweat as he swung the pick.

Ashe leaned wearily against the wall covered with dirt, his face lined with stress, his blue eyes having lost the poise of his theater demeanor. Callie was furious with him. During the hours that Rick had been working, Ashe had worked less than fifteen minutes. She left Jimmy and walked over to Ashe.

"Do something to help him," she hissed.

His eyes blazed. "I'm an actor, not a miner. I'm not accustomed to this brutal labor."

"Well, you'd better get used to it," Rick said, pausing and dropping the pick. "If you don't, you'll never see another stage."

Rick leaned against the wall using the cloth Callie had torn from her petticoat to wipe the grit from his face and neck. She looked over at Ashe. He sullenly removed his now dirty white linen shirt and grabbed the pick. He swung five times, gasping with each swing.

"I suppose you think you're a man just because you can break up this rock faster than I can," Ashe said furiously. "Well, there are more important things to being a man than mere physical strength."

"There are, Ashe, but they come from wisdom that begins with respect for the Lord."

"Nonsense. I have more wisdom than a gunslinger like you ever had."

Ashe threw the pick down. Callie picked it up and swung three times, and handed it back to Ashe, who tried again. This time he continued for several more whacks and brought down a section of rock. He looked over at Rick with satisfaction, and whacked it again.

"Very good, old chum, keep it up," Rick said, taking a swallow from the canteen.

Callie and Ashe exchanged the pick back and forth. Her hair hung loose and damp, sticking to her throat. Her expensive dress was dirty and torn, her hands had formed blisters that were now broken, wetting the pick handle. Rick struggled to his feet and took the pick from her.

"That's enough, honey. This is going to be a long haul, and you'll need to conserve your strength."

"My fiancée is not your honey," Ashe snarled.

Rick watched her. She was about to say something but held back. Ashe looked jubilant. He laughed. "You haven't won yet, Delance."

"I'm all right," she protested breathlessly, grabbing the axe away from Rick. "I'm strong. I can keep going." She looked down at her hands. "I should have brought gloves," she said dully, absently. "Aunt Weda's work gloves. I remember how she used them on the farm in Sacramento."

She felt Rick's hand lift her chin gently, and her eyes came to his. Something passed between them, something that sent a knowing shiver along her nerves. She knew how she felt about him and he did, too. She was merely delaying the inevitable.

"You're quite a woman after all, Callie. You're taking this like a soldier," Rick said.

Ashe took her arm and pulled her away from Rick. Rick shoved him, and he went back against the wall.

"Keep your grubby paws to yourself, Pelly. She doesn't like it. She doesn't belong to you any longer. Maybe she never did."

"I suppose you think she's yours now, is that it?"

"Stop it," Callie demanded. "This is not the time, Ashe."

"Have you gone soft on him after all?"

She tightened her lips into silence and walked back to where Jimmy remained unconscious. She sank to her knees before him and blinked the tears from her eyes, praying.

"Dear God, I've been wrong and foolish. I wanted my way no matter the price, and I've hurt others as well as myself. I never appreciated Uncle Samuel and Aunt Weda, but I can see they were wiser and more true to me than I had realized. I put the wrong emphasis on life and its goals. Now that my life may be taken from me, I see plainly how unwise I've been. Forgive me. Give me another chance at life. Help us to get out of here. I'll do anything You want me to do with the rest of my life with Your grace and strength to do it. Oh, Lord Jesus, help us."

Rick worked steadily, and she knew his muscles must be sore. She'd been wrong about Ashe. So much of what he appeared to be had come from the images he portrayed on stage. The Ashe Perry she had known was as much a masquerade as the black-bearded man she'd seen in the International Hotel. Ashe had wanted to marry her for his gain. But what about her? Could she say she'd been much different? She had wanted Ashe for his starry reputation, believing it would elevate her to the stage. They had, in fact, used each other.

How could I have been so blind? she wondered. *Here I am, like Jonah in the belly of the big fish. I've disobeyed God, though I knew about His ways. I wanted my own way instead. He said go one way, and I went the other. And now look at me!*

She measured the two men against each other, their commitment to truth, to honor, their beliefs about right and wrong and, most importantly, about God. There never should have been any real doubt which one she wanted. And there never would have been, were it not for her stubbornness. Her own plans had gotten in the way. She understood now why Samuel trusted Rick. Why Jimmy thought so much of him; why Brett Wilder had sworn him in as a deputy on that night so long ago. Regardless of his reputation as a gunfighter, there was solid character in Rick. He'd had his own battle with bitterness to deal with, and at age sixteen he'd turned the wrong corner. But even then, he'd only hunted to bring the guilty to justice. If he'd ridden with outlaws for several years it was in order to learn their ways and find his enemies.

She liked the way she could depend on Rick in a crisis. He hadn't panicked. He hadn't blamed anyone for the mess they were in—not even Ashe.

Whereas Ashe... Her mind went practically blank. Ashe had posed a threat, and all this time she hadn't seen it. He had said he cared for her, that he would have eventually told her who he was. But how could she trust him if he'd been willing to marry her to get rights to the mine without telling her the truth about himself? He'd lied about Elmira, too. His own aunt!

And that chandelier....Had it been Dylan Harkin or had it been Ashe himself...or even Elmira?

Callie looked over at Ashe asleep in the corner, his head on his jacket. Strangely, the death of his deceptive image caused her no severe disappointment or sense of loss. She felt as though she'd awakened from a long dream, and the fresh winds of reality were blowing through her soul.

How could she have been ashamed of Uncle Samuel and Aunt Weda, those two towers of strength and Christian love? All of their advice had been given to her in love. And they'd been right.

Rick... She could depend on him in a crisis.

Whereas Ashe...

She got up and went over to Rick, bringing the canteen that was growing lighter by the hour. He stopped and wiped his face. She looked down at the huge pile of rubble.

"It's feldspar and clay," he said with a measure of confidence. "I learned that from Threesome. I'm told most of the Comstock is made of it. Large sections are coming loose."

She wasn't as optimistic, but kept silent. Then she spoke.

"You complimented me earlier," she murmured quietly. "You said I was quite a woman."

His faint smile showed even in their predicament.

"That's right."

"Did I ever tell you you're man enough and gentleman enough to put Ashe to shame?"

His eyes narrowed. She dropped her eyes and handed him the canteen. "You can have my share of water," she murmured.

He took it quietly and drank a mouthful, then handed it back.

"Thank you for saying that, Callie."

She blinked hard and changed the subject. "How much farther do you think?" she made her question sound as though she believed he would break through to the Halliday-Harkin.

"Maybe just a few feet more."

He struck the pick into the rock and pulled away a big slab of blue-looking ore that fell to his feet.

"Silver ore," he whispered. "Looks pretty rich."

"Yes, but when a person is facing death it doesn't matter."

"No, it doesn't matter now, does it? What's really important shines the brightest then. Doing what brings honor to the Lord, what He wants you to do with the life He gave you, your family, the woman you love." He looked at her, "That's all that matters."

The base of the candle flame was starting to show some blue now. They were starting to run out of oxygen.

When his pick fell still there was absolute silence except for the sound of their breathing, more labored now.

"I'm glad Jimmy's unconscious. I wouldn't want him to be afraid."

He nodded. "A good boy...the best."

Any sounds from outside couldn't reach them in here.

"Do you think Samuel and Flint know what happened by now and are trying to dig us out?"

"Maybe, but I don't know what time it is. Seems like a week has passed."

"Ashe has a watch in his pocket. I'll find out."

She left the canteen on the floor and went to check on Jimmy, then went over to Ashe. She shook her head sadly. He was sound asleep. *Asleep, while Rick worked himself to death trying to save us. How could I ever have thought Rick had no character? I mistook Ashe's fancy clothes and manners in San Francisco restaurants for character. Character was Uncle Samuel riding miles out of his way to encourage a miner in the Scripture. Character was Aunt Weda rising up early to make sure they ate breakfast.*

Ashe and Broadway now embodied tinsel and fluff. Things that would blow away in the wind.

She listened to the heavy thuds of Rick's pick and winced with his wrenching gasps. *Character was Rick.*

Are we doomed? Her fears shouted in the dimness of the single weak candle flame that they were doomed forever and ever. Soon the air would be used up. Soon the flame would ebb and go out, and soon they would die slowly in total darkness. What mattered most was knowing that she belonged to Christ. She regretted now that she hadn't trusted Him very well during most of her life.

Slowly, heavily, she saw Rick swing the pick. In the beginning he had worked steadily, resting periodically. Now the air was such that all he could do was swing the pick twice for each minute of rest. She had helped all she could until her palms had again swollen with blisters.

Ashe had already given up. He had sunk hopelessly into a corner and lapsed into silence.

She went over to Ashe and knelt, shaking him, trying to get him up to take the pick but he did not respond.

The time, yes, Rick had asked what time it was. She picked up Ashe's jacket and reached into his pocket but instead of drawing out his watch she pulled out a small, ornate box.

This is the box that contained the sapphires!

Callie stared. She opened it, and the sapphires looked back. They showed no luster in the dimness, but they were the same jewels stolen from her dressing table in her room at the Stardust.

She stood. Ashe came awake and looked up, startled. She could see the dismay creep over his soiled face when he saw what was in her hand.

"You stole them!"

"Callie—"

Rick's pick fell silent as he leaned against the wall, resting.

Callie took a step back. "The sapphires are here in this box, Ashe. You stole them! It was you who hid in my dressing room, probably working with Elmira. You who shoved me roughly in the wardrobe. Again, you lied to me."

"I can explain—"

"Save your imagination. I no longer care to hear it." She struggled to remove the engagement ring. She took the ring, placed it inside the box with the other sapphires, snapped the lid closed with a decisive click, and—too politely—returned it to Ashe. "No thanks, Ashe. I've finally seen the truth."

She turned away from him with finality and looked at Rick Delance. She walked slowly toward him, and he set the pick down. His gaze spoke clearly and loudly, and she knew that hers did as well. She didn't hesitate, realizing that he was reluctant to touch her because he was so grimy. She moved closer and put her arms around him and pressed her lips against his.

"I've been a fool," she whispered. "I want you, Rick Delance."

His arms went around her so tightly that her breath was almost stopped. His kiss lingered, sending sparks through her mind and heart.

Was that her heart thumping so loudly?

He pushed her away, and she started. Rick turned to the rock face.

"Listen, Callie!"

She did. There was an unmistakable "clink, clink" sound.

"They're on the other side!" he said. "They're working in the Halliday-Harkin Mine to reach us!"

"Oh, Rick! Our prayers are answered!"

Ashe had gotten to his feet, his eyes showing life for the first time. "They're coming? They're coming to save us?"

Rick drew Callie close again, smiling, burying his face in her hair. She was laughing, thanking God, and feeling alive and free for the first time in her life. She reached up and mussed Rick's dark hair. He kissed her again and again.

"I love you Rick Delance," she said loudly. "Do you hear? I love you!"

"Sure took you a mighty long time to admit it, though. I thought I might have to go all the way to New York to convince you."

"Would you have gone?"

His dark gaze warmed her. "What do you think?"

"Now you won't have to. Because I'm going with you all the way to Cimarron to help you rebuild the Triple D."

"Would you?"

"What do you think?" she repeated, and held him tightly to prove it. "You'll never get away now," she whispered, kissing him again.

Ashe gave a short, brittle laugh. "So it's come to this has it?"

"You have the sapphires," Rick said smoothly. "That's what you wanted."

Ashe gave him a hateful look, then he smiled scornfully at Callie.

"All right, Callie 'dear,' have it your way. Just remember you're giving up Broadway."

Callie looped her arm through Rick's. "But look at what I've gained. I'm thankful this happened to me. This was my Jonah experience. I've learned what really matters the most."

"What?" Ashe asked impatiently. "Jonah?"

She smiled. "You wouldn't understand, Ashe." She looked up at Rick. "I'll enjoy living on a ranch in Cimarron. I'll be near Annalee and Brett, too."

Ashe said something under his breath and grabbing up his coat he turned his back and walked away from them.

Rick smoothed her hair. "Better wait with Jimmy, honey. I've still got work to do here."

The candle flame was flickering. With renewed hope and energy, Rick took hold of the pick and attacked the rock face.

Callie went and knelt again beside Jimmy. Again, she prayed, giving thanks for the help that was coming and asking fervently for Jimmy's life to be spared.

It could have been an hour later, or perhaps only fifteen minutes, but the sound of picks from the other side of the wall was becoming stronger and stronger. She saw a pick breaking through, then a small opening, next she heard a jubilant shout from Uncle Samuel and Rick's voice answering. Callie smiled and kissed Jimmy's unconscious forehead.

"Wouldn't you know it, Jimmy? It's our dearly beloved Uncle Samuel!" *Thank You, dear heavenly Father.*

Twenty-Eight

❧

Two days later the evening sun was setting, leaving a trail of crimson across Sun Mountain. Rick had returned to Threesome, and, after resting, he was doing well, though he was still a little sore. Callie had sent Flint to tell him that Jimmy was awake and that Dr. McMannis believed he would recuperate, but that he should be watched carefully for a few weeks. There was discussion of taking him to San Francisco to see other doctors, but now it seemed unnecessary.

Rick still could hardly believe that Callie belonged to him. But before he could think of settling down, he knew there was the unfinished business with Tom Hardy and his son-in-law, Zel. For the first time in five years he longed for a peaceful conclusion for Callie's sake. He wanted to return and rebuild the Triple D…and start his life with Callie. He now had too much to lose to want to risk dying. Yet, there was no choice. His enemies would not leave him in peace. They had come all this way, and they would not be satisfied until they saw him buried on Boot Hill.

Flint, Elmo, Fanshaw, and Everett were with him at the mine. He expected Zel to come here for the shootout and avoid the town. Rick had sent a message to Samuel telling him what he expected and to make sure Callie didn't come in the next few days. Callie didn't know Zel had arrived. Rick didn't want her to worry.

Flint sat at the table cleaning his rifle, and Elmo was boiling coffee. Rick was looking over the legal papers that Mr. Billings had mailed from Santa Fe to Bill Stewart, who'd sent them over from Carson. Rick was going to sign them and mail them back or bring them with him when he returned.

As he leafed through the papers he was surprised to see what his father had left him. He'd probably sell the line of riverboats, unless they'd already been confiscated by the Confederacy for the war. The land in Louisiana, too, may be worth little after the war. But land could be rebuilt, and so could the cotton plantation. He didn't know what to do with it yet. He'd talk about it with Callie. It was the ranch land he wanted. The land and the cattle. He wanted to turn the Triple D into one of the major cattle spreads in New Mexico.

"You heard about Dylan, didn't you?" Flint asked, tasting his coffee.

"Don't feel a bit sorry for him," Rick said.

"Me, neither," Elmo said crossly. "Had me so worried 'bout all you down in the Pelly mine, I almost had me one of them heart seizures."

"Don't do that," Rick commented. "You've got a heap of work yet to do back in Cimarron. For one thing you need to teach Callie how to make a good pot of coffee. She makes it like I do."

Elmo chuckled. "Always knew you'd get that gal. Mighty lucky man you are. Now that she's changed, that is. More like Annalee now." Then he looked quickly at Flint as though he remembered too late that Flint had once been sweet on her. Elmo cleared his voice and went on peeling potatoes to add to his stew.

Rick tried not to look at Flint. He wished it could have been any other man except his friend. As though Flint knew their thoughts he put his boots up on the other wooden chair and lifted his coffee cup. His amber eyes sparkled, and he grinned at Rick and then Elmo.

"Seen that pretty little filly who's come to town? She's the niece of that preacher at the other church. Her name's Becky, Becky Jones."

"I seen her," Elmo said. "She's seen you, too."

"So that's why you stopped going to Samuel's church," Rick teased. "I wondered."

Flint turned red. "C'mon, I ain't stopped going to Samuel's. I've just been attending every other Sunday is all."

Rick smiled. "Thought you were going with us to New Mexico."

"I ain't changed my mind. Doesn't mean she won't want to go into ranching."

"Is it that serious then?"

Flint set his cup down, looked from Elmo's amused grin to Rick's affected seriousness.

"It is," Flint said. "'Course, we won't rush things none. Everything will be done proper like. Her uncle will see to that."

"Thank God for uncles," Rick said and laughed. "If it wasn't for Samuel, I don't know what would have happened to Callie and me. He never gave up on either of us. Two prodigals have come home."

"The pa of that boy kept his eyes peeled on the road just looking for a sign of his boy coming home," Flint said easily. "Just like our heavenly Father."

It was early the next morning, and the sun was just coming up. Rick was awakened by the creak of a floorboard.

"Just me," Elmo said, "but you better get your guns strapped on. They're here, Delance. Ever' last one of 'em. Lined up out there on the hill."

Rick was up in an instant. He splashed water on his face and drank the black coffee Elmo handed him with a grave face.

"Where's Flint and the others?"

"At their posts. Soon as mornin' come up we saw 'em. They musta been there all night."

Rick dried his face on the towel and went to the window to look. They were there all right. He could see half a dozen riders on the low, brown hill overlooking Threesome.

"I'll get on the roof," Elmo said.

"You forget that. You stay inside this time."

"Yer foolin' me. Ain't no way. I been in this with ya since the first. An' I be with ya when it ends. One way or the other way."

Rick strapped on his gunbelt. He'd cleaned his pistols last night and reloaded them, something he always made sure of. As long as vicious coyotes prowled, the guns were needed.

He put his hat on and walked to the front door of the cabin. He didn't think Tom Hardy would allow an ambush. He had plans for running for political office, so Brett had said in the last message he'd included with Billings' letter and legal papers sent to Stewart. If he walked out on the porch and they filled him full of lead, the news would get back to Santa Fe. Both Brett and Billings would make sure Tom Hardy answered for it. No, Tom would want it fair, with everyone armed.

Rick opened the door and stepped out. The sun was higher, the morning fresh with a mild breeze. It was a good day to be alive, to make plans with Callie.

He walked to the edge of the porch and down the steps. A rider had broken rank from the five on the hill and came walking the horse slowly down toward the narrow dirt road into Three-some. Three other riders left the hill and followed. *Probably Zel and Bodene, but who was the third man?* Rick thought. *Could it be Thorne Wiley?*

Thorne Wiley. He killed Dylan, I'm sure. And maybe he killed Ralston, too. Ashe is somehow mixed up in all this, but he's maintaining his innocence. And he claims he didn't know Hugh Ralston was Walt Colefax until Ralston arrived in Virginia City and Elmira told him who he was. And Hoadly had been right when he'd mentioned that the real Ralston was dead. He was a gambler who was shot down for keeping an ace up his sleeve. He'd been related to Colefax, which is where Colefax must have gotten his name. He probably figured no one would remember him. Unfortunately for him, Dylan Harkin remembered. He just happened to be in Tucson the night Ralston was shot.

Rick's thought continued to wander as the four riders rode the trail to Threesome. *Ashe has to be involved somehow. He refuses to admit to any wrongdoing, but there's no way his hands are clean. I wonder where he got the sapphires? Maybe that will come out at the hearing Bill Stewart is going to hold next week.* Rick's focus shifted back to the task at hand.

The four riders from Santa Fe sat tall in their saddles and walked their horses forward single file in the direction of the cabin, the dust rising with the plod of the horses' hooves. As they came closer, Rick could see Tom Hardy in the middle. He looked older, grave, determined. He wore his guns. It was Zel that Rick watched closely. Like Tom, he too, had aged, but he was still a young man, handsome in a ruthless way. His smooth, black hair was still worn in the popular fashion of Kit Carson, and his mustache was oiled and trimmed with vain care. He wore buckskin, too, and the fringes tossed jauntily.

Here was a cold-blooded scoundrel who was mighty sure of himself, Rick thought.

The third man with them Rick hadn't seen before. He wore all gray. He must be around thirty-five, with a heavy cleft in his chin, a Roman nose, and a paunch.

"That's him," Elmo's voice came from the roof. "That's Bodene."

As they rode closer Rick's gaze swerved to Bodene. The man looked obstinate, his jaw and forehead narrow.

Bodene stared back, measuring him. Under Rick's gaze Bodene showed uncertainty for the first time. His Adam's apple bobbed as he swallowed. He was nervous.

The fourth man was big and slouched forward, muscles bulging in his too-tight black, dusty shirt. He had blondish hair and a wide, hard-boned face. He wore a humorless smile and his teeth were stained.

The Z scar. Rick saw it plainly on his wide, tanned neck. So this was Thorne Wiley. He, too, had been there that night.

Thorne, Bodene, and Zel spread out in horseshoe fashion with Tom Hardy in the center.

Flint made his presence known from the distant right of Rick, and Everett walked out at his left.

Rick saw Tom Hardy scowl as he saw them. Zel too, looked quickly at Flint. But Bodene just kept staring at Rick as though his eyes were glued there. Rick knew the man expected him to draw on him instead of the others because he'd been with Abner when Alex was murdered.

They all kept their hands on the pommel of their saddles, too smart to spook the firing too quickly. Tom must have given strict orders.

"Hello, Tom," Rick said. "Five years is a long time."

"I hear you're hunting trouble, Rick."

"Who told you that, Zel?"

Zel looked at his father-in-law. "Don't waste time, Pa. A crazed gunfighter like Delance can't be reasoned with."

"Still lying through your teeth, Zel? You've been lying to Tom all these years. I'm thinking now that Tom wasn't in the ambush you set up to kill my pa on the road to Santa Fe. I think you planned it all yourself. Just like you planned the ambush on the cattle drive."

"Words," Zel said. "He's buying time, Pa. Get on with it."

"Does he always tell you what to do, Mister Hardy? Seems to me the Hardy Ranch is yours. You made it what it is today. It was your work, and the work of the decent cowpunchers you once had working for you till Zel came riding in and took over. He had it all planned. To marry Tina, to take the Hardy Ranch. Trouble was, he wanted the Triple D, too. And he thought he knew how to get it. By dry-gulching my father, arranging for Bodene here to kill Alex, and stampeding our cattle. Then he sent those murdering hombres to burn the hacienda. Do you know he allowed Cesar to take Marita?"

"That's a lie," Zel said coldly, calmly.

"That's not what Cesar said before he died. I killed him, Tom. Zel hired him to come here and kill me. Cesar…Abner. Both are dead. How much more killing do you want before you deal with Zel yourself?"

At the mention of Abner, Bodene's eyes narrowed, and he looked quickly toward Zel. Abner was the acclaimed gunfighter, yet Rick had beaten him.

Zel looked at Tom Hardy. "He doesn't know what he's talking about. I didn't hire Cesar or Abner. Why should I?"

"Because you knew I was coming back to Santa Fe. Billings told you my father left everything to me and that I was going to claim it. And I am, Tom. I'm going home. I'm getting married, and I'm settling down. I've been fighting for one reason—justice. But now I've another reason—my own future. If I have to fight again to do it, I will. But this time I'm not a sixteen-year-old kid. There are those who are with me, Tom. Good men, all. Men who want nothing more than to get started in Cimarron in a new life. It's up to you. You're the patriarch. You should call the shots, not Zel."

Zel looked worried now. He was watching his father-in-law, not Rick. And evidently he didn't like what he saw written on his father-in-law's brown, lined face, because he turned his horse and faced Tom.

Rick didn't like that move toward Tom Hardy. He glanced at Flint who noticed, too. Flint's eyes moved from Zel to Thorne Wiley. Rick was now watching Zel.

"Are you going to digest all his lies?" Zel was saying. "What about Tina? What about Robbie?"

"Yes, what about them?" Tom Hardy spoke for the first time, his eyes leaving Rick to fix upon his son-in-law.

"I am thinking of my daughter and grandson, Zel. What about that night five years ago? The night outlaws attacked the Triple D and killed everyone there except Rick?"

"And me," Elmo spoke from where he lay flat on the roof, his rifle ready. "I wanna say somethin' Mister Hardy."

Zel and Bodene looked up sharply at Elmo's voice, and Rick could see they were worried now.

"Go ahead, Elmo," Tom said gravely.

"I was there, too, that night. Just like I was with Alex on the cattle drive the night Bodene there, and Abner, and Thorne rode in on Alex and shot him in cold blood. I saw ever'thing. If I hadn't managed to get away, I'd a died in the stampede. But the good Lord had other plans for me. I'm a witness. Now the Good Book says, 'You shall not bear false witness.' But I seen plenty of that with Zel here, Bodene, Abner, and Thorne. Cesar too. Cesar tried to kill me a few weeks ago. An' he got lead in Rick, too. But Rick got him. Thorne tried to shoot me back in Virginny Town when I was waitin' for Samuel to come treat Rick's gunshot wounds. I'm telling you, Mr. Hardy, that Zel's behind it all. He knew Rick was goin' home, and he hired these hombres to kill him and me before we leaves Virginny Town. I'll swear on the Good Book in any law-abidin' court in Santa Fe or Nevada that what I'm sayin' is the truth. And Zel knows it. So does Bodene and Thorne, if they had a mind to talk. That's why Zel wants me dead. He wants me dead so bad he can taste it. An' if'n it weren't for Rick I'd be dead now. Never had so much shootin' done on me in all my born years."

Zel, Bodene, and Thorne were staring up at the roof as though they saw a cougar ready to pounce on them instead of an old chuck-wagon cookie with a rifle.

Rick was watching. He saw Zel's eyes flare, his mouth tighten across his teeth. His hand dropped to his gun—

Rick was waiting. He palmed his gun and fired. The bullet went straight through Zel's heart. A rifle shot brought Bodene down from his saddle—Elmo's rifle. Thorne fired at Rick and missed, hitting the porch post, and Flint's rifle blasted Thorne from his saddle.

In seconds it was over, the loud blast of bullets ringing in their ears.

Tom Hardy looked stricken. He sat without moving.

Flint walked over to Zel.

"Straight through the heart. Dead." He kicked Zel's gun aside, stooped and picked it up.

Everett had walked over to Thorne and removed his guns. Bodene lay dying as Rick walked up to him and looked down. Bodene tried to say something but the words never left his lips before a final jerk of his body, then stillness. Rick took his gun and looked at it. The gun that had killed Alex and maybe his father as well.

Rick met Tom Hardy's eyes. "It could have been different, Tom," Rick said.

Tom Hardy said nothing. He gave a small nod.

"It can still be different," Rick said.

Tom Hardy remained silent.

"I'm going home. I'm taking my bride with me. I'm rebuilding. Does it end here once and for all or does it go on? Do you want Robbie Willard to grow up with vengeance in his heart and come looking for my son? Or do you want your grandson to grow up and manage the Hardy Ranch and live in peace with the Delances?"

Tom Hardy wiped the sweat from his forehead on the back of his sleeve. "It's over," he said.

Tom turned his horse and walked it across the yard toward the road. The two men on the hill rode to meet him. One of them came riding up. Rick had never seen him before. He was young, and he looked awed and frightened. "Name's Jake Hardy," he said. "Tom's my uncle. I'm livin' at the Hardy Ranch now. I come for their bodies and horses. Zel—well, he was a bad one all right."

Rick looked at him. He gave a nod. "You'll be welcome at the Triple D, Jake."

Jake gave a nod and wiped his sweaty palms against his trousers.

Rick gestured for Everett to help load the bodies on the backs of the horses. A few minutes later Jake Hardy was leading the horses down the road. The bodies of Zel Willard, Buck Bodene, and Thorne Wiley hung lifeless across their saddles.

Rick was still standing there a few minutes later when Elmo came down from the roof and walked up with his rifle.

"Did he mean it, you think? Is it over?"

"I think he meant it, Elmo. I think he wanted it to be over a long time ago. It was Zel who couldn't ride straight."

Flint was leaning against the porch post. "That kid, Jake, he has promise I think. Maybe take Tom's place when he dies. Take over till Robbie Willard grows up."

"Let's hope Robbie grows up a peace-loving man," Rick said.

"Dust," Flint said. "Someone's coming in an awful hurry."

Rick looked and saw a horse appear. As the rider drew nearer he saw it was Callie. She must have learned from Samuel of the expected gunfight with Zel and had wasted no time in getting here.

Rick stepped down from the porch to walk to meet her.

"Now ain't that a purty scene?" Elmo said. He scratched his whiskered chin and folded his arms across his chest. He and Flint watched as Callie got down from the saddle and ran into Rick's embrace. They held each other for a long time. Then Rick bent and kissed her. Her arms went around his neck. The wind blew against them and her skirts flared around her ankles.

Elmo sighed. "I was waitin' fer that fer a long time."

Flint laughed. "So was Rick."

Craig Parshall

CHAMBERS OF JUSTICE
The Resurrection File
Custody of the State
The Accused

Debra White Smith

SEVEN SISTERS
Second Chances
The Awakening
A Shelter in the Storm
To Rome with Love
For Your Heart Only
This Time Around
Let's Begin Again

Lori Wick

THE YELLOW ROSE TRILOGY
Every Little Thing About You
A Texas Sky
City Girl

CONTEMPORARY FICTION
Sophie's Heart
Beyond the Picket Fence
Pretense
The Princess
Bamboo & Lace

THE ENGLISH GARDEN
The Proposal
The Rescue
The Visitor
The Pursuit

KENSINGTON CHRONICLES
The Hawk and the Jewel
Wings of the Morning
The Knight and the Dove
Who Brings Forth the Wind